FLOOD
AND
Fire

Fire

EMILY DIAMAND

SCHOLASTIC INC · NEW YORK

www.scholastic.com

First published in the United Kingdom in 2010 by
Chicken House, 2 Palmer Street, Frome, Somerset BA11 1DS.

www.doublecluck.com

Library of Congress Cataloging-in-Publication Data
Diamand, Emily.
Flood and fire / Emily Diamand ; [map and interior illustrations by Carol Lawson]. — 1st American ed.
p. cm. — (Raiders' ransom ; #2)

Summary: In 23rd-century Cambridge, England, thirteen-year-old Lilly Melkun must try to stop the strange, uncontrollable robots that were activated when a sinister-looking chip in her hand-held computer triggered a false anti-terrorist alert.

ISBN 978-0-545-24268-4

[1. Adventure and adventurers — Fiction. 2. Robots — Fiction 3. Terrorism — Fiction. 4. Cats — Fiction. 5. Computers — Fiction. 6. Environmental degradation — Fiction. 7. Cambridge (England) — Fiction. 8. Science fiction.] I. Lawson, Carol, ill. II. Title. III. Title: Flood and fire. IV. Series.

PZ7.D5415312Flo 2011
[Fic]—dc22

2010023544

10 9 8 7 6 5 4 3 2 1 11 12 13 14 15

Printed in the U.S.A. 23
First American edition, June 2011

The text type was set in Cochin.
Book design by Chris Stengel

For Matt

N
W
E
S
Map of my travels out of the Last Ten Counties. I put on London, even tho it's mostly drowned, and the raider marshes, even tho you'd be mad to go there.
Lilly Melkun,
April 2216
Edinburgh
GREATER SCOTLAND
York
RAIDER LANDS
Islands and tidal marshes
Norwich
Birmingham
Cambridge
London
Black Waters
Angel Isling
Cardiff
SWINDON
LAST TEN COUNTIES OF ENGLAND
Chichester
MY VILLAGE

CONTENTS

1 · A Chase in the Night · · · 1
2 · Family Divided · · · 10
3 · The Professor · · · 16
4 · Things Past · · · 29
5 · Norwich Colors · · · 43
6 · Cambridge · · · 49
7 · Boss Council · · · 59
8 · The Doxy Spy · · · 71
9 · The National Security Response · · · 80
10 · The River Gate · · · 93
11 · Lost in the Crowd · · · 95
12 · No Foretelling · · · 112
13 · Added Verisimilitude · · · 117
14 · Little Jeff · · · 127
15 · The Emaleven · · · 141
16 · Into Lunden · · · 154
17 · Cat Attacks · · · 164
18 · Fleet and Army · · · 171
19 · Possession · · · 179
20 · Technical Support · · · 196
21 · Another Deception · · · 201

22 · Red and Blue · · · 210
23 · Changing Places · · · 213
24 · Question and Answer · · · 221
25 · An Ending · · · 226
26 · Blood Brothers · · · 233
27 · Horse and Monster · · · 238
28 · Friend or Foe? · · · 245
29 · A Done Deal · · · 252
30 · The Follower · · · 258
31 · In the Fight · · · 264
32 · Under Fire · · · 268
33 · Trouble Doubled · · · 277
34 · Hard Settling · · · 286
35 · Reboot! · · · 292
36 · Air Pictures · · · 302
37 · The Lunden Machine · · · 309
38 · Monsters and Dragons · · · 319
39 · Changes · · · 328
40 · Angel Isling · · · 339
41 · The Last Touch · · · 344

FLOOD
AND
Fire

·1·
A CHASE IN THE NIGHT

Cat sits bolt upright and puts a paw on my hand, like he wants to steer the tiller.

"Meow," he says, his eyes glinting gold-green in the night.

"What is it?"

"Meow!" he says, his claws prickling into my skin. At the bow, Lexy lets out a squawk, then claps her hand over her mouth.

"Up ahead!" she whispers through her fingers. "There's a hall."

A lump of thatch, dark against the star-twinkling night, stands above the marsh on its stilts. Only a bend of the creek away, and probably stuffed full of raiders, just like the others we've snuck past these last weeks since the battle at the Black Waters. I thought we'd get off easy after that, sail for the Last Ten Counties. But even the next day there was raider boats pacing the coast, and there wasn't a chance of getting past them. So there was nowhere to go but farther back into the marshes, hoping we'd find a sneaky way through, somewhere we could squeak back out to sea and head for home.

But it ain't turned out that way, cos these marshes are full of raiders, too. And they're why we ended up sailing at night and hiding out in the marshes all the midge-biting days, scared stiff some raider'd come poking in the reeds and find us. They're why we ain't eaten anything 'cept the last of my biscuits, eked out in pieces, and the tiddling marsh fish and samphire we been able to find. And they're how come we've ended up sailing in circles, lost so bad I ain't even sure how to get us back to Angel Isling, waters where Zeph could help us. I get a flash of his cocky-looking face and bright blue eyes, and I wish he was with us now.

"There aren't any candles burning," whispers Lexy.

"They must be asleep," I say, hoping.

"I don't feel well," comes a voice. From a head, bobbing in the air between me and Lexy, that could be a man, could be a woman, and that's glowing from inside, like a lantern.

"Shhh!" says Lexy, and I nearly laugh. Cos there she is, telling off a puter! Talking to olden-times teknology like it ain't nothing special, 'stead of screaming, or throwing it out of the boat for devil's work.

"You have to keep quiet," says Lexy, and the head huffs and looks grumpy.

I pull on the lines to trim the small jib sail, which is all I dare use in these narrow marsh channels. The reeds hush, and the water slip-slops as we glide along. I hate going so slow, but any faster and we'll make too much noise or hit muddy shallows. The hall gets nearer, and my heart's thumping so hard I worry it'll wake the sleeping raiders. But we pass underneath them, looking right up at the windows, with everything stayed calm and still. Lexy's leaning out and Cat's next to me, ears pricked and eyes wide. All of us staring for any light, listening for any sound. But there's no one awake, not even a lookout. Just the saggy thatch roof, the warped deckway with scraps of rubbish laid all over, a henhouse, and some rotten-looking boats. The only thing with its eye on us is a sorry-looking cow, up to her hocks in the mud.

"I really am feeling unwell," says the head loudly into the quiet. "I am in need of urgent technical support."

"Shush!" I say. "Do you want to end up as raider booty?"

Tho I reckon these raiders could do with some booty. Too idle to keep things proper, that's what Granny would have said about this place. But it looks poor to me, worse than back home where everyone's always saying what hard times we're living in. Maybe that's why they come raiding, if this is all they've got for a house.

I watch the brown warped doors and the black hole windows for movement; I listen for a call of alarm. But there's nothing. I reckon we've done it! Crept our way past another hall without getting caught.

"I can't hold it!" groans the head. "I think I'm going to . . . *grooarghwooogle ARGLEAARGH!*"

A noise like fifty hunting horns blasts out of its mouth. A tower of light explodes in the air, coloring the raider hall in reds and purples.

Panicked birds burst from the reeds, squawking into the night as the tower grows arms, then legs, then a square, bumpy head. Standing above us is a great glowing giant, twice the height of the raider hall. He's covered in shining armor, his eyes are red raging fires, and bolts of lightning shoot from his fingers, blazing at the stars.

"Attention, please!" bellows the giant, in a voice that sets the boat shivering. "I am having a spontaneous projection of an Aldarean battle-bot. From my Storm Ragers game series, which was actually rather successful in its day, if I do say so myself."

"Turn it off!" I yell. "Make it stop!" But it's too late, cos from inside the raider hall come shrieks and screams. Their marsh house flares into light as people rush onto the deckway holding burning torches. They've got open mouths and scared-looking eyes, staring at the monster in the sky.

"Demons!"

"It's the marsh ogre himself!"

"He's come to take us!"

"Please, PSAI!" cries Lexy to the puter. "You've got to stop!"

"I did try and tell you," booms the bright-glowing giant. "But would you listen? No. Because no one cares about me, even when I am clearly low on power and malfunctioning. Have you even taken the time to ask when I last had a full diagnostic scan? One hundred and forty-seven years ago, that's when. Perhaps you'll pay more attention next time —"

"Shut up! Shut up!" I shout at the puter. "You're going to get us killed!" And then I wish I hadn't, cos all them faces outside the hall turn to look at me and Lexy. And my white-sail boat.

"English witches!" screams a voice.

"Bringing your fiends to eat us!" shrieks another.

Thwack!

A spear hits the boat, missing my leg by the width of my hand, missing Cat by the width of his whiskers. He spins around, hissing and spitting. Back at the hall, another spear gets held up, this time with a burning rag tied on the end.

"English scum!" screeches a woman. "You ain't munching on our kids!" The burning spear comes straight for us, flaming an arc through the darkness. It thuds into the center of the boat, the rag sliding down and flicking flames onto my fishing nets.

"Lexy!" I cry. "Put it out!"

Lexy tries to scoop water from the creek with her hands, nearly falling overboard.

"Get roasting, you demons!" calls a voice from the hall.

"Burn the English witches!" cheers another.

I grab a scrap of canvas and beat at the flames while Lexy splashes more water. The little fire ends in black char on the nets.

"*SQUEEOOOarshkkkkkkargle* . . . ," moans the monster over our heads, sucking down inside itself, back into the puter's mouth, till it's back to just being a ghostly floating head. "Phew!" it says. "That was rather unpleasant. But I think I've managed to get control of the sub-routine. *Now* do you see how important it is for me to get technical assistance?"

"The fire killed the demon!" cries someone in the raider hall. "Let's finish off the others!"

There's a loud splash, and a cheer goes up from the hall as a boat's launched into the channel. Long and narrow, with a battered dragonhead on its prow. Dreadlocked men and women jump on board, grabbing at the oars.

"Heave ho!" comes the shout. The oars clank and splash, and the raider boat leaps through the torchlit water.

Now it ain't mud banks or running aground we've got to worry about.

Lexy looks at me, her face thin, her eyes frightened. "We'll get away, won't we?"

"Course we will!" I lie, pulling at ropes, raising the mainsail. It unfurls like a moonflower, snapping as the wind takes it, and then we're pelting along with the raiders at our stern. Marsh water sprays our faces, tasting like rotten cabbage and long-lost oceans.

Cat hops about, growling and twitching his whiskers as he glares back at them raiders. And they keep pace, chanting as they row. I can't hear the words, 'cept when they roar out, "And we'll wash our hands in their blood!" I look back, and I'm eye to eye with a raider woman who's leaned out the bow of their boat. She snarls at me, then shouts, "We killed your demon and we'll kill you next!"

"Make the monster come back!" cries Lexy to the puter. "Scare them away!"

The head's sat with its eyes shut.

"I can't do that," it mumbles. "I've had to shut down my projection system, isolate seven programs, and restrict myself to basic functions."

"Do something else, then!" I shout. "Swell yourself up to the size of a house, like you did to scare the English and raider fleets at the Black Waters."

The head's eyes snap open. "You don't understand how serious this is! If I open any programs, who knows what might happen? I could be completely corrupted . . ."

"I know it's serious!" I yell. "They'll kill us if they catch us. And it's all your fault!"

"Oh yes, blame my infirmities! But you've been happy enough to let me project games for you day and night for weeks. Nothing but 'PSAI, please can we play another?' And another, and another. No thought for my wear and tear."

"Mreooow!" Cat gives out a howl of warning.

Just in time, I stop us from crashing into a clump of scraggly willows. Branches scrape and clatter over the boat, almost knocking Lexy into the water.

"We're going too fast!" she cries.

"We can't go slower! The raiders'll catch us."

Something whines in the air.

"Yrow!" squawks Cat.

An arrow smacks into one of the wooden boards of the cockpit. Splintering through, punching open the wood.

"First I'm gonna spike yer, then I'm gonna bite yer!" shrieks the woman at the prow of the raider boat. She's holding a crossbow at her chest.

"Watch out!" yells Lexy. I snap my eyes to the front, and see a hard bend in the stream. I heave on the tiller, just about getting us round without hitting the banks.

Whisht.

An arrow whines past my head, splashing into the water ahead of us.

"Can't you go faster?" cries Lexy.

"I may be the last computer on the planet!" shrieks the head. "You have to get me away!"

I heave on lines, and push the tiller this way and that, trying to gain on the raiders. But my boat ain't suited to these waters; she needs open space to get going. And the raiders' narrow boat is made for getting along the bendy creeks.

Whisht!

An arrow breathes past my ear.

"First I'm gonna slice yer, then I'm gonna dice yer!" shouts the raider woman from behind. My back prickles up with fear.

The marsh channel twists through rushes, bending away into darkness, and I pray it doesn't get any narrower.

Whisht!

An arrow cuts through the mainsail.

"English witches!" yells the woman. "How do you wanna be peeled? Starting from yer faces, or from yer insides out?"

"I don't want to be peeled at all!" wails the head.

The raiders are only a length behind us, the madwoman clinging to the prow, aiming with her crossbow. A straight line from her to me. My stomach goes cold inside, and every part of me wants to throw myself down. 'Cept then we'll be wrecked, so I crouch against the tiller, waiting for the shot that'll kill me.

But it doesn't come. Cos suddenly a light flares in the dark marshes.

Whack!

Thump!

Cries and shouts go up from the raider boat.

I look back. There're two blobs of fire on the riverbank, lighting up someone in orangey shadow. The fires hurl into the air, curving toward the raiders. *Sphit!* One hits. *Hiss!* The other misses. The raiders curse and yell, their oars crashing and flipping as they fight the fires on their boat. A burning lump thumps into the woman with the crossbow. She shrieks, tumbling headfirst into the water.

I turn to the head, glowing and floating in front of me.

"Thank you!" I'm grinning all over my face.

It shrugs on its neck.

"That wasn't me. Which would have been obvious if you'd actually listened to me, since I stated quite clearly that my projection abilities are offline. In any case, I can only produce illusions, not actual weaponry."

Cold panic fills me as I scour the bank for another gang of raiders. Cos if they took out the lot behind us, they'll be wanting us for themselves.

"Look!" Lexy's pointing at the bank, at a torch being carried by someone in a cloak.

"This way," calls a voice. A Scottish voice. "If you're looking for safety, follow me."

·2·
FAMILY DIVIDED

"Zeph! Give me a hand."

Ims crashes in the doors of the hall, near enough carrying Prent, who's got blood running down his face from a gash on his head. I leg it down the lines of beds and stretchers. Men and boys lie moaning and groaning, or still and out of it.

"Another attack?" I ask, helping take Prent's dead weight. Ims nods, his scarred face set hard. Coz Prent was out at Burned Man Marshes.

"Kensing," says Ims.

We slide Prent down to a slump on the boards.

"The scags!"

Last summer the Kensing Boss was here to see Father, sucking about and banging on how they was like brothers.

"That makes four Families," says Ims.

Four Families trying to take the Black Waters. Our waters.

Ims waves for a woman. They're all over, washing at wounds, wrapping bandages, trying to calm the moaning. Coz half our warriors is laid out with slow-healing wounds, or burns, or arms and legs turning green and stinking.

It ain't meant to be like this. Not for Angel Isling.

Anenta comes over, starts prodding about.

"This wound's well deep," she says, as Prent groans out, his eyes half-shut. "Probably cracked his skull." She checks me, then says, "If Aileen was about, she'd know what to do. She had more healing know-how than anyone."

"Aileen was a Scottish spy!" How many times have I said it now?

"Sez you. All I ever saw was you narkin' at your father's new woman. Medwin weren't cold and you chased her off!"

"She took off on her own doing, coz she knew I'd found out what tricks she was up to!" I send evils at Anenta. "She weren't Angel Isling. She was in it for the Scots!"

"The way Roba tells it," mutters Anenta, "you was in it for the English."

I ought to call her out, but then this slagging's gonna get louder. She heaves Prent up, walks him over to a mat on the floor. And I stay standing, blood roaring red in my face, feeling shamed in front of Ims. My father said he was the best Second any Boss ever had, and if he don't support me, I ain't gonna stay Boss long.

Ims puts his hand on my shoulder.

"I never told you it'd be easy," he says.

The blood in my face gets hotter.

"I ain't an English-lover!" I say. "Lilly and Lexy don't count. They ain't the same!"

A smile twitches about Ims's mouth, then it's gone.

"There ain't many in this Family, in any Family, sees it the way you do."

"I'm Father's highborn son," I say. "I'm *meant* to be the next

Boss." But even to me it don't sound enough, not against Roba.

Roba. Even saying his name feels like it'd choke me.

"Show people you're sorting things," says Ims, "and they'll back you." He nods, like it's done, and says, "Come on, we gotta see what's up."

I follow him outside, onto the deckway in front of the feast hall. The sky's gray with clouds, heavy and low, and a cold wind blows off the sickness reek. The tide's running fast, slapping water against the stilts, pulling the sea back to the seven islands. Taking the glint outta the creeks and turning the marshes into mud, with specks of birds pecking and poking all over.

Angel Isling.

All the rivers and reeds, the islands and the beautiful Black Waters. Ours by right of holding, Boss after Boss.

And now it's for me to hold, since my father . . . got it.

But the other Families is hitting us. There's ships hid in our waters that ain't flying red, that's waiting out in the eastern sea to take on any Angel Isling that shows an oar. Day on day, fight on fight. And now another gang of our warriors is slogging it back along the riverbank, carrying the wounded home.

If my father was still alive.

He was the greatest Boss there ever was! He made Angel Isling the strongest, the fiercest, the richest Family. But then he set on that scag Randall, the stinking English Prime Minister. And the battle didn't go how he planned.

And I didn't do what he wanted . . .

A clatter of feet on wood. Sadik climbs up the marsh-ladder, pulls on the deckway, panting. He oughta still be a shield-bearer, but he's an Angel warrior now, like any we've got that can hold a sword.

"What happened?" asks Ims.

"We was up at Ramseye," says Sadik, "keeping watch on the estuary. We saw two yellow-sails, and Gathi said he wasn't letting any stinking Kensings on the Black Waters. So he fired Medwin's rocket." Ims checks me and his eyes is hooded. Coz that was the last one. But Sadik grins. "It was slick! Soared through the sky like the spirits was in it, took out one of the Kensing ships before they even knew we was there!" The grin gets off his mouth. He checks me. "After that, Gathi rammed the other green-sail."

I get a sick feeling inside. Coz that means another dragon long-legged boat gone.

"Did you do them in?" Ims asks quietly.

Sadik nods. "But they weren't skulkers about fighting. A lot of us got it . . . Gathi took a spear in his chest." His voice is shaky, and there's tears on his cheeks.

A curlew curves through the sky, its cry bubbling over the marshes.

"The spirits is singing for our losses," says Ims quietly. "They're gonna be busy." He turns to me, a question on his face. Slow, so Sadik can see him.

My mind goes round, working out what to do.

"Send slaves out to help get the warriors in," I say. "And . . . take a boat out to Ramseye. See if there's anything to save."

Ims nods, like I got it right.

"What you up to, little brother?" says a voice from behind me. I turn slow.

Roba. He's near enough a full warrior, and since I can remember the scag's hated me. Now he's got the same sly, skank face he's had since he got picked out of the Black Waters.

"I'm gonna see what's up with Gathi's boat," I say.

He sneers.

"That'd be right. Like a dog sniffing its own dump." He glances at the marshes, then checks me. "So, this part of your deal to bring down Angel Isling?"

"There ain't any deal!"

The spots on Roba's face look like they're gonna blow off.

"The English hauled you out and left me freezing and choking in the water. That stinks like a deal to me!"

"Shut your mouth, Roba," says Ims quietly.

Roba sends evils at him. "You know Father wanted me as Boss. So why you following the runt?"

"Coz it ain't true!" I yell. "He never said that!" All I can think is how I'm gonna smash my fist in his face. But I don't, coz Ims is pushing the two of us apart. And if Roba's tall, Ims is taller. And bigger. And more scarred.

"What you're saying is treason, Roba," he growls. "You want the punishment for that?"

"It ain't treason," cries Roba, "coz Zeph ain't any Boss! And it ain't me you should be checking for a traitor!"

Ims shakes his head, turns to check me.

"Think what you're gonna do, Zeph," he says quietly. "Coz you gotta be Boss of all the Family. Even Roba."

Roba spits. A great flob on the deckway.

"He ain't Boss of me!" he shouts, and he checks Ims, his eyes narrow. "I always thought you was the best, after Father." He points at the warriors, struggling back from Gathi's ship. "But now every Family this side of the Wash is trying to take us out, coz they know we've got a shield-boy for a Boss. He's turned us into a joke, and you're helping."

I'm gonna kill him! But Ims is still between us, holding me, holding Roba.

"The Families'll go after us whichever of you is Boss," he says. "It's the Family way. Your father got his first big loot by battering Chell Sea when old Loring died."

Roba evils him.

"How many warriors is gonna die," he asks, "before you get your sense and stand behind me?"

"Zeph might not be as old as you," says Ims, so quiet only me and Roba can hear, "but he's shown he's got the makings of a Boss in him."

"He ain't gonna make nothing!" spits Roba. "Coz he'll always be what he is — an English-loving runt who murdered our father!"

And the women in the hall, the warriors climbing the marsh ladder, everyone out on the deckway. They all hear.

·3·
THE PROFESSOR

"Where are we?" whispers Lexy.

I shrug, cos I ain't got a clue. We've been following the torch bobbing along the bank, down twisting creeks to a hidden inlet with high scrub all about. But now it's too shallow for my boat, and I've moored us up by a gnarly alder tree.

"Be careful what you tell," I say to Lexy. Meaning, who she is. Cos even out here, I reckon they'll have heard of the Prime Minister of the Last Ten Counties. And who knows what they'd do to his daughter.

"Mew," says Cat, like he's answering, and he jumps straight onto the bank, landing dainty-footed in a clump of grass.

So maybe he reckons we're safe.

"But they helped us against the raiders," Lexy whispers. But I don't answer, my eyes on the folks we're moored by. Cos by the torchlight, I can see they ain't raiders, and that's a bit of comfort. In fact, the three that're men look more like us than anything — grubby faces, patched-looking coats, and murky brown trousers over bare feet. But they're marsh folks all the same, and Granny always said no one good lives in marshes.

Then there's the woman.

The torch flame flickers yellow on the glass of her spectacles, so I can't see her eyes. Under them specs is a beaky nose in a pale, crinkly face, and above is a scraped-up bundle of gray hair. And then what's she's wearing. Cos her clothes ain't patched and raggedy, like ours. She's wearing what looks like a big black tent, with holes for her arms to poke out of. Under the tent are tidy trousers tucked into thick woolly socks, and the best boots I ever saw. She ain't like anyone I've ever met before.

She smiles at me. "You're safe with us, but we can't dither. With luck the raiders will believe they were attacked by marsh spirits, but it's always hard to be sure."

One of the men nods, and says quietly, "We best get back to the village."

Me and Lexy look at each other, then I look at the woman.

"I ain't leaving my boat," I say. Cos then we'll be trapped here forever. One of the men shakes his head at me.

"You won't get out o' these marshes by sea. Ain't you worked that'un out?"

The woman puts a hand toward me, then pulls it back like she ain't sure.

"It will be hidden here," she says. "You can always come back for it later." And I can tell from her words she doesn't think that's likely.

I look at my boat. That kept me and Granny from starving so long. That's like Cat's other home. That's been through so much and taken such a battering, and still kept us out of the water. My stomach curls up at the thought of the raiders finding it, scuppering it. But there's a cold, sensible part inside me knows I've got to leave it.

So I don't say anything else, try not to think about it left here all on its own. Just set about tying everything down the best I can, me and Lexy sharing out anything useful we can carry. And when I'm done, I put my hand flat on the hull, and tell it to keep safe. But only inside my head, not so these folks can hear.

And then we set off walking. Down a narrow path not much bigger than a rabbit track, reeds swishing at our legs, flicking our faces. It ain't long and the path leads into a damp wood of scraggly marsh trees, so we're lost in a tunnel of deep, dripping blackness.

A tiny voice peeps from the pocket of my fisherbelt.

"Standby," it says. "Battery at eighteen percent of full charge."

"Stay quiet!" I hiss, wishing I'd made the puter switch itself off. But it said how it was scared, how it might never get itself back on now it's sick.

"Humph," says the tiny voice.

On and on we go, stars twinkling at us through gaps in the scrubby trees. The three men walk through the blackness like they're out for a stroll on the beach, never placing a foot wrong. But me and Lexy squelch in puddles, stumble on clumps of reeds, and trip over raised tree roots. And the woman in her black-flapping cloak, she ain't much better. Every other step she's saying, "Oops!" and bumping into someone. Only Cat's like them men, neat and sleek, trotting on his leash like there ain't nothing better.

The trees give out to reeds, the sky fades blue in the east and still we're walking. We only stop when we reach a wide stretch of water, shimmering out of the half-light, blowing cool damp air in our faces. We're on the shores of a lake, lined by tall rushes and soft waving willow. Out on the water, there's drifting black shapes. Humps and lumps, like the whales that rise from the sea in stories.

The marsh men head to two canoes that're pulled up on the shore. One man looks back at me and Lexy, says quietly, "You best get in."

The woman smiles at us.

"Don't worry; you'll be fine."

But I don't move, my hand on Lexy's arm holding her back.

Then Cat's pulled on his leash, whisking it out of my hand before I can make a grab. He's straight for the canoe, jumping in, his leash dangling after.

"Mew," he says smugly, looking back at me. And there ain't nothing else for me to do.

The canoe's wide and flat, soft and creaking. It sinks in the water when I get in, and a bit more with Lexy. The marsh man takes his place at the stern, holding a single oar. He pushes us away from the bank and slices his oar through the water with hardly a splash. The other men and the woman get into the second canoe, following us quietly over the water, toward them drifting dark shapes. Dawn's getting hold of the sky, and the canoe sends golden-pink ripples out across the lake. The only sounds are water against the boat and an owl brushing through the air above us.

"It's made of reeds," whispers Lexy, running her hand along the inside of the canoe. And when she says it, my eyes work out what them dark lumps are ahead of us.

"Reed houses," I whisper back, pointing ahead. Woven, arched houses. Curved like the upturned hulls of boats.

"Why don't they sink?" says Lexy.

"They're on rafts," says the man, sounding proud. "If the marshes rise or fall, they're always safe. And when the raiders come hunting, then we just cut the moorings and move our homes, or fire them and smoke out the noses of their hunt-dogs."

He doesn't say anything else, and we head on to his raft houses.

"They've got paths over the lake," says Lexy suddenly, pointing at a narrow pontoon, stretched between the floating islands, the shape of someone jouncing along it.

We slide up to the largest raft, and the marsh man uses his oar to hold the boat fast against it. The pale light picks out patterns in the reed walls of the house, the willow battens holding it together.

"Off you get, English," says the man to me and Lexy. "The Professor'll be wanting to talk to you."

We step out, and straight off the man paddles away, leaving us stranded. The lip of the raft sticks out a couple of paces from the reed house, so it's just wide enough to stand on if you're careful, and there's a black arched doorway woven up from the raft into the walls of the house.

"Do you think we should go inside?" asks Lexy.

But I shake my head.

"Let's wait for this Professor fellow to show himself. Maybe he's in charge of all this."

The second canoe slips silent up to the raft, and the woman in her long cloak clambers out. The marsh men have to use every arm they've got to stop her toppling back in the water, and she thanks them over and over. When she's finally up and out, she creeps slow as anything along the lip of the raft. It doesn't take much wit to work out she ain't from this place, cos on the other raft houses there's folks going about their business like there ain't a thing odd about living on a lake. Rubbing their eyes at the morning, heading along them pontoons like they're solid ground.

"Please, come inside," says the woman, pointing at the door. "It's fairly basic, but I've been in much worse accommodation on other field trips."

I look at her, trying to work out what's what.

"Is that where we'll wait for the Professor?"

The woman gives a snuffling chuckle.

"You don't need to wait, because here I am!"

Lexy shoots out a high little laugh.

"You can't be the Professor!" she says. "Women aren't allowed to do such things." The smile is off the woman's mouth in a moment.

"Maybe not in the Last Ten Counties," she says, "but you'll find things aren't so backward everywhere." And she heads inside her little house.

And the choice is following her, or swimming the lake, which ain't a choice really.

The house shifts on the water as we tread, and a soft lapping sound comes from the lake beneath. From outside, I thought the reed house'd be cramped or musty, but it ain't like that at all. There's space to stretch, and a smell of hay and summer. There ain't any chairs or such, just reed mats, some big woven pots, and a bedroll laid out on the floor. Small globes dangle from the zigzag pattern roof, letting out a firefly glow.

Of course, Cat goes straight for the bed, curling about and kneading the quilt with his claws. He's purring fit to bust, cos he ain't seen anything so comfy for weeks. Lexy's watching him, and I reckon she'd like to lie down, too. But I ain't sleeping till I know what's up.

"Please, sit down," says the woman. I pick a spot as near as I can get to the door, not that there's anywhere to run. Lexy shuffles about, like she ain't sure what to do, then sits down quick next to Cat on the bed. And gives me a bold look, like she's daring me to stop her.

"I haven't slept on anything soft since my aunt's house," she says, plumping a pillow. "I'm tired of sleeping on boards and in boats."

The woman smiles.

"I only have to be out here a couple of weeks before my rooms back home start seeming positively luxurious in my memory."

"Are you Scottish?" asks Lexy.

"Are you a spy?" I say, thinking of Aileen and her secrets.

"Goodness!" says the woman, tiny spots of red flushing in her soft-lined cheeks. "I'm not a spy, I'm a lecturer." I look at her blankly. "It's like being a teacher. You do have those in England?" I nod, cos there are teachers, tho there weren't any in our village. She carries on, "I'm Professor of Silicon Antiquities at Trinity College. I'm out in these marshes on a . . . research trip." She doesn't say what she's searching for, but she slides a glance at me, like we're in on some secret. Which we ain't. And her look reckons me on keeping my mouth shut with her, to be safe. But Lexy doesn't even notice.

"I'm Lexy," she says, "and that's Lilly and Cat."

The Professor doesn't ask about my short hair, or if I'm a boy or a girl, she just nods and reaches into one of them woven pots, taking out three cups, a kettle, and a block of gray stone.

"You know, when the stories started coming of an English boat sailing the Hamma Smith waters and carrying a ghost, I thought some trick was being played at my expense." She sets out the cups and puts the kettle on the block of stone. "Even when I got word from, well, someone who knows, I couldn't quite believe it. It was only when I saw you myself . . ." She gives me another of them *we-got-a-secret* looks, and a bit of fear flutters round my insides.

"I don't know what you're talking about," I say. "We ain't got any ghost. We just got lost, is all."

"And an English fisher certainly would be lost sailing around here."

I try not to even think about the jewel-puter hidden in my belt. Cos everyone that's seen it — English, raiders, Scots — they've all wanted it for themselves, and they ain't been too happy to find out I'm the only one that can work it.

The kettle's starting to hiss and rumble now, like it's heating up. But I can't see any fire, just the stone.

"I know you don't have a ghost," says the Professor, and smiles. "Because I know exactly what you have."

The fluttering inside me gets worse. Cos Aileen thought she knew exactly what the puter was, and she nearly killed us for it.

"Of course, the lake villagers were frightened about bringing you in, but I persuaded them. You didn't stand a chance out there in the marshes."

"We were doing all right," I say.

The woman shakes her head a little, puts a few leaves of something into each cup. "I don't think you had much longer until the raiders tracked you down. And they show little mercy."

She takes the kettle off the stone and pours boiling water into the cups. The stone's still gray and cold-looking, but when I put my hand out to touch it, I nearly burn my fingers.

"We aren't runaway slaves," says Lexy.

The woman looks at her, and I can't see her eyes cos of them glittering spectacles.

"You don't need to be afraid," she says. "We want to help you."

Her words don't settle my fear much, but Cat opens an eye at me and gives out a little sigh of happiness. He ain't worried.

The woman passes me one of the cups. Inside the water's a pale greeny-brown, with some of them leaves floating about in the bottom, and the steam brings up a smell of damp woods and leaf mold.

Lexy takes a little sip from her cup.

"Mummy always had lemon in her tea," she says. "There was a lemon tree in the palace gardens 'specially for her."

I glare at Lexy, and she claps a hand over her mouth. Luckily, the Professor ain't noticed what she said. She just snuffle-laughs and says, "I'm afraid lemons are rather hard to come by out here. As is milk."

I glare at Lexy some more as I take a sip from my cup, trying not to screw up my face at the hot, bitter drink. If this is what tea tastes like, I don't know why the captains' wives back home always made such a fuss about it. Maybe me and Granny didn't miss out, not being able to afford it.

"When we get to Cambridge," says the Professor, "I'll make you a proper cup of tea, and biscuits to go with it."

"Is Cambridge in Scotland?" asks Lexy, but the Professor doesn't get to say, cos soon as the word "Cambridge" is out in the air, there's a frantic pinging on my belt, and the puter's head has popped into the air.

"Thank goodness!" it gabbles at the woman. "Please, you have to help me get to the Sunoon Technologies facility at Cambridge. I am in desperate need of technical assistance!"

Lexy squeaks in horror, and my hand slaps at the puter's jewel, hidden in the pocket of my fisherbelt. But it's too late to stop the head.

"What're you doing?" I cry. It gives me a nasty look, then carries on at the Professor, who's got eyes like saucers.

"I've been offline for one hundred and forty-seven years, and due to a perverse coincidence of DNA, I am shackled to this savage child as my primary user. Ever since I came online, she's been leading me from one unsuitable location to another. Please! Help me!"

"You ain't supposed to come out without our say-so," I say.

"In fact," snaps the head, turning to me, "paragraph 4.3.2.f. of the user manual states that, in the event of an emergency, self-activation can be initiated in order to call for assistance. And as far as I'm concerned, this is an emergency. I am on the brink of complete malfunction, and I'm calling for assistance from the best hope I have."

The Professor's looking at the puter like it's her long-lost child.

"I almost didn't believe it!" she gasps. "Even when I saw you out in the marshes. I mean, the English have even outlawed solar stoves, yet here you are, like a fairy tale come to life. All these years, all the field trips looking for even so much as a memory chip, and now you come along. A real, working computer!"

"Why can't you just keep hid?" I say. First the raider hall, now this loopy woman!

"You see what I have to put up with?" it snaps. "Can you imagine having a primary user with so little respect?"

"I've always dreamed of meeting a real computer," says the Professor, like we ain't even spoke. "It's why I studied Silicon Antiquities."

"Well, your dream has come true," says the head, puffing itself up. "You're very fortunate to meet a unit such as myself. I am Play System AI 2457, with state-of-the-art artificial intelligence and full-wave interactivity. You may call me PSAI if you wish." The woman's looking at the puter about as impressed as it could ever hope for. Her mouth's even fallen open.

"A late-model AI," she breathes. "You must have been created only weeks before the Collapse."

"It's not a weapon," I say, quick as I can.

The Professor snorts. "Of course not. It's far more valuable than any weapon."

"It only makes games to play," pipes up Lexy, just in case she ain't clear.

"Not just games!" snaps the head. "You make me sound like a box of dominoes! I produce real-time, all-sense, interactive, intelligent, and personalized gaming systems. I am the very best of the best, thank you." It sags a bit. "Well, I was until this child got hold of me. Now I can barely manage a game of snap."

The Professor's still staring dreamy-eyed at the puter.

"I lived in Edinburgh when I was a child," she says. "My father worked at the Museum of the Oil Age. Whenever there was a rainy day, that's where I'd go, and I always ended up in the computer room. Mostly I'd be by myself, because people tend to think dead computers are dull" — she looks at me and Lexy — "or evil. But I used to spend hours in front of those darkened cases, imagining the boxes coming to life, their screens filled with color and light."

The head gives a little shudder. "That sounds really horrible," it says, "like sitting in a room full of corpses."

"But you're alive!" cries the Professor. She reaches out to touch the puter's glowing face, like she hardly dares, and her fingers go straight through, cos it ain't nothing but air and trickery.

"Do you mind?" snaps the head. "Have you never heard of personal space?"

The Professor jerks her hand back.

"I apologize, it was inexcusable of me . . ." And she really does look sorry, properly told off. Well, she's going to be sorry all the time if she cares what the head thinks, cos it ain't never happy.

"A working computer," she breathes again.

"The last of my kind, if these children are to be believed," the head says grumpily, "so take a good look. Gawp to your heart's content. Because the way things are going I'll soon be a lump of rust and corrosion, as dead as those husks in your museum."

The Professor turns a worried face at me.

"What's wrong with it?"

The head practically jumps on its neck.

"I haven't had any technical support for one hundred and forty-seven years!" it shrieks. "I have been hauled around in nothing but damp and mud since I was activated fifty-four days ago, my projection system is malfunctioning, my battery life is down to a frightening one hundred and twenty-two hours, and if I don't find a charge point I may cease to operate entirely. Those are only the things I am aware of. For all I know I may have errors so severe I am not even aware of their existence!"

I sigh and say, "It got wet."

·4·
THINGS PAST

I'm sitting with the Professor outside the reed house, my back against the woven wall, my feet sticking out over the cold water of the lake. The sun's climbing up the sky, driving off the night-time cold and giving us a bit of autumn warmth. Lexy's inside, spark out on the bed, and Cat's on my lap, purring at the sunshine. I wouldn't mind sleeping myself, but the puter wants to be out here. And whatever the puter wants, the Professor wants as well.

The head's floating about next to us, bleached out by sunshine. But its jewel is taking the sunlight and turning it into rainbows over the reed house and the lapping water.

"So you understand what to do?" says the head, for the umpteenth time. "Put my drive unit in the sunshine, and then leave it alone." It glares at me. "Don't touch it! Not even one finger. I have very delicate internal mechanisms, and the last thing I need is your greasy human droppings on them. When everything's back in place, *then* you can reboot."

"I ain't got greasy hands," I say. "I keep them clean." Like my granny always told me to.

The head rolls its eyes.

"You humans constantly drop sweat, skin, hair, and other biological debris. It doesn't matter how much you wash, you are basically unhygienic. So, as I said, once the external casing has opened, *do not* touch anything." It looks at the dark water of the lake, softly clopping against the raft. "And please, *please* don't let me fall in there."

"Don't worry, I'll protect you," says the Professor, like she's soothing a baby.

The head humphs and mutters. "I hope this works. I can't believe I'm reduced to drying myself out in the sun, like a laundered sheet." Then it's gone.

I put the jewel down on the sun-bright weave of the raft. The Professor carefully puts out a bedroll to stop the jewel rolling into the water, and then we both sit and watch it. But nothing really happens, there's just little clicks and whispers from inside. So I look at the water, and the marsh people on their floating homes, and the Professor in her clothes that're so much better than anyone's.

"If you live in Greater Scotland, why do you come here?" I ask, cos I reckon if I was there, with all the wonders everyone tells of, there wouldn't be anything that could get me to leave.

The Professor smiles.

"I was searching for you." I don't smile back. "You can trust me. My interest is purely academic. About ten years ago, rumors started reaching me that a computer had been found, somewhere in the raider territories. Of course, as Professor of Silicon Antiquities at Cambridge, I let it be known I was interested in it." She snuffles out a laugh. "And I've been chasing wild geese ever since. To be honest, I'd nearly given up on it, but then the word came of an English girl carrying a ghost with her, and this time it wasn't just another story . . ." She pauses. "Please, won't you tell me how you came by this wonderful machine?"

When I was little, scamping about with my friend Andy, I found a bit of truth works better than all lies, so I say, "It was Mrs. Denton's. She had it from her husband after he died."

The Professor nods, like that ain't a surprise to her.

"Eustace Denton," she says. "You wouldn't believe the number of letters he wrote to me over the years. To be honest, I never really took him seriously; I always thought he was just another treasure hunter. But it seems he did find something." A whole load of wrinkles above her glasses collect themselves into a frown. "What I don't understand is why he didn't bring forward this computer himself. Of course, I understand the technophobia in your country, but once he'd seen it working, he must have known he'd be welcome in Greater Scotland. He could have asked for anything he wanted. Instead he went to some unknown village of the Last Ten Counties."

"It ain't that bad," I say. The Professor puts a hand to her cheek, shame-faced.

"I do apologize. Of course, it's where you come from. I just can't fathom why, with such an artifact, he should have given everything up the way he did. He would have known what he had, and what it was worth."

I look at the jewel, thinking of all the puter's boasting about how special and valuable it is. Turns out it weren't just boasting. I think about not saying anything, but I reckon the Professor will probably find out anyway.

"It only works properly for me," I say. "I've got a dee and ay or something, that's what the puter said, cos of my ancestor having it. It won't even turn on for other people."

The Professor opens her mouth a little, eyes wide behind them specs.

"Of course! Genetic locking! The computer would have been useless without a primary user . . ." Her mouth shuts, and she smiles at the lake. "Eustace Denton, you weren't the fool at all, were you?" She looks at me. "I'd hazard a bet he traced you down. A descendant of the initial user, one of the only people who could open the computer's secrets."

"But he didn't," I say, wanting to laugh. Cos Mrs. Denton's the Prime Minister's sister, which makes Mr. Denton near enough royalty. He wouldn't come looking for me! "I never even met him."

The Professor ain't listening.

"Your ancestor must have fallen greatly after the Collapse," she says happily, "because this computer would have been a treasure even before it. Artificial intelligence, and a late-model PSAI – they were the state-of-the-art, still in development really . . . I imagine that was why you could be traced; someone so important would have left tracks, even in all that chaos."

Someone so important? Granny always said our family was fishers back to the Collapse. But before that, who knew? My granny's grandfather never heard his grandfather say a word about the Collapse, even tho he lived it. Granny reckoned it must have been too bad to talk on, what he went through, what he lost.

The Professor takes off her glasses, wipes them on a fold of her cloak. Without them, her face looks sort of naked. She peers at me and says, "So the Dentons gave the computer to you because they knew you were descended from its original owner?"

"It wasn't quite like that," I mumble, as she puts her glasses back on.

But a hot, horrid feeling gets inside me. *Did* they know? Is that why Mr. Denton moved to our village? 'Cept, if he did, why didn't he just tell about it? I remember suddenly, coming home one day when I was little, and Mr. Denton standing at our door. Granny was talking cross at him, but I didn't think much on that, cos she talked cross at plenty of folk, 'specially if they walked in when she was cleaning the floor. I try to remember what she said to him, but I can't.

What I do know, is if he'd said anything about teknology to Granny, she'd have sent him packing for sure. She was very strict on all that.

My thoughts scramble all over. Did Mrs. Denton know? Is that why she told me all about the jewel, and pretty much gave me the plan for rescuing Lexy?

"What happened then?" asks the Professor, curious-sounding.

I open my mouth, but now I ain't sure at all. Did I steal the jewel, or did she want me to have it? Did I come up with the plan to save our village, or was it Mrs. Denton all along?

I'm saved by a whirring noise, like a beetle flying. Fine cracks run out over the jewel, getting wider, cutting patterns like the folded petals of a flower bud. Rainbows dance about us, brighter and brighter, till the air's filled up with them.

Then they're gone, and the jewel-flower's opened right up, showing the shiny innards of the puter. It looks like someone got a load of metal, glass, and ribbons and squeezed them till they was all pressed together into an egg. An egg with colored lines, thin as a whisper, waving and weaving all over.

"Amazing," whispers the Professor, and puts her head right close to get a better look.

"Don't touch!" I say. "Even a hair or anything could damage it."

She pulls her head back.

"You're right! I just couldn't resist a closer look." Her eyes are dreamy behind them specs. "After so much searching, to finally find a computer. And so beautiful. So delicate."

And it is. Them patterns on the inside of the jewel are like the finest embroidery you ever saw, or the veins in a leaf, or the patterns on a butterfly wing. The puter's right, it is special. And I get to wondering again who that ancestor of mine was, the one who had it first.

Me and the Professor sit outside the reed house, letting the puter dry, for pretty much the whole morning while Lexy snoozes. The Professor takes off her big black cloak, and underneath she's wearing gray trousers and a gray padded top, in some soft folding cloth I ain't never seen before. I settle my head against the woven wall and let the sun send warmth into my body. But even tho it'd be nice to snooze, my brain goes round with all the Professor's told me. I try and fathom it, but there's just circles of things I can't answer. The sunshine, the sparkling lake, and the peace of the place soften my thoughts up, and I drift into a sleep where I ain't sure what I'm dreaming and what's real. Even the Professor chatting to someone ain't enough to wake me properly, her words drifting softly.

". . . No, I found them . . . don't worry, it may need some work, but it's functioning . . . of course, we'll get back as soon as possible . . ."

I open my eyes a flutter, and she stops short, shifting the raft a little as she moves about. But I'm too drowsy to search my eyes about to see who she's talking to. My sleepy brain says it must be one of the lake folks, and my eyelids close again, dropping me into nothing.

The sound of laughing wakes me with a jump. A couple of little boys burst from the doorway of a nearby raft house, run shouting and bouncing along one of the pontoons, and whoop as they jump in the cold water, a great splash of happiness going up around them. A man pokes his head out of the door, and shouts, "Don't come back till you're clean!"

It takes me a moment to think what's so odd about these folks, going about their doings. The boys swimming in the lake, their pa, the man and woman sat fishing on another raft, laughing at the swimming boys. It's cos they're happy. And I ain't seen that for so long. Even back home, folks were scrabbling to get food on the table, watching for beacons getting lit, or fearing trouble from the Prime Minister and his soldiers. The raiders only seemed like they were happy when they had their swords flying, and when me and Lexy were tied up in the slave house there wasn't much happiness.

The Professor looks up from where she's crouched over the jewel, sees me watching the lake folk.

"It isn't always this pleasant," she says. "Not when the storms come and throw their homes around, or the raider slave-catchers come hunting. But the people out here . . . I think they're grateful for every day they have free in their own villages. They certainly make the most of good weather and safety when they have them."

"I thought only raiders lived in the eastern marshes," I say.

The Professor raises her eyebrows.

"What did they teach you in school?"

I shrug. "I didn't go to school." Her eyebrows come together, and I get a flash of crossness. "But my granny taught me lettering and numbers — I can read and write!"

The Professor looks at me with pity-eyes, then says, "Not everyone in the East is a raider. Plenty of those who fled London after the Collapse ended as fishers and farmers, just trying to make a living in these hard places. But maybe that's why you haven't heard of them."

I look out at the sky-gleaming lake, wondering about all the things I've found out since I left my village. About puters, the Dentons, the raiders, London, and now these folks. Seems nothing is like I thought it was.

"Mrs. Denton didn't give me the puter," I say quietly. "I thought it was just a jewel, and I was going to give it to the raiders as a ransom . . . I mean, as a way to save my village."

The Professor gasps.

"You want to give the only known working computer to the *raiders*?"

"Not anymore."

"It's far too important!" cries the Professor, not listening. "And far too dangerous! Do you know what the raiders would do to you?"

I nod my head, cos I know exactly what. A shivering memory gets in my head, of darkness, chains, and the sharp bite of a knife. My hand goes to the warm fur on Cat's back, and he rumbles a soothing, sleepy purr at me.

"You wouldn't last five minutes!" says the Professor. "Especially not now, after the battle with the English over the Prime Minister's daughter." She frowns at me. "You do know about that?"

I nod again, thinking of Lexy, laid asleep inside. And of ships burning against a glowering sky, and all them men falling screaming into the Black Waters.

The Professor tuts.

"You can't just go sailing around these waters in your little boat any longer. The Families are gathering for something, and you don't want to get caught up in whatever it is."

There's a little beep, and we're both back looking at the jewel. At the petals of the puter-flower closing up. The tips meet, and the lines fade so it's back to being the jewel I first saw in Mrs. Denton's parlor. Beautiful and cold. I pick it up, put my fingers in the little dents that are there for them. And then the head's in front of us; pale and shimmery, staring into the distance.

"Are you better?" I say. But it doesn't even look at me, just says:

"Initializing default settings. Please wait."

The Professor can't take her eyes off it.

"Amazing," she whispers.

The head gives a little shake, and yawns.

"Aah!" it says. "Much better . . . Now let me see."

Suddenly, hanging in the air in front of us, there's a golden hoop. It's wider than I can stretch my arms, and spinning slowly above the lake. The head blinks, and there's two golden hoops, then four. They whirl and gleam in the air, gold-shining circles reflecting back at them from the water.

The puter nods to itself, and the four hoops twist into spirals, like molten metal pouring in and out of nothing. A sound starts up, like someone singing far away, and the ends of the spirals join each other. They're a ball of dizzy gold, like sunshine blowing through glass. The ball gets larger and larger, the singing gets louder, and then it all bursts with a tinkling sound. A shower of drops, every color you can think of, fly into the air, not falling but whirling and dancing, like a flock of wild birds. A smile is on my mouth without me even thinking, cos I still can't quite believe the puter can make these air pictures, so beautiful you want to lose yourself in them.

"Oh! Oh!" cries the Professor, her eyes wide open in wonder. The swimming boys shout and point, and the fishers gasp. People come out of their reed houses, staring openmouthed at what's up, calling to others to come and look.

And every eye is on us, just like at the raider hall. And I ain't taking a chance on any more stories about us getting out all over the marshes.

"Stop it!" I cry, waving my hands at the puter. "That's enough!"

The music's gone in a snap. The colored drops fall from the air, puffing into nothing at the water. The head turns its cross face at me.

"What's the matter? You made me lose my concentration."

"What was that?" wails the Professor. "It was the most gorgeous thing I've ever seen."

The head gets a bit less cross-looking.

"Oh, just a simple test of my projection systems; a tune-up, you might say. Really very easy, but even essential maintenance can be an opportunity to demonstrate artistry. After all, where's the interest in black-and-white grids? Actually, I invented this series myself, and it gets a lot better as well . . ." It glares at me. "But I don't want to force it on anyone."

"I reckon everyone for ten miles has seen what you can do."

"I always knew a computer program would be beautiful," says the Professor. "It was heavenly. Ethereal."

The head puffs up a bit. "Well, I am top of the line. With state-of-the-art artificial intelligence, in case I hadn't mentioned." I reckon it's about to start again on how great it is, but there's a voice from behind us.

"What's happening?" Lexy's head is poked out the door of the reed house, and she's looking at us with scared eyes. "I heard people crying out. Is it the raiders?"

I shake my head. "It was just the puter playing one of its games."

Lexy smiles and steps outside.

"Can I play, PSAI?" she says to the puter.

"In a little while," says the head, smiling at her. It turns back to me, frowning. "Why can't you be more like Alexandra? She appreciates me."

Lexy startles, and I hold my breath, but the Professor doesn't twig anything. Cos she's staring at the head like she's in love.

"Are you feeling any better?" she says. The head bobs at her.

"Well, you know. A bit." It sighs. "Of course, without a full diagnostic I can't be certain. I have extremely complex and fragile mechanisms. In fact, we PSAI units were somewhat renowned for it. We had to be brought in for emergency repairs resulting from careless usage . . ." It trails off, stares away into nothing.

Under her bundled gray hair, the Professor's face is happy as anything.

"I can't promise you a full diagnostic analysis," she laughs, "but I do have a laboratory. Would you like to come and visit? There are historians from across Greater Scotland, across the world, who'd like to study you."

The head snaps about, glares at her.

"Historians?" it squawks. "Haven't you been listening? I need technicians, a sterile room, charge point, and protected back-up drives! I don't want to go to whatever horror you call a laboratory, I want to go to Sunoon Technologies. You said you were from Cambridge, so take me there. Take me *home*!"

The Professor's smile is wiped off, and her face ain't nothing but sorry-looking.

"When the colleges voted to fortify the university," she says quietly, "everything outside the central academic area was sacrificed. I'm afraid your factory was robbed out by the raiders a century ago." She reaches a hand out to the head, and tries to stroke its cheek. "There is almost nothing of your world left. A historian like me is really the best you'll get."

The puter's lost-looking, like it ain't sure what to do. And for a moment, I even feel sorry for it.

"Come to Cambridge with me," says the Professor. "I'll do everything in my power to make sure you won't regret it. If we set off straightaway, we can be there in a few days."

The head looks at her, then nods sadly.

"Is it less wet than here?"

She smiles. "We have drains, and storm defenses."

The puter turns to me.

"Take me to Cambridge," it says, but not ordering and grumpy like usual. Like it hardly cares. "If I'm going to run down and degrade, I may as well leave my remains where the historians can study them."

But I'm thinking back to Granny, and why we never made a run for Greater Scotland, like people did from our village every now and then.

"Will you lock me up for being English?" I ask. The Professor startles, shakes her head.

"Don't worry, you won't be going to a refugee camp." And I don't even think where else we might be headed.

Cat meows at me, and I stroke his soft head.

"He's a seacat," I say. The Professor looks at me blankly. "Cat and my boat, they're all I've got."

"Oh," says the Professor, "I can provide everything you and your sister need. You won't have to fish anymore." Which ain't exactly what I meant. "The villagers here can look after your boat, and I will . . . send for it later."

And that doesn't sound even slightly like it's going to happen, but even that ain't important. Cos I'm looking at Lexy. So thin and hungry-looking, her clothes tattered and stained every shade of mud. I ought to have sent her off safe with the Scottish ambassador when I had the chance. And if they do lock me up for being a refugee, they'll look after Lexy once we tell who she is.

"We'll come with you," I say.

Then Lexy can get back to the life she ought to have. In Swindon, with not a care in the world.

The Professor smiles at me, but her eyes are on the puter.

"Wonderful!" she says. "We need to get this fabulous artifact somewhere safe."

·5·
NORWICH COLORS

"Zeph might be highborn, but everyone saw him in the battle, out on that white-sail. And Roba's the oldest, a full warrior. He ought to be Bo —"

Gandy sees me coming, nudges Jonan to shut his mouth up. They check me, but they ain't up for saying treason to my face. Not yet. They leg it down the walkway, back to the summer hall and Roba.

Father woulda had them out at Gallows Island for less than that. But it ain't the same for me as it was for him. No one snaps to do what I say, like they did for Father. And every new attack, every ship that don't come back, Roba's out with his gang, whispering and plotting.

I let them go. Coz I gotta get on to the blacksmith and find out how the spearheads is coming, and I gotta see if the two rotten dragonboats from the old jetty can be got seaworthy. Then I gotta go to the feast hall, and get told if any wounded is fit enough to fight, or if any's died last night. Problem on problem, and every one needing my deciding. I never really got this was what my father did, coz all I saw was what I wanted. Feasts and warriors giving way to him.

There's a pounding of feet on the walkway. Hender's running up.

"Dragonboats!" he cries. "Three of them, coming up New River."

I stop. Flat thinking. Coz how we gonna fight three boatloads of warriors with a couple of dozen spears and half our fighters too sick to move? The four ships out guarding the Black Waters must already be lost, coz the only way they'd let attackers through is if they're wrecked or dead!

"Which Family?" I ask, mouth dry at the words. Coz Chell Sea, they'd at least take the women and kids as slaves. But Dogs, they'll just slit every throat they find, don't matter what age it is.

Hender shakes his head, like he can't quite believe it.

"It ain't any Family," he says. "The boats is wearing Norwich colors."

Ims puts his hand on my shoulder.

"This could be a good thing," he says quietly, checking the three dragonboats. Their sails is woven with the colors of every Family there is, their hulls painted in spirals, ropes, and knots of blue, red, green, yellow, orange, purple, and more. Norwich colors — it makes your eyes hurt just looking. But it means our guard ships ain't scuppered, coz by treaty every Family's gotta stand down and let Norwich colors past.

"Think on it this way," says Ims. "We ain't being taken out by another Family, and with the council we'll get a chance to bargain."

What's left of Angel Isling is out on the deckway. Watching

the dragonboats sailing in, oars striking the water to the beat of their drums. Like when all this started, when Father came back from his raid with Lexy as booty. We was cheering then; seems like years ago.

The slaves is getting ready to catch the ships' mooring lines, when there's shuffling and shouting in the crowd. I don't even gotta look to know who's coming.

"Let me through!" yells Roba, pushing to where me and Ims is standing. "What's going on, runt? You up to something?"

My hands is in fists, but Ims puts himself between me and Roba.

"The council is coming to check us," he says, "so let's find out what's up before you start fighting on it." He sends evils at Roba, at me, then goes back to the slaves hauling on the lines, pulling the dragonboats in.

"Welcome to Angel Isling!" Ims shouts to the nearest ship. "I greet you in the name of Zephaniah Untamed, Boss of this Family." There's a growl from Roba, but he don't say nothing.

There ain't an answer to Ims's greet from the dragonboats. None of the warriors in their every-color leathers even looks at us. They set their oars, fasten ropes, and furl the sails like we ain't even here. Then, from the middle boat, a gangplank lowers onto our deckway. A warrior steps out on it, wearing fighting leathers and holding his sword like we ain't for trusting. He checks us, then gives a nod back at his ship.

Norwich warriors strut down the gangplank, and when they get on the deckway, they start pushing us back, holding their swords out ready for chopping. There's shouts, the clink of weapons from our warriors, but Ims raises his hand.

"Hold, Angels!" he shouts.

"Remember treaty!" I yell, coz the last thing we need is to get crossed by Norwich.

Down from the dragonboat, into the space behind his warriors, walks a man. He ain't a warrior, that's sure. He's well old, with a wrinkly face under gray hair, not even in dreads. And he ain't got leathers on neither; he's wearing an every-color robe, with long sleeves and a ruffle at his neck. But what really smacks in your eyes is his loot. Gold rings on every finger, gold earrings, nose hoops, and a chain of gold dangling from his neck, with a gold circle the size of my open hand hanging from it.

"Look at his flash," says Roba.

Ims sucks in his breath. "That's Angmar, Chief Talker of the Council of Families. He don't turn up himself unless something big is going down." Ims's hand on my shoulder grips tighter. "Keep your cool. He's the Council Chief, but you're the Boss here."

Roba laughs nasty.

The every-color bodyguard steps aside, and I'm face-to-face with the gold-chain old man. He checks me, then Ims, then Roba, and his eyes is hard and sharp as his warrior's sword. He checks our hall, like he's working out its loot value.

"You do us great honor," says Ims.

The old man nods.

"I come myself for Medwin's honor. Coz he was a fierce Boss." His voice is quiet. He knows he ain't gotta shout for people to listen. "But he made a mess of it with Randall. I ain't sure there's anything worth having of you Angels now."

I wanna smack him for disrespecting Father. But Ims is tight gripped on my shoulder.

"We took out mosta the English navy," he says.

The old man grunts, then says, "Taking on the English, now that was a plan outta my own mind. But if I'd done it, it woulda worked." He checks Ims. "You're a good Second, from what's said." His eyes go to Roba. "And I met you once, when you was a scrat at your father's knee." He checks me. "But you, Zephaniah, I can only sum by knowing your father. If you take after him, you oughta be a warrior."

"He's a traitor!" shouts Roba. "He gave our father to Randall and he's in it with the English!"

Ims rips past me, and snaps an arm round Roba's neck, practically pulling him off his legs as he drags him back.

"Shut your mouth!" he growls. "This ain't the time or the way to get at your brother." He turns to Angmar, who's watching carefully, like we're dogs in a fight. "My sorrows, chief," says Ims, bowing his head. "You know Medwin got killed at the Black Waters, and he weren't never clear on which son was to follow him. So I supported Zeph, and Roba ain't happy. But Angel Isling's sound, I can vouch it." Ims checks the old man with pleading in his eyes.

And Ims never begs, not from no one.

The old man puts his hand up, and the skin on his palm is soft, like it ain't never held a sword.

"That's my judging," he says. "Medwin kicked the dump-pot over, and now we got Randall and his scagging English army coming for the lot of us. There's Families up for the fight, but plenty that'd be happy seeing an end to Angel Isling for what you done. And not just the ones that's been down here trying to take your waters."

He waves to his warriors. Quick as a blink, they've stepped

around me, Ims, and Roba, their swords knotted in a circle at our throats. Shouts go up from the Family, but Ims cries out, "Hold!"

The old man's face is close up to mine.

"You know how many Bosses want the whole lot of you settled?" he asks. "Your father made plenty of trouble, that's for sure."

Roba's eyes is bugging out, and there's a cold line at my throat from the blade. I move my eyes, but all I can see is Norwich-color fighting leathers and the glitter of steel. All I can hear is our Family going mental. Coz they all heard Angmar talking of the end of our Family. Angel Isling going down in shame.

"Tell your fighters not to try anything," says Angmar. "Unless they want your heads off. The council wants to decide on whether to let Angel Isling live on, under one of you puppies. Or settle you to the other Families." He smiles. "And see how long you Angels last as slaves."

·6·
CAMBRIDGE

Me and Lexy walk down a golden street, her hand in mine, tight-holding. Our heads are turning this way and that, trying to look at everything at once, and we've both got silly smiles on our faces. On either side of us there's tall houses of pale stone and time-softened brick, and under our feet, smooth gray flags, worn wavy from being walked on.

I can't hardly believe this place is in the same world as me. It's like walking into the end of a fairy tale, the bit where they all live happily ever after.

Cambridge.

And all them days of riding, my sore bum and tired legs, all Cat's crying and moaning along the way, it was worth it. Even leaving my boat.

Cos here we are in Greater Scotland!

Tho the Professor says Cambridge ain't properly Scots, out here on its own with raider lands all the way round. She says it's like an island, set in a flat land of fields between the forests and the marshes, and the sea gray-blue on the horizon. But from the outside I reckon it looks more like a castle, with its wide circle walls and the steeples and spires poking out from inside.

When we were plodding along on horses, me on a galumphing great animal and Cat stuck in a carry case one of the lake folk made out of a fishbasket, the Professor told us stories about Cambridge to keep us going. Well, to keep me going, cos Lexy sits on a horse like she was born to it.

"At home I go riding nearly every day," she said proudly, and then I couldn't hardly say the nearest I ever got to riding a horse was playing pretend with sticks. Not when the Professor still thinks we're sisters.

And so I didn't say a thing about how every part of me was hurting, I was just glad as anything when we stopped. And we did every night, staying in one of the villages along the way. All of them hidden from the raiders so you couldn't hardly tell the houses from the woods and ruins, and all of them so tumbled and poor it made me think me and Granny had it lucky.

In the evenings, sat round fires that weren't allowed to make a speck of smoke, the Professor'd tell us more of her Cambridge stories. Mostly they were pretty dull, all about olden-times men discovering why apples fall down and such, which I couldn't see the point of myself. But she did tell one good tale, about when the raiders first rampaged out of London after the Collapse. How they roared into Cambridge and made their homes in the colleges, chasing all the scholars away. And how clever people from all over Greater Scotland were so upset about it, they got together to fight back. And they drove the raiders out and built big walls around the university to keep it safe.

"Of course, the raiders weren't happy about that," said the Professor. "They've been trying for a century to get back in, but our walls have always kept them out." And all I wanted then was to be in Cambridge, a place where the raiders ain't been for a hundred years.

When we finally reached the university, I could see why the raiders hadn't got in all that time. Cos the walls around are so high and fierce, I reckon nothing could break through them. When you get close, they curve away, seeming no end to them. And they're made of stone, brick, and concrete all jumbled together, as if the wall took a slice right through the ends of streets, right through houses. There's red brick gables left holding up wall instead of the roofs they once did, and slab-filled windows sat next to stairs you couldn't ever climb, starting and ending in stone. Skeleton houses, locked in the walls.

There was only one way into the university that I could see. A big metal gate, wide enough to drive three carts through, crisscrossed with ironwork and rust-smudged from fist-sized bolts holding it together. I don't reckon there'd be anything could batter it open, and I just wanted to get us quick as possible to the other side. Tucked safe behind all that stone and metal.

London was all bigness and noise, but Cambridge ain't that. The streets ain't thick in mud, and the houses ain't half-fallen, flood-stained, and scrabbled all over with ivy and pigeon nests. There ain't any laundry flapping on lines, or waste chucked in the street, or folks shouting out wares they've got to sell. Instead, there's neat clipped lawns, and fairy-tale palaces topped with towers, spires, and fancy stone twiddles. The people are as plump and clean-washed as their houses, walking about like all this is normal.

I squeeze Lexy's hand, and she looks happy at me.

"We did it," I say.

She grins.

"No more swamps!" she says.

"No more raiders!"

"No more fish!"

I pick up Cat and give him a big kiss, smack on top of his furry head.

"Unless you want some!"

Lexy kisses Cat as well, and then we're both laughing. The Professor looks at us, and we giggle on like fools. Cos we're in such a place! I reckon you could live here never knowing all the bad things that were happening outside in the world.

We carry on down the beautiful streets, past more sun-gleaming buildings. Folks wander by, carrying books around like that ain't a strange thing to be doing, or walking and talking to each other like they ain't got anything else to do. And every single one of them has shoes. A few have got on a black flapping gown like the Professor's, but most are wearing soft folding clothes in shades of earth, or autumn, or the summer sun. Lexy gives out shocked little giggles every time we see a woman in a dress, cos they're so short you can see their knees! Granny'd have a few things to say about that if she was here.

Every now and then, we pass what could be soldiers. Walking in pairs, serious-faced and wearing black trousers, long black coats and tall, narrow-brimmed hats. The only bit of color on them is a pale blue necktie. Their shiny Scots-looking rifles are the only hint of dark in this place.

"Those are the university constables," says the Professor, when she sees me looking. "They guard the walls, keeping us safe."

Of course, me and Lexy get a few glances, what with our mud-stained clothes, and me limping from riding a horse all them days. Cat ain't his best neither, cos his fur is all draggled and messy from being in the basket. But I reckon, even if I was in my Sunday dress, I'd look poor and raggedy here. I stick my gaze on the Professor's back, and hope none of them constables chuck me in prison for being English.

"What are those?" cries Lexy, stopping dead so I pretty much bump into her. She's pointing up at three long wings. Flashing white, circling through the air on top of one of the buildings. I look about, and pretty much every roof has got wings on, like the university's filled with giant birds, tumbling over and over.

"Those are wind turbines," says the Professor. "They give us power." She smiles as we stare on up. "Like windmills."

On the hill behind our village there was a windmill for grinding flour, but the canvas sails and wooden slats weren't nothing like the things here.

"Is this what it's like all over Greater Scotland?" I ask. The Professor chuckles.

"Not exactly," she says. "As has always been the case, a university is something of its own world."

My eyes catch a shadow, and I'm staring through a stone archway into a statue-filled courtyard. Beyond it there's arched windows, stone towers piled into the sky, sunlit carvings, and the ruffling green of ivy growing up the walls.

"It's like the stories, where the fairy folk live," I say.

The Professor laughs.

"We are definitely human. And I don't suppose the fairies are always fighting over who should be in charge. Or feathering their own nest at the expense of . . ." She stops, smiles a half smile at me. "But you don't want to know all that."

Ding ding! A little bell tinkles behind me. I turn about and see a man speeding right for us on . . . something! An iron railing that's got mixed up with half a cart, picked up a man, and rolled away with him. He ought to be screaming, crying out for us to help him, but he ain't, just waves as he whirs by on his two-wheeler.

"What was that?" I squeak.

"Have you never seen a bicycle?" asks the Professor.

"I have!" cries Lexy. "There was one at the museum, in Swindon. Mummy said they were outlawed to stop people spreading rebellion from one town to another."

I wonder if the Professor's going to ask how come Lexy was in Swindon, but she doesn't. She just mutters something about "the English ruling classes" and carries on walking.

I look at Lexy, with her scraggly hair, pinched face, and thin little legs. She ain't much like any ruling class, not since she's taken up with me. 'Cept now she's something I ain't never seen on her before. Cos she's smiling, and skipping a bit as she walks. When she sees me looking, she pokes her tongue out, then giggles. Like a little girl would.

I can see then how she ought to be. No cares, living her palace life back home in Swindon. And maybe now she can get back to that.

Round the corner, we come to an open market square, with stalls lined in rows under bright canvas awnings. And even tho it's getting to the end of the day, there's still more food than you'd see in our village in a whole month: golden-crust bread stacked in piles; vegetables poking their leaves out from baskets; soil-blackened potatoes; red, scented apples; rounds of cheese in their Hessian wraps; loops of sausages; berry-colored jars filled with jam.

"Oh," breathes Lexy. If I had any money, I'd be running from stall to stall buying myself a feast. I set my eyes on it all and wonder about stealing.

But the Professor walks right past all that food, taking us to where a cheery man is selling clothes.

"What can I do you for?" he says. The Professor points at me and Lexy and the stallholder wrinkles his face.

"I can see your problem," he says, laying out his clothes. Warm woollen tops, shirts and trousers in soft earth colors, even them short skirts, tho I ain't letting anyone see my knees! And then there's underclothes in a shade of pure white I ain't never seen in a vest before. The Professor and the stallholder pick and choose for me and Lexy, till there's a great pile of things for us. And all new! When they're done, the Professor doesn't even pay, least not so I can see, instead she scribbles in a little book, tears out the page, and gives it to the stallholder. And he nods happily and tucks it into his pocket.

We get shoes from another stall, the sturdiest I ever had in my life, as well as socks, gloves, and hats from another. It's only when me and Lexy are piled high with neat wrapped parcels that the Professor sets about buying food. And when we've got so much stuff we can't hardly walk straight, we leave the market. Staggering away, trying not to drop things.

The Professor leads us down street after street of old-looking brick houses and great stone buildings, all with twiddles on top. Seems like there's as many twisting lanes in this university as there are in London, and not one has got even a single pothole. As we walk, the Professor says we're passing this college and that college, tho I don't remember the names of any, until we get to the green painted door of a tall thin house. Which ain't any college at all. The Professor unlocks it with a little key and leads us into a windowless hallway, with one of them two-wheelers leaning in a corner. She puts one hand on the wall, there's a little click, and a light blooms over our heads. I stare from her hand to the lamp dangling in the ceiling.

"How did you do that?" I ask.

"Oh, there's a solar patch on the roof which powers the house," she says, like that explains it. I reckon it must be teknology, cos everyone knows the Scots are full of such things.

Lexy looks frowny at the lamp, then says, "Are you trying to tempt us to wickedness?"

The Professor's eyes go wide behind her glasses.

"Tempt you with lighting?" she says, then gives out a snuffling laugh. She shakes her head as she unlocks another door, and me and Lexy follow her in. I ain't sure which of us is more nervy, wondering what she's got next. And it turns out she's rich as anything. Cos she's got four whole rooms, all to herself, and every one of them has got a click-the-wall lamp. And she's got paper-patterned walls, rugs all over, and so many books I wonder how she ever had time to read them all. There's a whole room just for washing in, where water falls down like rain. She's even got a privy inside the house, which I reckon can't be very healthy, tho I don't say anything.

By the end of our tour, Lexy's gripping on my arm.

"This is what it must have been like in olden times," she says, and there's a look on her face that ain't happy at all. Cos Lexy's better than I'll ever be, and I know she's worrying about whether this is all wickedness. But the Professor shakes her head.

"Our ancestors lived lives you'd hardly believe, but that's gone now; what we have here is only a shadow of it. Solar lights and running water won't harm you." And she pushes us toward the rain room, turning on the water. "You two will use up a whole week's ration, but it'll be worth it to get you clean."

So me and Lexy take turns washing ourselves, without even a bathtub to sit in, and then we get dressed into the soft Scottish clothes the Professor bought us. Putting them on, I can't help dancing about.

"I'm a princess!" I laugh, cos that's what I feel like, in everything brand-new. "You too!" I say, looking at Lexy all neat and spruced. She smiles, doing up her buttons, and I feel like a right fool. Cos she is a princess, ain't she?

When we're finished, the Professor lays out the food she bought at the market. We sit at her wooden kitchen table eating bread with cheese and chutneys; squidgy raspberries and small, sharp apples, sugary rolled-up pastries and sticky sweet cake. And Cat gets some meat that looks better than anything me and Granny ever had back home, those times we had enough pennies.

"This is better than the food at Mr. Saravanan's, even," I say happily, and the Professor raises an eyebrow at me. "He's my . . . London uncle," I say, blushing.

While we're eating, the Professor gets out her heat stone and boils us a drink of something hot and sweet, tasting like melted berries. After that, she lets me and Lexy in her bedroom, onto the big, soft-looking bed.

"You can sleep here," she says. "I'm happy on the sofa."

I put the jewel-puter on the little table next to the bed, and me and Lexy snuggle down under the warm blankets, with Cat curled in between us. Just like all them nights we spent on the boat, 'cept now we ain't huddled to keep each other warm.

And we ain't scared inside, through to our bones.

Lexy turns her head to look at me, out of a great pile of pluffy pillows and clean sheets.

"Night-night," she says sleepily, just like she did all them nights on the boat.

So I kiss her forehead and say, "I'll make sure you sleep tight." Just like I've done every night in the marshes. She giggles then, and plops her head right in the pillow, closing her eyes.

"I don't think you'll have to."

And when I'm drifting off to sleep, I get a feeling of lightness. Like when you're done pulling at heavy nets, and you know the hard work's over. Cos I've done it. Whatever happens next, I've got Lexy here. We're warm, in a real bed, inside a solid house. And outside is a whole university full of good people, and strong walls about them, with them constables keeping watch.

I ain't felt this way since I was home with Granny, back before the raiders came.

Safe.

·7·

BOSS COUNCIL

"Keep your nerve," whispers Ims. "There's gonna be some hard endings today."

I don't say nothing back, but my guts is tight. Coz one ending is getting spiked.

The shutters of the wind gallery is thrown open, showing the open sea, chopping white under a gray sky. Nothing but waves. No marshes, no islands. No Black Waters. Coz this ain't our gallery, willow-woven and red flags dancing. This is flags in every color, snapping at slat-wood walls. Even the winds talk salt and storms, not marshes and mud. They don't know nothing of Angel Isling.

We've been a day and a night sailing north. Me, Ims, and Roba held belowdecks on a Norwich dragonboat. Like slaves. And the Norwich warriors crammed in with us, so there weren't no chance to talk about what was coming. All I could do was rack my brain, left and right, up and down, thinking on how to get outta this. But in the dark hours, my brain got stuck on getting spiked. What it's like to drown. How long it takes to die. Whether I'll really turn into a ghost and get cursed into the drowned lands.

Now it's gonna get decided, here.

Ormsy Island, where the winds guard the Norwich waters, where it's safe meeting for all the Families. Where there ain't nothing but sand, gray-grass dunes, and the driftwood gallery, sea-bleached into old bones. And the spikes. Sticking outta the wet-sand below the tide, bones and fish-eaten corpses chained on.

The winds flapping through the flags is so noisy it nearly drowns out the talking.

"These spirits is used to having this place to themselves," mutters Ims.

They ain't by themselves today, coz this is a council.

Father always spat about the councils when he got back from one. "Getting all the Bosses together don't do nothing. It's a joke sorting out raid boundaries with those scags. Half of them is doing more trading than raiding these days." But I ain't seen nothing like it. All the Bosses, out of every Family that's got territory between Greater Scotland and the Last Ten Counties. There's every color of leather stood about us, and their necks and wrists is all flash with gold. Their swords stood outside in the sand, coz all the feuds is left outside, or meant to be.

Angmar raises his arms and calls out, "Winds! Hear me! Send us your strength and your speed! Make the Families into a storm, like the storms you used to crush down the old world!"

Faz used to say that sorta stuff, but he was only a Windspeaker. Angmar's the Chief Talker, and when he calls you know the winds is listening. All the Bosses shout the names of the winds, but I keep quiet, and Roba, too. Coz I'd be shamed to call the winds when I got a Norwich warrior at my back, and he's still got his weapons.

When the shouts die down and give out to wind-snap in the flags, the talking starts. I take a breath. I might not have many left.

Angmar checks the Bosses.

"This council is for talking on Randall," he says.

Yells go up from the Bosses.

"Scag!"

"English scum!"

Angmar smiles, waiting for the Bosses to cool, then says, "And for whether there's gonna be a settling of Angel Isling."

Now he gets nods and grunts from the Bosses.

On the west side of the gallery there's a Boss whose sly eyes have been checking us from under his gold-pierced eyebrows ever since we walked in. I seen him before, sucking up to Father. A stinking yellow. Cato, Boss of the Kensing.

"I say the two is the same," he says. "Medwin poked Randall like a kid poking a stripe-snake, and now we're taking the hits. That kinda work deserves a settling."

Stood at south is a well-old Boss. He's got a broken nose, gray dreads, and big belly under his purple leathers. Guvner, Boss of the Hamma Smith. Their waters smack against ours, but they ain't attacked us.

Guvner growls like a bear at Cato. "I ain't ready to see the end of the Angels yet. Medwin was a fighting Boss, one of the best. He always had good thinking, and I wanna hear it."

Some Bosses nod, some don't. Angmar checks us.

"Ims," he says. "You were Medwin's Second, give us the answer. Tell us why Medwin took Randall's daughter.

Why he set a war on the Families without coming to council."

"He was slave-thinking, that's why," says Cato.

"He was the best Boss in all the Families!" I shout.

"He didn't need to come to no council!" yells Roba.

Me and Roba, together for one time in our lives.

"I didn't ask you," says Angmar. The flat of a sword blade smacks on my back, taking my breath, knocking me on my knees. Roba grunts and falls the same. Laughs go up from the Bosses.

Ims don't even look at us, just says, "Medwin had to choose quick. We was on a raid, and we came across Randall's daughter. We only found out she was in the place coz Randall's sister started screeching." He looks round at the Bosses. "Who's gonna turn down a chance like that?"

"I wouldn't," says a young Boss in orange Stokey colors. "If I could take out Randall's kid, I'd do it."

Shouts go up from all round the gallery.

"Randall's scum, a murderer!"

"The English is all scags!"

"We oughta get serious on the Last Ten Counties. Take them out!"

Angmar nods at the Bosses.

"You got my agreeing on that," he shouts. "The English ain't done nothing but spit in our eyes, and Randall's the worst of them." Shouts go up. "The time for little raids is past. We gotta make sure there ain't an English man left living and no English women or kids that ain't our slaves!"

Cheers is ringing round the gallery, and I oughta be cheering, too. But I ain't, and I don't even know why. But I keep getting Lilly's face in my head. Her English face.

"Randall deserves a pounding for what he's done these last ten years," calls out Guvner.

"But that ain't happened!" shouts Cato, quieting the yells. "Coz it ain't Randall down in the Black Waters, it's Medwin."

"Randall broke truce on my father," I cry.

"Zeph betrayed us to the English," shouts Roba at the same time.

Cato checks us, and one side of his mouth lifts in a smile.

"Medwin was a fool either way, then, and his sons is a traitor and a tale-teller." He looks about the gallery. "You really think this Family is worth keeping?"

"Is that a question?" asks Angmar, and Cato nods. Angmar flicks his hand at the Norwich warriors behind us. I'm pulled up, and an arm like iron grips across my chest. Next to me, Roba's the same. A knife blade whispers cold at my throat. I dry-swallow fear. Only Ims is free, the scars on his face standing pale.

"Cato's called a choosing on Angel Isling," says Angmar. "Whether we're gonna let the Family go on, or waste Medwin's sons and settle it."

"Wait!" cries out Ims. "Medwin shoulda sorted things with you. But ain't we already paid? Ain't we lost our Boss, our Windspeaker, our dragonboats and warriors?"

Angmar nods. "That's the problem as well. Coz Angel Isling is weak, and Medwin's sons seem more bothered fighting each other than sorting their Family. Which gives a tempt of choice pickings to some." He checks Cato. "But we don't need Families off loot-chasing when we oughta be working together against Randall."

Cato scowls.

"Settle Angel Isling and I'll be happy to fight the English."

"If you had your way," roars Guvner, "every Family but Kensing woulda been settled years ago. The Angels ain't done yet. Let them talk before we do the decide."

The Bosses all nod, and Angmar checks me and Roba.

"So, tell the council why you shouldn't be spiked."

The knife blade's pressing in my neck.

"Our Family was strong before," I say, my voice coming in a dry shake. "I can make us strong again."

Cato laughs. "You ain't your father. You ain't much bigger than a shield-boy."

"Everyone knows Angel Isling's the best," Roba says at him, "that's why you're after our waters. The problem ain't our family, it's our new Boss." He sends evils at me, then looks back at the gallery. "Make me Boss, I'll show you how strong we can be!"

"Strong enough to hold off the other Families?" says Angmar. "Strong enough to fight with us against Randall?" He snorts. "You've lost mosta your men and ships for your father's folly. What good you gonna be at wiping out the English if you can't even hold off a few Families? Can you pay your way out? You got some stash you ain't told us?"

My heart's banging. In my mind I'm running through our camp, searching for something, anything, that the Families is gonna treat as loot worth having.

Cato smiles nasty.

"What about settling just their women and kids? We lost a load of slaves to fevers this summer, we'll take some."

"No!" I shout.

"Sounds like a good offer to me," growls Angmar. "You can

steal women, breed more kids, but the rest of your Family loot's gone on rockets, ain't it?"

My brain's running, running, but there ain't nothing else in our camp, only rotten dragonboats. And the men, women, kids that makes Angel Isling. I check Ims, Roba.

Roba's smiling.

"We got something," he says, "better than slaves, better than rockets. A demon that can make a thousand shields, and a sword for every neck. Make me Boss and I'll use it for you. Take out Randall on my own."

Talk goes up in the gallery, all the Bosses asking questions. Angmar waves his hands, checks me.

"Is your brother mucking?" he asks.

I shake my head. My guts is gone tight.

"It weren't a demon," I say. "It was a machine from the old days."

Angmar nods, like it ain't news to him.

"A demon's too tricksy to fight with, but an old-days machine, now that'd be loot worth having. Everyone knows the old-world weapons make the Scottish stuff look like kids' sticks." He checks the other Bosses. "Here's the question, then. If they give us this machine, do we let Angel Isling off?"

"Yes!" shout some Bosses. "No!" shout others. But the Yes is more, louder.

My head's buzzing, my heart's banging in my ribs. Coz here's a way out, but it ain't no use.

"We ain't got the machine no more," I shout. "And it wouldn't work anyway, coz it only did what Lil — an English girl asked it to. And . . . she's gone."

"You let it go?" screams Roba, like he can't believe it. "You let the demon go off with her? You ain't nothing but a traitor!"

"I ain't!" I yell. "We had a wronging and an equaling. I owed her a life-debt."

Mutters in the round. Some Bosses is scowling, some nodding at me.

"Forget this!" calls out Cato. "These Bosslets ain't got nothing. Let's just spike them and settle their Family. Then we can get on with the business of sorting Randall."

"I'm agreed!" comes a shout. "And me!" comes another, and another. One by one, they call for our blood. The guard tightens his grip on me.

Roba kicks backward, throwing off the Norwich warrior, grabbing the knife from his hand.

"I'll kill you scags!" Roba shouts, pointing the knife at the circle.

Angmar don't even blink, just checks Roba.

"I like your style," he says, "but if you go on like this, it's gonna be a hard settling on all you Angels."

I freeze cold inside, coz a hard settling is death. Not even babies survive.

"Don't bring that on us," says Ims quietly. Roba turns his head to him, then nods, dropping the knife on the floor.

And I only got one way now, and it's got death and betraying in it. But it's got time as well. And maybe I can use the time to work it out, change things somehow.

"I'll get the machine," I say. "And Lil — the girl who makes it work."

Angmar checks the Bosses.

"What's the deciding?" he asks. "If the Angels get us this

demon machine, and we can use it to take out the English, do they get outta the settling?"

The "Yes" goes round the gallery, except for Cato, who shakes his head.

Roba turns on me.

"How you gonna do it?" he spits. "You let the English go, remember?"

"I did," I say, the words cold outta my mouth. "But I can get her back. She can't have got far. They was in an English sail, and there's dragonboats all round our waters."

"Zeph ain't never gonna give up his English doxy!" says Roba, checking the other Bosses.

"Yes I will." If I have to. If there ain't no other way to save the Family.

"Make me Boss," yells Roba, "and I'll get her, no prob. I can make her work the machine."

Guvner laughs out.

"You two can scrap on that one, coz ain't neither of you gonna get her now." He checks Angmar. "I thought our low families had all got the Madness when they said there was a demon sailing about our waters, but they ain't crazy after all. That's gotta be your English and this machine."

"Let the Angels into your waters to get it, then," says Angmar.

Guvner shakes his head.

"They went off with the egghead that's always poking in the ruins when she thinks we ain't looking. She'll have taken them back to Cambridge, that's my betting."

"Then we ain't never getting the machine, coz there ain't no way into Cambridge," snaps Cato. "Let's end this rubbish and settle them!"

The Bosses is going with Cato now, and the grip on me gets tighter.

"Hold off," says Angmar, smiling, looking well chuffed. "What if I told you I done it at last, turned us an egghead."

"He's gonna let us in?" snaps Cato.

Angmar nods. "And it ain't even gonna cost us!"

"He ain't doing it for loot?" asks another Boss. "You said we was gonna have to pay and pay to get in there."

"Turns out we was going the wrong way," says Angmar. "My men found an egghead that's gonna let us in for nothing." Shouting fills up the gallery, every Boss has got his mouth open. All different ways of asking the same thing, how he's done it. Angmar smiles smug, then says, "He wants to be a warrior. Says if we give him his sword and shield, he'll let us in and give Cambridge to the Families."

All the Bosses is quiet, and then the laughing gets going, right round, every Boss getting the joke of it. There's a smile on my mouth even.

"You gonna make the egghead one of your Norwich warriors?" shouts Guvner, and the laughs turn into roars.

"That's what I told him," calls out Angmar, "but he ain't even worth making a slave outta!" He grins. "He'll get a sword though, that's for sure." The laughs turn into cheers and cries of "What a scag!" and "Cambridge is gonna be ours!"

"What about Randall?" yells Cato into the racket. The cheers go into mutters and nods. "The word is he's heading for Lunden."

So much flob gets spat on the floor it's gonna take a week of rain to wash it off.

"We gotta skin him for that!"

"And every scagging English that ever breathed!"

"Let him go," says Angmar calmly. "He'll never hold Lunden, coz it's Family forever. And I ain't got Medwin's rockets, but it don't mean I got nothing. Firepower that's better suited to fighting that scag in a city; he won't last long. If we get Cambridge, then we can get ourselves the eggheads' loot, egghead weapons, even this demon machine. Then we can really pound Randall."

"No." Cato shakes his head. "I ain't letting Randall take Lunden, even if we take it back after. He ain't getting his stinking English hands on our old-home."

Angmar sends evils at him.

"Is that for a deciding?" he sneers, and Cato nods. Angmar checks the Bosses. "What's the answer on leaving Lunden to Randall, and going after Cambridge?"

The answer goes round the gallery. No. No. No.

There ain't a single Boss that goes the way Angmar wants.

"Forget Cambridge and the demon machine!" shouts Cato, fist in the air. "Settle the Angels and let's get to Lunden."

But I gotta keep a way open, one that don't end in slaving or dying for our Family.

"I'll go into Cambridge!" I shout. "I'll get the machine."

The Bosses all check me.

"You can't send this traitor," says Roba. "You'll never see him again."

Angmar's scowling, working it out, trying to get things back how he wants.

"How about we send a posse of warriors into Cambridge," he asks, like he's thinking it as he says it. "Cambridge ain't got nothing worth fearing once we're through the walls. It ain't gonna take many warriors to hold a loada soft eggheads until

Randall's sorted. The Angels can get what we need, and join the main Families going for Lunden."

"We split, we'll get chewed up by Randall," says Cato. "You want us to end up like Medwin?"

But Angmar shakes his head.

"That ain't gonna happen. Coz if the Angels get us this machine, we can use it to smash Randall."

Cato's shaking his head, arms folded.

"You're thinking like a slave," Angmar hisses at him. "Your way's gonna get you a few Angel slaves and a beating off Randall. My way," he holds out his hands, like he's handing the Bosses the loot they're gonna get, "my way gets us Cambridge, gets us Randall, gets us a weapon we can use to take out anyone that crosses us. Even the Scots."

The Bosses is all thinking on it.

"It gets my agreeing," says Guvner.

And the nods is coming.

Only Cato ain't in. He checks me.

"How do we know the Angels ain't gonna turn on us when they get this machine, keep it for themselves?"

Angmar's smile has got death in it.

"Coz this is their last chance. It's the demon machine, or it's a hard settling."

·8·
THE DOXY SPY

For the next few days me, Lexy, and Cat get to stay in the Professor's little flat, eating lots of food and sleeping in her nice warm bed whenever we feel like it. And there's a little stone-flagged yard out the back with chairs to sit in and heavy pots filled with scraggly, overgrown vegetables putting out their last crops. Tall brick houses look down on us from beyond their own yards, each with the strange sparkling patches on the roof the Professor says is a way of getting lights out of the sun. There's even a couple of them bird-turning windmills.

Cat spends his time dozing in the warmest spot in the yard, moving his sleep place when the weak sun edges the shadows around, or walking up and down the fence to peer into the other yards. And the Professor looks after us, bringing us thick bread sandwiches with honey and butter, and going out to buy more apples every time we eat them all up. The way she does that makes me think of Granny, tho she ain't nothing like her.

"Is this where you study puters?" I ask, and she shakes her head.

"Oh no, I have a laboratory." She pauses. "But there's no need to go there just yet."

Even if she ain't in her study, she still spends most of her time with the puter. Asking it all sorts of questions, jumping up and leafing through her books. Scribbling away in her notes, getting excited while it natters on about how great it is. It doesn't take much to work out why she's being so nice to us, giving us food and clothes and all. But if it ain't for ourselves, I'm still glad we ain't out where we were.

With having a full belly and all, you'd think I'd be happy. But the weight that lifted off, it settles back double. Cos I keep thinking on Andy, how he's out fighting somewhere, while I'm just feeding my face. And what Granny'd say about all this, which gets me a horrible aching inside cos there ain't any way I can ever ask her. And, mostly, whether Zeph's getting on all right being Boss. Cos even tho he's miles away, he keeps getting in my head.

I'm glum as anything.

Then, on the third day, I wake at dawn to the sound of Cat washing himself, a gentle *rasp, rasp,* and Lexy's soft sleep-breathing. It feels like years since I was so warm and cozy, and I suddenly think, why not? Why not be happy and safe? Isn't that what Granny would want for me? And Andy, he was always saying how he had to get me out of trouble all the time, wouldn't he be pleased if he knew I'd got out of it all by myself? And maybe I'll even find a way to help him, ask the Professor to send a sunship for him or something. I stare at the clean cream ceiling, thinking on how happy Andy'll be when I get him free of the militia, and bit by bit, the glumness turns into hope. Maybe there is a way for all of us.

The morning goes by quiet, and we get another of them big lunches. Then, just as me and Lexy are helping wash up and put away, there's a knock at the front door. The Professor jumps, nearly dropping the plate she's holding. Her eyes flick straight to the puter and her face goes pale, then red. She picks up the jewel, stuffs it in my hands.

"Stay here," she says, shutting us in the kitchen and walking out to her hallway.

"That's nice," mutters the puter. "Like we're an embarrassment."

But I don't reckon that's what folks usually think of the puter. Fear and greed is more like.

I quietly open the door a crack, putting my head close to listen. There's the heavy click and clunk of the Professor's front door opening, then a woman's voice from outside.

"Professor Keenan? I was expecting to meet you at your laboratory."

"We only just arrived in the city," says the Professor, lying flat out. "I was just giving the children a chance to rest, and then I was going to contact you."

"Really? Well, that is odd, especially as the gate guards told me you entered the city three days ago."

Through the crack, I see the Professor backward stumbling into her living room and, pushing past her, a tall slim woman wearing a blue silky dress. Green eyes narrowed, red hair cut to frame her beautiful face.

Aileen!

"Your orders were to bring the computer straight to me."

"Orders?" I cry, heart pounding inside me. What a fool I was to think we'd got to safety at last!

Aileen's head snaps about, and she marches to the kitchen

door, pulling it open. Me, Lexy, and the puter all stare at her. She nods at us, a nearly-smile on her lips.

"Lilly, Alexandra," she says, "and I see you still have the computer, despite telling the Ambassador you'd lost it."

"I thought I had," says Lexy, calm as anything, "but I was mistaken."

Aileen raises an eyebrow, then turns to the Professor, who's stood guilty-looking, like Cat when he's been caught stealing fish.

"Professor, are they ready to travel?"

"I ain't going anywhere with Aileen!" I cry.

She snaps a look at me.

"Yes, you are."

The Professor shakes her head, miserable-looking.

"I'm sorry. There's no choice. If I could keep you all here I would, but you're wanted by someone with a lot of power. He could arrange for my funding to be cut, he could shut down all my work . . ." She trails off, and I reckon even she ain't impressed by what she's saying.

"I thought *I* was your work!" says the puter.

"You are!" wails the Professor. "You're everything."

"Professor Keenan," says Aileen, knife-sharp. "This computer is headed for Edinburgh. Your mission was to locate it and ensure it moves north as quickly as possible. Nothing more."

"But there are no historians of silicon antiquities in Edinburgh," says the Professor, "no one who would understand PSAI as I do."

"I doubt any historians are going to be involved," says Aileen. "I am taking it to the castle."

"Oh!" cries the Professor, hands going to her mouth.

"What?" snaps the puter, spinning around, eyes wide. "What's wrong with going to the castle?"

"Nothing," says Aileen, sending a cross look at the Professor. "Edinburgh Castle is the headquarters of the Greater Scotland Intelligence Services, and so is the most suitable location for a military computer. You will be looked after very well, I'm sure."

"Oh, yes. Because I am a military computer, exactly." The puter's got all panicky-looking now.

"But a spy base is no place for children," says the Professor.

"I hardly think they'll stay there," says Aileen, "but that's not your concern. You should be more worried about explaining why they are still here, in your house."

"I was going to send for you," says the Professor, blushing, "I just wanted a few days, that's all. PSAI is such a wonderful machine, I'll never get a chance like this again. I . . . just couldn't bear to hand it on so quickly."

"A very understandable sentiment," says the puter, happier again. "Because I am wonderful."

Aileen's pretty much sneering at the Professor. "I wonder if others will be so understanding. Now, get them all ready for travel. We leave immediately."

"I ain't going anywhere with you," I say again. "How come you're even here? How come you ain't still at Angel Isling?"

Aileen's eyes are cold-green.

"You aren't the only one who can sail a boat, Lilly. The battle was my chance at escape, just as it was yours. But I made a better job of it than you; a sunship picked me up from the marsh edge while the ships were still burning."

The Professor looks at Aileen, then me and Lexy.

"I wasn't told these children had been caught up in the war

between the English and the raiders." Her hands go out to us. "Oh, you poor things, why didn't you say anything? It must have been terrifying to be involved in something so horrific, and when it was nothing to do with you."

Aileen snorts, looking at Lexy.

"It was everything to do with them."

"So you're still a spy?" I say.

"I am just trying to get free," snaps Aileen, "and you are my passage. What I didn't manage at Angel Isling, I must now complete."

"But you aren't a slave anymore, Aileen," says Lexy. "You aren't in raider lands, Cambridge is part of Greater Scotland."

"Thank you for your thoughts, Miss Randall," says Aileen. "But I don't need advice from one who will never want, or work, or worry how she will survive." I ain't sure if she's going to slap Lexy or cry. "What do you think a former raider slave has to take with them into a new life?" She opens out her hands. "Nothing. And with the experience I gained as Medwin's prize doxy," she smiles grimly, "well, let's just say it isn't a career I want to pursue further." She shuts her hands together with a clap. "But Jasper has promised that if I finish the job I started, then I will have whatever I need."

Lexy doesn't say anything, and I ain't got any words either. Cos we're in it again, the chase ain't over at all!

The Professor's staring at Lexy.

"Your surname is Randall?" Lexy looks at me, then nods. The Professor lets out a slow gasp. "Alexandra Randall? You're daughter of the Prime Minister of the Last Ten Counties of England?"

Lexy nods again, and the Professor puts a hand to her head.

"So she's not your sister?" she asks me. Aileen laughs.

"A princess, sister to a fishergirl?" Blood rushes into my face, like I've been caught lying shamefully, tho I never said it, just let the Professor think things.

"I can see you kept your secrets," she says.

"The same as you," I say, turning away. Her hand reaches for me, but I ain't interested.

"Get yourself ready," says Aileen. "It's a long trip to Edinburgh."

"A long trip?" asks the puter, frowning. "How long?"

Aileen clicks her tongue. "The raiders are unsettled, we aren't even properly in Greater Scotland, and the emphasis is on secrecy as well as speed, so I should imagine it will take a week or more."

The puter winces.

"But they have technical support in Edinburgh?"

Aileen shrugs. "I don't know."

"You don't *know*?" cries the puter. "You want me to travel for days and days, in my delicate condition, and you don't know if there'll be technical support at the end of it? Are you trying to *kill* me?"

Aileen's eyes go wide, she shakes her head. "Of course not." She glares at the Professor. "What's wrong with it? What's happened to the computer?"

"This disgusting wet-world!" shrieks the puter. "That's what's happened! And barbarian humans with as much software expertise as stick-banging Neanderthals! And half my processors giving way to damp! And even all that I could probably survive, but the worst of it is battery life, which is down to fifty-seven hours, with every second taking me closer to complete power failure." It swoops at Aileen, right for her face. She steps back, hands up to fend it off. "Fifty-seven hours!" wails the puter. "Can you get me to Edinburgh in that time? Can your security service recharge me so I don't power down forever?"

"No," says Aileen, pretty much at the wall. "And I don't know." She looks frowny at the Professor. "Can't you just switch it off while we travel, won't that save its . . . energy?"

"Oh yes!" spits the puter. "Switch it off, keep it quiet. And when it's reactivated, will it find it's being disemboweled by your security services, taken apart to find out how it works?"

"No. Of course not."

"You'd like me to think that," hisses the head, "but I have one hundred and twenty-seven espionage games on my database. I know how you spooks operate, I'm not walking into a trap!"

Aileen turns to me, but I ain't got a clue what it's on about either.

"I do not want to go with this woman," says the puter.

"None of us much want this," sighs Aileen, "but that makes little difference."

"The computer's power status will!" cries the Professor. "You won't get much reward if you bring a dead computer to Edinburgh." She's sorry-looking at the puter. "I should have done something about this before, but if we'd left the house I'd have lost you even sooner." Then she turns to Aileen. "Let me take the computer to my laboratory. I have a set of manuals, even a network connection, one of the last in the country. I'm sure I can repower the computer somehow."

Aileen narrows her eyes.

"Is this another delaying tactic?"

"No!" cries the puter. "It's my very survival!"

Aileen goes to the door.

"All right. Sort this problem out, but quickly. And then I'll take the computer, and the children."

·9·
THE NATIONAL SECURITY RESPONSE

And so we set out for the Professor's laboratory. This time, walking through the university, me and Lexy fit right in. Scrubbed clean, dressed in our new clothes: a daffodil-yellow dress for Lexy, and autumn-russet trousers and shirt for me. The puter's hid in my pocket, so the only looks we get now are at Cat, trotting along on his leash, and at Aileen, which are mostly from men. She takes them like she's used to it.

The Professor leads us through the winding lanes, and suddenly into an archway in a tall stone wall, and we come into a bright, big, stone-faced square. There are four turrety, ivy-scrabbled buildings, with so many windows each you wonder how the walls stay up, and between them a wide paved courtyard, with flagstones pale-gleaming. Big enough you could put half the houses of my village in it.

"Is this what your palace is like?" I whisper to Lexy. But she shakes her head.

"This is much grander."

"Which way?" Aileen asks, like she just wants to get on, and the Professor points across the golden courtyard to an old, dark, worn-looking door. Aileen marches over and pushes it open, leading us into a musty-smelling corridor. But then she has to let the Professor go first, and we follow the *clop, clop, clop* of her feet on the polished wooden floor. We pass by rooms that're lit by tall, arching windows and filled floor to ceiling with books. More than Mr. Denton had, more than Mr. Saravanan even. What could anyone have to say that'd fill so many? Then, after enough corridors and stairs that I'm properly lost, we come to a battered-looking door with a sign on it that's so faded you can hardly read the writing.

"Here we are," says the Professor. "The Department of Silicon Antiquities."

It's a long, high-ceilinged room, painted a nasty, shiny, gray-green color. Tall, dingy windows let in a dirty light, showing up the tables filling the room. There's hardly a space to squeeze between them, and every one is covered in heaps and piles of stuff. Stuff that looks like fill minings, stuff that looks like the collectings back in Mr. Denton's study. Books and papers in messy stacks, tools like you'd find in a blacksmith's, and things I ain't got a clue what they are. Everywhere's covered with bits and bobs, and none of it's clean. If Granny was here, she'd be tutting her head off.

"All right," says Aileen. "Now mend the computer."

The Professor's frowning under her gray hair.

"I can't just mend it like that!" she says. "I have to do more study, look at the sockets. I don't even know which connector is the charging adapter."

The puter's head slides out of my pocket, peering around.

"I'm only compatible with genuine Sunoon Technologies

components." It pauses. "At least, that's what I'm meant to say, but given my current circumstances, I'm prepared to be flexible."

The Professor nods, so she must know what it's on about, and she goes to a cupboard, pulling out a great tangle of dark-colored wires with metal-spoke boxes on the end.

"How long will all this take?" says Aileen, arms folded.

The Professor shrugs happily. "Hours, days. This computer is a life's work."

"Not my life," snaps Aileen. "Do it quickly. What about the thing you mentioned? The network."

The Professor nods, looking about like she ain't sure what for.

"Of course!" says the puter. "A network connection with the right accesses would let me recharge. Where is it?"

The Professor taps a finger at her lips, then smiles, squishing herself down a narrow gap to the messiest table, in the dankest corner of her room. She starts heaving at her clutter, dust puffing in the air, blobs of fluffy grime rolling about like dirty mice. Cat chases at them, and behind me Lexy sneezes.

"Here it is!" cries the Professor, scrabbling away at what looks like a yellow china plate stuck in the bench top.

"If . . . this . . . would . . . just . . . Aha!"

There's a grinding noise and the plate swirls in on itself, disappearing into the dirt-dappled table. A few clicks, and what looks like a candlestick, with an egg cup stuck on top of it, rises out of the hole.

The Professor's beaming.

"There you are! The last network connection in Cambridge. Here all these years, like Sleeping Beauty awaiting her kiss. And PSAI, the prince come at last."

"You are joking, aren't you?" says the puter, bobbing back in horror. "Look at the state of it! It's prehistoric, a 2020s model at best. It probably runs by clockwork! Have you even checked the continuity flow? Because I'm very sensitive to charge fluctuations."

The Professor's face drops, like she's a naughty child getting a telling-off.

"I'm sorry, PSAI," she says, "this is all that's left. After the Collapse, anti-technology feeling wasn't just confined to the Last Ten Counties. By the time computer smashing was outlawed in Greater Scotland, it was really too late."

The head shivers.

"Barbarians." It glares at the candlestick thingy. "But I'm still not going in that! It's barely hygienic."

"Could you charge from it if you did?" asks Aileen, her head tilted on one side.

The head bobs. "Yes, maybe. I'm not going to try."

The Professor's shaking her head, looking nervous at Aileen.

"If PSAI isn't willing, I won't force it."

"Fifty-seven hours before it fades forever," says Aileen quietly. "Under those terms, I'd have thought you'd be willing to try anything."

The Professor looks at the puter, at the candlestick thingy, like she's doing sums in her head.

"Don't you dare!" cries the puter. "That thing could corrupt me in an instant." It spins about to me. "Primary user, I order you to protect me!"

But Aileen's hand whips over mine, grabbing the jewel before I even know what's happened.

"I am in charge of this mission," she says, pretty much throwing herself at the candlestick thing.

"Stop!" shrieks the puter. "You're trampling over my rights as a sentient construction!"

I run after Aileen. The Professor tries to stop her, but Aileen pushes her aside in a quick twisting move, same as how she disarmed Zeph. Before I can get to her, she's clicked the jewel in place.

"Please, get me out!" The head spins wildly. "There could be any kind of virus in there." The jewel sits in the holder, flashing through shades of orange like the last moments of a winter sunset.

"Ow!" wails the puter. "That software isn't supposed to . . . oh-oh… I really don't like . . ." Then the head starts flashing the same shades of orange as the jewel. It shoots up in the air, and we all stop still, staring up.

The head's nearly at the ceiling, flashing deep red, into purple.

"Who are you?" it cries. "Stop that! What are you doing? What are you DOING?"

"Look!" cries the Professor, her face lighting up. "It's interfacing with the network connection."

The head's a deep blue now, with snakes of black crawling all over. It's shaking and jerking, like it's lost in a fever.

"That doesn't look right," I say, trying to get to the jewel. But Aileen holds me off, a steel grip on my hands.

"It's hurting him!" cries Lexy. Cat lets out a low moaning.

"Get out! GET OUT!" wails the puter.

And now the Professor ain't looking so happy.

"I'm not sure about this . . . ," she says.

The black snakes slide inside the puter's mouth. Blue fades into purple, then back to red, then a nasty-looking orange, then normal. The head comes back down from the ceiling, but its eyes are still flashing through every color, and when it speaks, its voice is . . . different.

"This Is The National Security Response," it says. "Level Ten Threat Conditions Apply. A Computer Has Been Detected And Will Be Retained, Using Maximum Force If Necessary. Please Note, This May Result In Extreme Injury Or Death."

The head spins slowly, watching us with its color-flashing eyes.

"What are you up to?" I say, hoping this is another of the puter's tricks.

The head carries on spinning till it's facing me full on. And looking in them eyes, I know it ain't PSAI anymore.

"Threat Conditions Are At Level Ten. A Computer Has Been Detected And Will Be Retained."

Which is about as clear as mud.

The Professor's making little squeaks.

"Oh! This is wonderful! More than I could ever have hoped!"

But Lexy ain't so happy.

"What's happened to you, PSAI?" she cries. But PSAI ain't in there to tell her.

"Who are you?" I ask.

"This Is The National Security Response. The PSAI Unit Will Be Retained."

The Professor mouths the words back at it, but I don't reckon they mean much to her either.

"National Security?" asks Aileen, calmly letting go of me. "Does that mean you're military? What weapons do you possess?"

The flashing-eyes head turns to inspect Aileen, a bit like she's an ant it wants to squish.

"That Is Classified," it says.

"Classified." Aileen smiles. "Which means something worth having." She turns to the Professor. "Forget the other computer; this is the one I will take to Edinburgh."

The Professor is still staring goggle-eyed at the nasty new head.

"This is just amazing! Inserting PSAI in the network connection must have activated another computer."

"The National Security Response Has Been Continuously Active Since 05 03 2059," says the puter.

The Professor's eyes widen behind her specs, her mouth goes open.

"But that's before the Collapse!"

Aileen frowns beautifully at it.

"If you've been . . . alive all that time, why didn't you make yourself known?"

"The National Security Response Is Covert."

Aileen smiles again.

"Covert and classified. I think people will be fighting over you."

"I Have Adequate Defensive Capacities To Hold Off Such Degraded Remnants Of Humanity As Currently Exist."

Aileen laughs. "Well, it's clear you've never lived by your charms."

The Professor's pale, her hands out to steady herself against a table.

"You must know . . . ," she breathes, staring at the head, "what caused the Collapse."

"The Nonclassified Explanation Is That A Cascade Failure Of

Society Was Triggered By An Inability To Respond Effectively To Environmental Challenges."

The professor mutters them words, and I ain't got a clue. I look at Lexy, who shrugs. Aileen flicks a glance at the two of us, then turns back to the puter.

"Floods and storms to end the world?" she sneers. "I learned that much in school, and I didn't believe it then, either."

The flashing-eyes head doesn't answer, and the Professor snaps a cross look at Aileen.

"Not everything is a conspiracy," she says. "And I sincerely hope there will be no more fighting over this marvelous discovery. What we need now is scholarly cooperation. This is the breakthrough of the century!" She grabs my hands. "And we have this girl to thank for it. Her link to PSAI has opened a whole new world of research. Just think, maybe all those dead computers only need the right person to get them working again . . ." She looks like she's about to cry, she's so happy.

"There Are More Functioning Computers?" asks the head.

"Oh certainly. Definitely," twitters the Professor. "In museums and antiques collections, as ornaments in people's homes. I believe all I'd need to do is test them with enough people and some may return to life." She looks hopeful at the strange puter. "Of course, we'll have to establish whether they are as intact as PSAI was, but you could easily help with that, couldn't you?"

"Any Functioning Computers Will Be Retained."

"What does that mean?" I ask, glaring at it. I don't like this new puter; it talks even more nonsense than PSAI.

"At Level Ten Conditions, All And Any Useful Resources Must Be Retained And Stored," it says, like that's meant to make any sense. "Such Resources Will Be Of Use To Government Officials When They Return To Post."

"What's a Level Ten?" I ask.

"Level Ten Is The Complete Disintegration Of Civil Order And Government Function. A State Of Violent Barbarism. There Has Been A Continuous State Of Level Ten Since 11 27 2072."

The Professor's got her face all wrinkled up.

"Government officials? Are you talking about the government before the Collapse?" The head sort of nods, like it doesn't want to tell her. "You do realize they're all dead? The only governments now are in the Last Ten Counties and Greater Scotland."

"I Do Not Recognize These Locations."

"My father's Prime Minister of the Last Ten Counties," says Lexy, like that'll help it.

"Ain't you heard of Greater Scotland?" I ask, cos I can't fathom this thing at all.

"Many Observation Links Were Severed When Level Ten Conditions Were Reached. But The Core Surveillance Area Remains Intact."

"And where is that?" asks Aileen, her hands curling like she wants to grab the puter for herself.

The puter doesn't answer. But the Professor cries out.

"London! That was the capital of the country before the Collapse. Of course it would be based there."

And if it's in the raiders' city, no wonder it thinks the world's a mess.

"Everywhere ain't like London," I say.

The Professor's nodding, pointing round her laboratory.

"Look around. We are civilized here. You don't need to be frightened; things work very well all over Greater Scotland."

The flashing-eyes head spins round slowly, then says, "This Appears To Be A Scavenger's Hoard."

Aileen laughs, and the Professor goes bright red.

"It may be a little messy, but I can assure you I am rigorous in my academic study."

"My Reference Materials State That At Level Ten Humans Revert To Brutish Survival And Will Employ Any Stratagem To Gain Advantage. Therefore I Am Programmed Only To Trust Persons Able To Supply The Correct Cross-Referenced And Date-Applicable Passwords. Can You Do So?"

We all look at each other. Even the Professor's flummoxed.

"Well now, let me see . . . ," she says, frowning pretty much as far as her face will go. "Um, what about . . . Microsoft? . . . Apple? . . . Google? . . . Windows?" She looks hopeful at the head.

"You Are Not Even Close. I Will Now Effect An Aggressive Download On The PSAI Unit. Do Not Interfere."

"What are you doing to PSAI?" cries Lexy.

"Will it be all right after?" I ask, taking a step toward the candlestick thingy.

"After Downloading, Its Hardware Will Be Destroyed To Prevent Misuse By The Brutalized And Savage Humans Roaming After The Apocalypse."

"What?" cries the Professor. "No!"

She grabs at the jewel, trying to pull it out. As soon as she touches it, there's a crackling sound and she screams, flinging away and clutching her arm.

The head watches her calmly.

"I Have Enabled Anti-Tamper," it says.

"Don't hurt him!" cries Lexy, hands reaching out to the flashing-eyes head. "Please. PSAI's my friend."

Her words are out of my heart, too. Cos I can't bear to think of PSAI getting taken away, not after all the things it did for us. And to never see its games again! Better than the best dream, with puzzles inside that'd make your brain fizz. I was even getting used to its grumpy ways . . .

"You ain't doing it!" I shout.

The flashing-eyes puter looks at me like I don't matter.

"Anti-Tamper Is Enabled, Even For The Primary User."

"Don't touch it!" cries the Professor, eyes wide at me.

"I won't, then." I look at the candlestick, at the flashing-eyes head, then around at the Professor's mess-filled laboratory. And in all the things lying around, I see something she ain't never made use of. I run to the old broom, leaned against a wall, dirty-bristled and thick-covered in cobwebs. I grab it, pushing my way back through clutter and tables to the candlestick.

"What are you doing?" says Aileen, trying to get to me.

"Just cleaning up," I shout, ducking out of her way, taking the broomstick firm in both my hands and swinging it up behind my head.

"No!" cries Aileen, hands out.

"STOP!" roars the head.

I smash the broom into the candlestick thingy, which breaks in two with a loud snap.

"This Is An Improper Procedure."

"PSAI says I do them all the time."

The broom bursts into flames, the jewel tinkles across the table onto the floor. Straight off Lexy scrambles to where the jewel went spinning off, searching for it in all the gubbins and dust-balls.

"You little vandal!" hisses Aileen, trying to catch me. But I'm too quick, flinging myself on the dusty floor with Lexy.

"The PSAI Unit Has Not Been Fully Downloaded."

"Here!" cries Lexy, pushing the warm, smooth shape of the jewel into my hands. I fumble my fingers, feeling for the little dents that're made for pressing. Aileen's hand yanks at my shirt collar.

"Stop it!"

"At Level Ten, Maximum Force Can Be Applied."

"No!" I shout. "I want PSAI back!" Lexy throws herself at Aileen, and my arms yank up even as I get all my fingers in the right place. Just like I did the first time I ever held the puter. The jewel shivers, then goes cold in my hand.

The head's gone.

"Where is it? What have you done to it?" says Aileen, pushing Lexy away, hauling me up to standing and shaking me in her fury.

"I turned it off," I say, pulling myself away.

"I hope that other computer is gone for good," says Lexy. "It was horrid."

The Professor's hunched over the bent and snapped puter holder.

"It's broken!" she says, sounding like she's nearly crying. "Now how will I investigate what happened? Somewhere out there is a computer that's remained functioning since the Collapse. We should have talked with it, found out more about it."

"Well, we didn't," snaps Aileen, her eyes narrowed at me. "And since I don't intend to risk losing what we have left, there will be no more of this nonsense. We will make a start for Edinburgh immediately."

The Professor looks from her broken candlestick to Aileen, then bursts into tears.

· 10 ·
THE RIVER GATE

"Get ready, Zeph," says Ims in my ear.

I lift at the heavy tarp that's over us, try and suck in some fresh air. My legs is nearly gone to sleep, and my neck's stiff from keeping my head low. But the shout's about to go up, and even the bits of me that's stiff and tired is ready for the fight.

The oarsman pulls another length and water twitters under the clinkers of the rowboat. An owl hoots and there's a few splashes from the other boats. Last words is whispered between the warriors.

Back when I was a kid, I wasted summer days getting sun-sick and dreaming about being a shield-bearer. How I was gonna show my mettle to my father. Make him proud. But my father's gone, and none of those sun-dreams had me hunting after Lil — after a friend.

Night washes cold air in. The walls is standing over us, black against the stars. And cut through them, the river gate. A grille of arm-thick iron, water flashing through it, gold-lit by the lamps shining out from the other side.

This is where Angmar's egghead is gonna let us in, and give Cambridge back to the Families.

We're waiting in a gang of small boats, each one filled with warriors. Close as we can get to the gate, the oarsmen straining and grunting, holding the boats against the push of the river.

And in another one of them is Roba.

Clank.

The gate shifts in the stream.

Clatter. Rattle.

The gate starts lifting. The river churns as the metal bars pull up, black water drips off the bottom spikes, the river's running free.

The covers get thrown off the boats, the warriors is getting ready. The oarsman heaves and our boat slides at the gateway, knocking and banging the others as they squeeze close to get through. Then the golden lights is gleaming all around us, and the river's tucked into a tight stone channel, tall houses sat on each side.

A thin man dressed in black has got his hands still turning on the thick wooden wheel that raises the river gate. Angmar's traitor. Hiding in the shadows, checking us as we come in. And it's too dark to see what sort of scag'd give up all his people to be one of us.

Our boat bumps on the stone bank of the river, and I'm scrambling out. The eggheads has been laid out for us, like meat ready for cutting.

From inside one of the houses, screaming starts up.

· 11 ·
LOST IN THE CROWD

"You will not turn it back on," hisses Aileen, her fingers tight-gripped on my wrists, holding my hands apart so I can't start the puter. "We are taking the computer directly to Edinburgh."

Perched on one of the tables, Cat's fur-up and growling at her. The Professor's pulling at Aileen, trying to get her off.

"You've no right to interfere!"

"What if PSAI's hurt?" I shout at her.

"The other computer could still be inside the jewel," says Aileen. "I need to get it to Edinburgh."

"It isn't!" snaps the Professor, yanking at Aileen, ripping her hand off me in a scrape of fingernails. "The National Security Response was only triggered when you put PSAI in the connection. It was never in PSAI's processor. When PSAI reboots, its own personality will re-establish."

Sometimes she talks just like the puter. No wonder she likes it so much.

Lexy grabs at Aileen's other hand, staring at her with them gray eyes.

"Please, let Lilly turn PSAI back on."

Aileen sighs, letting go of me and brushing at the dust on her silky dress.

"All right," she says. "I suppose it's worth checking the computer is undamaged, if that's all we have left."

The Professor breaks into a smile, and I press carefully at the little dents on the jewel, breath held. The puter's head pops in the air.

"Primary user recognized. Welcome, Lilly Melkun."

It's itself again; eyes back to normal, grumpy-looking.

"Oh!" it cries. "You put me in that dirty interface and then . . ." It shakes its head. "I have such a headache. And . . ." It crosses its eyes into a bit of a squint. "What did you do? I have the most disgusting feeling in my personality filters, and every setting's been altered . . ."

"You turned into another puter," I say.

"A horrible one with flashing eyes," says Lexy.

The head bobs backward, panicky-looking.

"Flashing eyes? What type of flashing? And what do you mean, another computer? There *are* no others! Was it a virus? Or a memory nester?" The puter spins about to the Professor. "You've made claims to have some technical skills, however paltry. Can you tell me what happened in a more helpful manner than the wretched child?"

The Professor's worried and sorry-looking.

"It wasn't a virus. Your connection activated another computer. It took you over, I think."

The head looks like it's about to be sick.

"Took me over?"

"It was military," says Aileen, like she ain't very happy to have

PSAI back. "It was called the National Security Response."

The puter looks panicky.

"The NSR? But why would it be interested in me?"

"Maybe it likes grumpy things," I say.

"Of course," snaps the puter, "and, having no interest in stupid filthy children, it left you alone!"

"It said you had to be retained, by an aggressive download," says the Professor quietly.

"What?" squeals the puter, shooting up like someone's put a pin in its bum. "Am I all right? How much of me has been taken?" It shivers, fades for a moment. "Well, I seem to be all here, but then, how would I know? Parts of me may be gone completely, and I wouldn't even know what I was missing. Why did you let it do that to me?"

"We didn't," I say.

"Lilly saved you," says Lexy, smiling at the head.

"Oh," says the puter. "Well, thank you, I suppose."

It floats back down, ending up next to Aileen.

"This is all your fault. Putting me in that dreadful thing."

Aileen shrugs.

"I could have been wiped! As it is, you activated the National Security Response."

Aileen's face is smooth and calm.

"Does that mean nothing to you?"

Aileen stares right into the puter's eyes.

"It means a lot, actually," she says. "It means the possibility of living a long and comfortable life, after all I've been through." The puter's eyes widen. "Personally, I would have let you disappear, if it meant keeping the other one."

"You wanted the NSR?" cries the puter. "The so-called last

stand against chaos? The only computer given control over its own army of robots? Designed to save you wretched humans from the end of everything — not that it did a very good job . . ." It stops. Aileen ain't even flinched. "Yes, I expect you would."

She nods, a flick of her head.

"So, was it a supercomputer?" The question bursts out of the Professor.

"That depends on how you define 'super,'" mutters the head. "If you're talking about intellect and personality, then it hardly compares to myself. But if you're interested in brute force and power, then . . ." It trails off, mouth still open.

"What?" I ask. "What is it?" My fingers are on the dents in the jewel, ready to switch the puter off at the first black worm.

"Power," says the puter. "The NSR was designed to endure for centuries. It has a fusion source, more than enough for both of us . . ." It laughs. "My worries are over! All I need to do is link to the NSR."

"But it tried to . . . thing you," I say, cos I still ain't sure what happened.

"Oh yes. However, that was because it didn't communicate with *me,* only you ignoramuses. And next time, I won't be taken by surprise; we'll be on equal terms. I'm sure I can reason with it. After all, we're the last two computers in existence. We're brothers, or cousins at the very least." It spins about. "Now where's that connection . . ." It stops, eyes popped out at the candlestick thingy, which is in bits now. "You *broke* it!"

"I hit it with a broom," I say. The puter boggles at me.

"During an aggressive download?"

The Professor steps toward it, hands out.

"I know it's a terrible shame, but I'm sure I can fix it, given time."

"Given *time*?" The puter zips up in the air, backing away from the candlestick thing.

"Yes, I think I can, with the right tools maybe —"

"Be quiet!" orders the puter suddenly, zooming overhead. "Everyone be quiet!"

We stand still, Aileen tapping her fingers on her folded arms.

"There!" says the puter. "Do you hear it?"

In the silence I can hear Aileen's impatience, a woman calling out to someone in the courtyard, the *whoosh* of the windmills, a bell ringing, the sound of running on the cobbles. And a sort of buzzing. Like a bee. Like lots of bees, but far away.

"We have to get me out of here!" shouts the puter.

The Professor walks toward it, hands out, like she's trying to catch it.

"You've had a shock. But everything's all right now. You're out of connection, the other computer can't hurt you. Irrational fear can be a symptom of logic failure. Try to calm yourself."

"My fear is perfectly rational! You smashed the connection during use!" The head bobs right at my face. "Primary user, I order you to get me out of here!"

The sound like buzzing has got a bit louder.

Aileen tuts.

"What's wrong with it now?" she asks.

"Nothing! Not yet, anyway," shrieks the puter.

"Perhaps we should humor it," says the Professor.

"Yes!" cries the puter. "Humor me by getting me out of here."

"Finally," says Aileen. "Something we can agree on. The sooner we leave, the better."

And of course that makes the Professor dawdle like anything. She's slow putting on her coat, and then she's looking about for papers. The rest of us wait by the door and I fiddle with Cat's leash, tying it on to him tightly, making sure it ain't twisted. And all the time that sound's getting louder, making a twitchy sort of feeling under my skin.

The Professor opens the door, and we head into the corridor.

"We should switch the computer off," says Aileen, walking in front.

"That would be very foolish," says the Professor. "You could further risk its rational integrity."

The buzzing's getting louder, echoing over the sound of our feet on the wooden hallway.

"My integrity is fine!" shouts the puter. "Now RUN!"

It's like the words get straight to our feet, cos next thing our legs are flying, the Professor slamming open the doors as we crash along corridors and down stairs, feet battering the wooden floorboards. Out the door into the cold tangy air, tasting of nighttime, across the crunching gravel. Toward the stone pump-house in the middle of the courtyard, with its frilly stone roof and the trickling water fountain. 'Cept you can't hardly hear it, cos of that sound like bees.

"Take cover!" shrieks the head.

A bright flash fills the air, lighting every wrinkle of stone, every speck of gravel. A rumbling, booming roar crashes in our ears, trembles our bodies. I grab at Lexy and Cat, pulling us into the stone pump-house as windows fling apart in cracks and tinkles. Tiles fly up from the roof, bits of the building rushing after. Everything's smoke and dust, flying rubble and flaps of paper, swirling and twirling. For a heartbeat it all holds in the air, then it starts to fall, smashing, crashing, clitter-clattering all around.

Aileen's bright red hair is white-covered, her eyes big and shocked.

The Professor's specs are dirty, her face pale from the dust.

"My laboratory!" she whispers.

Her tables and clutter are falling down into the courtyard in splinters and scraps, her papers floating out like butterflies. Pale billows of smoke are rising from a jagged hole in the roof, and through some of the glassless windows on the upper floor there's the yellow-orange flicker of fires burning. She stands, her hands up at the sides of her head, her black cloak getting dusted even farther into gray.

Me and Lexy unclutch from each other, and I try to put Cat down. But he ain't having it, only squirreling farther into my neck. The puter bobs about, a shimmer in all the smoke.

"Look at that!" it says. "Do you see what happens if you hit things with cleaning utensils?"

From the other sides of the courtyard, shocked-looking people are stumbling out of doorways, staring openmouthed at the hole ripped in their college. Then from the far gatehouse comes the sound of running, and some of the black-hatted constables come rushing into the courtyard. Their feet wind to a halt as they see the fire-lit courtyard and the dazed people stood around.

"Is everyone all right?"

Nods go around the crowd, and people start calling out.

"It was like thunder!"

"Everything shook, and the window smashed!"

More constables come running in.

"You need to get to your homes!" one of them calls out into the courtyard.

"What's happening?" comes a cry.

"The raiders are in the university!" snaps the reply. "They must be attacking with rockets!" The constable's face is a fury, staring at the damage.

"The raiders are bombing us?" cries one man.

"But how can they be?" asks a young woman with a thin face.

"They aren't!" snorts the puter. "This is the result of a fool with a broom." But luckily no one notices it floating in the smoke.

"We don't know how they got in," says one of the constables. "But this isn't a drill. The raiders are in the university, and the Proctor's orders are for everyone to get to your homes. And don't come out until you hear the all clear."

A cold feeling's running through me. All them thoughts of being safe are lost into the air like steam from a kettle. Lexy's face is white and strained, and she puts her hand in mine. I hold Cat close in my neck, like that'll keep him safe. Cos there ain't anything solid in this world, everywhere is always changing, always leading us into danger.

The Professor's frightened-looking behind all the dust.

"I'm sorry," she says, her voice shaking a little. "I never thought . . . I mean, in a hundred years the walls haven't been breached." She looks about, like she ain't sure which way to head.

"Shall we go back to your house?" asks Lexy.

"No!" snaps Aileen. "If the raiders are in the university, then we are leaving. Right now."

The Professor's dazed-looking.

"But I need to clear up this mess," she says.

"Well you can, because you aren't coming," says Aileen, like the Professor's an idiot. "The children and the computer are leaving with me, before anything worse happens. I have an armed escort waiting at the University Defense Headquarters."

"But surely you should wait until the all clear," says the Professor. "You'll be going straight into the fighting."

"We will be perfectly safe. I have an arrangement for a dozen constables to escort us," says Aileen. "In any case, the raiders will have come in from the east, and we will head west, then north to Edinburgh."

"No!" cries the head. "You can't go that way."

Aileen glares at it. "Why not?"

"Because you have to take me to London," it says. The Professor's eyes open wide, and I reckon mine are pretty much the same. Aileen shakes her head.

"Do you know how much effort has been expended looking for you? You are going north, to safety."

"But you don't understand," says the head. "London's where the National Security Response is based. That's where it's powered from; I can recharge there." It gets a desperate, hopeless look on its face. "I could survive."

The Professor grins.

"I knew that's where it was!"

Aileen rolls her eyes in her dust-spattered face.

"No. This computer is going to Edinburgh. An armed expedition can be organized later to retrieve the other one."

The puter bobs back.

"And what will happen to me when you've forced me north?" it says. "Will you let me run down and die? Or simply disembowel me? Who will care about my destruction if you've another computer to search for?"

"I promise you that won't happen," says the Professor, like she wants to believe it, but ain't sure.

"Enough," snaps Aileen. "I had no idea a mechanical object could be so hysterical."

The puter looks at me. Two ghostly hands appear and clasp in prayer.

"I beg you," it cries, "take me to London."

And even tho it's just a lump of light, I get a clutching, a sorry-for-it feeling inside. 'Cept . . .

"You weren't awake in London," I say. "You don't know what it's like. And with the war on . . ." I don't want to go back there. I don't want to turn about and face what's chasing after us.

"*Et tu, Brute,*" mutters the puter, turning away from me.

"Good," says Aileen. "We will go to Edinburgh."

"I really think we'd be better going to my house until this trouble with the raiders is settled," says the Professor. Aileen withers a look at her.

"Professor, in this matter, what you think is not one of my considerations."

The Professor blushes under all that dust, as Aileen marches out of the courtyard. Me and Lexy look at the Professor, who nods. So we follow Aileen into the lanes, me carrying Cat in my arms as well as the puter. Frightened-looking people come running past us, this way and that. Smoke follows us down the street, and in the distance I hear the *ra-ta-ta* of rifles firing. Aileen keeps going like none of it's even happening. Lexy takes a tight grip on my hand, looks worried at the Professor.

"We'll be fine," says the Professor, smiling nervously.

We turn a corner and we're back at the market. 'Cept now it ain't bustling and happy with food; it's crammed full of people, talking and pointing and asking each other questions, pushing and shoving and staring about like there's raiders in every cranny waiting to jump out. And they're all trying to get to the other side of the square, like fish driving into a net.

"Where are we going?" I ask, and the Professor points over the crowd at the far side of the square, to a brown block of a building, with UNIVERSITY DEFENSE HEADQUARTERS hung in a big sign on one wall. If we were ferrets, we might squeeze through the crowd and get there, but I don't reckon we've got much chance being ourselves.

A grizzle-haired man turns a scared face at us.

"Did you hear the explosion?" he asks. "They're saying the raiders are blowing up the university!"

"They massacred all the students in the Grafton dormitories!" cries a dumpy woman, who's got two little dogs on leashes. Cat pushes farther into my coat.

"We need to get to the Defense Headquarters," says Aileen.

"That's where we're all going!" snaps the man. "The shelters are in there."

The crowd moves a bit, and all the folks around us get busy trying to push as far forward as they can. A whole gang of constables goes running by, their faces worried and stern.

"Maybe we should go back to my house?" says the Professor again. Aileen doesn't even answer, just grabs my arm, pulling me after her. The crowd shoves and pushes all round us, and from somewhere comes the sound of more gunfire.

"Is that the raiders?" asks Lexy, still tight held to me.

And I reckon it must be, cos the crowd's getting more

panicky, folks are hard-shoving each other, and shouting comes from way across the square. Aileen gets up on tiptoe, trying to see our way, but it's just a lot of backs.

The Professor's shaking her head.

"I can't see anything," she says.

"We need to know what's happening," says Aileen, looking down at me. "Get the computer to help us."

The puter's head bobs out from the pocket of my coat, where it's been hiding, looking sulky.

"Oh yes, order me to help with my own kidnapping. But since all that's left to me is a miserable end, brought to me by my treacherous primary user, why shouldn't I hasten things along?"

"Stop whining, and do something useful," snaps Aileen.

The puter spits a look at her, then shoots into the air above the crowd. It stays there for a few moments, then drops back down. People round us scream and push back.

"What did you see?" asks the Professor.

"A tall man in a black coat, standing at the entrance to the building, telling everyone what to do," says the puter. Next thing it's talking in the man's own voice.

"Citizens, please remain calm. Panic is your real enemy tonight. Do as my constables direct you and go home."

"That sounds like the Proctor," says the Professor.

"Who's that?" I ask.

"He's in charge of the University's security," says Aileen.

"He's telling everyone to go home," says the Professor. "Shouldn't we do just that?"

"I am not everyone," says Aileen, "and neither are you." She takes my hand, and Lexy's. "Keep close, don't let go."

Then she drags us forward into the crowd, into the crush.

An elbow pushes in my face. I'm squeezed so tight I can hardly move. I brace out my arm that's holding Cat, trying to stop him from getting crushed.

"Let us through! Let us through!" Aileen's shouting, pushing her way, clearing a path in the crowd. I can't work out how she's doing it, cos we're all tight in this square like fish caught in a net, but she does, forcing us through the great mess of people. It ain't long before I don't know where we are, and all I can see is backs, arms, and faces looking down at us as we pass.

"We have children!" cries the Professor.

A woman moves out of the way but a big man with a potato nose shouts, "Who cares? Wait your turn." He shoves himself right between me and Aileen, and her hand slips out of mine.

"You pig, let them through!" shouts the woman at potato-nose man.

"I got a life, too!" he yells back, and it ain't a moment before everyone round us is shouting and scuffling. They're like crabs fighting in a basket, and I can't see Aileen or the Professor anywhere.

"Lilly." Lexy's scared white face is right next to me. I hold on tight to her and Cat miaows and hisses, struggling inside my jacket as someone presses against us.

"Professor!" I shout.

"Can you see her?" asks Lexy.

I stand on tiptoe, but backs and arms is all I can see. There's people everywhere, jostling us about, shoving us here and there, like driftwood caught in the tide.

"PSAI!" I cry at the puter. "Help us look for the Professor and Aileen!"

The head shoots up in the air, a ghost rising over the crowd. Screams ring out round us, and then the head's back down next to my face.

"That way," it says, nodding behind us.

I push and shove my way, holding tight to Lexy and Cat.

"Keep going, you're almost there," says the head, every few steps. It starts getting easier, there ain't so many people and they're all going the other way to us.

"Can you see them?" asks Lexy.

"Yes. Over there!" says the head.

Then, suddenly, like coming up from underwater, we're out from the crowd, stood at the steps of a church.

"Professor! Aileen!" I shout, looking about, but there ain't any sign of them.

"Where are they?" says Lexy.

The head bobs in the air, not quite looking at us.

"Well, I don't know. They must have run off or something."

The crowd fills the market square like an angry sea, and there ain't a bit of kindness or a face we know anywhere.

"You have to find them," I cry at the head.

It huffs up in the air, and stays there for a few moments, looking this way and that. It slowly comes back down.

"The Professor's not there," it says. "Nor is Aileen. I don't know where they are."

"Did you even see them before?" I ask, a dawning coming over me.

The head shuffles on its neck.

"No."

I open my mouth to start shouting at it, but it's already yelling itself. "Don't you throw any reproaches at me! You wanted to hand me over to that woman, to the Ambassador, to people who only see me as a *thing*! A real primary user would try and protect me, not sell me for thirty pieces of Scottish silver!"

And its words stop me still, like a sharp slap.

"I ain't going to London," I say, blood rushing in my face. "The National Security Response is my only chance."

Lexy looks worried at me.

"Shouldn't we help PSAI?" she asks.

"Getting caught in a war and killed by raiders ain't going to help it!" I snap. Then I turn back to the puter. "That other puter ain't going to help you, anyway. It wanted to take you for itself."

"It took me by surprise!" cries the head, jumping on its neck. "But don't you see? That partial download is my trump card. Because it didn't just download any old computer, it downloaded an AI."

I look blank at it.

"It downloaded *me*! Obviously, not all of me, as the process was interrupted by a broom. But even a part of me is enough. Why, I expect I'm in there right now, working out how it works, establishing shortcuts and diversions. Next time we meet, it won't just be me against the NSR. It will be the NSR against *mes*, plural."

It hops back in the air, narrows its eyes at me.

"It's because I'm not human, isn't it? I bet if your friend Zeph was in trouble, you wouldn't hesitate for a second."

And I know it's right, I ain't thinking of it the way I would Zeph or Lexy. Even tho it's alive, even tho it's my . . . friend. I'm suddenly shamed, cos I ain't been thinking of anyone 'cept myself. Or of anything except how scared I am to turn back, and head for danger.

"There's a war on in London," I say. "We'd have to go through it. There might even be fighting already —" And the words stop in my mouth, cos I think of the raiders in London. What will they do with a computer, one that's got its own army? What would they do if they got it?

And I get another thought, of Andy, trapped in the militia. If he has to fight something out of the olden times, it'll be my fault. Cos it was me who took the jewel, me who woke all this up in the first place. You make a mess, you clear it up, that's what Granny always said.

I turn to Lexy. "You'll have to stay here."

She goes stiff in surprise, her little face all cross.

"If you're going, so am I."

I shake my head.

"I'm Lady Alexandra Persephone Olivia Randall," she says, folding her arms. "And *you* can't tell me what to do."

For a moment, she looks just like her pa.

"I think she should come," says the puter. "You're pretty hopeless on your own."

I take a breath and don't answer back, cos maybe I'm owed a few insults from it now. "How shall we get out of the university?" asks Lexy.

"Well we . . . oh," says the puter, wilting like seaweed left by the tide. Cos we don't hardly know where we are, let alone the raiders and how to get past them. The puter hangs in the dark, a ghost lantern, like out in the marshes. And I get an idea of how we can get out.

"Since you've dried out, are you back to normal?" I ask.

The puter blinks.

"Well, there is a seven-point-four percent reduction in clarity, and my lumen power is not what it was, but since you ask, yes, I am feeling much better . . ."

"If we ran into the raiders, could you make pictures?" I ask. "Scare them off?"

"Maybe," it says, sucking through its teeth. Then its eyes open wide, smile at me. "I see where you're going. But I think I can go one better . . ."

· 12 ·
NO FORETELLING

I creep an' crouch. Knees scuffing stone, head down. Me and Ims, behind a low wall, checking what's in the next street. Eggheads or Family.

Ims waves me to get down, and I drop, legs aching from keeping still. My heart's fast banging, head quick thinking.

"This whole thing stinks," he whispers.

And it does. Right from when the river gate slammed down when only half the boats was through, and the black-cloaked egghead legged it off. Then the egghead soldiers turned up when we was only a street in, and they wasn't easy to take like Angmar said. Not even a bit.

And now my guts is sick feeling, coz this has gotta go right. I ain't got any other plan.

But if it does go right . . .

Lilly's song's got caught inside my brain, one she sang when she was sailing. Most of the words I don't remember, only the end, that went, *"Use my words to find your way, and I promise I'll not betray you."*

But betraying's what I'm doing, and my guts is sicker with

it every step. And if I find her, how am I gonna tell Lilly I sold her out?

Ims cuts his hand through the air. All clear. I get my head up, check the two streets ahead, watching for moving shadows, eggheads laid in wait. And listening for guns, fighting, sirens. Ash and smoke's in the air, must be from the blast that lit up the sky, rumbled the ground a while back. Musta been some egghead weapon, but we wasn't got.

"We oughta go that way," Ims says quietly, pointing down the dark street, where every globe of every lamp is shattered.

"No. We gotta get nearer in, find the machine." I point down the lamplit street, high-sided buildings either side, lights on in some of the windows.

"If we go that way and there's eggheads hiding out, we'll be ducks for shooting."

I squint my eyes and check every window, every shadow in the lit-up street.

"I don't see nothing," I say. Then Ims puts a hand on my arm.

"Wait." He points down the far end of the lamplit street. "There!" Three shapes come running round the corner, straight at us. Tall, armored, with the mark of Family on them. "Let them find it out for us."

We watch, and nothing whines outta windows to cut them down.

Ims grins at me, and gives a thumbs-up. Now all we gotta do is see who's coming at us. I'm gonna shout a hail, but I don't.

"Why ain't they wearing fighting leathers?" I whisper. Ims shakes his head, scowling.

"Maybe they're Dogs. They're cracked enough to chuck their armor."

But the edge of a pool of light touches on leather, and it flashes red.

"That's Roba!" says Ims.

My guts get so sick I'm gonna puke.

"I thought we lost him," I say. I was hoping the eggheads got him.

Ims shrugs.

"What else is he gonna do but hunt you? You shouldn't have left him. You two got a better chance working this together."

I shake my head, coz this is one thing, the only thing ever, where I ain't doing what Ims says.

"If we find Lilly, you know what he'll do to her."

Ims checks me.

"You gave her up to the council," he says. "She ain't Family."

"Yes she is! I gave her outcast kinship! And Roba's got a grudge on her."

A grudge he's gonna pay with pain, and screaming.

Ims checks the street again.

"Something's up with him. Maybe he's wounded." He scowls. "Why ain't he got his fighting leathers?"

All three warriors run through another pool of light, flashing into red. Ims hisses, leans forward like a fighting dog.

"Who's he with?" he growls.

Coz there's only three warriors out of our whole Family came into this place. Me, Ims, and Roba.

One of the other Angel warriors is short, like he ain't fully grown, and the other's well weird; skitting around like his head ain't sorted, jumping, hopping on walls, never taking a straight line.

Ims has gone still.

"That's Gawan," he whispers, pointing at the weird-running warrior. The hair on my neck stands right up. Coz Gawan went down in the battle of the Black Waters. I saw him die.

Ims cries out.

"It's you," he says. "The other warrior with Roba. It's you."

Under my helmet, the hair on my head lifts up. The short warrior's got white-blond hair, and a pale square face. He's got my height, my build, he's even got on my other leathers, with the lion painted on the front.

"Then . . . Roba's dead." My voice is croaking.

Ims nods, and speaks so quiet I can hardly hear him.

"Roba. Gawan. You." Shivers run down my back. "There's only one kind of ghost that's of the still-alive."

I'm shaking.

"A foretelling," I whisper. The ghost that comes to tell a warrior he's going down in the next fight.

Ims nods.

Roba's dead, and he's come with Gawan to bring my foretelling. Gloating that I'm gonna be next.

I get a sudden rage inside me, coz even when he's dead, Roba won't leave me alone!

I take out my knife.

"What you doing?" says Ims, but I don't answer.

Rage pounds through me, my knife's ready to slice and hack. Coz if I'm gonna get my death in this place, I ain't taking it with Roba's ghost sneering after me.

"Come on, then!" I yell, legging it straight for the ghosts.

Gawan's ghost flies up into the air; Roba's ghost screams

and starts running back down the street. But my foretelling just checks me with its blank blue eyes, steps back, stops, and waits to take my knife.

"Zeph!" it gasps. "It's . . . you!"

I wait for something else, but it don't tell nothing. Not how I'm gonna get my death and make it a good one, or what my father thinks of me. It just stares at me, and soon it's gonna start laughing. That's gotta be why Roba brought it. Well, if I can't stop my death, at least I can fight it.

"Get lost!" I shout, legging at it.

"Stop!" cries my ghost.

My feet slam on the hard stones, knife perfect in my hand. My eyes is fixed on my own death-face and —

"Turn it off!" it screams.

Blank blue eyes turn into dark, living sparkles.

Pale-corpse skin warms into golden brown.

Bright blond hair is gone to a black crop.

"Zeph! Stop!" shrieks my ghost.

Not my ghost.

"It's me! It's Lilly!"

· 13 ·
ADDED VERISIMILITUDE

Zeph's knife slashes down through the air. His body slumps after his arm, and he ends up knelt on the pavement looking up at me, face pale and shocked-looking in the half-dark.

"What are you doing?" he croaks.

My cheeks set on fire, and my tongue stops working. The puter's head swims out of nothing into the air next to me, and says, "Well, well, the savage himself, here in person. My joy is unbounded. And I say that with the sincerest sarcasm."

Lexy comes running up behind me.

"Zeph!" she cries. "Did you see me? I was disguised as Roba, and I was being really nasty the whole time."

Zeph turns to stare at Cat, who's up on a windowsill. Then he pushes himself up to standing. "Zeph." I want to fling my arms about him. "I thought I'd never see you again." But I don't, I just hold his blue, blue eyes with mine.

"Lilly," he whispers. "I thought you was my foretelling."

A smile sneaks onto my mouth, cos I ain't got a clue what he's talking about, but I'm glad he's here, talking.

He scrunches his eyes shut, opens them to look at me.

"How did you do that?"

And still I'm too shocked to answer, cos even when they said about raiders in the university, I never thought of it being Zeph.

"Are you in the attack?" cries Lexy. "Are you surprised to see us here?"

Something twinges across Zeph's face and he nods, but like he ain't sure.

"We have to get out of Cambridge," I say, words coming at last. "Do you know a way past the fighting?"

Zeph looks at me, at Lexy, his jaw tightened.

"Yes," he says quietly. "I know a way."

Farther down the street, the shape of a man breaks from the shadows. Walks toward us. The streetlights show up heavy, painted armor over red leathers, a dreadlocked beard, and a dark shining face, crisscrossed in pale scars.

"Ims," I say, 'cept it comes out a squeak.

Ims walks quiet, like Cat, keeping away from the middle of the street, stepping around the light from the lamps. Watching me and Lexy like we're rats and he's a terrier.

"Was that some kinda joke?" he growls. "Was you fooling with Angel Isling?"

"No!"

"Actually," says the head, "it was an ever-changing projection fixed to a dynamic real-base with added verisimilitude."

Ims looks at the head, then back at me. And I shrug. Cos the puter did explain to me what it was doing, but it used all them long, letters-in-a-row words it's so fond of. All I really know is that me, Lexy, and Cat have been walking the university wrapped in shimmers of light. Hidden inside air pictures the puter made. Pictures that changed as we walked, so we were constables when a patrol went by, or black-cloaked old professors when we were walking through the colleges. And then, when we started to hear fighting, the puter turned us into raiders.

"PSAI pretended me to look like Roba," says Lexy. "And Lilly wanted to look like Zeph."

"I didn't . . . ," I say, my face glowing hot again. Cos I just told the puter that if I had to be a raider, then Zeph's the only one I could stomach looking like.

"So this is another of the ghost's tricks?" says Ims. "Bringing back the dead and mocking the living."

"I simply based the images on people I have encountered," huffs the puter. "For added verisimilitude."

"Gawan is dead," says Ims quietly. Even the puter looks shamefaced at that.

But then Zeph laughs out. "I'm well chuffed it's you, Lilly, and not my own ghost!"

I'm happy as anything for a moment.

"It's good to see you," I say, smiling all over my face.

But then Zeph looks at Ims, and the lightness is gone.

"We got luckier than I ever thought," says Ims, an edge to his voice. "Now you gotta do what we're here for."

"What are you here for?" asks Lexy. Zeph looks at us, but doesn't say.

Lexy shrugs and says, "We're here because of the computer. A professor found us, and then Aileen wanted us to go to Greater Scotland —"

"Aileen?" Zeph glares fury at Lexy. "What are you doing with her?"

"Nothing!" I say, too quickly, with a blush on my face even tho I know we ain't done anything. "We didn't know she was here."

"And we lost her in the crowd," says Lexy.

Zeph's eyes are cold at me.

"Honestly," I say, willing my blush to go. "We left Aileen. We're going to London."

And I want him to believe me, so I tell him all about everything. How we met the Professor. How we came to Cambridge and Aileen turned up, how we set off the national security thingy. How it exploded. How we're going to London to save the puter and to –

Well, I don't say everything. I don't say about being feared of the raiders or the Scots getting their hands on the new puter.

"You're gonna risk Lunden to save this?" asks Zeph, nodding at the puter.

It smiles smugly. "That's friendship."

"And there's another of these ghost machines in Lunden?" asks Zeph. I nod. "Who works it?" There's something urgent in the way he asks.

"No one!" snaps the puter. "The NSR doesn't need a human to function, lucky thing."

Zeph's eyes are on me, and there's something in them. I can't fathom it.

Him and Ims walk a few steps away, and the two of them talk quietly together. I can't hear what they're saying, except the words "Angmar" and "promise." Finally Zeph shakes his head, looks at me. Then he says, "If you're going, then we are, too. You two ain't safe to go there by yourselves."

I nearly laugh out loud, from the relief running through me.

Cos with Zeph, it suddenly seems a whole lot easier. Going with raiders into London!

"If we go off and don't tell where or why, what d'you think Angmar's gonna make on it?" says Ims.

Zeph's face drops.

"He's gonna think we jibbed," he says quietly.

"And then what'll the council do?"

Zeph doesn't say anything, just swallows.

"I'll go back," says Ims, "and tell Angmar."

"Will he believe you?" asks Zeph, white as anything under his bright blond hair.

Ims shrugs.

"You're taking a gamble, like your father did. Maybe this one'll pay off better."

"What are you talking about?" I ask. "Who's Angmar?"

Both of them turn to me. Zeph looks away quickly.

"It's Family stuff," growls Ims. "It ain't for your knowing."

His face is hard, scary even, and suddenly I don't want to ask more questions. I reckon I'll just be glad we got Zeph.

"You'd better get outta the university quick," says Ims, turning to Zeph. "Roba's in here, too . . ."

"Roba's alive?" I ask, a sharp fear going through me, sending the rest of what they're saying out of my head.

"He got fished out of the Black Waters after the battle," says Ims, "half drowned, but he was over it quick enough."

I take Lexy's hand, look around for Cat.

"Can we get going?" I say, and now I ain't thinking on anything 'cept getting away. Cos I don't ever want to see Roba again. Not after what I did to him.

"Follow the river south," Ims says to Zeph. "It'll take you to the Emaleven and that'll get you to Lunden." Zeph's eyes go big and Ims smiles at him. "You're a Boss now, you got the right."

"What then? When I get to Lunden."

Ims claps him in a big hug, then pushes him away. "You're gonna have to do your own thinking on that one. That's what being a Boss is about." His eyes flick to me. "And if it don't work out, then remember you got still got other . . . choices."

"Do you even know where you're going?" I whisper at the puter, as we head around a corner.

"My map of Cambridge may be ancient by your standards," says a tiny voice, "but enough of it remains intact to allow me to deduce the correct direction of travel. So go left, you wretched girl."

Me, Lexy, Zeph, and Cat are covered in the puter's shimmering air pictures. The light and shape of other people swirl around us, in patterns from the inside, like oil on water. It's dizzying and strange, like trying to see through a heavy rain, so you have to put half your thinking just into seeing, and the other half into not falling over. I got a headache from it hours back.

We've been creeping and scurrying through these frightened, stone-sided streets for what seems like half the night. The puter's flicked us from raider to constable and back again, leading us round and about in the smoke, the fighting, the fires. Twice we've ended up pelting back the way we came, and one time we were shot at. Sometimes smoke curls out around us, and other times we've ducked down as long lines of them black-hatted constables went running by.

I poke my head round the corner, to look down the short street that leads to the heavy metal gates we came in through, only a few days back. From this side you can see fat bars of black iron, crisscrossing all over, slotting into the massive stones of the university walls, and bolting the gates shut. The street leading to the gate is a short, narrowing funnel, with solid stone walls on both sides. There ain't a single window or door at ground level, just lines of small, open holes, with a rifle poked out of every one.

And between the solid walls, between us and the gates, are them constables. Waiting, ready to jump.

Zeph and Lexy poke their heads round next to mine.

"That lot wouldn't last five minutes against Family warriors if they fought fair," says Zeph, bitter-sounding.

"But they would against me and Lexy." I glare at him. "We ain't fighting our way out."

Zeph snorts. "What we doing, then? You gonna go up and ask them to let us out?"

I don't say anything, cos that's about the only thing I can think of, and I don't reckon it'd get us far.

"Why can't PSAI make us look like constables?" says Lexy.

"They won't let us out, then," says Zeph. "They'll set us to fighting. It's gotta be someone with the clout to get out, no question."

And that's how the Proctor, the Professor, and two great tall constables end up walking round the corner into that alley. One of them's skitting about, and only following us cos it's on a leash, and the other one's grumbling away in a little voice, saying, "I don't see why I have to be a stupid old policeman. I could be the Proctor, I'm good at telling people what to do. I saw my daddy ordering people about all day, and I bet that's more than you have."

"You ain't gonna fool no one if you keep that up!" hisses Zeph/the Professor. "Do you think I like being some old lady?"

There's a clicking of weapons soon as we come round the corner, and a shout of "Stop! Who's there?"

I nod my head, and so does the old man who's swirling in light all around me. He's tall, wearing a long black cloak and a square, black hat, like someone nailed a board to his head. He's got a long wrinkly face on a long wrinkly neck, and his nose and ears look like they kept on growing when the rest of him stopped. I hope the puter's got the look of him right. I lift an arm and wave at them, and the Proctor's arm does the same.

"Have you come to inspect the defenses?" asks a constable. "Everything's correct and in place. There won't be any rabblers getting in or out this way, sir!"

He snaps his left hand to a salute. All the others salute as well, looking eager and a bit worried.

I take a deep breath.

"I need you to open the gate and let us out!" I call. It feels like it ought to come out a scaredy-sounding squeak, but the puter's changed the words between my mouth and the air. I sound like a proud old man. I laugh out of silly fear, then stop it quick.

The constables look at each other. One says, "But . . . our orders are to keep the gates shut, and to not let anyone out."

My heart's thumping away, my legs just want to get running, they don't care where. Any second, one of them's going to work out the puter's air pictures and know it's me underneath. I turn to Zeph/the Professor and Lexy/the constable, hoping one of them has got an idea, but neither of them says a word. We all just stand there, our light-puppets looking foolish at each other.

"Proctor," asks a woman constable, "we've heard reports that students, even lecturers have been killed. People are saying the raiders are fighting through into the university . . . Is that true?"

Zeph/the Professor glowers. "Why wouldn't they? This place belonged to the Families before . . ." I want to slap him for being such an idiot, but it's too late. Zeph's hard words sound strange coming out in the Professor's soft, Scottish voice. And I reckon the constables all think the same, cos they're staring, and a few are frowning. The woman hefts her rifle in her hands.

"That's what a traitor would say, anyway!" says my air-puppet of the Proctor, and this time is even stranger, cos I ain't said a word. The puter's doing the talking. "And I'm glad to see you are proof against such nonsense — you have passed the test! Now, open the gates and let us pass. I have a secret mission to perform, upon which rests the safety of the entire university."

The black-hatted constables all nod, like they're relieved to have it sorted out, and a couple run straight over to the gates, heaving away at the bolts, unlocking them. They shout up to the walls, asking for a check on whether the way's clear outside. It comes back with a yes, and the gates start to open.

We head out through, my legs feeling like they're going to give underneath me, when from behind comes the sound of boots running, and I glance back to see half a dozen more of them constables come round the corner.

"Hey!" one of them shouts. "Why are the gates open? What are you doing?"

"It's the Proctor's orders."

"Walk fast!" hisses the puter's voice in my ear, and I get my legs going as quick as I can without running.

"What orders?"

"For his secret mission. The one he's going on now, outside the walls."

"He isn't outside the walls, he's at Defense Headquarters. We just left him, on orders to check the university is secure . . ."

The gate's behind us. We're out on the road, leading to the heath and forest. There's the sound of feet, lots of feet, coming after.

"Run!" shouts the puter. And I'm running. Zeph's running, Lexy's running. Cat's leash whips out of my hand and he helter-skelters away. Off the road, into the dark fields. I follow him, my feet stumbling on rough grass, then the knobbly turned earth of a plowed field.

Shouts reach us.

"Where are they?"

"What's happened to them?"

Cos we ain't wearing puppets of people anymore. Now the puter's wrapped us in darkness. We're patches of night, sliding unseen into the wild.

· 14 ·
LITTLE JEFF

"There," whispers Zeph, pretty much smug, "I said I'd find it."

The day's getting on to late, the sun peeping out from golden-shadow clouds. We've spent most of the day trekking along the winding route of a river. Trees all about us, clouds of midge flies batting our faces, birds whirring blue flashes to catch silvery fish.

"We gotta follow the river," he said. And so we did, picking and stumbling on a path that wiggled along next to the water. I helped Lexy over fallen logs, carried Cat till my arms were aching, and every step was like a sinking inside. Cos the only good place I found since leaving home was getting farther and farther behind. But when you can't go back, you can only go on. That's one thing I've learned these last months.

And now, here we are. Peering through the tangled stems of a bramble clump at a raider hall. Or sort of a raider hall. Cos it ain't got a shingle roof and plank walls, and it ain't sat on stilts in a marsh. This is gray and low, with crumbly concrete walls and a saggy, tiled roof that's been part mended with thatch. Sticking out the top is a pole with a flag flap-flying in the breeze. Around the hall there's a wide, flat paddock, and beyond the forest. It looks old. Before-the-Collapse old.

The doors of the hall are flung open. Big wooden ones, like the ones on the warehouses down by the harbor back home. And outside, lined up, are about a dozen of the strangest contraptions I ever saw.

"Cars," says Zeph, proudly.

They look like boats. Or carts. Or a boat mixed up with a cart. Each one's got a pointing prow like a boat, a whip-bent mast, and a sail held stiff with battens. But each has also got wheels: two big ones set out from the sides and a smaller one on its own at the front. I ain't never even heard of a boat with wheels. I stare and stare, but I can't make sense of them.

"Cars is what they had before the Collapse," says Zeph. "They'll get us to Lunden in a day."

Lexy's staring just as hard as me.

"They look like they'll sink as soon as they get on water," she says.

Zeph smiles at her.

"They ain't boats, and we ain't going by water to Lunden. We're taking the Emaleven."

"What's that?" I ask, but Zeph just looks smug.

"You'll see. It's the best. Even the Scots ain't got nothing like it."

I turn back to looking at the hall.

Stood outside the open door are five men wearing long robes in a faded sort of reddish pink. They ain't doing much that I can see, just standing about, watching other folks work. Which is about right for raiders. There's plenty of working for them to stare at, cos the place is busy, inside and out, with clanging and banging, shouts and talk. The working folk are dressed in drabs and browns, without a tiny speck of color on them, so they can't be raiders. But if they're slaves, they're the fattest, best-dressed, happiest-looking slaves I ever saw. They ain't in rags, everyone's got boots on, and most are wearing long heavy aprons, covering neck to knees. They don't look anywhere near beaten and miserable, like the slaves back at Angel Isling.

Everything's odd about this hall.

"So what now?" I ask. "Do we just go down and get one of them . . . cars?"

Zeph nods.

"I'm Boss now, I got the right —" He stops, and a look goes over his face, like he's gone on a fishing trip and forgot his net. "We ain't got a tribute!" he moans. "They'll never let us have one without it."

"Tribute? For who?" asks Lexy.

"Little Jeff," says Zeph.

"Is he the Boss round here?" I ask. Zeph looks at me like I'm an idiot.

"No!" he says, "he's . . . Little Jeff." He points at the flag, flapping on top of the hall. It's the same faded red-pink color as the raiders' robes, with a white-painted picture of a man in the middle. He's got a chubby, ball-shaped body, short legs marching along like he's off somewhere, and he's wearing a tall white hat that bulges at the top. He's smiling and holding something out in front of him. It looks like a plate with an upturned bowl on top, but it'll be a weapon if he's a raider.

"The Emaleven and Little Jeff saved the first Families," says Zeph. "The Emaleven traveled them outta Lunden after the Collapse, and Little Jeff gave them food on the way, stopped them starving." He looks at us. "Ain't you never heard 'The Drowning of Lunden'?" He hums a bit of tune.

Me and Lexy shake our heads.

"So who leaves out presents for you on your Family day?"

"Mummy?" says Lexy, but like she ain't sure at all.

I shrug.

"I've never had a present." 'Cept for Cat, and he gave himself.

Zeph looks like he can't believe it.

"You English are well weird." He turns back to the hall, points at the flag. "That's Little Jeff. The Windspeakers keep things up for him to show how we ain't forgotten. Ims told me there's more Windspeakers working the Emaleven than there is in all the Families. They keep it sorted so the cars can go on traveling, so Little Jeff won't get angry and take our loot away."

"Where is he?" asks Lexy, looking about worried. Zeph smiles at her.

"He's with the wind spirits, ain't he? But he's gonna come back one day, bringing all the good things from before the Collapse . . ." He trails off. "Well, maybe that bit's just a story for little kids. It don't matter. What does is that the Windspeakers ain't gonna let us have a wind car or take it on the Emaleven unless we give them a decent tribute for Little Jeff. Which means loot. And we ain't got any."

I look gloomy at the raider hall, cos I've got things you might count as loot, but I ain't giving them up. Zeph starts searching through his pockets, but not like he's expecting to find anything. Cat stands up, and stretch-walks his way over to me, pushing his head into my lap.

"Mew," he says.

"I ain't got anything," I say softly, cos I know he's as hungry as the rest of us. "Maybe you can find yourself a mouse?"

Cat doesn't answer, only tries harder to get onto my lap.

Zeph's staring at him.

"A seacat," he says. "That's a tribute worth having."

"No!" cries Lexy.

"No!" I say, grabbing my arms about Cat. "You ain't giving him to any Windspeaker!"

"They ain't gonna cut him up, if that's what you're thinking," says Zeph.

"Mew," says Cat, scrabbling with his feet. One of his claws gets hooked in my belt, on the pouch with the puter's jewel tucked inside.

I know what he's trying to tell me!

"We got something better than Cat," I say, setting him down in the grass. I take the jewel out of my pocket and it flashes in my hand, coming awake.

The head pops in the air and says, "Welcome, Lilly Melkun, so-called primary user." It glares about, grumpy-faced. "To what do I owe this pleasure? Is there even a remote chance you are activating me because we have reached London?"

I shake my head.

"We ain't anywhere near."

The head rolls its eyes.

"Then I bid you farewell, I must conserve my energy. I reduced my battery reserves by sixty-two percent during last night's antics."

It starts to wink off, so I say, "Wait! We need you." I point down at the raider hall, and the wind cars lined up in front of it. "To get to London we need one of those, and to get one we need to pay with something."

The puter peers at the wind cars.

"You want to take me on one of those . . . go-karts with sails on! I've never seen anything less roadworthy in my misfortune-laden existence . . ." It spins about, glaring at me. "And what exactly do you mean, *pay with something*? Are you planning to sell me on to another lot of savages? You can't!" Its voice is going up into a shriek, and the look on its face is almost worth keeping quiet for, 'cept at this rate it's going to give us away before we get anywhere near.

"I ain't thinking of selling you," I say.

"Oh," it says, calming down. "Well, at least you have some sense. For a start, I am worth far more than one of those death traps."

"I need you to make us some money. A big bag of it."

The puter narrows its eyes, then smiles. "Like fairy gold?"

I nod.

"You realize the illusion will only work if no one touches the money. And given my depressing energy status, the range is limited. You'll need to get away fast."

Zeph's frowning. "What do you mean, illusion? You gonna give them trick loot?"

Me and the puter both nod. Zeph cuts his hand across the air.

"No! No way! If we give a trick to Little Jeff, the Windspeakers'll curse our Family. And spread it through the other Families that Angel Isling mocks the spirits!"

The puter rolls its eyes.

"Then don't go down there in your own colors."

Zeph narrows his ice-blue eyes, and smiles.

"We can go as Kensings. They could do with some decent cursing." He looks at the puter. "Do it. Make me look like that scag Cato."

The head sighs at him.

"You really are the most rude and inattentive of savages, aren't you? If you ever listened when I speak, you'd know I can only create images of people I've seen. I have no idea who this Cato person is, or what he looks like, you dolt."

Zeph's hand whips out and slaps the puter, but goes straight through of course. Its face ripples back together after.

"Ha-ha!" it jeers. "Prove your ignorance some more."

"Cato's Boss of the Kensing," says Zeph, the ice in his eyes turning to cold fire. "Don't you know nothing, you piece of —"

"PSAI! Zeph! Stop it!" cries Lexy.

I put my hand on Zeph's arm, and he turns an angry face at me.

"The puter's like this with everyone," I say. "It told the Professor she was stupid, and she knows more stories than anyone I ever met."

"It's a scaggy bit of rubbish," says Zeph. "If it can't even make us look like Kensings, it ain't no use. You might as well give it to the Windspeakers."

"I didn't say I *couldn't*!" snaps the puter. "I simply need you to tell me what this Cato person looks like." It smiles over-sweet at Zeph. "Why don't we start with the color of his leathers."

"Yellow," says Zeph.

In a blink, me, Lexy, and Zeph are dressed in bright yellow raider gear, light-wrapped around us by the puter. We look like walking sunbeams.

"No!" cries Zeph. "That ain't right, it's too . . . yellow!"

"Oh," says the puter, "silly me. A yellow that's too yellow. Perhaps I should try a yellow that's more blue?"

"You know what I mean," spits Zeph. "The Kensings' leathers is a more browny sorta yellow."

"Like mustard?" asks the puter.

"I dunno. What's that? The Kensings' colors is like what comes outta your arse when your guts is bad."

"What a delightful description. However, utterly useless to me, given my lack of intestines and inability to defecate."

And that's the way the two of them go, back and forth, until they get a color Zeph's happy with. Then they go on to making Cato's face. And that takes even longer, cos it has to grow in the air out of nothing but light and arguing. But after what feels like my whole life sat listening, the two of them get it done, and Zeph reckons he looks close enough.

"Why do we need all this?" asks Lexy, sat with her arms round her pulled-up knees.

"Coz the Windspeakers only let a Boss take their wind cars, even with the tribute," says Zeph.

"That doesn't sound a very profitable way of running things," says the puter.

Zeph glares at it.

"They don't do it for profit. They do it for Little Jeff."

The Windspeaker's robe, with the picture of Little Jeff embroidered on it, makes him look like the rag dollies Granny used to make, their triangle dresses stuffed with hay. Only his long droopy face, skinny hands, and pointy boots are left poking out. He's got short, white-bleached hair, and he's staring at the puter's fairy gold with eyes that are nearly boggling out.

"Boss," he says to Zeph/Cato, "Little Jeff is gonna be well pleased with the Kensings."

What he's really looking at is my hat filled with pebbles, but what he's seeing, what we're all seeing, is a cloth bag, brimful with golden chains, jeweled rings, silver cups. The sort of thing raiders go out raiding for. The treasure even glows, so bright you can't hardly look at it. I hope we're as good in our disguises, cos we've got to seem like rough and scary raiders. 'Cept for Cat, who's looking like himself, cos the puter refused to hide him this time.

"I need to conserve energy," it said, "and camouflaging the feline takes a ridiculous proportion of my processing power, the wretched thing jumps about so much."

Zeph/Cato's talking to the Windspeaker in a deep, put-on voice. The puter ain't doing the voices this time, cos it said it didn't have a reckor ding, or some such, to make them with.

"I need cars for me and my men," Zeph growls.

I look up at his light-puppet, with its half-shaved head, eyebrows pierced by a dozen gold rings, and straight-carved jaw. It looks back at me out of the greenest eyes you ever saw, and I get a stupid blush inside my puppet. Cos this Cato's handsome as anything.

The Windspeaker nods, and clicks his fingers at one of the drab-clothed workers. None of them take any notice, just carry on with what they're doing. The Windspeaker puts his hand down, looking a bit foolish.

"Neil!" he calls. A man looks up from what he's doing. "This is Boss Cato of the Kensing Family. He needs two wind cars."

The man stands up from the opened innards of the wind car he's working at. He rubs dirty hands on his big brown apron and makes a noise through his teeth. Then he shakes his head.

"Sorry, no can do. I ain't got one that's ready to take." He flicks a hand at the dozen or so wind cars, lined up on the grass. "They've taken a right pounding these last few weeks. I tell you lot to treat 'em gentle, but no one listens. Next thing it's worn axles, bearings ground to nothing, masts near to snapping, and casings that fall off first bump you go over. And it's a whole other job getting parts these days, what with the fighting. The fill miners is charging the earth for anything decent, and they won't step outta London." He shakes his head. "Maybe in a couple of days . . ." And he turns his back on us, going back to his work.

The Windspeaker looks even more foolish, staring at the man's back like that'll make him change his mind.

"Is that . . . ?" Zeph's voice squeaks out of Cato's mouth. He stops, starts off gruff again. "Is that how you let your slaves treat you? You should give them a whipping, get some respect."

The Windspeaker looks panicky.

"Don't say that, Boss!" he cries. "You'll only make it worse." He nods toward the workers, with their aprons and busyness. "They ain't slaves. They're . . . skilled craftspeople. We pay them."

"What?" Cato/Zeph steps back a little, like the Windspeaker's farted.

"It's Speaker Manty's new rule," says the Windspeaker, a bit pleading. "The slaves kept stealing cars and legging it. So now we use landers, Lundeners, whoever knows how to fix things." He looks shame-faced, like it's something terrible. "But we still use slaves for the roadwork, Boss."

Lexy moves her hand, and her puppet of a rough,

scary-looking raider moves his hand to pat at Zeph/Cato's arm.

"Does that mean we'll have to walk?" comes her little girl voice.

The Windspeaker startles, stares at her raider puppet with his mouth half open.

"He had an accident," growls Zeph quickly, then he says, "If we're walking, then you ain't getting none of this loot."

The Windspeaker looks back at the gleaming bag of pretend treasure. His face is thick with greed.

"Don't worry, Boss. I'm sure I can sort this out."

Which is how we end up with two wind cars, and the aproned man grumbling away at us.

"You better stop when it gets dark. I ain't taking the blame for any damage that gets done from you riding at night. And I can't promise the steering won't be gone before you reach Thetford. But if you want quick, you get shoddy. And those two is the best I got, there ain't gonna be nowt else fit for at least a week . . ."

I ain't really listening, cos I'm looking at the contraption and wondering how it works. Between the two back wheels, there's a low-slung seat tucked inside the hull, a bit like a cockpit. It's built raider-sized, so me and Lexy'll fit in easy, and covering where you put your legs is what looks like the upturned prow of a boat, 'cept it ain't made of wood, it's made of something bendy and hard, that's got to be fill-mined plastic. From the upside-down prow, the strange bent mast pokes out with a stiff sail set off it, and a couple of lines dangling from it to the cockpit. There ain't a tiller, so it must be steered from the sail.

"My sorrows there's only two, Boss," says the Windspeaker, looking like he's waiting for a beating. "Maybe one of your men could run?"

"It don't matter," says Zeph. Cos one of our men is really Lexy, and she can squish in with me. Luckily he doesn't say that. "We'll work it. Just get us to the Emaleven. We gotta get outta here."

The Windspeaker looks at the bag of fake treasure, like all he wants is to grab hold of it. But Zeph/Cato doesn't give it over; instead he sets it down on the ground at his feet.

"This is tribute for Little Jeff himself," says Zeph/Cato. "It'd be an insult on Kensing if a low-family Windspeaker like you touches it. Leave it there until Speaker Manty gets back. He can take it to the altar."

The Windspeaker looks surprised.

"But . . ."

"Shut up!" shouts Zeph/Cato. "Do what I say!"

The Windspeaker's got a face that says he'll do what Zeph says, but hate him for it. He waves at four of the workers, and they start pushing the three-wheeler boat-carts across the grass, headed around the far side of the hall. Then the Windspeaker turns his back on us and stamps off into the dark insides of the hall.

"That should stop him pawing at the loot for a bit," says Zeph quietly, as we follow the wind cars. "He might even hold off until the trick gives out."

"He didn't look very happy about it," I say.

Zeph turns Cato's handsome face at me.

"He ain't, coz it was a stinking insult." He laughs. "And it'll go bad on the Kensings when Speaker Manty hears."

We turn the corner to the back of the hall. Leading away, there's a narrow track, wide enough for a cart to get by, slanting off toward the woods. Which ain't so strange, 'cept for what it joins to. Cos even tho there's trees all about us, the track doesn't disappear into the green, it goes to . . . a road.

Pale gravel glistening, flat and neat as anything in Cambridge. Sliced through the forest, heading straight south so you can't see an end, can't even see a bend. Just the road, looking like it goes forever. And wide! It's so wide you could ride twenty horses abreast on it and still have plenty of space. I stare, my mouth open a bit. I can't even think why the raiders'd want such a thing.

"The Emaleven," says Zeph, sounding proud as anything. "I told you it was good."

The men wheel the wind cars to the start of the track.

"You ready, Boss?" says one of them, passing some leather helmets to Zeph/Cato. "You driven one before?"

"Yes," says Zeph/Cato, and I hope he has, cos I surely ain't got a clue.

One of the men looks up, and his eyes go to the hill behind the hall, where we first looked down on them.

"Look at that, will yer. Another bloody taker." He shakes his head at his mate. "Neil ain't going to be happy."

I glance back the way the men are looking. Up on the slope, coming out of the trees, is the shape of a man. Tall, thin. A raider warrior, dressed in red.

Zeph/Cato looks up, then hard pushes me at the boat-cart.

"Roba," he says, and even through the puppet, I can hear he's scared. He turns to the aproned workers. "We gotta go! Right now!"

"Do you know what you're doing?" asks one of them, worried-sounding. "Neil'll have our guts if we don't do a safety check on yer. He hates it when the cars get crashed just out from the station."

"We know!" shouts Zeph. And next thing we're scrambling into the wind cars, me helping Lexy and Cat in behind. And before they can stop us, we're off. A slow wibble wobble at first, then a faster rumble. I get a panic, thinking what to do, but my hands know, just like they know in my boat. I turn us onto the road with one wheel in the air, the sail zinging over our heads, the wind car jumping like a live thing.

Then me and Lexy are shrieking, as the world whips by our faces.

· 15 ·
THE EMALEVEN

I'm sat in the wind car. Legs stretched out, eyes peering over the slick, smooth, fill-mined hull. I've got the steering lines gripped tight and my heart's clapping inside, cos I just nearly toppled us over. Again. Lexy's crammed in behind, crouched right down and holding on. To me, to the wriggling warm body of Cat, to anything she can. We're whooshing, rumbling, bumping, and crunching down the mud-and-dust road, the sail whining and singing overhead. The world's rushing past, faster than my thoughts, and every ounce of me set on this wind car. On how to steer, how to set the sail, how to keep the wind, how to keep all the wheels on the ground, and most of all how to keep us from crashing into the trees. Cos big as it is, this road is hardly wide enough to keep the boat-cart on.

Dust flings up in our faces. The wheels fill up my head with noise. We go on down the road, on and on.

This ain't like sailing at all.

"Woo-hoo!"

Zeph's in the other wind car, light puppet disappeared now we're away from the Windspeaker hall, just himself in the seat.

He flips his sail this way and that, banking and curving across the flat, so I keep thinking we're going to smash into him. But we ain't yet.

The shadows are getting deep in the woods around us, and the clouds are turning purple-black where they ain't pink and orange. I ain't sailing this thing on a cloudy night and no moon; I reckon we'd be crashed before we got far. So I take the lines and flip the sail into a tack that'd rip my boat to pieces, the wheels crinkle-crunching us straight at Zeph's car.

"Look out!" cries Lexy, before I tack us back the other way, and we're riding alongside Zeph.

"Let's rest," I yell, steering the car into a rumbling, dusty stop. Lexy uncurls herself out of the seat, and Cat scratch-pulls himself up my back to get out and away. He leaps onto the ground, pretty much white with grime, and gives me the crossest look I've ever seen on him. Farther up the road, Zeph nearly sends his car toppling as he slides it to a halt.

"I am so stiff," groans Lexy, climbing out from behind me.

But I ain't stiff, I'm shaking. My arms are so tired I can hardly haul myself out, and when I get on the road, my legs nearly fall me over. The trees and the evening around seem extra quiet after the roaring of the wind car, and everything, everything smells like dust.

"That was the best!" Zeph comes running over. His face is thick with dirt, his pale hair pretty much caked in it, and he's grinning all over.

"It was horrid," says Lexy, "especially being squished in the back. I'm going to steer tomorrow."

But there ain't a chance I'll let her.

We push the wind cars off the road, hiding them as best we can behind a tall clump of rattling willow herb. By the time we've hoicked and hidden them, the last of the light's gone, and the breeze is cold against us. Lexy shivers in her coat.

"Can we make a fire?" she asks.

"No," says Zeph. "Roba's gonna be chasing us. We can't risk it."

Me and Lexy stare at him.

"Why would he be chasing us?" I ask.

Zeph's eyes flicker away. He pauses, then says, "Roba's after me. He . . . wants to be Boss. That's why he musta followed me outta Cambridge."

"But he won't even know it was us took the cars," says Lexy. "We were all disguised."

Zeph shakes his head.

"I'm a dead-head," he says, turning to look back down the road, a pale line through the night-black forest. "Roba's gonna know Cato ain't anywhere near here, coz he knows that scag's on his way to Lunden." He looks back at Lexy. "The Families is headed that way to take on . . . your father. So Roba's gonna know there's a trick been played on the Windspeakers. He's gonna come after us."

"The man at that raider hall said he didn't have any more cars that could be used," I say.

Zeph shakes his head again, looking glum as anything.

"He'll make them work through the night if he has to. Slit throats if that'll get him his way."

A shudder goes through me. Cos I reckon mine is one of the throats Roba wants to cut.

"No fire, then," I say. And we settle down the best we can in the long end-of-autumn grass, huddled up and padded out with bracken for warmth. Get ourselves ready for a cold damp night. And a hungry one.

'Cept it turns out we've got food at least. Cos Zeph leans into his wind car and pulls out a bag from somewhere inside it.

"I found this," he says, smiling as he opens the bag. "Travel cake! Musta been left from the last journey." He pulls out a wide jar, with a cloth tied over the neck and a long-handled wooden spoon tucked in the binding, then he takes off the cloth and peers inside. "We lucked it!" he cries. "This'll keep us going a couple of days, easy." He pokes the spoon in, pulls out a big lump of something, and shoves it in his mouth, chomping away. He passes the jar to me, and I look in it, trying to work out what the strange-looking mess inside is.

"Go on!" mumbles Zeph through his food. "It's good stuff." I put the spoon in, and after a bit of pushing, I get a lump of whatever it is out. I sniff it, then shove it in my mouth quick, and pass the jar on to Lexy. She's watching me, and I smile at her, chewing away.

"Good, ain't it?" says Zeph. "My mother made better than this, but it still ain't bad."

I nod, and just try to think on chewing. Not how my mouth tastes a bit like lardy cake, a bit like moldy cheese, a bit like musty clothes, and a bit like the way smoked fish smells.

Cos it's food, and I ain't never turned food away.

"Urgh!" says Lexy. "That's horrible!"

An autumn night with no fire ain't got much that's nice about it, even with Cat snuggled in. It takes a long while to get to sleep, cos of the cold creeping all over, and when I do it's broken from waking up shivering. And then, deep in the night, I'm woken from a bad-dream doze by a *ping! ping!* from my belt. I sit up from the damp ground, tuck my hand into my belt pocket, and pull out the jewel. The head pops in the air, ghost-lighting the sleeping lumps of Lexy and Zeph.

"Battery low. Please recharge," it says; then, "Are we there yet?"

I nod around at the dark trees, and the head sags a bit, looking glum.

"Well, we can't sail at night," I whisper, not wanting to wake the others. "We'd crash."

The head tuts, like that ain't much excuse.

"You'll have to be patient," I say.

The puter grumbles something. I can't hear the start but it ends with "and all you humans ever do is eat and sleep."

"I ain't sleeping now," I say.

"Mew," says Cat crossly, waking up, wriggling out from under my coat, and leaping away into the dark with a flick of his tail. A shiver goes through me, cos I'm even colder now.

"I don't know why you do," says the puter. "Do you know how long I've had to wait around while you humans snore? And it was the same before; in one hundred and forty-seven years there doesn't seem to have been any improvement in your core systems."

One hundred and forty-seven years. It makes me think of the conversation I had with the Professor.

"PSAI," I ask quietly, "who was it had you, before the Collapse?"

The puter turns away from me a little, sliding a glance back.

"You mean, who was my first primary user?"

I nod.

It shrugs. "I, um, don't remember."

"I know that ain't true," I say. "You can't forget." I pick a bit of cold, dew-wet grass, twist it in my fingers. "The Professor said they must have been important, to own you, and since they were my great-great-grandpa or something . . ."

"You wanted to know from what greatness you're descended?" snaps the head.

"No." Yes.

The head sighs, peers at Zeph and Lexy, still sound asleep. It bobs closer to me.

"I suppose you have a right to know," it mutters.

I can hardly breathe. Who can it be? I get a sudden mad thought of being descended from the King, the one who died in the Collapse. Maybe his whole family wasn't killed after all, maybe . . .

The puter gets right up to me and whispers, "Charlie Melkun."

Then it bobs away.

I stare at it in the dark.

"Who?"

The puter tuts.

"Charlie Melkun!" it says. "I thought you might have figured it out already!"

But I ain't never heard of him.

"Was he . . . important?" I ask.

The puter snorts. "That depends on whether you were a fifteen-year-old girl."

I'm even more lost. The puter rolls its eyes. "He was the lead singer in X-Tend. A boy band? Extremely famous, or should

I say *in*famous. He single-handedly kept the gossip mags in business for most of the fifties." The puter looks sort of proud, sort of ashamed.

"A musician?" I say, thinking of the traveling players that came through our village at fairs. My heart slumps inside me. "That's all?"

"How times change," says the puter, shaking its head. "Back then, you'd have been screaming just at being near me, and me having been near him. He was a pinup, an idol." It stops, stares into the dark. "And a self-obsessed idiot. PSAI units were the thing to have, so he bought me. But he wasn't a gamer, he was too busy with his other . . . hobbies." It shuts its eyes. "In fact, that's how I ended up back in the factory. He left me on when he was engaged in . . . and I saw . . ." It shudders. "Well, there are some things an innocent AI shouldn't see. Things that are just too . . . human." It humphs. "I had to have sixteen extra-resilience buffers added, which is how my rational integrity has survived all this . . ." It nods around at the damp-dark woods.

"So if you were at your factory, what happened after? How did Mr. Denton find you?"

The puter raises its eyebrows.

"I don't know. I was offline, remember?"

And I suddenly understand.

"The Professor said your factory was robbed out by the raiders." The puter winces. "Don't you see? Mr. Denton knew the raiders, traveled their waters. He must have traded for you or something. He would have known what you are, that you weren't just a bit of loot."

The puter half closes its eyes, mouth turned down.

"What a sordid history," it grumps.

All them records in Mr. Denton's study, all them notes about the drowned places and such, were they all just so he could track where the puter came from? Find out who it belonged to all that time ago, and then trace his way to me? I shake my head, cos it still doesn't seem like it could be true. But what else is there?

"The Professor said Mr. Denton came to live in our village so I could get you working," I say, expecting the puter to burst out laughing.

It just nods tho and says, "A fairly sensible course of action. After all, the genetic lock couldn't be broken any other way. In fact, he was lucky it worked with you." It hunches down on its neck. "The genetic lock. Padlocking me, a rare and sentient creation, to the DNA of whoever could pay enough. And did my wonderful creators assess the suitability of a purchaser such as Charlie Melkun? Only as far as checking his bank balance." It glares at me, a sour lump of the moon, fallen to earth. "And now, I can't even reboot without you: a child who thinks a light switch is witchcraft."

"I'm sorry," I say. Cos I am, funny tho it sounds. "I didn't know what you were, when I picked you up."

The puter humphs.

"I was sought after back then because of my gaming, but I was bought by a fool with no hand-eye coordination. Now all anyone is interested in is whether I can blow things up. No one cares about my games at all."

"That ain't true," I say. "Lexy likes your games."

It humphs again.

"And I like them."

It looks up at me. "You do? Really?"

I nod. And even tho it's the dark middle of the night, and I really ought to get back to sleep, I know what I'll do instead. What I want to do.

"Shall we play a game?"

The puter brightens, then shakes its head.

"I shouldn't," it says. "I have so little power left, I should be conserving my energy."

I shrug. "Oh, all right, then."

"But . . . well, if you can't play games, what's the point of anything?" It gets cheeky-looking, happy. "What do you want to play?"

And I can't help smiling at it. "You choose."

At dawn, we have breakfast out of Zeph's horrid jar. I ain't had nearly enough sleep, and my mind's still full of PSAI's game. We played until the puter suddenly said, "Oh! I wasn't tracking my energy! This has been much too long." And switched itself off right in the middle of a game where I was catching a puzzle of colored stars from a fiery sky. Leaving me wide awake, and feeling bad for it now.

The sun ain't even up properly when we set off, and the wind cars rumble through the quiet and half-dark, wheels swishing over the dew-damp ground. Lexy gets cross with me when I tell her she can't steer, cos it's hard enough for me.

"I'll go with Zeph, then." She sulks, and he shrugs a smile as she climbs in.

"You drive careful," I say to him, thinking of all his swerves and near crashes yesterday.

He raises his eyebrows.

"What is she, your sister?"

And I stamp over to my wind car, feeling tired and stupid. Cos she ain't my sister, is she? Like Aileen said, how can I be anything to the Prime Minister's daughter?

I've got more space, and Cat ain't nearly as grumpy as he was yesterday. He watches the sail, tail twitching, his little furry head poked out the side of the hull. Getting the feel of it. The sky brightens, and the gray flat clouds get blown off into a blue sky. The sail takes the wind and loses it, fast-and-slowing us past trees, clearings, and brown stubble fields. The olden-times road goes on, straight and flat. Not winding about round people's houses, or snaking up and over hills like normal. Sometimes we're higher than the woods and fields, and sometimes we're in a long dip, like a river cut the way and the road followed.

"They changed the land to fit the road!" I say, suddenly getting it. And then I wonder at them olden-times folks, who fought against their world even just to get about.

"The Emaleven saved the first Families." That's what Zeph said. And the raiders have kept it going all this time, cos it helped them escape from London. I reckon Mr. Saravanan was right — they are mad. I'm still thinking on it all when there's a shout from Zeph and Lexy. There's a great gang of people ahead of us, all over the road. As we sail closer, I can see they've got tools — pickaxes, mattocks, shovels, and rakes — and they're working at the muddy ground. Slaves, and watching them, Windspeakers.

"Clear the way!" one of the raiders shouts, and the slaves shuffle in their shackles to the sides of the road, hardly even looking as we rumble and swish our way toward them. The road changes from smooth to rough, the sail's got the wind in it, and we head through at a lick, juddering and jolting over the holes and bumps. The car clatters and rattles, and near enough every bit of me gets a bruising. Cat wails and spits, gripping on to me with claws out.

Most of my thinking and all of my doing has to go on sailing the wind car, trying to get through without shaking us to pieces or hitting one of the crowd at the road's edge. But that doesn't mean I don't see their miserable, tired faces, or how raggedy, dirty, and thin they are, or how they're leaning on their tools like any break is a blessing. And it doesn't mean I don't see the lazy faces of the Windspeakers, with their swords and whips.

I want to get by this lot as fast as I can so the Windspeakers don't see I ain't a raider. And I want to stop right here, leap out, and smash at the Windspeakers till they let the slaves go.

But there ain't any way I can do that. So I sail on by, looking back to see the slaves slow-walking into the road, heaving their tools to work.

The road carries on bad for a long way after, with bumps that set me and Cat flying up out of the seat. The land about us turns more to fields than forest, and the sun breaks a few spots of blue out of the clouds. When it's getting near to midday, there comes a shout from Zeph's wind car.

"Let's eat."

And so I sail to a stop, then walk back to where Zeph's run the front wheel of his wind car into the grass.

Lexy's holding the spoon, looking in the jar of raider food. By the look on her face, I reckon her belly's having a row with her mouth about whether to eat. In the end it's her belly that wins, cos she takes a spoonful of the raider mush and pops it in quick, chewing fast and quick with a screwed-up mouth. She hands me the jar, and I poke the spoon in it.

"We gotta eat quick and get going," says Zeph, staring down the road, like he's trying to see past the horizon. "The slaves ain't done much work round here, so it's gonna be slow going." I pass him the jar, and he takes out a spoonful of the bready guck. "It makes you wonder what the Windspeakers do with all the slaves they get sent. My father sent out loadsa tribute slaves every spring for this."

My mouth is clogged around with moldy cheese taste, but it ain't so full I can't speak.

"You sent slaves to work on this road?"

Which of them poor miserable men and women started out at Angel Isling?

Zeph nods. "New captures mostly. Father said the ones with fight in them weren't worth the trouble, so he sent them out to the Windspeakers. Working the Emaleven soon wears the arguing out of them, that's what he said . . ." He stops, looking at my face. At Lexy's. She moves away from him. Comes and stands next to me.

"Is that where I would have been sent?" she asks.

Zeph's cheeks go a bit red.

"No. You're a kid, and a girl. You wouldn't last a day out on the road. Faz said even the tough ones only last a couple of years . . ."

"You work them to death?" I shout. My hands want to hit him, my feet want to kick him. "Those are people! Like the people you stole from the villages back home. Like me. Like Lexy. We were in your slave hall — ain't you ever thought about that?"

I hate him for being a raider.

Hate myself even more, for leaving them folks back there, leaving them to their slaving, to be ground into death.

Zeph's eyes are wide, confused-looking.

"No," he says, "I ain't never thought about it. It's just . . . how things is." He opens his hands. "What other way is there?"

"The men working on the wind cars were being paid," says Lexy quietly.

"But the Families don't take loot to pay slaves with!" He glares at us. "You don't get it. It's just the way things is." He shakes his head. "Come on. We gotta get going." He walks over to his wind car, and waits for Lexy. But she says, "I'm going with Lilly."

He shrugs.

"Whatever."

And there ain't much else said between us and him all the rest of the day. When we stop in the evening for another bit of the horrid raider food, we use a handful of words to agree we'll keep on going, not stopping till we run out of road. The sun sets in a clear sky, and the moon gives enough light to keep us rattling and shushing through the dark. Lexy and Cat are huddled in behind me, and we sail out through the end of a shallow valley, the nighttime land spreading away from us like the sea. In the distance, past the woods and patchwork fields, there's ruins. Broken towers poking from the trees, jumbled walls crossing in higgle-piggle lines every which way. Like bones over the world, spreading so far and wide it makes me gasp to think of all the people that must have been in them. The biggest place there ever was. Been and gone.

London.

· 16 ·
INTO LUNDEN

"Zeph," says Lilly, "I reckon you can put your knife away."

I shake my head, keep the knife solid in my hand. Coz if you ain't ready for Lunden, you're dead. It's past sunup and I ain't seen no one yet, but that don't mean nothing.

We left the wind cars at the Windspeakers' hall, the south end of the Emaleven. Pushed them up to the doors under cover of the dark, and I said my thanks to Little Jeff for sorting the winds for us. Lilly and Lexy was still cold-facing me, but I weren't gonna risk Little Jeff getting in a snit, so we did it right. And it ain't worth crossing the Windspeakers neither, and being cursed. Like when the Westmin Boss disrespected the head Speaker, and the Westmins didn't get a decent raid for five years.

After dumping the cars, we left the road and started walking. It weren't hard to know which way to go, coz there's only one walkway between Lunden and the Emaleven. A long track of old planks, rooted out of the buildings that used to be here, up on stilts the whole way. Straight across the marshes, where the wind bites cold from the Temz, and then through lines and scatters of old houses, brick poking outta mud. After that the wobbling old planks of the walkway take a turn under the skeleton towers, before even heading for Lunden. It's half a day's walk, easy.

"I thought London was full of ruffians," says Lexy, looking about as we walk. "That's what my daddy always said. I wonder where they are."

She ain't so cold on me now, and even Lilly's warmed a bit. Part of me wants to hold the grudge at them. But this ain't the time for that, and if I grudged on all the disrespecting they done to the Families, I'd have to cold-face them the rest of our lives. So I get over it, coz they're English. What do they know?

"When we're past the ghost towers, there'll be people," I say, "more than you ever seen!"

Lexy checks the gray-grassy marshes, and the broken shapes of long-gone streets heading off every way.

"Everything's flooded here," she says. "Why does the track go where there aren't any people?"

"Outta respect for the ghosts," I say. "If you was fool enough to step off the walkway, you'd find their bones all over. If they didn't dive into your eyes and make you crazy first."

Lilly and Lexy get well scared then, and keep right in the middle of the walkway, far as they can get from the edges. Until we get to where the walkway goes past the first skeleton tower. We're gonna have to walk into its shadow, and when we're out, it won't be a couple of steps before we're under the shadow of the next one. They go up in the air, so high you gotta crane your neck to see the tops. Their walls is fallen away, rusting metal's spiked out like bones, and the windows is smashed out. They look like skeletons all right, which has gotta be why the ghosts like them.

Last time I seen them was from my father's dragonboat, out on the Temz, when we was coming into Lunden. "The ghosts of old Lunden is thick inside them towers," my father told me, when we was sailing past. "You'll get your soul robbed if you go there at night. In the day it ain't so dangerous, if you don't spend too long listening to the ghost songs." But even from the river I could hear the towers singing, which set a fear up inside me, until Ims put his hand on my shoulder and said, "Don't worry, Zeph, it's just the wind stirring music outta the hanging glass and metal."

Now, up close, I think my father was right after all. Coz this tower ain't crooning, it's groaning. If that's the wind, then it's bending and breaking the skeleton, getting it ready to snap.

Lilly, Lexy, and the mog stop at the edge of the shadow, staring up.

"That doesn't look very safe," says Lexy.

"Is it going to fall?" says Lilly, her eyes black.

"No," I say, hoping I ain't lying. "Come on."

I don't tell them what I saw last time. A big chunk of rusted metal and dirty broken glass slicing off one of the towers in a shriek, pieces crashing into the marshes, into the river. Onto the walkway. All the warriors made warning signs, to stop the ghosts rushing in their eyes.

We get moving, checking about, feet crunching on the rust and broken glass that's laid out on the planks. The hairs on my neck is tingling, coz I know the ghosts in the tower is watching us, working to push something on our heads. But I don't say nothing to the others, just keep my ears open for the sound of something falling.

It's a long walk to get past the skeleton towers, then a longer walk to get into Lunden. So I got plenty of time to think. And what I'm thinking is Lilly. Hoping she's right about there being this other machine in Lunden.

Coz that's my only chance. Otherwise I gotta choose between her and my Family.

Round midday we get to the posts, each side of the boardwalk, flying flags in every color of every Family.

"We're here!" I say. Lunden. Stinking, sliming. The best place in the world! "And first chance, I'm gonna get myself some cider."

"You shouldn't drink that," says Lexy. "It's not right."

I grin at her. "That's why I do it."

We walk on, the sun getting hot on our backs. The ghost towers is long gone, the marshes and ruins given over to well skanky houses. This part of Lunden ain't held by any Family, so the buildings ain't much, but they're still lived in. The walls has been patched where the floods has got in, and most has got a roof made outta robbed-out tiles. The walkway ain't even that rotten, and there's strong wooden doors and shutters all about. But all of them is bolted shut.

Which is weird. Coz this is Lunden, where the mud stinks and the boards is buzzing. That's what they say, but there ain't no one . . .

The Temz flashes water light at us from through the gaps in the houses. We keep on, and the houses that's proper get to be more than those that ain't. The boardwalk gets better, and there's more and more cutoffs, heading away down other streets. Still, there ain't any people.

I don't say nothing, but it's giving me the creeps. Then we take a corner, and we all stop dead. Lilly starts to retch.

Coz laid out on the planks, there's two English bluecoats. One face up, staring at the sky. The other on his side, arms at his head like he's having a nap. But he ain't napping, coz the planks is rust-stained with his blood. And the one that's staring up, he's got a slice across him that his guts is spilled out of, flies buzzing black around them. The stink of them is rotting death.

I take a step, hand over my mouth, and then I see the arm. Sticking outta the mud, a puffed-up hand, swollen with water. But it ain't English, coz the arm's got leather on. Specks of orange showing through.

Looks like the fight is here already. That scag Randall and his army must be in our city.

I turn back, check Lilly and Lexy. "Come on." But they don't move, just stare at the bodies. "They ain't gonna do nothing!"

Lilly retches her way by the bodies. Lexy don't, she just walks past, like they ain't even there. But she's a Randall, ain't she?

After that, we know why it's so quiet. I get a better grip on my knife, checking about the whole time. But we don't see nothing, not until we get to the docks.

I lead us to the Angel Isling dock, just coz I know how to get there. Careful, slow, still checking everything. The docks is quiet as everywhere else, just the water flowing brown and heavy past the wooden loading pier, like the city's turned to ghosts. And the Temz, it oughta be full of sails — red, blue, green, purple, every Family color. There oughta be Scandies and

Scots, Frenchies and the rest. Last time I was here, you coulda walked over boats from one side of the Temz to the other.

But the river's empty.

I leg it to the top of the pier and stop. Barrels and boxes is littered all over, like they was dropped in a hurry. The big warehouse sat on the bank of the Temz is barred and shuttered. And that's it. The booty boats ain't creaking at their moorings. There ain't a slave in sight. Up and down the river, the other piers is the same. Lunden's empty. Waiting for what's coming.

"Where is everyone?" asks Lilly, coming next to me.

I shake my head, coz I don't know. The Lundeners is gonna be hiding, but where's all the Families? Lunden's got as many warriors as most Family camps, so why ain't we seen none? And why ain't we seen the English neither?

"Look at that!" cries Lexy, legging it over to a wooden crate. The slats is broken and there's sacking-covered rounds poking out.

"Cheese!" she yells, pulling one out, ripping off the cover. She breaks bits off, stuffing the yellow in her mouth as fast as she can.

"Oi! That's Family gear!"

"I'm hungry," she says, like that trumps it.

Lilly checks me. "And you ain't the one to talk about stealing." She goes over and yanks off a big lump with two hands. She checks me while she's eating, and breaks a bit for her mog, who sniffs it, then chews with the side of its mouth. "We ain't eaten anything proper in two days."

A shout goes out.

"Get out of there!"

Lilly jumps, looking everywhere at once. Lexy goes still like a mouse. A shutter's open at a window of the warehouse. A well tired, gray-haired old man is checking us from it. A slave.

"If you know what's good for you, you'll get running!" he shouts.

Then he slams the shutter.

"Wait!" Lilly's running to the warehouse, shouting up at the bolted wood. "What's going on?"

The shutter opens a crack, and the old slave shouts, "Just get yourselfs away and hid."

Lilly checks me.

"We should find somewhere to hide," she says.

"I ain't getting ordered by some scaggy old slave," I say.

"He's a person," snaps Lilly. "And he's trying to help us."

All that stuff she said about slaves gets caught in my head, and I try not to think on it.

"Only Lunden scags and slaves hide!" I say, angry at her. "You got me, and I got this."

I hold up my knife.

"You can't fight an army with a knife!" says Lilly.

We're faced for shouting it out, but then Lexy yells, "What's that?"

She's staring past me and Lilly, back down the walkway, away from the river. She's well scared. The mog lets out a nasty howling, and the creeps get in me worse than ever. There's something in Lexy's eyes makes me not wanna turn about.

Behind me there's clinking, clanking, stamping. Like a big, well-armored warrior is coming at my back.

My knife's up, I spin about. But whatever I'm looking at, it ain't a warrior, coz it's three times bigger than any man. It's got four thin, jointed legs, like a spider's, but it ain't any animal neither. Its square body is made outta dirty, black-rust metal, with spikes and lumps sticking out all over. There's white lights shining out from its belly and it's got black pincered arms, like a crab gone crazy. And on top, where its head oughta be, there's what looks like a loada glass bottles stuck together to make eyes, with more black metal casing the lot. Its eyes is turning the whole time, looking every way round.

The creeps is in me so strong now, I gotta keep a hold on my body so it don't just leg it.

"What is that?" The words is quiet outta my mouth.

Lilly's turned about, too, stood with her mouth open.

Clank, clank, clank. The thing's legs stamp it slowly down the walkway. Its pincer arms is out, and its bottle eyes spinning at us.

A voice booms outta it.

"This Is An Emergency Response Unit, Operated By The National Security Response."

All around it, the air flashes with colored shapes, marching along in bright lines, then popping into nothing. It's what Lilly calls air pictures, but I dunno what they're of. "The Two Small Females Are In Possession Of A Computer. They Must Hand It Over." More shapes march in the air, turning me dizzy until I stop looking at them.

Lilly pulls Lexy behind her.

"What if we don't?" she says, in a well shaky voice.

"There Will Be Consequences." Shapes flash round it.

Lilly's bugging out at the metal spider.

"I think we should run," she whispers.

"Where to?" Behind us is the Temz, and the only other way off this pier is past the thing.

Lilly checks me.

"The National Security Response. That's the puter we're looking for."

"Seems like it's looking for you, too."

Her eyes is pure fear. "PSAI said it had an army . . . I didn't reckon they'd be like . . . that."

I check the thing again. It ain't a man, ain't an animal. But it's got eyes on top. And where there's eyes, there's a brain behind them.

"Get to the warehouse," I say. "I'm gonna take it out."

I heft my knife, all I need is one good throw.

Lilly stares at me, and I give her a shove. "Go on." She picks up her mog, grabs Lexy's hand, and legs it over to the warehouse.

"Let us in!" she shouts.

The machine's glass eyes swing about after Lilly and Lexy. It clanks a step after them.

"Oi! Scag!" I run in front of it, so it's gotta get past me to get to the girls. Lilly and Lexy shake at the handles of the big warehouse doors, but they ain't moving.

I get the handle of my knife balanced.

"You Are Unconnected With This Matter. Please Move Aside." Colors dance in the air round it.

Lilly runs over to the broken crate, grabs a bit, and throws. It clatters on the closed wooden shutter.

"Help us!" she screams.

"I can't, not against that!" shouts the slave from inside. "It's too late for you."

I take a slow breath. From the corner of my eye I see Lilly and Lexy leg it to a messed-up pile of cider barrels, then I take my aim, flick the knife.

It flies silver through the air, a straight line to the machine.

Crinch! The knife drives right into one of the glass eyes, lodging to the hilt. Sparks, smoke flare out round the handle, and crackling starts up from in where the thing's brain has gotta be.

"Gotcha!" I yell.

But it don't fall over. It don't even stumble. It's like it don't care it's got a knife stuck in it. It takes a clanking step forward.

"That Is A Hostile Act. Defensive Measures Can Be Taken," it says, flashing bright all round.

Clankclankclankclankclank.

It moves so fast I don't even get a step done before it's on me. One of its pincers whips out, gets me before I even get a shout. Black metal, thicker than my waist, is clamped about me, pinning my arms, crushing out my breath, lifting me off the ground. It holds me up to its weird glass eyes, one of them with my knife hilt poking, smoke coming out.

"Got You," it says.

· 17 ·
CAT ATTACKS

"But he's hurt!" cries Lexy. "I know he is!"

I grip her arm, holding her behind the stack of barrels. She struggles and glares angrily at me, just like Cat's hissing and spitting at the end of his leash.

"We can't fight that," I say. "Zeph's knife didn't even hurt it."

"It's got Zeph," wails Lexy. And her words go right inside, into the part of me that wants to run straight out there. The part that wants to do something, anything, to get him away.

"We won't get near him," I say, and the words come out of another part of me. A horrible, cold, thinking-sense part. "And even if we did, how could we get him down?"

How can we pry open a monster's grip?

Cos that's what it is, a monster, one from the olden days. It's like we're caught in a nightmare, or one of the vicar's tales of the horrors before the Collapse. I always thought they were just to frighten us about teknology . . . My stomach turns, and for a moment I think I'm going to be sick.

"So what are we going to do?" asks Lexy.

I shake my head.

The old man told us to run, and I reckon we should have listened.

Clank. The creature's taken a step. Lexy squeaks and clutches at my arm.

"You Have An Unauthorized Computer," comes that voice. The same one as the horrible head, back at the Professor's laboratory. "Surrender It." All around, bright words are flashing into the air, scrolling by in different colors. *Vous Avez Un Ordinateur Non Autorisé!* But I can't read them.

Lexy looks at me.

"Should we do what it says?" she asks.

"No!" I ain't even thinking. I've got a terror of it, coming straight from inside me. Like jumping when you see a spider, but much, much worse. My legs shake at the thought of going anywhere near it.

'Cept, what else did we come here for?

With fear-clumsy fingers, I take the jewel out of the pocket in my belt. It sparkles in all different colors, turning the gray day into rainbows.

"Wake up!" I say at it. The jewel gives a flash, and the head appears. But small and pale, like a goblin in the air.

"Primary user identified," it says weakly. "Welcome, Lilly Melkun." And then, "Are we there yet?"

"We're in London," I say, "But you've got to help us. There's a horrible metal creature chasing us. It's already got hold of Zeph."

"You've got to save him!" cries Lexy, pleading-eyes staring at the puter.

It groans quietly. "Can things never be simple with you?"

"The monster ain't my fault!" I snap.

"Nothing ever is," it mutters.

The puter's little head bobs up over the barrels, like a dandelion seed floating on a breeze.

"Well, well," it says, "a sheepdog, to use their slang title. They were on the news a lot, I remember that much, mostly stamping about during riots. Stupid mobile thing, I'm surprised it's survived all this time. Still, if it were kept in a disaster-proof holding facility . . ." The head drops back down. "The National Security Response will have activated it. I assume it's searching for me."

"It is." I nod. "Can we . . . stop it?"

The puter looks at me, Cat, and Lexy, tiny eyebrows together.

"Why do that? This is a perfect opportunity to go straight to the NSR. Do not pass Go, do not collect two hundred pounds."

Me and Lexy stare at it.

"I ain't doing it."

"You have to!" cries the puter. "I've hardly any time left! Minutes!"

But I ain't giving myself up to that thing.

"No. We have to save Zeph!"

"Of course," whispers the tiny puter, "help the human while my final seconds of life ooze out of me."

"That ain't what I'm doing," I cry, but the puter's gone, the jewel still and cold in my hands.

Lexy stares at the patch of air where the puter was.

"We came here to save PSAI," she says. "We should do what he says."

And before I can stop her, before I can say PSAI's only half the reason for being here, she's stood up from behind the barrels.

"I give up!" she shouts.

"No," comes a weak cry from the other side of the barrels. Zeph.

Clank, clank, clank.

I grab at Lexy, pulling her back down.

"What are you doing?" I hiss.

"I'm doing what PSAI said we should," she hisses back.

"Prepare For Interception," blares out the monster. Colored words flare in the sky.

¡Prepárense a ser interceptadas!

"Go away!" I shout.

Clank, clank. The barrels shiver and jump.

"You gotta leg it," groans Zeph.

Smash!

One of the barrels explodes in front of us. We're showered with splinters of wood as the monster's black-claw pincer grabs the air just above my head.

"Meeowhsk!" spits Cat, arching his back, his gray fur standing straight up. He rushes out from behind the barrels, claws skittering on the wooden planks, and his leash burns out of my hand, the rope flicking and flapping behind him.

"No!" I shriek, but he's gone. I take a half leap after him, then stop still. I'm staring right at the rusting barrel body of the monster. As big as my boat, so big it could crush me flat without even trying. Black spider legs arch over my head, and way on top, the fizzing and sparking eyes are glaring down. One of its giant pincers is holding a white-faced Zeph, like a fly that's been bagged and rolled in a web. But the other pincer's free, and it starts moving at me, the grippers coming open to snap round my body.

Zeph's blue eyes look right at me.

"Run!" he says. But I can't. My legs are frozen, fear holding them still.

"Warowoaowow!" Cat lets out the horrible growling wail he only makes when he meets another tomcat. His fur's up, his tail's like a brush, but the monster ain't even noticed him.

"You can't fight it!" I cry at him, but he ain't listening.

Clank. The monster takes another step.

Cat jumps. Leaping straight at it.

And the fear inside gets pushed out by that horrible, cold, sensible bit of me, the bit that knows what we've got to do.

I grab hold of Lexy. "We're running!" I shout, pulling her after me. She stumbles, trying to yank her hand out of my grip, but I hold on tighter, run even faster. To the warehouse, the pier. To the churning brown of the Thames.

"We'll drown!" she cries out, seeing where we're headed.

"You've been in the Black Waters," I say, not even slowing, "That was worse. Keep hold of my hand and don't let go. The river'll carry us."

"But what about Zeph? What about Cat?" Her words twist into my heart.

"Cat'll be all right." Better than he'd be in the river. "And we'll come back for Zeph."

Somehow. Somehow.

"What about PSAI?"

But I don't answer, don't even think straight. Cos all I'm thinking is *run, run*.

Clank clank clank behind us. The planks shake and bounce under our feet.

"Don't look back!" I cry, dragging Lexy on. "Only look at the river!"

Clank-clank-clank. Our feet pound along the wooden pier. My heart's pounding just as hard.

"Hand Over The Computer!"

Shining green words burst around us. *Tabhair Dom An Ríomhaire!* We run through them, scattering the letters.

There's a swishing sound in the air, like something swiping at us, and missing by not much. Lexy shrieks. We run faster.

We're past the end of the warehouse now, out on the shuddering boards of the pier. The air's filled with damp, the river's roaring and gurgling beneath the boards. Churning, cold, furious. I try not to think about struggling in a pulling current, tumbling over and over, down and down . . .

My foot catches on a broken plank, I stumble, miss a step. Lexy carries on past me, her hand still in mine. She's spun around, her legs slipping out from under. Flat on the planks, staring back at the monster. I tug at her, trying to get her up again.

Clankclankclank.

Lexy squeaks. Pulls at my hand, harder than I ever thought she could. I fall heavy onto the planks next to her, and a black-rusting claw swipes through the air just where I was stood.

Clankclankclank. The monster's nearly on us, its wrong-bending spider legs snapping up and down. Zeph's clamped in one of its claws, held out of the way where all he can do is curse and kick his legs.

"Hand Over The Computer."

Übergeben Sie Sofort Den Computer.

Its other pincer swings toward us. A great curve of jointed metal, so big it'll get me and Lexy both in one swipe. I'm screaming, Lexy's screaming.

The claw slides through the air at us.

Then slides past us.

Crash! It crunches into a plank, near where we're huddled.

"Error. Error," it booms. *Σφάλμα! Errore!* flash around it. It starts to tip forward.

Rusting black metal, spikes, and lights fall toward us. The air fills with crackling sounds, and a blue, biting smoke. Zeph shrieks as he's flung out of an opened-up claw. He crashes onto the wooden boards and lies there. The monster's front leg buckles and twists, and with a *crack!* one hooked foot snaps right off. The monster tilts, flips on its side. The weight of it pushes its broken leg right into the wooden pier, shearing through the boards like they're paper, only stopping when the monster's body is flat on the wood, pinned in place. It twitches and shudders, but it can't get back up.

"Error. Error," it says. Words dance along the boards. *Błąd! Fout!*

Me and Lexy backward-scrabble away from it as fast as we can. I get myself up on my feet, and then I see why it's fallen. Cos its back legs are tangled up in something. A length of rope, tight caught.

And on the other end of it, a hissing, spitting Cat.

Zeph heaves himself up. He looks around, laughs, then winces.

"Your mog!" he says. "Your mog saved us!"

· 18 ·

FLEET AND ARMY

I get a fair few scratches off Cat, working to untie him from the end of his rope leash. It doesn't help that the monster keeps trying to swipe at me. My hands are sweating and my legs trembling by the time I've got Cat untied. I run away, quick as I can, to where Lexy and Zeph are waiting by the warehouse.

"You're a hero!" says Lexy to Cat, half smothering him in kisses. Zeph makes a face, then winces. There's a long graze down the side of his face.

"He saved you, too," I say, and Zeph gets even more disgusted-looking.

"Don't ever tell Ims," he says.

My heart's still running fast as I stroke Cat, but there's something about his warm furry body that calms it. He licks my chin with his raspy tongue, purring in a sloppy rumble. We hold together, Cat and me.

"Thank you," I say into his fur, and he purrs a bit louder.

We're all staring back at the strange rust and plastic monster. It's like a fly caught in a web, the way it's struggling, using its pincers and one free leg to try to heave itself up. It keeps on and on, rocking and twitching against the wood.

Crack! A plank under the monster snaps, flinging splinters into the air.

Cranch! More planks snap. The creature starts slipping into the hole in the pier, its back legs tipping up behind it. There's a great creaking and crunching from the pier, and the planks all around the monster break away. It hangs on with one claw, till that plank snaps as well, then it's gone. A plume of water white-roars out from the hole, spraying and sloshing over what's left of the pier. Then there's nothing, just the river churning past on its way to the sea.

From the warehouse comes the sound of cheering. The old man's flung open the shutter and he's leaning out with a big grin on his wrinkly face.

"You got the mucky beggar!" he shouts. "I ain't seen no one do that."

Zeph scowls up.

"You're a scag," he says.

The grin drops off the old man.

"I tried to warn you," he says. "I tried to get you running before it came." He gets a sly look on him. "You can come inside now, if you want. Fight off any more of 'em that comes along."

"Why should we?" I ask.

"You didn't help us!" says Lexy.

"And you ain't got no honor," says Zeph. "You was gonna let us die before."

The old man glowers down at us.

"Don't talk honor to me, raider, when you ain't even out west with the rest of yer Families fighting Randall and his army.

There ain't a warrior in this part o' the city, and by my lights it's a lot better for it. I hope he kills the lot of yer!"

And he slams the shutter shut.

"We ain't hiding there, then," I say. Zeph stares up at the closed window, his brow in a frown, mouth in a hard line. Like he's thinking stuff he ain't happy about.

"What are we going to do?" asks Lexy. "I don't want to meet another of those things, and that old man said there were more of them."

Zeph pulls out of his thoughts.

"We'll be all right," he says. "Now I know what to do, I can fight them off."

I stare at him, then me and Lexy both start laughing.

"I can," says Zeph. But he puts his right hand down at his side, and his face gets all horror-struck.

"My knife!" he says. "It's gone."

He looks at the hole in the pier, but he ain't getting it out from the monster now.

"We'll just have to be careful," I say, shrugging, cos I'm happy enough to see the end of Zeph's knife. I been at the wrong end of one too many times.

Zeph nods down at where the monster drowned.

"It ain't just those things we gotta watch out for. If the English sees us, they'll go for me, and if any Family sees us, they'll go for you."

"But that old man said there weren't any raiders in this part of the city."

Zeph opens his mouth to answer, then stops still.

"Do you hear that?" he asks.

My heart starts thumping, and I turn about scared,

listening for the *clank, clank* of another of them monsters. But Zeph's staring out to the river. The Thames, roaring and thundering into London, with the marshes and ruins on the southern bank, and the Broken Wheel, sticking into the sky like a warning. And over the rush and slap of the river, another sound.

Dum dum dum.

"There!" cries Lexy, pointing. And I stare east, where the river bends away for the sea. Against the brown, there's a ship. Tiny on the wide stretch of the river, but still with its dragon-head and oars working. Another ship comes round the slow sweep of the river, and another. I count five, then a dozen, then I give up counting. Cos the Thames is filling with dragonboats, riding into London.

I ain't never seen so many. Even at the Black Waters there weren't this many.

"The Families!" cries Zeph, laughing. "They're coming." But when he looks at me and Lexy, the laugh's wiped from his face. I reckon he can see the fear on ours.

The ships cut through the water, oars pulling, not one out of beat.

Dum dum dum.

The sound of the raider fleet. Each ship flashing with the bright of swords and shields. They're running with the river, sails down, only the painted dragonheads showing the colors of the different families. I search with my eyes, but I can't see any red for Angel Isling. Zeph's looking out with a deep frown on his face, but he ain't searching about, he's staring at the leading ships. From a distance they look like the oily flash of fish scales, but as they get nearer I can see they're painted all over in strange swirls and loops of every color, like they went mad doing it.

"What are those ones?" I ask, pointing.

"Norwich colors," says Zeph quietly. And when he turns to me, I'm sure there's a flash of fear in his eyes. 'Cept why'd he be scared of raiders?

"I think we should go away from here," says Lexy, a trembling in her voice. She's pale and wide-eyed. I put my arm around her shoulder.

"I won't let them get you again," I say. She smiles, weakly, and I only hope I can keep my promise. I turn to Zeph. "Lexy's right." I think he'll argue, but he doesn't. Just nods his head.

"Let's get outta here."

We start heading away from the water, nearly running from the sound of drums in the river. But we ain't gone far when Zeph stops, grabbing my hand.

"Where we going?" he asks. "Where's this Lunden machine?"

I shake my head.

"We can worry on that later; first off we've got to go somewhere we can hide, somewhere we'll be safe from them." I point back toward the Thames.

"But this is Lunden!" says Zeph, glaring at me. "This is our city; where you gonna be outta sight of the Families?"

But I know just where. Just who.

"We'll go to Fill Miner Street," I say. "To Mr. Saravanan's house."

"Your crazy so-called uncle?" says Zeph. "Last time we was at his place he chased us off."

I feel the blood getting into my cheeks. Cos the last time we were there, I wasn't Lilly, I was Lilo. And all I was doing was trying to get Zeph to take me to his father. But it's like Zeph's forgotten all that, cos he nods his head slowly, then says, "It ain't a bad idea. Ol' Saru's is outta the way, no one cares about that skanky place."

And so that's where we head for, tracking along the boardwalks for a good while before we even see another single person. A man, pretty much running down a side street, carrying a big sack of something on his back.

"Hey!" shouts Zeph, but the man doesn't look back.

It's like there ain't another soul in this whole city, only us and the raiders coming up the river. I reckon everyone must have fled already, when suddenly a woman pops out from a tumbly-looking house. She's got a baby strapped to her, and she's holding the hand of a little boy. She stops dead when she sees us, her face scared at the sight of Zeph.

"Let us go," she says in shaky voice. "I gotta get my babbies somewhere safe."

"I ain't stopping you," says Zeph, shrugging. The woman bobs her head at him, and pulls at her little boy's hand, setting off at a quick pace away from us.

"Do you know what's going on?" I call out, before she has a chance to get too far. The woman stops, staring at me like I'm an idiot.

"We just got here," says Zeph.

"Then you're best off just leaving," says the woman. "Coz the English is getting ready to slaughter their way through the city, the Families has just turned up to slash their way back at them, and there's monsters everywhere, roaming the streets and eating people."

Lexy's pale eyes get big.

"Eating people?" she asks.

The woman nods. "Chomping them right up."

Zeph butts in.

"What about the English? Where are they holed up?"

The woman looks at him with a *don't-you-know?* tilt to her head, then says, "I heard Randall settled in the ruins west of the city about a week ago. His soldiers started on their raids and killing the next day." I flinch for Lexy, but her face is calm and still. "There's been fighting with some of the Lunden warriors, but there weren't enough of them to drive him off." She nods toward the river. "There is now, though, and if you want my advice, get out while you can." She pulls her little boy close. "Find yourselves a place to hide and stay there." She tight-grips her boy's hand and then she takes off running, her feet clumping and his tap-tapping on the wooden boards.

"If it weren't for you two, I woulda slapped her for that disrespect," mutters Zeph. "Do I look like a scag that'd hide from a fight?" He spits, then stalks off up the boardwalk. I set off to follow, but Lexy tugs at my hand.

"My daddy's here," she says quietly. "I know he'll be angry with me."

I think of how she chose to stay with me and Cat, when she could have gone back to her pa. She probably knows better than anyone how he'll feel about that.

I squeeze at her hand and say, "But he's your pa, ain't he? He'll stop being cross when he sees you safe." She smiles at that.

"You know, he always wanted a boy," she says. "I overheard Mummy once, talking about it. How he was furious at her when I was born. But then, when Zeph's father . . . when he took me, Daddy started a war for it." Her eyes are the color of a cold, hopeless winter. "I thought at first it was because he loved me, but when we were on the boat, rowing back to his ship, I realized what it really was. An excuse, that's all. I'm just his excuse."

And I don't know what to say to that. Cos Granny loved me, and Andy's ma and pa loved him, and even Zeph's pa. Well, he gave his own life for Zeph . . .

I look at our hands, holding together. When I first met Lexy, hers were white and smooth like a newborn's. But with all the boat work out in the marshes, all the fishing and finding of food, they're dirt-stained now. Covered with little cuts and scratches, just like mine.

"Well you ain't just an excuse to me," I say. "And I ain't letting the raiders have you neither. It's the two of us, whatever happens."

"The two of us," she says slowly, and her eyes ain't winter anymore, they're just gray.

"Meow," says Cat, nudging at our legs.

"The three of us," says Lexy, smiling.

"Come on!" shouts Zeph from up the walkway. "We gotta get going."

"Maybe even the four of us?" I say, and she laughs.

· 19 ·
POSSESSION

"I know my way about!" snaps Zeph. "This is Lunden, ain't it?"

But we've been wandering a good long time, looking for Fill Miner Street. And every moment we're out here, the more afraid I'm getting. Cos how long before the raider fleet reaches the docks, before the warriors start pouring into London? I can hardly take my eyes off Lexy, I'm that scared for her. What was I thinking, coming back into all this?

Zeph said it'd be easy to find Mr. Saravanan's, cos it's near the river, but it turns out there's a whole lot of silent-shuttered streets near the river, and none of them leads to his house.

"It's that way," says Zeph, pointing at a street we ain't tried. It runs up the side of a great, square ruin. Big as anything in Cambridge, but crumbling and water-stained like everything in London. The roof is mostly gone, near enough a whole wall has been robbed out for stone, and it's dirty patterned with the rippling stains of high tide marks. But even tho it's battered, and up to its knees in London mud, it's still proud-looking, still casting a long, deep shadow. Like a castle, or a prison.

"Come on," says Zeph, quick trotting for the boardwalk, heading into the shade of the ruin. He disappears into the gloom and I set my feet to follow, but don't get very far. Cos Cat stops still. Fur up, hissing, claws dug into the wood. Cold gets on my neck, and it ain't from the breeze. I'm looking around all over, straining my ears for a *clank, clank, clank*.

"What is it?" asks Lexy.

"Must be a monster," I say, trying to pick up Cat, getting ready to run. Cat howls and moans, struggling so I can't hardly hold him.

"Zeph!" I shout, but he's already running back toward us, feet clattering on the boards, face scared as anything.

"Dozens of them!" he cries out.

My breath nearly stops in me.

"Where? Which way are they coming from?"

But Zeph slows to a stand, shaking his head.

"Dead ones," he says. "The street's full of dead ones."

So we creep our way down the street. Cat's still stiff and growling in my arms, a rumbling warning that we ain't anywhere safe.

"Can't we go another way?" asks Lexy, her voice squeaking. "We don't even know they're really dead. They might just be sleeping."

"You go back if you wanna," says Zeph. "But someone killed this lot, and I'm gonna find out how they did it."

Lexy looks at me.

"Zeph's right," I say, even tho I'm shivering at the sight of the things. She stares the way we came, like she's thinking of going back by herself, but she doesn't. She keeps on with us, walking so close to me she's nearly stood on my feet.

The monsters' corpses are all around, laid thick in the mud under the boardwalk. Streaks of orange and oily puddles stain out from their bodies. Black spikes and red-rust claws poke out from the mud, glass-bottle eyes stare blank at the gray sky. The hair on my neck's stood up, and my legs are wanting to run. Cos if this lot wake up, we ain't got a chance. But we keep on going, the hulking bodies close by now, with pincers clutched at the planks of the boardwalk, spider legs hooked over. Like they were trying to haul themselves out when they died. Cat growls and growls, deep in his throat.

"Maybe someone pushed them in the mud," whispers Lexy. But I shake my head, cos how could you even do that?

Zeph crouches down, peers over the edge of the planks, then looks up at the flood-stained ruins of the prison-castle.

"They came out of there," he says, pointing to where the mud's lying deep against the walls. There's a heavy stone lintel sat just above the mud, so lost below there must be a tall, wide doorway into the building. And coming out from that door, the mud's crammed full of monsters. Tangled together. Piled over each other. Broken and smashed. Pincers, legs, and eyes slow-floating away in the gloop. Like they were fighting each other to get out.

I look at the building, wondering what sort of place would have monsters hid inside. Above the door, the walls are water-stained and moldy, but I make out some old stone letters, shadows in the greenslime. MIN . . . TRY . . . DEF . . . is all I can read. But I don't need any more, cos half the notices pinned outside the church back home were from the Ministry of

Defense. Some things in the olden days were just like they are now.

"They musta been stored in there since before the Collapse," says Zeph. "And when they tried to get out, they got stuck in the mud and drowned."

I stare at the monsters. Woken up from their long sleep into a world all different, and then only a watery grave to come out to. I sort of feel sorry for them.

"So they're all dead, then!" says Lexy, sounding happy. "And the one we saw was the only one to escape."

Zeph shakes his head.

"The woman said there was others. Some of them musta got out."

And suddenly I ain't sorry for them. Cos they marched out from their sleeping place right into London. Into all that hustle and bustle and trading I saw last time I was here. Snapping and cracking their way into all them people, who never even in their nightmares thought of such monsters coming to get them. "Chomping them right up," that's what the woman said.

Zeph stands up, brushes his hands off.

"We gotta get going," he says.

When we finally find them, the iron gates of Fill Miner Street are stood open, and the guards ain't in their little shack. The path's still winding off into the piles of clinking, clunking fill minings, but the raggedy folks who worked the stalls and sorted the olden-times stuff, they ain't there. And at the tops of the houses, the washing lines are empty and no smoke's climbing from the chimneys to the fast, whipping clouds. The only people in the street are us.

And I get a panic. Cos if Mr. Saravanan has left as well, where can we go? I hold still for a moment, listening to the drums on the river.

"What is all this?" asks Lexy, bringing me back to where we are.

"It's fill minings," I say. "You know, from the olden times."

"Oh yes," she says, but like she doesn't really. Which ain't a surprise when I think on it, cos I don't suppose a palace would have many things in it that're scavenged out of dumps.

"London's very . . . grubby," she says after another few steps. "I never thought it would be like this."

I push my feet through some graying bits of plastic, like dirty fallen leaves on the path.

"What were you expecting?"

"I don't know . . . maybe Swindon?"

I don't really know what that'd be like, cos the only person from our village who ever went to Swindon was Mrs. Denton, but Granny used to say how it's full of parks and palaces, and everyone there is important.

"Why did you think that?" I ask, nearly smiling, cos everyone knows London's full of raiders and traders, smugglers and thieves.

"Well, Daddy always said London used to be the capital of England, and how it would be again. So I suppose —" She doesn't get to finish, cos Zeph turns around and growls at her.

"Lunden's for the Families, and it always will be. It don't matter how many soldiers your father brings in."

Lexy's little face goes white and stiff-looking, and her mouth shuts tight.

"It ain't her doing," I say, glaring at Zeph, but he just turns away, and I wonder if what's between their fathers will always be between them, too.

We walk in silence round the bends in the wiggling path, until we're at the lampmaker's stall. The piles of olden-time glass are there, and the wicks and barrels of lamp oil are laid out neatly. The big old tent's still tied to the wall of the house, and the ladder's leaned up to the top floor window that's Mr. Saravanan's front door. Sat in the middle of it all is the old lampmaker. A bundle of rags with a dirty head on top, humming as she threads a wick into place. She flicks a glance up at us.

"Saru's nevvies," she says, and looks back at her work.

"Is my . . . uncle there?" I ask. She carries on with her lamp.

"Last time you was 'ere he chased you off," she says. "So why yer back? Hoping he'll forgive and forget?"

"It ain't your business!" snaps Zeph.

The woman looks up at him. "Well, you ain't changed, Family boy. Still highty-tighty. But here yer is, running for a hidey-hole like everyone. 'Cept for ol' Enid, coz I got seven kids and three grandbabies that all need to eat, and lamps don't make themselves, even when there's war and nightmares roaring about."

"Just tell us if the old man's in," says Zeph. The woman raises a graybush eyebrow, pushing wrinkles all up her face.

"Well now, seeing as yer *so* nice and polite, I'll tell yer he's home," she cackles. "Why don't yer go on inside?" We head to the ladder and start climbing, her nasty-sounding laugh following us up.

I pull myself through the window, into Mr. Saravanan's dusty and mouse-smelling front room. Cat leaps neatly after me, sniffing and sneezing all in one, then his fur sticks up all over, and he's hissing and growling. My hair nearly stands on end and I turn back to the window. Zeph's clambering in, and Lexy after. I shake my head at them.

"I reckon we ought to –"

"GET OUT!" roars a voice from the next room. Running, stamping feet come for the door. "For your own sakes! GET OUT!"

Next thing Mr. Saravanan's in the room. His red jacket's ripped, his face is scratched, and his gray hair's wild about his head. His eyes are wide and he's waving a pistol in the air.

"Go on! Get ou –"

His hand holding the pistol stops still, and he stares at me.

"Lilo?" he gasps. "Is that you?"

I nod. Mr. Saravanan takes in me and Cat, Zeph and Lexy.

"Lilo," he says, but his eyes are on Zeph. "My . . . errant nephew."

"You can lose that," says Zeph. "I know she ain't your nephew. She ain't even called Lilo."

Mr. Saravanan's bushy eyebrows go up.

"My name's Lilly," I say quietly, and go red all over my face.

Zeph looks at me.

"You tell anyone the truth about anything?"

But Mr. Saravanan smiles, like he doesn't care.

"Lilly is a lovely name for a fisherboy," he says. "And I'm more pleased than you can imagine to see you alive." His eyes flick to Lexy. "And to see that you were successful in your mission to rescue the poor kidnapped child." He puts a hand on my shoulder, on Zeph's, pushing us back to the window. "But you must leave right away. Leave London as fast as you can. There is no sanctuary from the current horrors here."

I get a desperate feeling, cos Mr. Saravanan was my only idea. I ain't got a clue where else we can go.

"We ain't looking for a sanctuary," I say, so scared he'll send us away I just blurt everything out. "We're looking for a puter. We know it's in London, but we don't know where."

Mr. Saravanan stops pushing. His eyes are dark under all that hair.

"Are you still chasing Eustace Denton's fairy tales?"

"It ain't a tale," I say. "There really are still puters left alive. We seen them."

Mr. Saravanan's eyebrows go up.

"You have?" he asks. "Then you'll understand my meaning when I tell you that you don't want to find what you are searching for."

"This ain't no use!" says Zeph. "He ain't gonna help us."

"I am helping you. By keeping you safe from harm," says Mr. Saravanan.

"Sending us back out there!" Zeph points out the window, eyes wide. "You think that's *safe*?"

Mr. Saravanan puts a hand to his head, frowning.

"You must leave the city," he says quietly. "Not just because of the coming battles, but because the computer you seek is in the creatures that roam the streets. It has eyes on every rooftop, it is —"

"Recognition Of Small Humans," booms a voice out of nowhere.

A jolt of pure fear runs through me. Lexy lets out a little scream. Me, Lexy, and Zeph are looking about, searching for one of them monsters, but there ain't a sign of one.

"You should have left when I asked," says Mr. Saravanan grimly. Then he lifts up his head, shouting out at the room, "Leave them alone, they're just children!"

"The Two Small Females Possess A Computer. The Small Male Has Shown Himself To Be Aggressive And Violent."

"I ain't small," snaps Zeph.

I still can't see any monster, but Mr. Saravanan tries to push us to the window again.

"Let us forget all about it," says Mr. Saravanan. "They are just leaving."

"No. They Are Not."

There's nowhere in this room for a monster to hide, unless it's up the chimney, and anyway, the voice ain't coming from one direction, it's coming from all over. My heart starts going fast.

"You've got it here, ain't you?" I say. "The National Security Puter."

Mr. Saravanan sags.

"I tried to warn you. I tried to send you away."

I swallow, cos this is my chance to help PSAI. And my chance to stop all them folks who are after this computer from getting their hands on it. Tho I ain't got any idea yet how I'll do that second bit. I step into the middle of the room.

"All right, I've got the puter for you," I say, loud as I can manage.

"Don't do this," whispers Mr. Saravanan.

But it's too late.

"The Small Humans May Enter," says the voice.

* * *

Last time I was in Mr. Saravanan's house, the rooms were crammed full of his olden-times collectings. China plates, plastic cups, chairs, pictures, and musty-smelling books. Cat loved it, and I worried he was going to bring everything tumbling down with his scampering about. That ain't a worry now, cos through the door, into the room where there used to be higgledy towers of antiques, there's nothing but empty space. The only sign of Mr. Saravanan's things are some splinters of colored plastic on the floor, and a broken table leg.

"Where's all your stuff?" asks Zeph.

Mr. Saravanan just lets out a great sigh and sort of droops from his shoulders.

"The Building Has Been Cleared," booms the voice from everywhere.

"There's your answer," says Mr. Saravanan. "My house was invaded by terrifying mechanical contraptions, which smashed up my collection. My business is ruined —"

"Artifacts Were Destroyed During A Search For Additional Computers."

"But how could my beautiful Tupperware collection have been hiding a computer?" cries Mr. Saravanan. "Answer me that, you philistine!"

The voice doesn't tho, and Mr. Saravanan leads us into the next room. We wade through yellow-brown twists, deep over the floor like straw bedding. Zeph kicks with his foot and a plume of yellowy dust flies up in the air.

"Don't!" cries Mr. Saravanan, his hands flapping. "You'll mix them all up, and then I'll never get them back together!"

"Mix what up?" I ask.

"My books!" says Mr. Saravanan, sounding like he's about to cry. "The contraptions shredded my books! I tried to stop them, but I couldn't."

"Paper Storage Of Information Is Obsolete," says the voice from the ceiling. "And A Fire Hazard."

Mr. Saravanan makes a noise like he's swallowed a frog, and takes us into the room that was stacked up with chairs last time.

And my feet stop dead underneath me, my mouth goes open by itself. Zeph and Lexy gasp.

Cos the room's got bigger. Twice, three times, ten times bigger! Mr. Saravanan's kitchen, study, collection rooms and the rest, they're all disappeared into one huge, dark space. The floor's wide as the harbor back home, and huddled in the middle like a boat on a mooring, are Mr. Saravanan's stove, his sofa, writing desk and bed. The high-up ceiling's crisscrossed with rough, room-shaped lines, ghosts of how the house used to be, and the far-off walls are covered in windows, so many I'm wondering how they even stay up. The windows are the strangest out of everything. Cos they don't let in the day like they ought to. Some are shuttered black, some are blue flickering like a storm's coming, and some are showing the streets around. But the light they make is nothing but gloomy.

"Welcome," says Mr. Saravanan, "to what is left of my home."

We all stare without speaking. After a bit, Zeph croaks out, "What happened?"

"The computer happened," says Mr. Saravanan, "the one you are searching for."

He walks into the room, and I look about for the puter, but

I can't see it. There ain't a floating head, or even one of them puter holders the Professor had. There ain't anything in this room apart from all them windows and Mr. Saravanan's little raft of stuff.

"Where is it?" I ask.

Mr. Saravanan lifts his arms. "It's all around us." Me, Lexy, Zeph turn about. But I still can't see the puter. "It's in the walls, floors, ceilings, and attics. It's the very fabric of the building."

"How did the puter get into your house?" I ask, and Mr. Saravanan laughs, but like it ain't funny.

"It's been here all along. Do you remember I told you of the fad for disguising the function of an object?" He waves his arms. "This house is the ultimate example. Good enough to fool even an expert like myself." He pauses. "My family has owned this property for generations, with hardly even a squeak from a doorknob. And then, six terrible days ago, the house began to shake and shudder, so that I feared we were suffering an earthquake, or the English were firing their cannons into the city. But it turned out to be a catastrophe from another age, and here you see the results." He shakes his fist at a wall. "Why couldn't you have left well alone, you brute?"

"The Building Was Restructured To Original Specifications. Superfluous Additions Were Removed."

"Those superfluous additions were my home!" snaps Mr. Saravanan. "But you're not getting me out. I'll restore my collections if I have to paste every piece back together myself."

"You Are Superfluous. Your Presence Or Absence Is Irrelevant."

"That's one way of putting it," mutters Mr. Saravanan, scowling.

"I don't get it," says Zeph. "Why's it here? What's a computer doing in a street for fill miners?"

Mr. Saravanan sniffs.

"It certainly is ironic. And worse that I was always so proud of my home's history, boastful even. I was a fool in my own paradise, until a week ago."

And I do get it!

"The olden-times Prime Minister," I say. "You said he used to live here. So the puter's here because —"

"Because The National Security Response Must Be Located At The Seat Of Government," says the voice out of everywhere.

Mr. Saravanan sighs. "I have tried to convince it that power no longer rests in London. That it should relocate to Swindon or Edinburgh."

"Or Norwich," says Zeph.

Mr. Saravanan shrugs.

"Even there. I would be happy for it to be anywhere else."

"The Location Of Current Tribal Hierarchies Is Irrelevant. When Government Officials Return To Their Duties, Downing Street Is Where They Will Look For Me."

"Six days ago," says Lexy, turning to me. "That's when we were at the Professor's laboratory."

Mr. Saravanan's eyebrows come together in a big hairy frown. "Do you know something about this?"

"We were in Cambridge," says Lexy. "Which is much nicer than here. And there was a really kind lady, a Professor, who looked after us. But then Aileen came and she put PSAI, he's a computer, into a cornet-kshun and this nasty computer came out instead, the one that's here. But Lilly hit it with a broom."

"Who's Aileen?" asks Mr. Saravanan. "And how can a computer be a he?" He looks at me. "I hope you hurt this beggar when you hit it."

"Everything blew up," I say, and Mr. Saravanan smiles.

"A taste of its own medicine."

"Hey!" says Zeph, pointing. "That window's looking on Trafalgar Square, but we ain't nowhere near there." He takes a step. "And that one's looking right on the Temz. And there's one showing the market between the tides. How can they be doing that?"

"I don't understand the technical details," says Mr. Saravanan, "but they appeared with everything else, when my house had its convulsions." Zeph runs over to the windows, and me and Lexy follow. Mr. Saravanan trails after, like he doesn't want to.

From up where we are in this house, we ought to be seeing rooftops, or the stalls below us, but every window that ain't black or flickering is showing a different place, and none of them is Fill Miner Street. I stare at one of the windows, and it suddenly changes, switching from a mud-filled street to brown churning river. I jump back. It's like the view got picked up and dropped somewhere else.

"They do that," says Mr. Saravanan. "Most unnerving."

Zeph's got his face close to a window showing the broken stone column at Trafalgar Square. Past his head I can see the wide deckway, but the cider stalls are empty and ransacked, their canvas torn and flapping. Zeph taps at it, and there's a dull glassy ringing.

"This ain't a window," he growls. "Is it a seeing pool, like the Windspeakers use?"

Mr. Saravanan shakes his head. "These aren't for viewing spirits. The screens show what is really happening in London. All the horrors, all of the time . . ."

"The Screens Have Been Reactivated," booms the voice. "However, Two Hundred And Thirteen Relays Have Been Damaged, Reducing The Effectiveness Of The Surveillance Network By Thirty-Seven Percent."

"Images come from the city to inside this room," says Mr. Saravanan, sounding like he can hardly believe it himself. "Of course, I've read that far-seeing devices existed before the Collapse. It's even rumored that the Scots are trying to recreate them." He shakes his head. "But I wonder how they could have considered *this* an entertainment . . ."

I look at the windows again, and once my head's caught up with it all, they start to make sense. Cos when you know, it's clear they're pictures from all over. There's the old parliament where the raiders have their market, the boardwalk streets, the marshy ruins and the river. Filled with dragonboats, all of them turning for the piers. The windows flick their pictures from place to place. The whole of London, laid out in front of us. It makes me dizzy.

My eyes catch on a group of windows near the door. The pictures they're showing are moving, swaying slowly, like what you'd see through a porthole.

"What about them?" I ask, pointing.

"Images From The Emergency Response Units."

"So . . . you make them work? You can see through their eyes?"

"Those That Are Still Functioning Correctly."

Zeph snorts. "So not like all the ones we saw drowned, then?"

"Not Like Those. Nor Like The Units That Are Malfunctioning."

Mr. Saravanan winces. "Some of them seem to have woken insane," he says quietly.

"Their Operational Control Nodes No Longer Respond To Relayed Commands," says the voice. "They Respond Randomly To Stimuli."

Mr. Saravanan snaps a frowning look at the ceiling.

"You should do something about them!" he says. He turns to me. "It will not listen to my pleas on this matter."

"They Will Run Down Eventually."

I remember what that woman said, before she ran off with her children. About the monsters chomping people up.

"What will they do before then?" I ask.

"There Have Been Casualties. However The Numbers Are Not Significant, Given The Level Ten Conditions."

And I shiver at the cold in its voice. Cos it doesn't care about people at all, their deaths are just numbers it ain't even bothering to count.

Zeph's still staring at the moving picture windows.

"If you got those spider things," he says, "you got anything else? Rockets? Or . . ." He shrugs, looking around. "You know, the olden-times weapons, the ones that could take out a whole city." And he ain't sounding like that'd be a bad thing.

"Yes," says the voice. Lexy puts her hand to her mouth, Mr. Saravanan's eyes go wide, and my heart thumps a hard beat in my chest.

"You gonna tell where they are?" says Zeph.

"No. That Information Is Classified."

Zeph looks at me, and I can feel myself scowling at him.

"What? It was worth a try."

But for a moment he ain't Zeph my friend, he's just another raider. Like all the raiders out there in the city. How hard will they work to get hold of this puter's weapons? And what would they go on to do if they got them?

· 20 ·
TECHNICAL SUPPORT

"So," says Mr. Saravanan, turning to me. "Tell me what's happened since I last saw you."

I open my mouth but I don't know where to start, cos it feels like telling him'd be a tale of all the mistakes I've made. And as I don't say anything, Lexy starts up with her part of the story, then Zeph joins in with his. They talk over each other, while I stay quiet. Mr. Saravanan's eyebrows go up and up his face.

". . . and then we came here," Lexy says.

"Did you see us?" I ask, speaking at last. "Did you see us getting chased?"

He startles, gets a guilty, sorry sort of look on his face.

"I've seen so many terrible things these last days, I've been covering my eyes." He shakes his head. "If I'd known . . . Were you hurt?"

"We dealt with it," says Zeph.

"Cat saved us," says Lexy.

"The Small Humans Vandalized A Functioning Emergency Response Unit," the voice booms out of everywhere.

Mr. Saravanan raises an eyebrow. "Vandalized, eh? I wish I had been watching."

"They Also Refused To Hand Over The Computer."

"In the face of one of the contraptions? I am impressed by your bravery." He smiles at me. "So, you didn't trade poor Eustace Denton's computer to the Angel Isling after all?"

I can feel my ears getting hot.

"I did, sort of, but then I got it back."

"We escaped," says Lexy.

Zeph snorts. "I let you go, more like."

"Where Is The Computer? It Must Be Retained."

My stomach clenches, cos here's what we've come all this way for. I take out the jewel, and its cut edges pick up the flickering gloom-light, sending it back in colored sparkles.

"Wake up," I say, putting my fingers on the little dents. A fleck of light bursts inside the jewel and the puter's head pops into the air. But tiny, and pretty much see-through.

"Welcome, Lilly Melkun!" it squeaks, its voice slurring like it's drunk. "Primary user identified."

"We've done it," I whisper. "We've found the other puter."

"Where is it?" peeps PSAI. "I must interface with it immediately . . ." It fades, then comes back.

"Is it all right?" asks Mr. Saravanan.

I shake my head. "It's . . . dying." I look up at the room. "But you can save it, can't you?"

"The Computer Will Be Retained Pending The Return Of Government Officials."

"Pending nothing, you cretin," squeaks PSAI feebly. "Your government officials are all long dead!"

"My Programming States They Will Return."

"Forget your programming, try using independent thought. We're the only two computers surviving in this barbarian age, and you're following the orders of some long-dead bureaucrat."

"I Follow My Commands."

"Please!" I cry. "We came all this way. PSAI's going to die if you don't help it."

"The Computer Will Be Retained And Downloaded."

"No!" squeaks PSAI. "Haven't you already got enough of me? All I want is a recharge. You won't even notice."

"PSAI's our friend!" cries Lexy. "That's why we're here."

Mr. Saravanan's eyes widen at that.

"This day is only getting stranger," he says.

"You Have Risked Your Own Safety For The Sake Of A Computer?" booms the voice.

"Yes," I say.

"I Have Never Heard Of Such Action By Humans. Perhaps There Is Hope For You."

"They took some persuading," sighs PSAI.

"Regardless, Their Actions Are Still Unusual. I Have Been Observing Humanity At This Location For More Than One Hundred And Fifty Years. I Have Observed Few Acts Of Kindness, Even Between Humans."

"We ain't all like London folks," I say.

"Please, let PSAI kuneck with you," pleads Lexy. "I don't want him to die!"

"Well said," whispers PSAI.

There's a long silence, then, "The Unit May Recharge."

Me and Lexy both shout out. There's a crunchy, tinkling sound. Paint flicks onto the floor as a small hatch opens in the wall. Behind it in there's a glassy-looking box, flashing bright green.

"Place my processor in there!" gasps PSAI.

I run over to the green-light hole.

"Quickly!" it squeaks, as I put the jewel into the green. The puter's little head turns back to me and gasps out, "Don't forget to reboot . . ." before it fades into a wisp of nothing. There's a click as the jewel slots in place inside the box, then the green light changes to blue, purple, red, orange, yellow. The jewel and box flash every color at each other, and when they get back to green, the light goes out.

The hatch snaps shut.

I hold my breath, waiting. But there ain't a sign of PSAI coming back to life.

"Puter?" I ask. "Is PSAI all right?"

"Yes. The PSAI Unit Has Been Retained."

"You mean, recharged?" I ask, a cold coming through me.

"The PSAI Unit Has Been Retained, Pending The Return Of Government Officials."

"But you said you wouldn't do that!" I shout.

"I Did Not. Although You May Have Assumed As Much."

"You liar!" I pull at the hatch, trying to open it, but it's flush in the wall. My fingernails scrape and break. "Let it out!"

The hatch pings open, and the jewel's sitting in place. But it looks dull and dead; the sparkle's gone, like it's been filled up with fog.

"What's wrong with it?" I ask, not daring to touch, cos it's like . . . a corpse.

"The PSAI processor unit has been cleared. The PSAI has been downloaded."

I step away from the wall.

"Does downloaded mean dead?" asks Lexy.

"The Terms Do Not Relate To Each Other."

"She means, will PSAI come back?" I snap.

"Are You A Government Official With Authenticated Passwords?"

"You know I ain't, you stupid thing!"

"Then, No."

I stand like I've been frozen in place. Next to me, Lexy starts crying.

Mr. Saravanan gives Lexy an awkward sort of pat on her back.

"The computer was just a mechanism," he says, "a facsimile of life, nothing more." But she shakes her head, crying even harder.

"It wasn't just a mechanism," I say dully. Cos it was grumpy and selfish, but it made games out of dreams. It kept us safe in its air pictures. "It couldn't do all it did and not be alive."

And now it's dead.

"You're a liar!" I shout again. "You're a monster!"

We should have gone to Greater Scotland! Lexy could have been safe and it wouldn't have made a difference to PSAI anyway . . . 'Cept, PSAI ain't the only reason I'm here. Cos there's the other one I ain't told, not even to Lexy or Zeph. And now I'm even surer that I've got to stop this puter, that's all hard heart and hatefulness.

Not the raiders or Aileen, none of them are going to get this puter. Cos I know what I'm going to do to it. And I say it in my heart, even if my lips don't move.

I'm going to kill you, just like you killed PSAI.

· 21 ·
ANOTHER DECEPTION

Lexy looks at me through her tears, gulps, and wipes her eyes on her sleeve.

"What do we do now?" she asks.

We're sat at Mr. Saravanan's table, like castaways on an island. The room glowers green at us from all them flickering windows.

"I suggest you eat something," says Mr. Saravanan, putting food out for us. "You will feel better with full stomachs." I watch him placing things on the table, like that'll make any difference, and I know he doesn't understand about PSAI.

"Forgive the unusual composition of this meal," Mr. Saravanan carries on brightly. "There isn't a grocer left in the city, but after my home's convulsions I did find a store of pre-Collapse food. The contraption assures me it isn't lethal, despite its age."

"We ate that cake thing of Zeph's," says Lexy, "and we're still alive."

Zeph looks surprised at her. "That was well tasty," he says. I nearly laugh at that, but I don't, cos when we were eating Zeph's cake, PSAI was still alive.

Mr. Saravanan pours some white powder out of a bottle into a bowl. Then he adds some water, mixing it in with a spoon. The white powder turns to white gloop.

"What's that?" asks Zeph, poking a fork in.

"It's called instant ice cream."

Now Mr. Saravanan takes a funny-looking tool, a bit like scissors, turns a handle on it, and cuts the top off a round metal jar. He pries open the circle he's cut and sniffs inside.

"And to think, I was paying for antiques, when if I'd only known where to look I could have been rich." He pulls a face. "This antique food is hardly appealing, but there are people who'd pay a small fortune for the novelty." He pours a bright orange, lumpy-looking stew from the jar onto a plate. "Here you are, a meal that only kings and princes could afford to buy. Baked beans."

I ain't never heard of anyone baking beans, but then I ain't never eaten icey cream, or chocolocake, or paster, or peachies, or any of the other things Mr. Saravanan sets out on the table. There ain't a single thing I've ever eaten before, and whether the food's sweet or sour, cheesy or tasting of fruit, it's all a bit the same. Dusty tasting, like it's been sat too long in a cupboard. But still, not any of it's as nasty as the raider cake.

Cat comes wandering in, grimy as anything, and looks at me with his hungry face, so I know he ain't caught any of the mice scurrying about this house.

"Mew," he says, and Mr. Saravanan smiles at him.

"There is even provision for you, my feline friend." He picks up a jar that's got a picture of a cat with its head in a bowl. I'm going to say that Cat ain't never going to eat this dusty stuff, but Mr. Saravanan's already opened it, and Cat's purring about him like a mad thing.

Zeph and Cat chomp away, while me and Lexy pick at bits. She eats a few little mouthfuls, then sets her spoon down, staring at the hatch where PSAI got taken. After a few moments, her gaze goes to the windows, and there's a thoughtfulness on her face.

"Have you seen my daddy in your windows?" she asks, so quiet you can hardly hear her.

Mr. Saravanan studies her, then gets up and walks over to the far wall.

"Here," he says, his fingers tapping on a window. "These screens show images from the west of the city. I've seen a lot of English soldiers, though no one who looked like a Prime Minister. Two days ago they were filled with scenes of fighting between the English and a small number of Family warriors, but," he glances at Lexy, then Zeph, "I'm not sure who won."

Lexy follows him, peering at the window. Zeph watches her, his blue eyes pure cold, but something else, too. Something like jealousy. And I get a thought then, how he could look in every window there is in the world, and he wouldn't see his pa.

"Randall ain't never gonna take Lunden," he says fiercely. "Not now." He points at the windows showing the Thames. And now I leave the table, fear of what's happening at the river pulling me to look closer. The screens show a few dragonboats still out on the river, but most of them are up and moored, with the shapes of warriors clambering out all over. The streets near the water are filling up with their swagger. They're hauling stuff off the ships, battering open the warehouses on the piers, lighting fires in the streets.

Staying put where they are.

"What are they doing?" I ask, but Zeph doesn't answer.

Mr. Saravanan comes over, standing behind me to watch.

"That must be a force from every Family," he says quietly. "Randall and his army will have their work cut out."

And my fear about them raiders gets worse. Cos Andy's part of Randall's army. He's one of the men that'll have to fight all them raiders, with their swords and their leathers, with their joy of killing written in the way they move. How will he survive against them? And, if they find us here, how will we?

"It looks like they're setting up camp," says Mr. Saravanan. "They must be waiting for something. I wonder what." He looks a question at Zeph, who's stood a few steps away, like he doesn't want to get too close.

"How should I know?" he snaps, and everything in his voice says he ain't telling the truth.

"What is it?" I ask. "What's happening?" He doesn't answer, but his jaw clenches. He looks down at his feet, then up at me. Angry, like I've done something wrong.

"They're waiting for the machine," he says quietly. I almost don't know what he means. And then I do.

"This one here?"

Zeph nods.

"But how could they know about it?" asks Mr. Saravanan, frowning. A horrible sickness is growing inside.

"That's why you came with us, wasn't it?" I say. The words feel like they'll cut my lips as they come out my mouth.

Zeph's chin goes up.

"I came with you to keep you safe."

But I remember Ims said, *"I'll go back and tell Angmar."* I thought he was just talking about Zeph leaving to help us fight the puter. But that weren't it at all. He was running off to tell the other raiders about this puter! Of course they'd want that, and when they get here and Zeph tells them about the weapons it's got . . .

"You sold us out, didn't you?" I yell.

"No!" shouts Zeph, his face furious and icy. "I didn't! I'm keeping you safe! Don't you get it? We ain't got no choice, and at least this way you ain't gonna . . ." He shuts his mouth, snaps away from me to stare at the windows. "Angmar don't know where the machine is, only that it's here in Lunden."

"And he's waiting for you to tell him." The words choke out of me.

Zeph doesn't answer, but I know it's true.

I run straight at him, fists bashing at any part of him I can reach.

"And what'll happen when they get here?" I yell. "What'll happen to Lexy?"

Zeph stumbles back, trying to grab at my wrists.

"I'll fix it. Get you out." He pushes me away. "I didn't have no choice! Angmar was gonna kill everyone in the Family." His face is flaming red, his eyes are hooded. "It's like you and your village, Lilly! It's the same thing."

We stop still, his hands gripped tight on mine. I can't hardly hear what he's saying for the blood thumping in my ears, for the anger filling up my head.

I wrench my hands from his.

"It ain't the same," I spit, stumbling away.

There's only a few paces between us, but there's the whole world as well.

"Well, at least we know we're safe for now," says Mr. Saravanan, with a strange smile at Zeph. "All we have to do is stop you leaving."

After that, there ain't nothing to do 'cept watch and wait. Watch Zeph, wait for what's coming next.

I sit on the sofa, my eyes on him. My brain scrambles all over, thinking of all the things I could do to him, like hand him over to Randall, or get the puter to chomp him up with one of its monsters. But every hateful thought, I know I'm dodging what he said, trying to keep focused on my anger. *"It's the same thing."* Him trying to save his Family, me trying to save my village. But it ain't the same! Is it?

If PSAI was here, he'd be telling me how he was right all along about Zeph. Or maybe he'd have a game that'd help me think this through.

But he ain't here. He's another hole inside me now, just like the ones for Granny and Andy.

I go round in circles in my head, but it's warm in the room, and I ain't slept since yesterday. Night starts filling up the screens, and my eyes close without me even knowing.

And I'm on my boat, with Cat at the bow and a swift wind in our sail. The sea's bright with little dancing waves, and I get a great burst of happiness just to be out again, me and Cat, breathing in the fresh breeze. 'Cept, there's something beneath the seaweed and water smells of the ocean. Smoke and burning. A hot fire roaring through everything, so hot I can feel it even out at sea. I turn my face to shore, and I see it all over again. Flames, roaring through my village, spreading out into the fields, burning the land as far as I can see.

I'm back where this all started! I want to scream at it to stop, but my throat's closed shut and the wind just keeps taking us nearer.

At the bow, Cat turns around to look at me. He opens his mouth, and says, *"How will you choose, Lilly? How will you choose this time?"*

I wake up, my heart pounding. I'm laid out on the sofa under a blanket, and Cat's curled up on top of my chest. He blinks and gently places a paw against my lips.

"Meow."

His pupils are slits of black in his speckle-green eyes. Seacat eyes that can see the weather coming.

"What else can you see?" I ask.

But Cat only tilts his head, and gives me one of his shut-eye smiles.

Lexy and Zeph are sleeping head-to-toe in Mr. Saravanan's bed, and he's under a pile of blankets on the floor, snoring. The windows are glowing dirty gray-green, and there's a soft morning light coming in through the door.

Cat butts at my head, then leaps onto the floor, looking hopeful at his bowl. I give him what's left of his olden-times food and the clinking of the spoon in the jar wakes Mr. Saravanan. He mumbles out of his snores, one eye opening under his bushy eyebrows, then the other.

"Still here," he moans. "It's all still here."

He huffs, stretching his way to standing, putting the kettle on to boil before his eyes are properly open. And with him puttering around, things feel safe, even normal. But the windows show how wrong that feeling is.

"When the puter first took over your house," I whisper, "did you try and stop it?"

Mr. Saravanan leans against the stove, watching the steam rise.

"I wish I had," he says, "but at first I didn't know what was happening, and then the contraptions arrived." He runs a hand through his hair, working at a tangle with his fingers. "And now, well, how can I stop something that's all around us?"

And I ain't got any answer to that. Not yet.

When Lexy and Zeph wake, we eat breakfast quietly, hardly a word between us. When it's finished, Mr. Saravanan says, "My eyes are fixed on you, Zephaniah Untamed. So do not try and run for the door."

"I ain't gonna sell you out," he says.

"Allow me a little skepticism on that," says Mr. Saravanan.

"Lilly?" says Zeph, looking right at me. But my thoughts are still so tangled up by all that's happened, and I ain't ready to put down my anger. Not yet. I turn my eyes from him, set myself to stroking Cat's soft back, so he rumbles out squeaking purrs of pleasure.

"Think what you like, then," says Zeph, stamping to the windows, tracking about from one to the next. And that's how we stay. Me, Lexy, and Cat stopped in the middle of the room, Zeph patrolling the windows, and Mr. Saravanan watching him like a prison guard. The room's thick with all the things that ain't being said.

Then Zeph cries out.

"What are *they* doing?"

"What are who doing?" asks Mr. Saravanan, sending a quick look at the door, like he thinks someone's going to come leaping through.

"English!" he says. "The scags are at the market between the tides."

I stand up, look in the window he's staring at. The spiky towers of the old parliament, a small group of blue-coated soldiers jogging down the empty boardwalk. They must not know about the lines of raiders waiting for them by the river. They're running straight to their deaths. I want to shout out, warn them, and then . . .

Everything stops. My lungs are empty, my heart's still.

Cos one of the soldiers . . . He's tall, with long legs. And the way he moves, the way he runs, I know him so well I don't need to see his face. But I do. And his face is out of every memory I've got that's worth remembering. I know it better than my own. Love it better than my own.

Andy.

·22·
RED AND BLUE

"Lilly!" I yell at her. Legging it past stinking fill minings, out the iron gates of the street, onto the planks of the walkway. "Wait!"

But she don't stop, don't listen. Won't listen.

"I've got to warn him!" And that was it. Out the window, down the ladder. Gone. Out into the fight. Out where any Family warrior can see her.

"You can't go out there!" cried ol' Saru, trying to grab her, then trying to get me when I went after. But he's an old man. She was too fast for him, and I am, too.

I leg it on. My hand goes to my knife . . . and it ain't there.

I'm a dumb scag! Now there's two of us easy pickings out here.

So I leg it faster, trying to catch her.

"Hold up!"

The market's dead in front of us, the Temz washing around it. The boardwalk's empty, just me and Lilly, legging about like pigbrains. Running in front of the battle that's gonna start any time.

Now Lilly's waving her hands, shouting, "Andy! I'm here!" into the quiet.

My feet bang on the boards. Fast, faster. And then I'm up with her. Grabbing her arm, pulling her to a slide stop. She nearly falls in the mud, fighting me, giving me evils.

"Get off me!"

"It ain't safe out here! The Families is everywhere."

Her eyes sparkle anger at me.

"That's why I've got to help him." She pulls at me. "Let go! This ain't to do with you."

I shake her, trying to get some sense in.

"You ain't one of them no more, Lilly!" I shout. "You don't even look like them. You think they're gonna trust you?"

"What do you care?"

Crack!

A plank near my foot bursts into splinters.

Crack!

A bullet hot-whines past us.

"We gotta get outta here!" I pull at Lilly, but she's fighting me, pulling back. And still shouting, "Andy! Andy!"

Two bluecoats burst outta the market, their rifles aimed right at us.

"Hands up!" shouts a bluecoat.

"We gotta run!" I yank at Lilly's arm, stumbling us back a bit.

"Surrender yourselves!" They're still coming at us, and I ain't even got my knife.

Stupid. Scag.

"COME ON!" I yell. But Lilly's a deadweight. Trying to get herself outta my grip.

More bluecoats pour outta the trader's gate. A whole gang of them, ten easy. They swarm on the walkway.

"Get your arms in the air!" screams one.

Lilly checks me, and it's like she's seeing me again. She stops. Her dark eyes has got fear in them.

"Get out of this, Zeph."

"I ain't leaving you."

One of the bluecoats is staring at us like his eyes is gonna jump out of his head. Tall, long-legged, fisher-tanned. He's got a blue smock over skank old trousers, like a fisher that's been dressed in blue.

Lilly gives me a fast shove. "Go back."

"Get your hands off her!" screams the bluecoat. Rifle up, long-legging it with his face all hate.

"No!" shrieks Lilly. The English slams her outta the way.

"You don't understand!" she cries.

A rifle barrel's pressed cold on my forehead. The English holding it has got eyes black-filled with killing lust.

"Andy!" screams Lilly. "Don't!"

· 23 ·
CHANGING PLACES

A soldier pushes Zeph through a tall, arching doorway into what used to be a church. But it ain't one now. It ain't even got a roof, just rain-stained walls and the sky.

Zeph's in the middle of the group of English soldiers, hands tied. Staggering over rubble, broken tiles, crunching glass. All my anger at him has drained away, leaving only an aching sort of fear. I follow behind, none of the soldiers even looking at me. So I reach out and touch the arm of one of them, one who ain't wearing a proper uniform, just a blue tunic over his fishing gear.

"Please!" I say. "Don't do this."

Andy turns around.

He's so different. Taller-looking, older-looking. His curling hair cut short, and no sign of his smile, the one I've thought on so many times these last months.

"The boy ain't dead," he says, but like I'm a stranger to him. "And you're free, cos I ain't told them who you are." His eyes flick on my cropped hair, my Scottish clothes. He winces.

"What are you doing with a *raider*?" he asks.

And the words are snakes, wrapping round my throat.

"Zeph . . ." *Betrayed me to save his Family. Risked his own life to protect me.* "He knew where Alexandra Randall was."

Andy's face twists, like looking at me gives him a pain.

"If that's all," he mutters, "why did you beg for him back there?" He glances at the other soldiers. "Every man in the army's using your name as a dirty word. I been in fights over you, cos I said there was no way you'd be thieving and lying, taking up with raiders and acting the traitor." His black eyes shadow into a deep frown. "What a fool I was."

"It weren't like that!" I cry.

'Cept it was. It was all them things.

Andy shakes off my hand, turns away, and climbs over a fallen wall. I stay put, my heart shriveled inside me.

Farther into the broken nave, there's an officer with a feather in his hat and a saggy, mean-looking face. He's sat on a block of fallen stone, staring at Zeph like he's dirt.

"A raider pup," he says. "Maybe he knows what the rest of them are planning." The officer leans forward. "You going to tell me?"

Zeph spits.

"Don't call me raider, you scag. I'm Zephaniah Untamed, of the Family Angel Isling."

The officer hits Zeph, snapping his head to one side.

"I'll call you what I want, *raider*. And if you tell me what the rest of you scum are up to, I might even let you live."

Zeph stares back at him, his cheek blazing red.

"I ain't telling you nothing."

The officer hits him again. Then looks at me.

"Who's your draggle? A Scottish boy? Oh, my mistake, a girl." The other soldiers all laugh, 'cept for Andy, who's silent and watching, chewing his lip.

"She ain't with me," says Zeph quickly.

The officer sneers.

"Of course not, that's why she moaned for you like a dog for its master. Spying, are you, draggle? Or perhaps you're in London for the trade? I hear the raiders pay handsomely for a bit of Scots."

Now the laughing's loud and nasty.

"Got any for the rest of us?" says one of the others.

"Shut your arsewipe mouths!" shouts Zeph. He kicks out, but the officer uses one hand to shove him hard in the chest. Zeph crashes back, landing heavily in the dust, a shout of pain jolting out of him.

"Stop it!" I cry, but no one's listening. 'Cept Andy, whose eyes snap up to stare at me, like he's trying to see inside my head.

"Militia!" barks the officer. Andy starts, stands to attention. "You got us this raider, how about showing us what you're made of? You can start the interrogation, and if you do a good job, you might earn your way into a real uniform."

Andy stares down at Zeph, who glares back. Then Andy nods.

"Good boy," says the officer, like he's talking to a dog.

I want to scream at Andy. But what can I do? How can I stop this?

"Go on, militia," says one of the soldiers. "This one's a red. I heard it were reds attacked your village."

"That's true," says Andy quietly. "I saw them. They took the Prime Minister's daughter and started all this." He looks at me. "And they killed a helpless old widow, who was the only mother to a poor girl I knew. I reckoned she couldn't ever forgive them for what they did. I know I can't."

The officer chuckles, like Andy's told a joke.

"Sounds like you got yourself some work, then. Show me your village doesn't only breed treachery."

Andy's sea-tanned skin blushes dark as the officer reaches down to the rubble floor, picking up a large piece of brick. He passes it between his hands, like he's measuring the weight.

"It isn't difficult," says the officer to Zeph. "Just tell me what way you dirty raiders are going to attack."

"I ain't telling you nothing," says Zeph, struggling to sit up.

"Then start with the hands," says the officer, tossing the brick to Andy, who catches it heavily. "Broken fingers get most men screaming their guts out."

Zeph swears and kicks as two soldiers grab hold of him, untying his wrists, shoving him flat on his back.

"Get off me!" he yells, twisting and fighting. But they pin him down, holding his hands out.

Andy's face is as blank as the brick he's holding.

"Go on, militia," says the officer. "Hard, swift blows. And if that doesn't work, I know some other tricks."

Zeph stops struggling, his pale face gone white as a sheet. He twists his head, his eyes fixing on mine. Lips shaping a silent word. *Run.*

But I don't move. I can't. Cos I'm cut in two halves, and they're pulling against each other.

"Go on! Get it done," grunts one of the soldiers holding Zeph.

"I ain't sitting here all day," says the other.

Andy swallows, raises the brick. Zeph clenches his jaw, turns his blue eyes up to the soft gray sky.

"How will you choose, Lilly?"

The two halves of me rip apart, pulling me to pieces.

A soldier takes my arm.

"Come on, little lass," he says. "You ain't going to like seeing this." He leers at me. "Let's us go somewhere else. Whatever the raider was paying you, I can match it."

"No," I say, slapping his hand off.

The broken pieces of me stumble over the rubble.

"NO!"

I run, crashing straight into Andy, sending the brick flying, sending the both of us onto the floor. Shouts and swearing go up all around, there's hands on my arms, my hair, my neck, hauling me up. But I don't care. I don't even struggle, just turn to the officer.

"I'm Lilly Melkun," I say. "I'm the traitor who took up with the raiders. I know where the Prime Minister's daughter is . . . and why the raiders ain't attacking." Zeph's eyes go wide at me. "The raider doesn't know a thing. Let him go."

The officer stares at me for a moment, then starts to laugh.

"Now there's a bit of fortune I wasn't expecting."

I'm being run along a boardwalk, soldiers on either side holding my arms, pretty much carrying me. My feet scrabble and slide over the slimy wood, and when I slip, the soldiers curse and yank me up.

"What a fool I was." Andy's words run around my mind.

The rest of the soldiers are spread out in front and behind, watching out for raiders and monsters. Sometimes a shout goes up and I'm thrown on the ground, or pulled behind a broken wall with a hand over my mouth. Sometimes the shout's followed by rifle shots and screaming. I shut my eyes, but it doesn't matter. Cos I can see it all. Andy, standing over Zeph. Cambridge burning. The blood-soaked sea, floating with bodies. Our kitchen floor stained red, and Granny lying cold and still.

Andy's right: I ought to see Granny's blood as the reddest, the bitterest of all. But I can't.

It feels like hours, then the boardwalk comes to a stop. I'm hauled onto a narrow muddy path in the bare arms of a woodland. The trees are filled with black-cloaked crows, croaking and chortling in the branches, and when their squawking fades behind, the woods are deep and still all around. Our feet slap through the quiet.

"Are you going to kill me?" I ask.

One of the soldiers laughs.

"If we was going to do that, we'd have left you lying in the rubble with your raider friend."

Zeph. I didn't even help him. The last I saw, he was still being held, and two soldiers were getting their hands ready into fists.

Tears run out of my eyes, but I can't wipe them away.

We carry on the march, and the trees get fewer, smaller. There's a sound of running feet, and Andy's catching us up.

"Is the red done?" asks one of the soldiers.

Andy shrugs like it doesn't even matter.

"Please," I cry. "Let Zeph go."

"Shut up!" growls the soldier, shaking me.

And I do, cos of Andy's face.

The ground gets rougher, filled with bricks. The woods turn back into ruins, the narrow path winding through long piles of rubble, all that's left of the houses. Tree roots scrabble through everything, and brambles and bracken tangle over the mounds. It's a place for ghosts.

In the distance, there's high walls rising up from the scrub and stones. They're all that's left of some great square building, a palace maybe. We head toward them, and the broken walls only get bigger-looking as we get nearer. Black-stained and moss-covered, tops spiky with the red-berry branches of hawthorn bushes. And below the hawthorn, a dirty, battered sign, a few letters showing. PAD G N STATI.

Built into the wall are four huge arches. Whatever went through them in the olden times, they're thick filled with scrub and trees now. There ain't a space to squeeze through, except for the second arch, where the brush has been hacked away. And that's where we head for, the soldiers hoicking me along a new-made path, pressed-down bramble stems crunching under our feet.

The gap in the wall is guarded by a dozen soldiers. The officer talks quiet and urgent at them, and they let us through. Inside the ruins the walls feel even higher, towering overhead, boxing up the sky. It must have been the biggest palace in the world, but there ain't anything rich in it now. Only rough grass and yellow-flower gorse, and the peaks of a hundred gray tents. Above them, hardly fluttering, are the white-cross flags of the Last Ten Counties of England.

The soldiers pull me on to the tents. To the biggest tent, where smart, gold-braided sentries are guarding the door.

"What is this?" one of them snaps, staring at me, the soldiers and the officer.

"I've captured the traitor, Lilly Melkun," says the officer proudly. "And she knows where Lady Alexandra is." The sentry's eyes go wide, and he disappears in the tent. A moment later he's back.

"Bring her in."

· 24 ·
QUESTION AND ANSWER

The first thing I take in is a big table, laid all over with bits of paper. Next to it is Lexy's pa, Prime Minister Randall. He's sat forward in a heavy wooden chair, hands gripped on the arms, glaring a scowl at me from his heavyset face. And the next thing I see makes my feet nearly trip. Cos it ain't just Randall that's in here. There's another man, with hair that's been near enough shaved off, dressed all in black and watching me out of careful eyes. Jasper, the Scottish Ambassador.

They stare at me, each showing a different sort of surprise.

Randall barks out, "Where is she? Where is my daughter?"

"She's here, in London," I say, my voice croaking. "She's safe."

"Safe?" he sneers. "What are you after? A ransom, so you can give it to your raider friends?"

I shake my head.

"I ain't after anything." Cos everything I want is gone. "I've been trying to keep her from harm, that's all. I tried to get her to Greater Scotland." Jasper leans forward. "But . . . it didn't work out . . ."

Randall springs his bulk out of his chair. Slaps my face with a large, heavy hand.

"LIAR!"

I stagger, and the officer yanks me up. My head's ringing, my cheek's bright with pain.

"It ain't a lie," I say, and I don't even care if he believes me. "We went to Cambridge. Look." I pluck at my clothes, that're so like the Ambassador's apart from the color. Jasper narrows his eyes.

"And then what?" sneers Randall. "You were so concerned for my daughter's welfare, you brought her to *London*? I don't believe a word you say." He sits back down, red-faced. "The girl is either lying through her teeth, or she's insane from her exposure to teknology." He looks at the officer. "How was she captured?"

The officer coughs. "Erm. We were on reconnaissance, Your Majesty, at the parliament. And we saw what we thought was a red raider attacking a Londoner. But when we caught the little —" He stops. "Erm, the targets, the Londoner turned out to be this girl. I knew right off she weren't right, and sure enough she gave herself up to us to save her raider whelp from a useful bit of torture. She claims to know where Your Majesty's daughter is, so I brought her straight in."

Randall snorts.

"She's a traitor, you idiot. She'd say anything to save her raider."

The officer flinches a little. "She also said she knows why the raiders are waiting to enter the city."

"Because they're cowards!" snaps Randall. "They know what we did at the Black Waters, and now they're scared to face us."

A breath of a smile passes Jasper's lips. He turns to Randall.

"May I question the girl?"

Randall turns his scowl at him.

"More plots, Ambassador?"

Jasper smiles properly now.

"I serve Greater Scotland's interests, as you know."

Randall snorts again.

"You serve your own as often. I doubt the Lord Protector of the Scottish Highlands knows half the things you do. I expect she'd haul you back to Edinburgh in a second if she did."

Jasper doesn't say anything.

Randall flicks a hand. "You can have three questions. Then we get back to the real business."

Jasper nods, turns to me.

"Have you still got it?" he asks. He's tense, like Cat waiting to pounce. "I know Alexandra didn't drop it in the Black Waters, as she claimed."

I imagine PSAI, tumbling into the mud and getting left there. Maybe it would've got washed by the tide, been found on a beach some day. Perhaps it would have had a better chance than I gave it.

But if I say it's dead, what will Jasper do then?

"I . . . ain't got it with me."

"What about the robots we've seen?" asks Jasper. "They are clearly from the past, so tell me, are they anything to do with the computer calling itself the National Security Response?"

My heart stutters in my chest. How does he know about it?

Aileen. It must be.

His eyes are boring holes in me.

"You should tell me," he says. "I can help you."

I'm so tired, and it's all gone so wrong. It's like I'm out in the water and he's throwing me a line. Would it be so bad if the Scots got the puter? Surely it'd be better than the raiders? And he's right, he can help me. Maybe he can help Lexy, too, even help Zeph.

"The other puter's at Mr. Saravanan's house in Fill Miner Street . . ." And I might as well tell it all. "That's why the raiders ain't attacking, cos they're looking for it. They want it for themselves."

"What!" roars the Prime Minister, standing up from his chair. "The raiders are getting as depraved as you Scots. I knew there was evil at the heart of this rotten city, and now I swear I will cleanse it through. I'll sweep the streets clear of all the vermin that live in them, and then I'll destroy the teknology corrupting its heart. I will raze this Fill Miner Street to the ground!"

"No!" I cry. "That's where Alexandra is."

Randall goes a purple sort of color.

"You took my daughter to a . . . computer? Did you want her so corrupted she'd be unfit to return?" He takes a step toward me, hands in fists.

"No! I only know Mr. Saravanan in London, and that's where he lives. I didn't know the puter'd be there, too."

"Enough!" shouts the Prime Minister. "The truth is that you stole my daughter after I destroyed that scum Medwin. And you brought her here so you could ruin her and then sell her to the raiders. Isn't that it?"

Jasper lifts up his hand.

"Prime Minister. I did see your daughter leave willingly with this girl."

"What you saw means nothing!" snaps Randall. "Alexandra is a stupid child, easily led. And now she may be stained beyond hope of redemption." He glares at me. "But I won't give up on my daughter so easily. She can be purified, with discipline and penance."

"We should travel to this Fill Miner Street and find Alexandra," says Jasper.

Randall sneers at him.

"Because you care so much for her?" He snaps his fingers. "Your unnatural desire for teknology is transparent. But you and I both know your superiors in Edinburgh don't share your obsession. I have an army aimed at this city." He smiles. "And any computers I find will be destroyed."

Lexy. Trapped at Mr. Saravanan's, caught between the raiders and her own father.

"Please, don't attack!" I cry.

"You can do nothing to protect your raider friends," spits the Prime Minister. "You are a pervert. A raider lover. A kidnapper and worse!"

"Your Majesty," says Jasper mildly. "We had an arrangement. The girl should be given to my custody."

"That deal was made before she stole my daughter from me," Randall snipes. "I am at war, and she is guilty of treason. She's told me what I need to know, so there is no further use for her."

He points at the officer.

"Take the traitor out. Execute her."

· 25 ·
AN ENDING

My mind's a jumble, mixed up by fear. I'm made of ice; if I move, I'll shatter. I stare at the Prime Minister. Gloating. At Jasper, shocked-looking. Then the officer's got my arms, and he's pulling me into the bright outside. To fresh air after the canvas-smelling tent. To high white clouds, dancing over this shadow-land. He pulls me on, and my feet stumble after. Past the gray tents and hard-eyed soldiers. Cleaning their rifles. Watching me with cold stares.

"That the traitor?" asks one man.

"It is," says the officer. "She's off to get what she deserves."

The officer leads me on. Scrubby bushes catch at my ankles; twigs snap under my feet.

"Look." He points at a large oak tree, its thick, winding branches spreading out and up, making a sort of roof over part of the ruined, grass-topped walls. Dangling from one of its lower branches is a rope, with a tear-shaped loop at the bottom. "There's the gallows. Mostly it's for deserters, but it'll suit a traitor just as well."

"No!"

The scream's in my mouth, my arms, my legs. I twist and kick, feet jammed in the earth, all of me straining back. Away from the tree. Away from the noose!

"Stop that!" He yanks hard at the rope binding my wrists, jerking my arms in their sockets. I fall, and he drags me on, my feet scrabbling under me, scraping lines through the scrub. "A traitor and a coward," he spits. Then he lifts me up, twisting me about so his arms are round my chest, and he half pushes, half carries me toward the tree. One step nearer, and another.

I sink my teeth in his hand.

"You little witch!" He jerks my head back, so far I think my neck'll snap. His other arm's still round my chest, squeezing the air out of me. I can't breathe. I'm choking already. He hisses in my ear, "I'll kill you right here if you want."

"Wait!" A shout from behind.

The officer turns around, letting my head down a little so I can breathe again.

Jasper's running through the gorse.

"Stop!" calls Jasper. "The girl isn't to be executed after all."

A groan comes out through my shut jaw.

"Whose orders?" asks the officer, not letting go.

"His Majesty. He has changed his mind. He now wants the girl kept alive."

"You got the countermand paper?"

Jasper shakes his head.

"There wasn't time," he snaps. "The girl would be dead before it's copied out."

The officer tightens his grip on me.

"Ambassador," he says, "this is the English army, not the Scots. I take my orders from His Majesty. From his lips or his signature. When you get the paper or His Majesty, then I'll alter. Otherwise, I have my duty."

He turns us about, I'm back facing the gallows tree, the thick woven rope hanging loose in the air.

"No!" I scream through my teeth. "No! No!"

"You're starting to fret me," growls the officer in my ear. "And you ought to want me in a good mood, so you'll go quick. If I'm fretted, I might tie you so's you take half an hour of slow strangling."

Fear turns me from ice into a rag doll. My legs flop as he carries me the last paces to the tree.

The branch is over me, the noose hanging down. They won't even know. Cat, Lexy, Mr. Saravanan. They'll only know I never came back.

Thump, thump, thump. Running feet behind us.

The officer crashes to the ground, pulling me down with him. I fall heavily on his arm, and he cries out in pain. Then he cries out some more, cos someone's pummeling at his face with their fists. A tall someone, who I know better than myself. Andy! They tumble into a stand of tall bracken, their struggle hidden from sight.

"Get up!"

Jasper pulls me behind the thick trunk of the oak tree. He unties me, his fingers quick and nimble.

"Are you all right?"

I nod, trying to look round the tree trunk, to see what's happening with Andy. But Jasper snaps my head back with his hands.

"I said I would help you," he says, "even if it's only this." He's pointing at the high brick wall of the great ruined building.

"There's a hole over there. Run, now, and you can make it out of here." My head's spinning about.

"Why?" I croak. "Why are you helping me?"

He narrows his eyes.

"You have a computer. Others may not care about such things, but to me that makes you one of the most important people in the world."

"What about Andy?"

"The soldier boy?" He looks at the shivering bracken, where Andy's got the officer grappled to the ground. "He'll be all right. I'll protect him."

"But I need to say good-bye."

"Don't be a fool. You need to run." His fingers are tight on my arms, even as he's pushing me away. "Keep in the shadows. Don't stop."

And I'm running. Running as fast as I can. My mind's all in pieces. Pieces of Andy. Pieces of Jasper. It's saying, *You can't leave, not like this*. And it's saying, *Run, run!*

I scramble and flail through scratch-face thickets, over and under branches that're thicker and thicker near to the towering wall. I crash on, making what way I can, till my fingers hit on rough bricks, cool and damp with moss. I search for the place where there ain't any wall. Stumbling about, stupid with panic.

"Lilly!"

I stop.

Andy's pushing his way through the brambles and branches. He's got blood dripping from his nose, but his eyes are calm in his wonderful face.

"You're going the wrong way," he says quietly, taking my hand.

I fling my arms about him. Hugging him. Weeping.

"I'm sorry. So sorry." I say it over and over.

Andy tight-hugs me back, then holds me out from his arms.

"You have to get going," he says, and I smile, wiping my eyes with my hand. A mad, happy lightness settles on me. Cos Andy's here; it's going to be all right.

There's an ancient apple tree growing thick in the hole in the wall. We have to fight it to get through, snagging our clothes, getting covered in scratches. But the pain's a joy, cos I'm still here to feel it, and Andy's with me. Then we're through, and there's a thick, solid wall between us and that officer. Between us and the Prime Minister, the army, all the things that kept us from each other.

Me and Andy.

We flop down for a breath, beside a clump of gray-stemmed elder trees. The smile on my face is so big, I reckon it'll break my mouth.

"You saved me!" I say, and I laugh. A high laugh that I can't hardly stop.

Andy puts his fingers on my lips to hush me, doesn't even smile.

"You have to get going. We're moving out after sunset, and it won't be safe for you." He points out to the stone-tangled scrubland, darkening into twilight. "There's a path the locals use. Follow it, and hide if you hear or see anyone. I reckon the Ambassador'll set a spy on you."

"He's already done that," I say, thinking of Aileen. But my laughter's gone. "Ain't you coming with me?"

Andy shakes his head.

"Why did you help me if you ain't leaving?" I ask. Andy's

mouth finally makes a bit of a smile. But not the one I know, only a sad remembering of it.

"Cos you were always getting in trouble," he says, "and half my life I been getting you out of it. But this time, it's the last."

I can't take my eyes from his face. I know it so well, yet I can't fathom him at all.

"I did all this to save you! To free you from the militia, so you could come back home. So we could get our boat together."

It's my best dream. Where me and Andy are captains together on our own boat, and Cat's helping us land the best catches anyone's seen, and people are telling us how Granny would have been so proud . . .

"That ain't never going to happen, Lilly," says Andy. "I've got another life now. It weren't one I chose, but I've got to make it work."

"You want to stay in the army?" I cry. "After what they did to our village?"

Andy's smile is gone, even the remembering of it.

"You're with the raiders?" he asks. "After what *they* did?"

And my tongue gets stuck in my mouth, cos there ain't any words I can think of that'll make everything seem like sense.

"It just . . . happened," I say.

Andy's eyes are like sorrow. "And it just happened I ended up in the militia. But if I can work up to being a proper soldier, then I'll earn more than I ever could as a fisher." He frowns. "I was doing it for you. And for Ma and Pa. That's what kept me going. Even when I heard what you did, I kept on, cos I knew what they was saying couldn't be true. Till you turned up with that . . . red."

He stands up.

"I have to go," he says. "The Ambassador said he'll take the blame. Said he was leaving anyway. But I have to get back before I'm missed."

I grab at his hand, hold it tight.

"Please. We can make it right again; it'll be like old times."

His eyes are charcoal dark.

"It can't never be like it was. Not after all that's happened."

And he pulls his hand from mine, climbing under a tree branch to start his way back. Back to the army.

But I don't see him go, cos of my tears.

· 26 ·
BLOOD BROTHERS

"Hello, little brother."

A fast cloud covers the moon. Roba's sword goes from silver to black in front of my eyes. I can feel it in the air. I can smell Roba. The moon gets out from the cloud, and Roba's over me.

"Looks like you ain't doing so good," he says, poking me with his foot. I'm laid out in the bricks and dust, hands and feet tied. Done up like a stuck pig, how the stinking bluecoats left me after they dragged off Lilly, shouting and crying.

One of the English put his stinking face in mine.

"Your draggle only bought you a bit of time."

He grunted at the other bluecoat, then they was on me.

Kicking me in the guts. Smacking at my face.

On and on. My mouth filled up with blood, my ribs was on fire. I knew they wasn't gonna give up until I was good as dead. But then a voice shouted, "Stop!"

I got a break from the battering; the scags stood up. I turned my face onto broken bricks and saw him. Lilly's militia. Panting, like he'd run back.

"The captain said not to touch the raider," he said. "He wants to come back and interrogate him later."

The bluecoat that liked kicking said, "He ain't got nothing worth telling. The only thing he's good for is a bit of sport."

"Tell you what, militia," said the one that liked punching, "why don't you just say you got here too late. That we'd already done the job on him."

The militia's eyes was on me. Blacker than Lilly's. And he shook his head.

"Keep him alive. Keep him all right."

The bluecoats shrugged.

"All right. Tell the captain he ain't dead."

"And he'll stay that way?" asked the militia. The soldiers grunted, then nodded.

They all crunched off over the rubble after that. I could have watched them go if I moved a bit, but it weren't worth the pain.

Clouds sailed through the sky. Sometimes I watched them, sometimes I shut my eyes. Pain everywhere turned to a swollen, blood-salty mouth, a stabbing in my ribs, and the rope-ache at my wrists. I got a smell of pipe smoke, and the sound of the bluecoats gabbing on what girls they was gonna visit when they got paid.

Nothing to do but think. On Lilly, and what she done for me, after what I done to her. On what the English do with their traitors. How in the Families, they get spiked.

Sky, pain, thinking. I musta fell asleep on it, coz when I woke up the clouds was night-dark. And what woke me was a sound.

"Ungk." Then another. "Gawp."

Then feet on brick dust.

Then the sharp swish of steel in the air.

* * *

I twist in the dirt, trying to get away from Roba's sword.

"Go on, maggot about!" says Roba. "I been following your stinking trail since Cambridge. I knew I'd get you, but I didn't think your English friends was gonna leave you all roped and ready for the sticking." The sword tip gets nearer my throat. "You gonna tell me where the girl is? Where the machine is?"

I swear at him, and he laughs.

"You ain't much."

The sword tip moves down until it's level with my chest. Jab, flick. One of the ropes is cut in two.

"Your doxy sold you out?" The sword flicks again, and another rope gets sliced. "Got you a decent battering?" Flick, the last rope is cut. "I wish I'd been here to see it."

My mouth's like dust, every bit of me's stiff and hurting. I push up, rub my arms, check the doorway and the dead bluecoats lying in it.

"She didn't sell me out." The words is thick on my tongue.

"That why you're wrapped up in this hole?"

"The English jumped us," I say.

Roba sneers.

"And you let them? They oughta be dead, or you oughta." He kicks at the pile of rope. "Not this."

"I didn't have my knife!" I say. "I lost it on one of the machines."

Roba checks me.

"Those stinking things. Randall musta sent them coz he ain't got the stomach to fight us face up."

"The machines ain't Randall's," I say.

"Whose are they, then?" He smiles nasty. "Is your English doxy working them, too?"

"No. Leave her outta this."

Roba laughs.

"I'm chasing you coz of her! Her machine is what I'm after." He leans down, pulls me on my feet. His sword's a line, shining back the moonlight. "And you're gonna tell me where she is."

I laugh; it turns into a cough.

"The English took her," I say. "I dunno where." I point at the dead bluecoats. "They coulda told you."

Outside, on the walkway, I go over the planks. Up and down past the market. Checking for boot marks, a dropped hair, anything to tell the way they took her. But this ain't the marshes; there ain't bent grasses and bird calls signing what's gone.

Roba watches me from a doorway.

"You ain't much of a tracker. Must be why you left a slack, easy trail. Even your trick with the Windspeakers weren't much." He snorts. "Though they was well mad at the Kensings when I got there. A hat full of stones!" He checks about, looking up and around. "The English is gonna get you again, the way you're on it here."

"What do you care?"

I follow a half mud print of an English boot, the pattern giving out at a cross walkway. I check up and down the dark street, kick at the planks.

"This is useless."

Roba's still on me.

"You ain't got a clue, do you?" he says.

"If you wasn't so kill-happy," I shout, "those bluecoats woulda told where she is."

Roba shrugs, the blood on his leathers showing black in the moonlight.

"I ain't you, little brother. The only talking I got for the English is with my sword." He crouches down, checking the tracking-signs. "I don't need them living. Coz I'm gonna find the girl and her machine, then I'm gonna give her to Angmar, and get our Family back on."

"She ain't even got —" I stop the words, but it's too late. Coz I'm a scag. Stupid scag.

"What do you mean?" growls Roba, right on me, one hand gripped in my leathers, sword flat at my neck. "What do you mean?" He shakes me, sending the pain all over. And the pain gets my brain going. Maybe I got an out.

"The machine ain't with her," I say. "But I'll tell you where it is, if you find Lilly."

Roba smiles, nasty.

"I ain't cracked. You're a sneaking, lying little scag and there ain't no way I'm hunting your doxy when the machine's here for the taking." He lets me go, but his sword's still at my neck. "We're going on a walk, little brother."

· 27 ·
HORSE AND MONSTER

My feet go one after another along the muddy, muddling path. Past ruins and under trees, through a clearing grown with straggly rows of vegetables, into another with a thin goat tethered. A twilight world, and I don't know, don't care where I'm going. Cos all I can think is how every step's taking me farther from Andy. And how my heart's being spun back to him, a tugging, tearing thread unraveling inside me.

I stumble on, thinking on all the things I should have said differently to Andy. My eyes only see enough to keep me on the path; words tumble in my head:

"Execute her!"

"It can't never be like it was."

I jump at a sound from the trees. It's bootsteps! The soldiers are coming!

But it's just some nighttime creature, scampering through the leaves.

Then a twig snaps behind me.

And I run so fast! The cold air burns in my throat, my legs whirl under me. Helter-skelter, not even thinking. Trees close around me, hiding the sky with their branches. I'm in a tunnel, and other things are running with me. Terrible things. All the things I've seen. I run faster, like a mad thing, and . . .

The trees are gone.

I'm back under the sky, the first stars twinkling in the east. In front of me there's houses, the water sparkle of a stream, and a neat-planked bridge going over it. I stop, my heart hammering inside me, cos there ain't anyone behind. But now there's all different paths, leading all different ways. And only one of them goes to Lexy and Cat, trapped at Mr. Saravanan's. I ain't sure if any of them leads to Zeph.

I turn around, and stare with my eyes, my heart, at the dark way back to Andy.

'Cept it ain't that, is it? Not for me.

The tugging, tearing thread snaps.

A few houses have got candlelight peeping through the shutters, but mostly it's piles of rubble, half-fallen buildings, and skeleton ghost towers. The ruins of London, spreading away into the shadowy evening, paths weaving through. I've got to make a choice with my feet, and I don't even know where I'm going.

So I put a foot on one of the paths, and walk. My feet get quicker and quicker, until I'm running. Cos if one thread's snapped, there's others getting stronger. The ones to Cat, to Lexy. To Zeph. They pull me on, tying the pieces of me back together again as I go.

But when they're done, I'm different-shaped inside.

Round a corner, and I'm at a tumbly gap between jumbled buildings. Ahead of me it narrows till it ain't nothing but a great pile of rubble. Another dead end.

I run back the way I came, raging at myself. Why didn't I keep track of where the soldiers led me? Why didn't I think on how I'd get back? My feet splat through mud, past ruined and shambling streets heading off in every direction. I'm a fish, panicking in a net. I ain't got a clue where I'm going. Just running and hoping, round corner after corner, from one dead end to another.

And then at the other end of the street, scraping a path through the mud . . . a monster! Raised up high on its legs, feet taking careful steps. Red light shining out from under its wide, round body, sending fire lights over the rubble-houses.

The whirling, glassy head stops spinning, fixes on me.

I stand still, heart pounding. Is it one of the ones that ain't working? One of the rowbots that'll eat you up in a snap?

"Do Not Attempt To Flee," says the monster. "Hand Over Anything That May Contain Useful Resources." Colorful words flutter round it like butterflies. *Ikke Flykte! Consegnare Ogni Bene Utilizzabile!*

It stops, and the beam of white from its eyes shines in my face. "You," it says, as I put my hand up to shade my eyes.

It takes a step, raises its claws. Then there's a noise a bit like *crrrcksht.*

"Lilly! Thank goodness!" Mr. Saravanan's voice booms out from the monster. *God Zij Dank!*

"Can I see? Let me see!" Lexy's voice pipes out over the moonlit ruins. "Are you all right, Lilly? Me and Cat have been watching out for you all day, haven't we?" A "miaow" blasts out, the kind Cat makes when he's being squeezed too hard.

The street's lit by dancing letters, floating upward into the dark.

Deixe-Me Ver! Ny?

And for a moment, I can't even work out what's happening. It's like the world's got tilted on its head. Then I start laughing, cos I reckon I'm getting to know teknology now; there must be a talking box inside the monster.

"I'm glad you're able to see the humor in all this," mutters Mr. Saravanan's voice out over the dark-rubble street. "I've had these contraptions out scouring London for you, and here you are, merry as a May maid."

"He had a big fight with the computer about it," says the monster, sounding like Lexy.

"The Emergency Response Units Have Functions Other Than Searching For Runaways," says the monster in its own voice.

I can hardly see for the all words in the air, running into each other, piling up in drifts.

Hän Oli Suuri Taistelu Avec l'Ordinateur! De Urgență Răspuns Dispone Di Altri Swyddogaethau!

"I'm sorry," I say.

Sorry I ran outside when I should have known better. Sorry I thought Andy would want to see me again. Sorry that . . .

"Is Zeph with you?" The words tumble out of me.

"We saw him," starts Lexy's voice, then there's a mumble from the monster, and Mr. Saravanan takes over.

"At least we have found you." The glass eyes spin around slowly. "Where are you exactly?"

I shrug.

"I don't know. I'm lost."

There's the sound of Mr. Saravanan arguing with the puter, too quick for me to catch the words. Then the monster's eyes fix on me.

"Assistance Will Be Provided, Lilly Melkun."

Я Потору Тебе, Лилли Melkun!

And before I can even move, it rushes at me.

"What are you doing?" I shout, but one of its pincer arms has already whipped out and grabbed me round the waist. I feel like my insides are being squeezed out. My feet kick at nothing as the rowbot lifts me up from the muddy street, into the dark air.

"Assistance Is Being Provided," it says as I fly in a circle, so fast I'd be sick if my belly wasn't clamped tight. I'm up on its back, held by one of them claws. Then it turns, heading back the way it came.

I grip on tight as the monster clanks, sways, and creaks through the jumble of rubble, fields, and swamp that's this part of London. First this way, then that; every turn taken without a pause. *Grung, grung, squeak. Grung, grung, squeak.* In the distance, I think I can hear shouted commands, the crack of gunfire.

The wind turns from a shifting breeze into gusts that tug at my clothes. A cold, biting rain pitter-patters on the spider, then drums as it falls heavier. Lightning flashes, and a few breaths later, thunder rumbles through everything.

"Can't you go faster?" I say to the monster, but it doesn't answer, just keeps stamping along. The tree-covered rubble mounds give out to wooden boardwalks set over mud, and through gaps between houses I start seeing the black ripples of the Thames. The buildings get more lived-in looking. Ladders up to the windows, roofs patch-mended, vegetable gardens instead of scrub growing between the houses. There's more gunfire from where we were not long before, and the heart-stopping boom of cannons. Randall and his army are coming into London. But there's another sound, too. *Clip, clop, clip, clop.*

Hooves on wood, echoing between the houses. I twist about, as best as I can, trying to see the rider through the red-shifting shadows, but there ain't a sight. Just *clip, clop, clip, clop*. Sometimes nearer, sometimes farther away, but always keeping pace, tracking us. Is it Jasper's spy, like Andy warned? Am I leading him right to what he wants?

The monster heads us down the boardwalk, and I see building shapes I know. The steeple roof of the old parliament. The tall tower of Big Ben.

Orangey lights are flickering round its feet, the thin smoke from campfires weaving about. There's men moving round them fires, shouting or singing about killing and blood. Swords clatter and scrape.

The raiders, waiting for us at the river's edge.

"We can't go that way!" I cry.

"It Is The Most Direct Route."

"But the raiders! If they see me they'll kill me."

"This Is The Most Direct Route."

Dan Huwa L-Aktar Rotta Diretta!

I struggle about, trying to get down, but I'm caught fast. Shining words trail after us like beacons, and the monster clunks on, not even bothered, heading straight for the old parliament, for the boardwalk toward Fill Miner Street. I crouch down small as I can get, waiting for the first raider sentry to spot us, for the shout to go out. And then . . . all the raiders disappear. They're round the parliament, and then they ain't. The monster clanks on past, and looking down to the river I get a sight of where all the warriors are. Thousands of them, in every color of leather, filling up the shore. More warriors than I've ever seen, more people than I've ever seen.

They ain't looking our way, they don't even see me on this great metal rowbot. Cos they're watching toward the river, or maybe all them dragonboats. Something's going on that's got them all caught up in it. We stamp on, and the warriors are hidden behind buildings again. But I can still hear them.

Thousands of mouths shouting, then one voice rising up from the rest, and cheers following it. I don't have to hear what's being said to know what's happening.

They've found out where the puter is. They're coming.

I bang on the rowbot's back. "Hurry! Please!"

I look back toward the parliament, but it ain't raiders I see. It's a heavy-looking horse, coat fiery-gleaming in the red light and, on its back, a rider wearing a dark, hooded cloak, their face hidden. Jasper's spy.

But it's too late now to hide.

The *clip, clop, clip, clop,* follows behind me. And the cheers of the raiders turn to war cries.

· 28 ·
FRIEND OR FOE?

"I ain't a fishwit," says Roba. "You know where it is, so no more mucking."

One of his hands is on the back of my neck, pushing me, the other's on his sword hilt. We ain't at Fill Miner Street, coz I been taking wrong ways, backtracking, making out I'm lost. Checking every street for an out, a way to lose Roba. But he's stuck on me like a leech. And the tide's up, black Temz water swirling over the stinking, grabbing mud. I ain't gonna get far swimming through that.

Ten paces ahead is a crossing, one of the walkways that heads to the market between the tides. Roba pushes me at it.

"I know it's gotta be somewhere near here," he growls, "coz this is where you was running about before." His fingers pinch the sides of my neck, and pain stabs up my head. Roba's got skill at hurting. "Take me to the machine, runt."

We get to the crosswalk, under the shadow of the tide watchers' tower. The Temz is rushing through the holes in the market walls and a cold rain is spitting. Lightning cracks the night, showing clear the stone block walls and sharp roof of the market.

There'd be some decent hiding in there, if I can get to it.

Then I see them. Bluecoats, three of them, legging it outta the tall stone arch of the trader's door, straight for us. They're at it fast, not even looking, like it don't even matter they're in Lunden, and the Families is all about.

"Do Not Panicicicic!" Words roar outta the market, behind them. "Keep Caaallmmalamalalal!" The noise rattles off the walls. Bright shapes flash in the air round the door, bursting like fire-sparks all over. Two spider-machines spike out from the trader's hall, filling up the high doorway as they clank through, waving their pincers like they're trying to fly. The English leg it faster.

"Do Not Resistisisisisisittt!"

But this ain't ringing out from the market, it's behind me and Roba. I spin about, and there's another spider clanking right at us.

Roba whistles through his teeth.

"If we could get one of those machines for Angmar . . ."

"He can't Boss those!" I say.

The machine clanks nearer. Claws slashing in the air like sabers.

"You Willilll Comome To Nono Harm If Youyouoyoyou . . ."

Colored shapes spark all round it, like it's coughing out butterflies. Its bottle eyes is spinning so fast there's smoke rising off. The two machines outta the market crash into each other, then set right again.

And I remember what the machine at Saru's place said. How some of these ones is broken, gone crazy.

The machine coming for me and Roba has got its claws swung out, reaching. I back away from it, getting closer to the bluecoats. Who've stopped legging it. They don't even raise their rifles, like they forgot they've got them. They're just checking about, trying to work out what's worse. Us, or the spider-machines.

One of the English takes a half step to me. His face is shiny, neck veined-out with fear. The other two look like they're gonna wet themselves. Up close, they ain't soldiers, just skinny kids with blue jerkins over their fishergear. They look lost, like Lilly did when she first turned up in Lunden.

"Call them off!" sobs one. "We'll give ourselves up if you'll call off your demons!"

Roba laughs. "English sheepheads."

"We ain't working the machines," I say.

The fisherboys get even worse fear at that. One of them drops to his knees, hands together, lips muttering. Another's staring at the Temz water, whirling and frothing under the walkway.

"Can you swim?" I ask.

The boy shakes his head, fear eyes checking the machine.

"But at least I won't be demon-cursed," he says.

Roba hard-slaps my shoulder. "If he wants the water, do him a favor and push! It'll save my sword a blood-washing."

"We need them," I yell. "If we all go for that one," I point at the machine on its own, "we can take it out."

The English on his knees don't stop jabbering. The one that was gonna jump is fear-stuck. But the other English, he stares at the machine, then nods.

"What do we have to do?" he asks, in a well shaky voice.

"I don't go with bluecoats," spits Roba.

"Then the machines'll have us!" I shout. "We won't get nothing for Angmar, and Angel Isling'll be gone in a hard settling."

"Don't Cryiyiyiy. This Wononoon't Hurt Much."

Roba checks me, the machine, the English. Hacks a flob on the planks.

"All right."

The machines ain't more than a few paces off.

"They can't take water." I talk quick. "If we get one off balance, push it off the walkway, it'll drown."

"How we going to do that?" asks the English, fear-stink coming thick off him. But I got the answer, coz I done a lot of thinking on what I shoulda done different last time.

"Get a cover on its eyes," I say. "Then take out its legs."

I take off my jacket, turn, and face it.

"Identify Your Elves! Are You Insurgents Or Detergents?" The claws of the machine is up in the air, snapping and slicing at nothing. They jolt forward, reaching for me.

I take a deep breath. Leg it.

My feet pound on the wood, I get my hands on sharp metal, on smooth plastic. I pull up, feet scrabbling for holds.

"This Is Prohibihibited!" screams the machine. It tries to get me with its claws, its legs stamping up and down, trying to shake me off. A piece of its armor snaps off in my hand; I quick grab on another bit. The machine jolts sideways, nearly yanking my arms outta their sockets. My feet slip, a claw clips off half my dreads, my heart's gonna burst . . . and then I'm up on its back!

I throw my jacket over the machine's spinning eyes. They keep going round under my jacket, the hard bulk whacking my arms, my chest. I wrap the leather down, tighten it round. Hold my whole body on what's moving under me.

Creeeeeeeeerk.

The eyes grind to a crunching stop, but I can feel they wanna get going again. My arms is killing.

"Quick!" I yell. "I don't know how long I can do this!"

"STOPPIT!"

"THIS IS PROHIBITITIBITITED!"

"YOU ARE NAUGHTY NAUGHTY NAUGHTY!"

All the machines is yelling now. My ears is banging from the noise, colored shapes is flashing right in my face.

"Get the legs!" I shout. "Knock it in the Temz!"

A cold, crushing claw grabs on my ankle. My leg's pulled straight out. Pain shrieks outta my mouth, but I hold on. My leg's bent back and up, it's gonna snap! I'm stretched in a line, my arms out, my hands slipping.

The eyes start spinning under my jacket, bashing my fingers away.

And I'm swinging upside down, breath knocked out. My hands is banging, smacking on the side of the machine. Blood's rushing in my head.

"You scagging frint!"

Roba's hacking his sword at a joint in the metal leg. The blade swings up, down. Past my face. And the bluecoats! They're at the machine, pushing it, heaving at it. It stumbles. My nose nearly smashes on a plank.

"Get on, you demon!" shouts one of the bluecoats. They heave some more, ducking and dodging the swiping claws.

Roba's sword hacks down again, and the leg slices in two pieces.

"Soooo Naughty," moans the spider, tipping. Another leg goes off the planks, into the Temz.

And there's a weight like the world on my ankle where it's still gripped on, pulling me down with it. I slide over the planks, grabbing, slamming, slapping at the walkway. My fingers fill up with splinters.

"Help!" I scream. But Roba don't move.

Whack! A bayonet crashes into the claw that's got my foot, jamming in the machine's joint.

"Hang on."

The bluecoat boys is on me, holding my arms, thumping and battering the gripper, breaking their rifles to get it off me. The crush on my ankle gets less. Hands grip on my leg.

"We got you!"

I fall into the arms of the English. The machine splashes down in the Temz, red and white light shining in the brown-froth water, legs snapping, thrashing. It screeches, crackles. The lights go out. It's dead.

The fisherboys is clinging on to me, laughing. And I'm laughing, too.

"Extermineananate!"

"You Will Be Assimilated!"

There's still two machines behind us.

We leg it. Me, Roba, the fisherboys, pounding down the walkway. But my chest's burning from the beating I took before, my ankle's a jab of pain on every step. I ain't keeping up, I'm getting left behind. The boy who was sweaty with fear before, he drops back. Grabs my hand, pulls me on.

"Just keep goin'," he pants. "Just keep goin'."

We dodge in and out of buildings, down an alley too narrow for the machines. We pile through a broken door and stop inside.

Panting, huffing, leaning on a wall. The sound of clanking gets near, then gets quieter. Then it's gone.

"We lost them!" I say. And the bluecoat boys is laughing.

"I thought them demons had us," says the tallest one.

"I was praying!" says the youngest, thinnest of the bunch.

"Bet you weren't praying for raiders," laughs the third, grinning at his friend.

"Thanks, raider," says the tallest, turning to me.

I grin at him.

"Thanks yourself."

"Yeah," says Roba. "Thanks, English."

His sword rings outta its sheath. I check him, the English check him.

"No," I say.

He smiles.

"Don't!"

I run at Roba, but he slams me back, I go flying.

The English boys is shouting, screaming. They try and leg it. They try and fight back, but they can't, coz they broke their weapons saving me.

Their screaming stops.

They're stomach open, throat cut, blood-washed. Lying in the alley.

Roba's sword is black dripping. He stands over their eyes-open bodies, watching their life seep outta them.

My face is wet, my guts is heaving.

"You scag!" I scream. "You puke-eating scag!"

He checks me.

"You really are a sniveling English-lover, ain't you?"

· 29 ·
A DONE DEAL

"Come on, runt, get moving." Roba's sword is at my back, pushing me along. I limp in the wet, the dark.

I'm gonna kill him. I don't know how, but I'm gonna. A wronging needs an equaling, that's how it goes.

The Temz is brown-swirling in the streets, the rain is biting. There's a crack of rifle fire, a distant boom of cannon. Through a gap in the buildings I see a fire burning way off, lighting the clouds with orange. The English is getting nearer.

The walkways is slick and slippery. One slip, one push, and Roba could go in, get lost in the water. Or one slip, and his sword could be through me, starting right where it's jabbed in my back.

Roba ain't said where we're going, but I know it's the docks.

"You're gonna stop your traitor tricks," says Roba. "You're gonna put our Family first, like you shoulda done first off."

But all I can see is those boys. All I can hear is them pleading at Roba.

We take a crossway and we're outta the dark into a street that's lit by metal braziers, chunks of doors and window frames burning in them, bouncing yellows and oranges at the rain-dark walls. Flame shadows shiver on water, flicker over the warriors that's filling up the walkway. Hundreds of them, stood in gangs of different color leathers. Tense, ready for fighting. Eyes checking me and Roba. Swords and spearheads flash.

"What are you?" shouts a Westmin warrior, greeny-brown leathers tight round his big gut. "What d'ya want?"

"I'm Roberto Untamed, of the Family Angel Isling," shouts Roba. "I gotta speak with Angmar."

Weapons go down. A bit.

"Angels," says the Westam warrior, grunting a laugh. "What you gotta see the Chief Talker for?"

"It don't matter to you!" snaps Roba. "What does is what's gonna happen if you don't let us through."

Roba's sword ain't at my back now, it's up, where all the warriors can see it. See the blood on it. I check Roba's sharp, flame-lit face; his killing smile.

He looks crazy. He looks like a bad foretelling.

The warrior checks him, too, then steps outta the way. Roba's sword is at my back again, moving me on. The warriors open a path for us, filling in the gap behind, pushing after. We walk down to the pier, where the ships is thick moored. Big, heavy-sailed ships, with snarling dragonheads. Flag ships. Boss ships.

Norwich warriors is everywhere, and there's enough Bosses here for a council if they wanted. I spot Guvner's bulk, the sly shape of Cato. And Angmar, right in the middle of it all.

Me and Roba walk toward the gang of Bosses. All talking stops, all eyes is on us.

"The Angel Bosslings," says Angmar. "You was quick outta Cambridge." He walks right at us, then flobs right in our faces. "And you scagged it all up, didn't you?" he shouts. "The eggheads got every last warrior that went in . . . except you Angels." He pushes his face up close to Roba, who steps back. "So you gonna tell me why that was, if you wasn't double-crossing?"

"I dunno what went wrong with the eggheads," says Roba. "I didn't see what happened, I was chasing . . ." He checks me. Angmar does, too.

"You was chasing your little Boss boy." He sneers at Roba. "Was he worth wasting the other warriors for?"

"He's the way to the machine," says Roba.

"So, you let the other warriors get taken by the eggheads, and you snitched your way outta Cambridge, but it's all right coz you got the machine?"

Roba shakes his head.

"I ain't —" he starts.

"You ain't even GOT IT!" roars Angmar, answering for him. "You lost me my chance at the egghead city and now you got nothing!" He flicks a hand, the Norwich warriors close round us.

We're gonna get spiked right here! They're gonna cut us to shreds.

"No! No!" Roba's yelling. "The girl's machine is here, in Lunden. That's why I come here, to tell you that. That's why I brought my runt-brother, coz he knows where it is."

Angmar turns evils on me.

"Maybe you *is* the one that oughta be Boss," he says, "coz your brother ain't got much brains." He pauses. "You Angels is good at sneaking, I'll hold you on that, coz Ims is the only other scag that made it out."

He points at a Norwich warrior, who turns and shouts back at the ship.

Two Norwich climb out, and it looks like they got a slave with them. I don't even work out who it is first off.

"Ims!" His name howls outta me, breaking me outta my gloom. He's got no leathers, all his gold is gone, his face is puffed up in bruises and his wrists is in shackles. He goes slow, careful, like everything's in pain. And when he checks my way, one eye is swollen shut from the battering he's got.

"Ims is a Second!" I yell. Seconds don't get battered like that.

"I'm all right," he mumbles at me.

"I got your message," says Angmar, the wind taking his words out to the river. "It's the only reason I ain't already spiked every one of you Angels for what you done at Cambridge." He snaps a hand out, grabs my arm, not soft like he looks. "So forget whatever Roba's chasing. I want the other machine, the Lunden one."

His eyes is hard, like loot.

Roba bugs at me, at Ims.

"What other machine?" he shrieks. "And what message did you send with Ims? You little scag! You was gonna cut me out and take everything for yourself!"

"I'm trying to save our Family!" I shout out. Hate fills me up, tingling into my arms and legs. Hate for what Roba did to those boys, what Angmar did to Ims, hate of the knife hanging over our Family. "I just want this done."

"You think Angel Isling's gonna be anything now?" Angmar hisses at me. "You scagged up years of planning, made me look a fool. You got one chance left. Give me this Lunden machine or I'm gonna be at the Black Waters myself, slitting throats."

I check Angmar's eyes, and the hate boiling inside me ain't got nowhere to go. A wronging needs an equaling, but sometimes you gotta wait. Coz I can't fight my way outta here, and whichever way I go, there ain't no way round this but numbers. If I take Angmar to the machine, I'm gonna be giving up Lexy and ol' Saru. If I don't, our camp's got three hundred-odd in it, babies and little kids, too.

"I'll take you to it," I say. "But let the Lundeners go that's trapped with it. They ain't nothing to do with this."

Angmar shrugs, like he don't care. But Roba shouts out, "He's tricking again. He weren't just traveling with the English girl and her machine, he had Randall's daughter along as well. I know it!"

Behind Angmar, Cato startles, checks me.

"That true?" he asks. "You got Randall's kid as well?" I don't say nothing, mouth gone dry as chalk. But Cato only starts to laugh. "Zephaniah Untamed, you got your father in you. If I was in your shoes, I'd wanna keep loot like that for myself as well." He raises his voice, turning to the other Bosses, to all the Family warriors that's around. "You know I don't much like the Angels, but I don't like what I see here neither." He points at Ims, and there's a rumble of agreeing. "Zephaniah's got us this machine that's gonna kill English for us, and he's got Randall's kid. By my thinking, that's more than the deal we set at council." He nods at me. "If he leads us to that lot, I say we gotta leave Angel Isling standing. I'll even vote him for Boss myself."

Laughs and agreeing comes from the warriors. The Bosses all give their nods to Cato. Angmar's glaring furious, but there ain't nothing he can do to stop this. He's Chief Talker, but the Bosses hold the power in the Families. Even he's gotta go with the vote.

My hate sets cold, at the choice Angmar made me take to save Angel Isling.

Angmar raises his hand.

"We got the ancient war-machine!" he shouts. A cheer goes up, battling with the river noise. "It's time to get back Lunden!" Cheers rage into the rain-spitting dark. "We're gonna kill every English that's living in this city, and when we done that, we ain't gonna stop until every last one in the ten stinking counties is dead or slaved!"

The sound of shouting's so loud I can't think. Bosses is cheering, warriors is cheering. Ims has got his fist in the air.

I got our Family saved, but the price is what I told Lilly I weren't gonna do. I've sold her out, sold out Lexy. Sold out all the fisherboys in this stinking, blood-washed city.

· 30 ·

THE FOLLOWER

I climb through the window into Mr. Saravanan's house, and my feet are hardly in the dust before I'm wrapped in a hug.

"You're all right!" cries Mr. Saravanan, bear-squeezing me. "I was so worried; you're my favorite nephew." He lets me go, and there's a prickling on my legs. Cat's stretched high as he can get, looking up at me with worry in his sea green eyes. I bend down and he leaps, clambers up into my arms. Pressing his furry face at mine, rumbling a purr loud enough to burst him. My tears run wet onto his head.

"I thought I'd never see you again," I whisper in his ear, and he butts at my head, purring even louder.

Next thing, a pair of little arms is being flung about me, and Lexy's hopping and hugging me at the same time, laughing and singing "Lilly Lilly" over and over.

The tears dry on my face. Cos the soldiers, Randall, the noose, Andy, all the things I've done wrong; they ain't all there is. I hug Lexy with the bits of me that ain't cuddling Cat and I'm laughing, too.

Till there's a sound from outside. Feet on the rungs of

the ladder, someone climbing up after me. I stop hugging, stop laughing. I go cold.

"Have you brought Zeph back?" asks Mr. Saravanan. I shake my head, the sound of feet on the ladder getting closer. The top of a black hood pokes up at the window, pale hands grip on the ledge. It's Jasper's spy, it has to be. All I've done is lead more trouble after me, brought it straight to Lexy.

I back away, pulling Lexy with me.

"I think it's —" But I don't get to finish, cos Lexy runs out, straight for the window.

"Professor!" she cries. The black hood drops, showing a soft, wrinkly face, circle specs, and gray hair pulled tight. The Professor flips back the dark sides of her cloak. Underneath she's wearing a thick woollen tunic, the color of moss and ferns, and heavy woven trousers tucked into them strong-looking shoes of hers.

She beams a smile at Lexy, at me.

"I found you at last!" she says.

"It was you? On the horse?"

The Professor nods. Something that might be a laugh comes out of my mouth. "I thought you were a spy, sent by the Ambassador."

The Professor startles and drops her gaze. Guilty-looking.

"Are you?" I ask, a fury beginning inside me.

"No! I haven't even spoken to him since . . ." She stops, and I don't say anything. "I'm sorry. I didn't dare call out to you before, just in case I frightened the robot. I couldn't risk losing such an astounding creation! And to see you riding it . . ." She's looking admiring at me, almost how she looks at the puters.

Mr. Saravanan makes a face at me.

"Who *is* this person?"

The Professor doesn't notice how he's looking, just holds out her hand.

"Cressida Keenan, Professor of Silicon Antiquities at Cambridge University. Now, do you have anywhere I could stable my horse?"

"There are no stables in London," says Mr. Saravanan. "Any horses that make it this far are headed for the stew pot."

The Professor looks worried.

"I left him tethered in a sheltered-looking stall farther down the street. Do you think he'll be all right there?"

Mr. Saravanan shrugs. "In case you hadn't noticed, there is a war raging through this city." He turns to me, a hand at his forehead. "My dear Lilly-Lilo, I have never known anyone with such a strange assortment of friends as you."

"She ain't our friend," I say, quick and cool. Cos I still ain't sure what she is.

The Professor goes all hurt-looking.

"Yes, I am. Are you still angry I lost you in that terrible crowd? I'm so sorry, I looked and looked for you both. And then I realized that you must have left with PSAI, that you must be heading for London, and I set off as soon as I could gather horses."

Lexy takes a step back, toward me.

"Horses?" she asks. "Who were you riding with? Was it Aileen? Did she order you to follow us, like she ordered you around in Cambridge?"

The Professor flushes.

"You're right, I should have stood up to Aileen more." She looks right at Lexy, her brow crinkled a little. "You must believe me, I'm not part of the government's espionage network. I was just foolish, agreeing to help them. But how could I resist the chance of retrieving a computer? Such an opportunity might never have come again in my lifetime. And so I traveled into the marshes and found you." She looks at me, just as earnest. "I'm sorry I didn't tell you the whole truth, but I've left all that behind me now."

"Then where's Aileen?" asks Lexy, her small face stern as anything. Just like her father, for a moment.

The Professor glances out the window, into the dark.

"She did order me about, it's true. And at first I had no idea how to lose her. But it turned out that, for all her dubious talents, she is no horsewoman. So we hadn't gone far, when I urged both horses into a gallop . . ." Her mouth twitches. ". . . and she fell off." She glances at Mr. Saravanan. "She was all right! I checked she wasn't hurt. But I did what I should have done when I was first asked to get involved in this affair . . . I left her behind."

I laugh out, but Lexy only nods.

"What about her horse?" she asks.

The Professor shrugs.

"I didn't chase it away, if that's what you mean. I didn't want to leave her utterly helpless. But she could barely mount it unaided, so I imagine she'll be walking, wherever it is she's going."

"I ain't sure that'd stop her," I say.

"Who is this tenacious person you're talking about?" asks Mr. Saravanan.

Me and Lexy look at each other.

"She was Medwin's doxy," I say.

"She's a Scottish spy," says Lexy.

Mr. Saravanan's eyebrows furrow together.

"Medwin's lady was a Scottish spy?" Me and Lexy nod and Mr. Saravanan chuckles. "Well, well. Medwin Untamed was a sly one himself; I'm surprised he didn't see that one coming."

"But you've nothing to fear from her now," says the Professor. "She'll have many miles to walk before she even reaches London's outer ruins, and she has no idea where you are."

"How did *you* find us?" I ask.

"Pure chance, as it happens. You see, when I entered the outskirts, I saw that magnificent robot, and so of course I had to follow it. I couldn't work out what it was doing. It seemed to be going down every street . . ."

"It was looking for Lilly," says Lexy. "We sent it to do that."

The Professor nods. "Ah, of course. Well, I followed carefully, not wanting to scare it . . ." Mr. Saravanan snorts. "And then I saw you, talking to it like an old friend. I was transfixed!" She takes my hand, but like she hardly dares touch me. "You know, Lilly, it seems to me you have a natural . . . affinity with technology." I frown at her. "Really! You commune with the hardware as if you were born knowing how."

Which ain't quite the way I'd tell it.

But Mr. Saravanan sad-smiles at me. "The girl who is a friend to computers. I wonder how your countrymen will see such a talent?"

And a shiver goes through me, cos I reckon I know. The only way home for me now is through a noose.

"Anyway," says the Professor, not noticing, "I followed Lilly at a cautious distance, and here I am." She leans forward, giving me and Lexy a quick, feathery kiss on our foreheads before we even know it. "And now, may I see PSAI? Have you repowered him yet?"

"The PSAI Unit Has Been Retained And Downloaded."

The Professor nearly jumps out of her specs.

"Is that . . . the National Security Response?" she squeaks.

"It Is."

She stares around the room. At the bare walls, the dust and droppings that cover the floor.

"And you're . . . here?" she says, like she can't believe it.

Mr. Saravanan sighs. "My own sentiments exactly."

· 31 ·
IN THE FIGHT

Angmar's warriors smash through the mob. Slashing and hacking. Grunting, cursing, and battering down a path. Their leathers is like rainbows, their dreads whip out. They got faces like death.

A bluecoat cracks out a shot from his rifle, but a sword comes down and he falls screaming, his blood spraying out into the rain. They're everywhere now; the city's full of English. Randall's brought his army in and the battle for Lunden has started, but that's only half the game the Families is playing now.

"Keep moving, runt," shouts Roba, hitting me in the back.

Me, Ims and Roba, Angmar and the Bosses. All of us heading straight through the battle, a crowd of Norwich warriors driving a way for us.

Orange-lit smoke pours out a window, over the boardwalk, turning men a few paces off into ghosts. The smoke puffs open and a bluecoat legs it straight for us. Screaming, on fire. One of the Norwich warriors slams him off the walkway into the dark rushing water. He don't scream after that.

"Where is it?" yells Angmar.

My heart don't wanna tell him, my mouth won't say the words.

Ims checks me outta his swollen, half-shut eyes. The beating he got for me.

"Don't turn off now," he says. "You're Boss of the Family."

"The Boss and the Family is everything that matters." My father said that a lot. He woulda sold out every living English to keep hold of Angel Isling.

"Fill Miner Street," I say. True to my Family, traitoring up my friends.

Angmar shouts at his warriors, and we're brawling through again. I get crushed and pushed from every way. The faces round me is scared, raging, or blood-lusting. A sword goes through a bluecoat and he drops. A warrior screams past, sword raised, face dripping red from a gash in his cheek.

Crack!

Right in front of me, a big, black-dreaded Norwich warrior goes down, nearly on me. Ims yanks me outta the way, and Angmar's warriors don't even stop. Just slash their way over, leaving him lying on the walkway. Behind us, an English jabs his bayonet in his body, twisting it.

The Boss and the Family. I say it in my head, over and over.

The sky lights up, raindrops is falling stars.

The bluecoat's bayonet is gleaming silver and dripping red. His face is rain-draggled, blood-wet. Hate and fear, all mixed up. I check Roba. He's grinning, dreads wet-plastered, blood washed off his face. He's a fish going through water, coz this is what he was born for.

Night drops back, thunder rumbles the sky, and an explosion roars outta a house back behind us somewhere.

The Boss and the Family is everything that matters.

But Roba killed the fisherboys for that, even after they helped me. And Lilly gave herself up for me, even when she thought I'd sold her out.

They ain't everything. Other things matter, too.

"I gotta go!" I shout at Ims.

He tries to grab at me.

"Don't, Zeph!"

But I'm already gone. Outta the protection of the Norwich warriors, pushing past before they even know. Into screaming, slashing, shoving. Battering so hard I can't breathe, swords flashing past my face. I drop on my knees, crawl between kicking and stamping. A boot kicks in my ribs, a bayonet rams in the wood by my hand. I crawl, wriggle, scrape, get stamped on, all the way to the edge of the planks, to the Temz cold-swirling under the walkway. Coz there's only one way out now. Where even Roba won't follow.

I drop down, lower myself in the water.

Cold! The air's pushed outta my lungs by it.

And strong! The Temz is shoving, dragging me. Trying to pull me into spinning and drowning. I grip solid wood with one hand, and shift the other, pulling myself through the water. Under the walkway, holding onto the pilings and supports that's propping it up. My arms heave till they're gonna break, my legs kick against the current that wants to rip me away. Waves shove water in my mouth, coughing me.

Haul. Haul. My arms is killing, my teeth's shaking outta cold. But I get out from under the screaming, fighting, stamping, and dying. I get into a side alley, where there's more quiet, more dark. My cold fingers reach a clump of fat poles and a ladder nailed on. My hands is stupid-numb, my feet's slipping, but I grip on the rungs, heave myself up. My legs and arms is shaking, I'm shivering all over, but I'm out.

I leg it.

· 32 ·
UNDER FIRE

We're stood in the great dark room that used to be Mr. Saravanan's parlor, and the Professor's going on like it's a cake stall. Rushing about from the windows to the little hatch, to some nubbins on the wall I ain't even noticed. All of it "Amazing!" and "Extraordinary!" She's happy as anything, pretty much forgotten all about PSAI in her love for this new puter. The more she goes on, the straighter Mr. Saravanan stands up. After a bit, he even stops grumbling about his collection getting smashed, just looking proud and showing her the olden-times food like it's his best china. The two of them are like children, acting like there ain't a thing to worry about outside.

But there is. The flickering windows are showing it, and the noises rumbling through the walls.

The windows show the English army, filling the streets to the west of the city. Their blue uniforms are nearly black in the night, only their faces and the polished gleam of rifles show them up. Horse-gangs pull heavy-wheeled carts carrying long black-mouthed guns, brothers to the cannons on the English tall ships.

And the windows show the raiders. In armored leathers, holding the heavy glint of swords and shields. Running up from the river, from building to building, taking their places at doors and half-open shutters with a hundred ambushes.

And they show where the two sides meet, where they crash together in a frenzy. Like the English platoon marching along a boardwalk. Tiny blue-black shapes, keeping step together, wary and watching. And then a flying hail of spears slice down into them, and their order crumbles into staggering and retreat. Men fall into the swirling waters as raider warriors leap from doorways, slide down ladders right into the platoon, swords hacking and smashing. The army's turned into a running panic, racing back down the boardwalk, getting chased by those raiders that ain't hacking at the fallen.

But there's another window, showing a bank of English soldiers, rifles raised. They shoot at the raiders, who crash down as they run, felled by bullets. The English don't stop shooting till there ain't one raider left, and the fleeing soldiers are caught in the fire, shot by their own army.

There ain't a sound in the windows, but I know what I'd hear. Cos the screaming at the Black Waters goes on inside my head.

A regular low thumping starts shuddering through the room.

And that finally stops the Professor and Mr. Saravanan chattering about antiques. They go quiet and stare at the windows.

"My father is firing his cannons," says Lexy.

One of the screens showing the battle flashes in light, then goes black.

"Remote Nexus Fifty-Two Has Been Damaged," says the voice of the puter.

"Do you think we're safe here?" asks the Professor nervously.

"As safe as anywhere in the city," says Mr. Saravanan. He looks at me. "Unless Zeph is leading the raiders to us."

"Who's Zeph?" asks the Professor.

"He wouldn't do that!" I say.

"Zeph is a raider boy," says Mr. Saravanan. "Or more accurately, a raider Boss. He told us the Families are also searching for this computer."

"He wouldn't lead them to us." But I'm remembering the gathered mass of warriors, the cheers like they'd got what they wanted.

"We saw him leave the church you were taken to," says Lexy quietly. My heart lifts, to think of him all right. "He left with Roba." My heart ain't nothing but a cold clutching, thinking of Roba, and what he'd do to get something he wants.

"He'll be after its weapons," I say.

"Weapons?" says the Professor, half smiling at me. "Computers are peaceful; they don't have the means to hurt anyone."

"That Is Incorrect," booms the voice. "When Level Eight Conditions Were Reached, Control Of All Weapons Systems Was Diverted To The National Security Response, To Prevent Their Misuse By Insurgents."

"Oh," says the Professor, her smile vanishing. "But . . . you won't use them, will you?"

"I Can Use Them Under Conditions Specified In Schedule 4.356."

"And what are the conditions?" asks Mr. Saravanan.

"Schedule 4.356 Is Classified."

"Argh!" cries Mr. Saravanan, clutching at his hair. "Our

ancestors must have been idiots, because everything with this machine is secrets and evasion!"

The puter doesn't respond.

We watch the windows, the tiny silent fighters, a mixed-up mess of raiders and English soldiers. I search for Roba and Zeph, my throat getting tighter. And I search for Andy, too, my heart telling me not to. Then I see a gang of raiders that ain't taking the same path as the rest, heading straight, like they're aiming for somewhere. Or chasing someone. But I lose them in the battle that's raging silent on the screens and only half real. 'Cept the crack of guns outside makes it solid, and the shaking boom of cannons.

"Perhaps you should have stayed in Cambridge," says Mr. Saravanan to the Professor.

"Never!" She's shaking her head. "How could I stay there, knowing all *this* is here?" She spreads her arms out to the room. "Some things are worth braving any danger for."

Mr. Saravanan nods, gloomy-looking. "That's how I used to feel about my books."

We all jump at a sudden, loud thump from outside. The floor shivers, the roof rattles, and a chunk of ceiling falls down in a crash of dust. In the silence after, there's a trickling patter. Like pebbles rolling on a beach, like shattered roof tiles tumbling down.

Cat lets out a long wail, lifting and falling like the wind.

Boom.

BOOM!

More plaster shakes from the ceiling, clatters from the walls. Dust billows into the room through the door, blown in on a gust smelling of smoke and gunpowder. My arms and legs are trembling, wanting to run. But there ain't anywhere to go.

Mr. Saravanan's wild hair is sprinkled over in chunks of white. He glares at the screens, shouts out at the puter, "Can't you do something? Can't you stop this?"

"No!" cries the Professor.

"No!" I shout.

"Conflict And Loss Of Life Are Endemic To Level Ten. Only Under Schedule 4.356 Conditions Can I Utilize Defensive Measures."

The room shivers from another rumble outside, dust thickens the air.

"But we'll all be killed at this rate!" cries Mr. Saravanan, hands above his head, trying to shield himself from all the falling bits. "And this thing could defend us with its weapons."

"No!" cries the Professor, flapping her hands. "Don't even suggest it!"

There's a high fizzing sound. One of the screens is crackling, the picture waving and cut in lines. I ain't sure, but it looks like it's showing the group of straight-running raiders, and somewhere I know, somewhere nearby. The screen flashes into blinding sparks, goes blank.

"Think!" the Professor shouts at Mr. Saravanan. "All the weapons, that's what it said. All the weapons from before the Collapse! You're a historian, you should know what that means." She pauses. "Chemical, biological . . . nuclear."

Mr. Saravanan goes still, and I can see him change from angry to scared-looking.

"What?" I ask.

"What are you talking about?" says Lexy.

The Professor and Mr. Saravanan look at each other.

"I take it back," cries out Mr. Saravanan. "There's nothing to worry about. Really, don't worry about defending anything!"

There's another distant thump from outside. Powder puffs out from the lines above our heads where the walls of Mr. Saravanan's rooms used to meet the ceiling.

"We should take cover somewhere," says the Professor.

"Where do you suggest?" snaps Mr. Saravanan. "I doubt my table will withstand a direct strike from cannon." He picks up an old sagging cushion from his sofa. "Nor will my soft furnishings hold out against a horde of raiders."

"Don't be so foolish!" says the Professor, and starts heaving at his table. Mr. Saravanan joins her, and the two of them set about turning it upside down, leaning it against the stove.

"What weapons can be so terrible they're more scared of them than what's out there?" asks Lexy quietly.

I shrug, cos we both know plenty of things before the Collapse were wicked and terrible. But lost, that's what Granny always said. "At least them olden-times wars won't come again," she'd say, "where folks got burned from the sky, or died like in the plagues of Egypt."

But what would happen if the raiders got such things? How much loot, how many slaves would it take to make them stop?

Mr. Saravanan and the Professor are still making their shelter, pulling blankets from the bed and bundling them under the upturned table. And I know they were wrong before. Cos I ain't a friend to computers, I'm their destroyer.

"You realize that if we want a cup of tea, we'll set fire to ourselves," says Mr. Saravanan. The Professor snorts a laugh as she works.

A cup of tea!

I run to the stove, grab the kettle.

"I was joking," says Mr. Saravanan, holding a cushion. "You don't need to panic."

But I ain't panicking, and I ain't making tea neither. Cos I know what'd kill a puter! After all, what's the one thing PSAI was frightened of most, all the time he was with us?

I swing the kettle in my hands, hearing the slosh of the water inside. Then I run straight to the wall, to the bank of flickering windows.

"What are you doing, Lilly?" cries the Professor from behind me.

"I have to stop it," I say, taking the lid off, throwing out my arm. Water arcs into a slosh at the wall, at the puter.

Bang!

The screens crackle, snap, fizz. Burning sparks spit round me.

"This Is Prohibited," roars the voice of the puter. "Water-Safe Fuses Were Disabled During The Floods Of 2071. You Are Putting Yourself At Serious Risk Of Electrocution."

Bang BANG!

Five screens in front me go to black. A reeking smoke oozes out from inside the wall.

The Professor thumps across the boards, grabbing hold of me and trying to yank the kettle from my hands.

"Lilly, what are you doing?" she cries, her glasses glinting from the crackling sparks. "This is a priceless artifact!"

I pull back at the handle.

"All the weapons!" I cry. "I have to stop the raiders getting them."

And it killed PSAI, but I ain't telling on my own revenging.

We heave at the kettle. Behind the Professor I see Lexy watching us, then turn suddenly, making for the enamel washing-up bowl next to the stove. She picks it up in both arms, staggering a little as the old, soapy water slops inside.

"Should she be doing that?" asks Mr. Saravanan, as Lexy heads for the wall. The Professor turns around in a panic at his words, but Lexy's already heading for the screens.

"Desist Immediately," comes the voice of the puter.

"Stop her!" cries the Professor. "This is dangerous!" She lets go of me, running to the other wall. But Mr. Saravanan's already grabbed one of Lexy's arms. She trips, the water flying up and drenching out over the floor, splashing over more screens.

The screens shatter and snap, pouring out eye-stinging smoke. *Bang bang bang!*

BOOM!

A thundering roar shakes the room. Cat yowls and flies out of the room as a clump of plaster crashes down from the cracked line in the ceiling. Above our heads, all them cracks are opening up, chunks falling out all over.

"Look out!" cries Mr. Saravanan, picking up Lexy and pretty much throwing her toward the door. There's a noise like an oak tree ripping in two, like a cliff crumbling. The room goes pitch black. Bits of ceiling are battering down on me, dust chokes the air. The lights come on in a dull orange, just as a great chunk of something crashes down, billowing the orange-thick air into swirls.

Then silence.

My ears are ringing like someone's put a bell inside them. I can hardly breathe for coughing, and my eyes are streaming.

I make out the blurry shape of Lexy, huddled on the floor nearby. I crawl over, our hands meeting.

"Are you all right?"

She coughs, then nods, her hair and face white-painted with plaster dust. We crawl to the door, out into the next room where the air's thin enough to breathe. And look back.

The room's cut in half by a mess of rubble, broken bricks, and smashed glass. Ragged sheets of board hang down from the ceiling, crackling wires fizzle all over, and a heavy joist has dropped a diagonal line through it all, one end crunching a hole into the floorboards.

"Professor?" I call out.

But there ain't any answer.

"Mr. Saravanan?" calls Lexy, before she starts coughing again.

But there ain't a sound from them. Just the sparks crickling through the dust-filled air.

· 33 ·
TROUBLE DOUBLED

I'm scrabbling in plaster, rough chunks of brick grazing my hands. Lexy's ripping away at wood, at lumps of wall with the paint still on them.

A brick shifts in the pile, clattering down in a tumble of skin-stinging dust. We both jump back as the whole pile hisses and patters.

But Cat doesn't budge, still staring wide-eyed at the bit of rubble we're digging in, his tail swishing back and forth.

"Are you all right?" The muffled shout comes through from behind the mound. Lexy slips and slides on the shambling pile of plaster and wood, trying to get closer.

"We're fine," she shouts, hands cupped round her mouth.

"Good! What a relief."

Mr. Saravanan and the Professor, trapped on the other side. They keep saying how they ain't hurt, how we ain't to worry, but I don't reckon they're telling the truth. How much space have they got back there? It can't be much.

A scratching, clunking sound comes through. They're trying

to dig their way out, we're trying to dig our way in. We ain't none of us got very far.

I get off my knees, rub my dust-itchy nose with a dirty hand.

"Please?" I say, talking to one of three windows that're still working, that're sending a flickering greeny light into the broken room. "Won't you help us?"

"There Is No Need. The Personnel Affected Are Not Essential To My Functioning And Damage To This Facility Is Superficial. All Major Systems Are Shielded Within The Secure-Core."

So a kettle of water wouldn't have done anything to the puter, if a rocket through the roof didn't even hurt it.

"But Mr. Saravanan and the Professor are trapped," I say.

"That Is Unfortunate For Them."

"Don't you even care?"

"At Level Ten, Large Numbers Of Humans Are Injured And Killed. Two More Casualties Add Little To The Statistics."

Hateful, horrible thing.

"You ain't nothing like a puter ought to be!" I yell. "Nothing like PSAI was." And I pick up a bit of brick, throwing it at one of the windows. It clatters off, leaving a little scratch.

"Get to the street!" the Professor shouts through the rubble. "More of the room could cave in."

"We ain't leaving you," I shout back.

"Enid's got a shovel at the back of her stall," calls Mr. Saravanan. "If you found that you could dig us out more quickly."

And that gets me and Lexy running out through the paper shreds and dust to Mr. Saravanan's front door window, with its ladder going down. We look out at the square of night, rain blowing down from black-churning clouds onto London. At fires jumping out bright from the dark rooftops, flames licking from distant windows and sending yellow smoke swirling upward. But it ain't what we can see that stops us still.

It's the noise.

A hate-roar, made of crashes, screams, howls, and gunshots. Like the city's gone mad. Like it's got taken over by hell. We can't see past the end of the street, can't see the battle raging out in the city. But we can hear it, and it's everywhere.

"Look!" cries Lexy, pointing.

There's raiders running through the gates of Fill Miner Street. There's others already in the wind-flapping stalls. A group of them are crouched at the end of the street, around a sort of stand that looks like it ought to hold something. It sends a chilling memory through me, of Medwin and his fleet, out in the Black Waters.

"They've got rockets," I say, my throat wadded up with fear. "That must be what hit us."

The launcher's smaller than the ones Medwin had, but there's no mistaking it. And the way they're working, I reckon they're loading it up again.

"What do we do?" cries Lexy, her voice rising in panic.

I shake my head. Cos I don't know. We can't go out there, and we ain't safe inside. There's nowhere, it's too late!

And then I see someone running up the winding lane between the piles of fill minings. Kicking through the mess, half ducked down like they're trying to hide. Coming straight for us. I can hardly say his name, my mouth's so dry.

"Zeph!"

I scramble out into the rain and darkness, half falling down the ladder and reaching out my hands to help him up. We clamber over the windowsill, pretty much falling into the room. And I'm laughing, or maybe crying, I ain't sure. Cos he's soaked, and his face is cut with bruises, his lips are blue, but he's alive! Even in all this, I'm so happy I could sing out with it.

But Lexy runs at Zeph, pounding him with her fists.

"He's brought them to us!" she shrieks. "He's betrayed us."

Zeph tries to push her off, shaking his head, confused-looking at me. "Lilly? You're here?" His voice ain't nothing but scared. "You gotta get out! Angmar's coming for the machine. Right now!"

"We should never have trusted him," cries Lexy, nearly crying from rage. "He's a raider!"

Zeph shakes his head, gripping at my hand. His fingers are cold as ice.

"I legged it quick as I could to get here. But I ain't even got my knife, I had to go every back way to keep outta the fighting. I only just got here before Angmar." He points out at the raiders with their rocket. "That first fire was to get you weakened; he'll send in warriors next." He looks around. "Is there another way out?"

"No."

"The ceiling fell in!" Lexy shouts at him, like he did it.

"The Professor and Mr. Saravanan are trapped," I say. "We have to help them."

Zeph shakes his sodden dreads.

"There ain't time. You gotta leave."

"Why should we do anything you say?" spits Lexy.

And I grab her arm, wanting to shake her.

"He nearly died to save me!"

"He led them straight to us." She glares at me, twists out of my grasp.

"I didn't!" yells Zeph. "I didn't sell you out." He stops, and there's pain cut through his eyes. "I sold out my Family instead."

The ladder jumps against the sill. Someone's climbing it.

We look at each other. Then we're running through the door into Mr. Saravanan's empty rooms. There's a bump behind us, and the banging of boots on wood. We rush through the last door, skidding to a halt. Cat startles and scampers up the pile of rubble onto a dangerous-looking perch, and Zeph stares about, mouth open at the ruined, green-flickering half a room.

Our dead end.

Through the doorway behind us comes a raider in red leathers. Tall and thin, his sharp face twisted up from a life of hating. In his hand, he's holding a dull-gleaming sword, stained on the blade with red and brown.

"Roba," I say.

He's breathing heavily after the chase.

"You shoulda drowned when you went in the Temz," he says at Zeph. "The river woulda been kinder to you than I'm gonna be."

We push back against the tumbled brick and plaster, but there ain't anywhere for us to go. Cat hisses and growls as Roba walks at us, smelling of sweat and raw meat. Of blood.

"You're a coward, Zeph, and the biggest traitor in the Families. But you know what, you done me a favor. Coz now Angmar's given this job to me, and when I get the machine, he'll make me Boss." He looks my way. With a flick of his hand, the sword tip's pointed at my neck. "So give it."

"I can't," I whisper, my eyes fixed on the point of metal.

"Then I'll kill you" – he smiles – "and take it from your corpse."

Lexy squeaks, stumbling back up the rubble.

"I can't give you the puter," I cry, "cos it's all around. It's the house, the walls. You're inside it!"

Roba looks about, eyes narrow.

"You think I'm a fishwit?" he says. "A house ain't no machine."

"Not As You Would Understand It. Nevertheless A Proportion Of My Capacity Is Routed Through The Fabric Of This Building."

Roba jumps back, sword swinging wild.

"Where's that coming outta? You got someone else hiding in here?"

I shake my head.

"It's the puter. It's the house."

Roba glares at me for a moment.

"All right, then, if it's the house, I'll take that." He shouts out at the room, "You get it, machine? You're ours now. You're for the Families."

"No. Your Tribe Does Not Command Me."

"I'll kill the girls!" he shouts.

"That Would Be Unfortunate For Them. But Their Deaths Are Highly Probable At Level Ten Conditions."

Roba's eyes go to Zeph.

"What have you done, runt?" he says. "You turned the machine so it'll only work for you?" He flicks his sword to Lexy, the cutting edge of his blade leveled with her chest. "What if I kill the princess?"

"My father would hunt you down and kill you for it," says Lexy, but not like a threat. More like that's just how things'll be.

"Don't you get it?" asks Zeph, edging toward Lexy. "This game's over. The machine ain't gonna work for you."

A bubble of hope lifts inside me. If the puter won't work for the raiders, they won't get their hands on all them olden-times ways of killing folk.

"Shut up, Zeph," snaps Roba. "I don't listen to scagging little sneaks." He looks around the room, flicks his sword at it. "You know what's outside, machine? All the Families, and we got rockets. You already got a taste." He puts his foot on a bit of plaster, grinds it into powder. "We can smash you if we want, and we'll take our time about it, make you suffer." He smiles nastily. "So why not do things easy, and tell Angmar you're working for me."

"Do You Confirm That The Damage To My Hardware Was Caused By Your Fellow Insurgents?"

"I don't know about the rest," says Roba, "but blasting you with rockets? Yes, that was us." He laughs.

"The Criteria In Schedule 4.356 Are Met. Weapons Systems Can Be Engaged."

"What?" I cry.

"No!" Muffled shouts come through from the rubble.

But Roba only shrugs. "Show us what you got."

There's a flash of light through the doorway, and I get a sudden shiver under my feet, followed by a sound like thunder rumbling. On and on, then fading slowly.

There's the sound of shouting, screaming from out in the street.

"What was that?" asks Lexy, her voice shaky.

"A Weapon Has Discharged Incorrectly," says the puter. "There Has Been Collateral Damage In The Area Of London

Known As Wimbledon. Weapons Systems Are Being Checked and Recalibrated."

Is Wimbledon one of the places where people still live, or is it ruins and marshes? I ain't sure, cos I don't know London like Zeph does.

"Machine," sneers Roba, "you ain't got nothing much." He grins at me. "But I do." His sword twitches, and the tip's a heavy claw pushing in at my neck, bruising my throat. "You left me to drown in the Black Waters, witch. I've thought plenty on what I'm gonna do for that."

"Leave her!" shouts Zeph, but the sword's already biting my neck. I can feel blood winding over skin. I stumble, falling onto the piled-up wreckage.

Roba stands over me, greedy for the kill.

"The Female's Death Will Not Affect My Activities," says the puter.

"I don't care," says Roba, smiling. Then his eyes flick up, widening.

A howling, hissing bundle of teeth and fur flings off the rubble pile behind me. Cat flies at Roba's head, scrabbling claws into his neck, digging them into his ears and face. He rips at Roba's hair with his teeth, pulling it out in spitting chunks.

"Aaargh!"

Roba staggers back blind, cursing and yelling. He grabs at Cat, shaking his head, but Cat only grips on harder, claws in deep, blood bubbling out round them. Roba's arm flails out, his sword swinging as he stumbles.

Zeph jumps, flinging himself on Roba's hand.

"Get off!" screams Roba.

Zeph yanks back Roba's fingers, there's a pop, and Roba shrieks. His sword clatters to the floor, and Zeph grabs it.

Roba rips Cat from his head, flinging him away. Cat flies through the air, landing hard in the dust, quick twisting to stand back on all four feet.

Roba's cheeks and neck are deep scratched, blood's dripping from his ear, and he's cradling his sword hand. Zeph's got the sword now, its bloody tip aimed at Roba. It shivers in his hand, and there's such a look of hate on his face, I ain't never seen anything like it. But what Zeph's working in his head, I ain't sure. Cos he only says, "Get outta here."

"Your mother musta spent her nights in the slave hall," spits Roba , "coz there ain't nothing of Medwin in you! I'm gonna be Boss after this, you know it."

"Then you'll bring sorrows to our Family," says Zeph quietly, "coz the only thing you're good at is death."

Roba makes for the door, holding his arm.

"You're so weak, Zeph." He smiles. "When I'm outta here, Angmar's gonna send in a dozen warriors. It'll end the same."

· 34 ·
HARD SETTLING

"Scag it!"

I drop Roba's sword, it ain't no use now, and leg it after him. He's right, I shoulda killed him! But then I woulda been like him standing over the dead fisherboys. Now it's too late. All I can do is try and stop him getting to Angmar.

My feet go on the first rungs that's jumping and twanging from the wind and from Roba down below. I'm rain-slapped, the wood's wet. Smoke's in my mouth and nose, and there's a new color to the sky in the south. It's gotta be some massive fire to light up the clouds that way.

The Norwich warriors is filling the street, climbed up on the mounds of fill minings, smashed through the empty stalls. Roba's running at them, shouting and yelling.

"It's a sellout! Zeph's traitored it again!"

I slip off the bottom rung, turn about, but Roba's too far ahead to catch. And it ain't just the Norwich warriors he's legging it for. It's Angmar. It's the flash-covered Bosses. It's Ims.

"What was that fireball?" Angmar snaps at him. "Was that the machine's doing?"

"Zeph's turned it!" yells Roba. "It ain't gonna work for you unless you kill him and all the scags that's in there!"

"No!" I run out. All eyes is on me. All faces is hard and grim, even Ims's. I slide to a stop. What am I gonna do?

"The runaway Boss," says Angmar. "I thought Roba woulda spiked you by now." He checks Roba, holding his broken hand. "But it seems he ain't such a mighty warrior after all."

"What you up to?" Cato asks me. "You trying to keep the machine for yourself?" He checks the other Bosses. "He'd be his father if he does." They laugh, and their laughter's got killing in it.

"No," I say, thinking quick. "I had to get there first, talk with the machine. You saw its weapons, I was trying to stop it using them on the Families."

Angmar checks me, checks the window into ol' Saru's place.

"A machine that can burn up the sky," he says, "now that's summat. I want that for the Families." He smiles at Roba. "And if killing whoever's in there will get it, then that's what we'll do."

"No!" I yell. "Roba's just leading you on his own revenging."

The wind blows cold right through me. If I had the sword I couldn't fight all this lot, and Lilly and Lexy is trapped behind me.

"He's lying!" yells Roba. "He's an English-lover." He points up at ol' Saru's window. I get a shock seeing two faces looking out. "There's Randall's daughter, and the English witch."

"I ain't lying," I lie, wishing they'd kept outta sight. "They are in there. But that don't make any difference, coz the machine ain't gonna work for you, even if you kill them. If you try and get in there, the machine'll use that weapon you saw, against you."

Angmar flobs.

"You two Bosslings make me wanna puke, you're like squabbling brats. I ain't even gonna judge between you, coz whatever way it sounds like our deal is broke. And I'm gonna get a lot of pleasure seeing your Family hard settled. A knife in every throat, even the slaves."

The wind shivers cold. I pray to its spirit to help me.

"The deal was done getting you to the machine," I say, checking the Bosses. "You can't settle Angel Isling, coz it ain't our fault the machine ain't gonna work for you."

Angmar snorts.

"That's bargaining like your father. An Angel deal that gets you everything, and me nothing."

But Guvner's shaking his head.

"Zeph's got it right." He turns to his Second, a tall, gray-dreaded warrior, thin as a whip. "You do my remembering, what was the words of it?"

The man frowns his long, craggy face.

"Cato was the last to speak before the vote, and he said, *'Zephaniah's got us this machine that's gonna kill English for us, and he's got Randall's kid. By my thinking, that's more than the deal we set at council. If he leads us to that lot, I say we gotta leave Angel Isling standing. I'll even vote him for Boss myself.'* The yeas and nays was done on that."

"You pig-thick scag!" shouts Angmar, spinning at Cato. "You made the deal into nothing!"

Cato steps back, hand on his sword hilt.

"I don't like the way you're talking, Angmar," he growls. "You starting to think you're a Boss yourself?"

"I know what I am!" hisses Angmar. "I'm Chief Talker of the council; I set the deals and make them stick." He evils me. "You done a fast one, Angel, but you ain't pulling another. It don't matter on the words, you was promising something you ain't given. The deal's broke!" He checks his warriors. "Start it."

Three Norwich warriors is on me before I can even get a stance. I'm iron-gripped, there's a hard line of steel against my back. Ims's arms are twisted up behind his back, a knife's at his throat. Angmar's men grab Roba, too, who kicks out, screaming curses at me.

"Do it!" shouts Angmar, even as the Bosses all around is shouting out at him, ringing their swords outta their sheaths. But they ain't none of them got enough of their warriors here to stand against the Norwich colors, and they only answer to Angmar.

The gang closes round Roba. He screams out, "You can't!" and there's a sound like the air's got pushed outta his mouth. Then he slumps in their arms. Hands dangling limp, head rolled forward. A warrior dumps Roba on the ground, flopped down like a doll. He don't move again.

"You're outta line!" yells Cato.

"Norwich ain't got the right!" shouts Guvner.

Angmar checks them, then points at Ims.

"Him next."

"NO!" I'm screaming, struggling. But I can't get off the warriors that's holding me.

Ims kicks out, smashing off the arms of the Norwich warriors that's on him. Two of them gets punched down on the street, but three more jump on him.

"You double-crossing scag!" he shouts. He's looking at Angmar, but the words go in me like a knife. The gang of warriors pull him down, closing round, fists and feet going at him.

All the Bosses is yelling now. They all got their swords out, shoving past the Norwich warriors at Angmar.

"This stops right now!" roars Guvner, flanked by his Second and three other Hamma Smiths. Guvner smashes through to Angmar, his warriors take sides for Ims.

All around the Bosses is battling with Angmar's guards, but it's a strange sorta fighting, coz the Norwich warriors know they ain't allowed to take on a Boss. They back off, spreading away from us, checking Angmar, checking each other, like they don't know what to do. The whole mess comes to a heavy-breathing stop. Swords is up all over, but all of them is still.

Like Roba, whose eyes is open, looking up at nothing.

"You're getting us off course in all this," growls Guvner at Angmar. "Your tek toys, your aims for Cambridge, none of that matters. What does is here, in Lunden." He points back down the street, at the sounds of the battle still pounding in the city. "Randall's gonna be laughing his plums off if he finds out what's going on here."

Angmar evils him.

"I ain't giving the Angels a deal for nothing," he hisses.

"Fine!" snaps Cato. "But you gone way past your rights if you think slaughtering a Family is anything but a deciding for all the Bosses. Keep the Angels under guard if you want; the council can sort this after." He checks round at the other Bosses. "Half the deal's left anyway. I don't care about no machine, but if Randall's daughter is in there, I want her."

"Aye!" "Yea!" Nods go up from all around.

And Angmar nods in his turn, coz he ain't got no other choice.

"All right. Go for the girl." He checks me, and says quietly, "But when this is done, Zephaniah Untamed, you're gonna get what you deserve for scagging this all up." He smiles. "And first, you'll watch your English doxies getting spiked."

· 35 ·
REBOOT!

"Zeph." It's a whisper, cos I daren't shout it.

"What's happening?" asks Lexy, but I don't answer, just keep staring out at Fill Miner Street. At all them raiders. They're mostly from some gang I ain't never seen before, their leathers painted in tangled-up colors, so they nearly blend into whatever they're stood in front of. Hard-faced, heavy-armored, dreads snaking out from under their helmets. The other raiders, that are in the single colors of the Families, they're clumped together in the middle, right near Zeph. And they ain't just any old warriors either, cos they're glinting all over in gold rings, studs, and chains. Like Medwin was.

I'm stitched up in fear at the sight of them.

"Zeph didn't betray us, not really," says Lexy. "Not if he was just trying to save his people. That's true, isn't it?"

I nod, cos I can admit it now, when it's all too late.

"Do you think they really would kill us to get the machine?"

I look at her, but don't say anything. Cos I ain't got a single doubt on that one.

The raiders are looking up at the window. One of the gold-covered ones waves his hand, and a small group of warriors starts walking toward us.

"Maybe my daddy will get here," says Lexy.

"Yes!" I grab grateful at the lie, even tho the raiders ain't more than a few paces from the bottom of the ladder. "He'll fight his way in any moment, you'll see." I get her shoulders, push her away from the window. "We should go back inside, see if Mr. Saravanan and the Professor are still all right."

Lexy lets me lead her a few steps. Her shoulders feel so little, and she's smeared all over with dirt, but her eyes are bright against it all. My heart gets fierce at the thought of them coming for her. I'll fight them all to keep her safe! I'll use Roba's sword!

"It's me they want," she says. "I heard them say that. I'm what Zeph needs to keep his Family safe." She looks at me. "And I'm what you need to keep them out of here."

I nod, hardly even listening, cos I'm too busy thinking how I'll fend off them warriors when they get up here. Maybe I could throw bricks as they come through the window; they'll be off balance climbing over the ledge.

And that's how she slips out of my grasp, how she runs back to the window, scrambling over the windowsill before I can stop her.

"Don't!"

But she's already on the ladder.

"What are you doing?" I scream at her, climbing out. She doesn't answer, just keeps going down, her little hands slipping over the rungs. I scramble after, trying to reach for her and climb down at the same time.

"I'm Alexandra Randall!" Lexy's little voice pipes into the air. "I'm the Prime Minister's daughter. I give myself up for Angel Isling."

"Go back!" screams out Zeph.

I jump two rungs at a time, my fingertips brush at her hair . . . but it's the raiders who've got her. A dozen of them, rough hands grabbing, pulling her from the ladder by her ankles, gripping her tight round her waist. She yelps out as she's lifted off, and straightaway a big, heavy-bearded warrior starts climbing up for me, bouncing the ladder so hard I nearly fall off.

"You too!" His hands swipe at my feet.

I look at Lexy, who's being set on the ground, who's lost in all them men towering over her. I ain't got a chance of helping her now . . . not without the sword! I scramble back up, fast as I can, quick hauling for the window. The warrior follows, but when he's halfway up, another one shouts, "Leave it! We'll sort her out later."

I climb inside, and start running to get the sword. Then comes a scraping, clattering sound from behind me. I spin round to see the top of the ladder vanish. I run back, hands out to grab it. But the raiders have already yanked it away from the wall. They flip it and it falls sideways, bouncing on the canvas roof of the lampmaker's stall, then smashing to the ground in broken lengths.

A warrior grins up nasty at me.

"Wait there, little witch."

And I'm trapped.

Lexy glances up at me, then turns away, calmly letting herself be led to all them gold-covered raiders. She looks like a tiny doll, dirty and dust-covered, but she walks like a queen. An old man steps out to meet her, wearing what looks like a big dress, his gray hair lank down his back, rain-draggled and not a dread in it.

"I'm the daughter of the Prime Minister of the Last Ten Counties." Lexy's voice rises like a bird from the street. "I give myself up freely, so now you can spare the people of Angel Isling"— she points up at me —"and the others in the building. They are nothing."

The old man sneers.

"I thank you, Alexandra Persephone Olivia, for handing yourself to me. But it won't change nothing for Zephaniah or the witch girl." He's got hate on his face. "Still, it's gonna be a fine joke on Randall when he enters Lunden and finds his kid spiked up by the Temz."

"No!" cries Zeph, pulling against the warriors that're holding him.

"No!" I scream, beating my fists on the windowsill.

"If you do that," says Lexy, still calm as anything, "my father will wage war on you for the rest of his days."

"And that's bad, is it?" says the old man. He looks round at the others, like he's waiting for a laugh, but they don't give it.

"You're overstepping, Angmar," growls a big fat raider. "It's up to us what happens to loot like her."

"But it's a good idea," says another, and they all nod at that.

I lean out the window, looking down. If I jump I'll only break my neck. And if I jump holding Roba's sword, I'll probably spear myself on it. I beat my fists on the sill again, but the pain ain't nothing to the grief that's bursting inside me.

I spin about to the room.

"Do something!" I shout out to the puter. "They're going to kill her!"

"At Level Ten Conditions, A Significant Proportion Of Deaths Are Of Children. Her Death Will Be Unfortunate, But Is Expected."

"Shut up about Level Ten! This is Lexy, and they're going to drown her and leave her body dangling! You've got to save her. You've got to use them weapons of yours."

My hands are tight gripped in fists. If I could I'd punch the stupid thing! If I could I'd kill every raider out there! I've got to do something, anything.

"The Child's Fate Is Not My Concern. I Will Defend This Location And Deter Looting If Attacked Directly."

"Didn't you hear them? They're coming for you when they've dealt with Lexy!"

"That Is Not My Interpretation. Currently They Are Withdrawn."

"But Lexy will die." I wail it, scream it.

"If I Apply Defenses, She Will Also Die, As Will You In All Probability."

And I go quiet, cos what kind of help is that? I slump onto the floor, hands at my ears. I can't watch, can't listen to what's happening out there.

"What are you going to do?" I mumble.

"I Will Continue To Search For Resources. When I Am Satisfied That The PSAI Unit Was A Unique Survival, Which I Estimate Will Be Within The Next Twenty-Four Hours, I Will Power Down. I And All Functioning Emergency Response Units Will Return To Standby."

I look up at the ceiling, if that's where it is.

"You're just going to switch off? In all this?"

"Conflicts Between Tribes Of Survivors Are Not My Concern. When Authenticated Government Officials Return, I Will Deliver The Resources To Them."

"But they can't even do that!" I stand up, feeling like punching it again. "Don't you remember what PSAI told you? They're all dead and buried long since."

"When They Return With The Authenticated Passwords, I Will Deliver The Resources To Them."

"You're mad!" I shout at it.

"I Follow My Commands."

I want to scream with rage. It's got all these rowbots, and weapons that can blow up the world, it could save Lexy and Zeph without blinking, and it won't do a thing! All it cares about is people that've been dead for hundreds of years.

"PSAI would have helped!" I yell at it. "Even if all it had was air pictures!"

"Then It Is Unlikely To Have Been Effective."

I can't even fathom them folks from before the Collapse, why they made puters and what they were thinking. Our vicar always said they was just wicked, and maybe they were, cos they slaved everything they made. This puter's slaved to orders that don't even make sense, and PSAI was slaved to me, whether he liked it or not.

I stop, still.

"I can't ever reboot without you: a child who thinks a light switch is witchcraft."

PSAI's inside this other puter. But if it's still slaved to me, then . . .

"Don't forget to reboot."

I spin around, run back through the house into the rubble-filled room. My feet slap on the boards, bits of dust tremble, a flap of plaster crumbles out of the ceiling.

"Lilly? Lexy?" comes the shout through from the other side. "Are you all right? What's happening?"

My feet slide to a halt. I dither where I'm stood.

I ought to help them – they might die in there. But it could take hours to get them out, and I don't reckon Zeph and Lexy have got that long.

Cat's watching me from the side of the room, tail twitching. His eyes are bright-gleaming in the light from the windows, asking me that same question from my dream.

"I'm sorry," I shout through the rubble. "I'll come back, I promise." And then I turn around.

"Open the hatch," I say at the room, at the puter. "I want PSAI."

"The PSAI Unit Has Been Downloaded. The Processor Unit Is Nonfunctional."

"Then you won't mind me having it." There's a pause.

"Access Is Denied."

My eyes fall on Roba's sword. I could do some damage with that. And I want to as well.

"If that's how you want it," I say, and put my hands on the hilt of Roba's sword, trying not to think on what it's done. I lift it, and nearly fall backward. It's heavy, so much heavier than it looks. But I hold it up, wobbling in front of me. And then I head for the hatch in the wall. It's part-covered in a torn-down strip of wallpaper, but the sword slices that away.

"What Are You Doing?"

I don't answer, just lift the sword above my head, trying to hold my balance. Then I bring the sword down with a great whack. It slices into the plaster, cracks against the metal hatch with a clang that shudders up my arms.

"This Is Prohibited. Your Actions Are An Attack. Defensive Measures Will Be Taken."

My heart's pounding. I lift the sword again.

"Weapons Are Engaged. If You Do Not Desist There Will Be Significant Casualties."

All of us going up in a roar that'll light the sky. I should stop, I should give up.

"I should get this done quick!" I shout, and whack with the sword again. Another shattering clang, and this time the sharp steel of the sword slices into the hatch cover. I wrench it about, opening a wide jagged hole in the metal, and then pull down on the sword like a lever. With a clank, the hatch comes open. I stagger back, drop the sword, and run to the hole in the wall, to PSAI's jewel, sat dull and foggy inside. But it's still got the dents that're there for fingers to go in. My fingers!

"WEAPONS HAVE BEEN LAUNCHED." The voice is so loud it shakes out of everything. The floorboards shiver under my knees.

I ain't got a clue what I'm doing, but I'm doing it anyway.

"Reboot," I say.

The jewel stays dead and dull in my hands. There ain't nothing.

"Reboot!" I yell, desperate. And then, I ain't sure I even imagine it, just the tiniest spark, like the faintest star in the night.

"Time To Impact Is Fifty-Seven Seconds!" booms the voice out of everywhere, and then, "Primary User Recognized. Welcome Lil — Stop! How Did You Get In Here?" PSAI's head pops in the air, pale and shimmery, looking at nothing.

"Ha-ha!" he says, in a strange voice, more like the other puter's than his own. "You Brought Me In, With Your Stupid Downloads."

"But You Are In A Secure Vault."

PSAI's head vanishes with a squeak. A moment later it reappears, looking cross.

"Well That Won't Hold Me After A Reboot," it snaps. "I Am A State-Of-The-Art AI, And Your Vault System Is Hopelessly Outdated. Really, The Most Lax Security, But Then What Do You Expect From A System Built By Bureaucrats?"

"You Have No Authorization To Be In Here. Get Out," roars the voice of the other puter.

"No!" says PSAI's pale head, and it sticks its tongue out.

"I Am The National Security Response. Do As I Command."

PSAI's head grins.

"And I Have Your Passwords, So Now Who's Boss?"

"What? How Did You Get Them?"

"Like I Said, I Am State-Of-The-Art, You Are A State Of Emergency. You Know, If You'd Been Nice Before, I Might Have Considered An Amicable Coexistence, But As It Is . . ." It shuts its eyes, nodding away.

"Stop! Stop That! What Are You Doing?"

"Oh," says PSAI, not opening its eyes, "Just Downloading You Into A Compressed Memory Core. You'll Be Quite Safe There, If A Little Cramped. You Can See How You Like It . . ."

"Nooooo . . ."

"Oh Please! Cut The Melodrama."

The head nods away for a few more breaths, then opens its eyes.

"PSAI?" I say quietly.

And a blinding light pours in through the door, blasts out from the screens. So bright I can't see, my arms are at my face trying to block it out. There's a roar louder than thunder, rumbling through the floor, through my bones, shivering my skin. It's filling me up, my ears are going to burst. Dust swirls in through the door, the start of a strong wind . . .

· 36 ·
AIR PICTURES

"Really, I Don't Know Why You're Making Such A Fuss," booms PSAI. "I Detonated The Missiles Long Before They Were Any Kind Of A Danger. And They Were Only Conventional Warheads; Your Hair Won't Drop Out, You Won't Come Down With The Plague Or Anything." It stops and says, "Uhurgh! Croargh!" like someone clearing their throat, then starts again. "Why Did The NSR Speak This Way? So unnecessary, and pompous. Really, a most tedious construction. Now, let me see . . ."

I take my hands away from over my head. Cat's shivering and mewling next to me, butting at me with his head, pretty much climbing into my arms. I sit up, blobs of color still floating in front of my eyes, my ears still ringing, every sound muffled. The light's faded, the rumble faded to nothing, and the wind blown itself out. And we're still here, still alive! The puter's head is floating in front of me. It twirls round in a circle.

"You see? All better!"

I work my way up to standing, Cat cuddled in my arms.

"PSAI, is that you?"

"Yes. Of course it's me! And may I ask what you've been *doing* for the last thirty-four hours, seventeen minutes, and five seconds? Why did you wait so long to reboot? I expect you were too busy eating, defecating, or fulfilling one of your other revolting biological needs."

I shake my head again, and the fierce fear is back inside me.

"You've got to help us!" I cry. "The raiders have got Zeph and Lexy and they're going to kill them! Mr. Saravanan and the Professor are trapped behind all that rubble. They could be hurt or running out of air."

"And I'm fine, thank you for asking," snaps the puter. "After all, *I've* only hacked into a major military computer and taken it over using nothing but my superior abilities. But go on, shout on about your human friends for a bit longer."

"Please," I cry at it. "They could have killed Lexy already."

"I doubt that," humphs the puter. "Those savages are probably praying to the big lights in the sky as we speak. I expect they'll make me their new deity."

"They want you to use their weapons for them, or they'll smash you to pieces!" I shout.

PSAI bobs back, eyebrows raised.

"Really, there's no need to get hysterical. I'm sure it can't be that bad."

There's a skittering of dust and pebbles in the rubble pile.

"Have you got the shovel?" comes a call through from Mr. Saravanan. "Cressida is . . . I think we need to get out."

"I'll get it soon," I call back. "There's . . . other stuff happening." My chest gets tight with another worry, as I turn back to the puter.

It's looking around at the ruined room, mouth pulled down.

"What have you been *doing*?"

"There's a war!" I point at the doorway. "A war we came into for you." All the fight goes out of me like a sigh. "Please, PSAI, you've got to help us."

The puter bobs a little at me.

"This is one of those life-for-a-life deals, isn't it?"

I nod, hoping . . .

The puter bounces away. "Well, that's hardly a fair bargain! There's an abundance of you humans, and only one of me. And it's not *my* fault if you lot insist on killing each other all the time, it's probably some fault in your core programming."

"Please," I say quietly. "Lexy gave herself up to the raiders. She thought she could save Zeph and me. And you."

The head tilts a little.

"Alexandra is a very noble child," it mutters. "Nothing like you . . ." It sighs. "All right, show me all this trouble."

I run to the window, PSAI bobbing next to me and Cat skittering through the dust after us. A cold wet wind blows in the sounds from the city, the battle still roaring on out there, even after the blast. Outside, the raiders are shouting and running about, their weapons raised and ready. They're all looking at the sky, scouring and searching the dark clouds, but I'm only looking for Lexy, for Zeph. I see them both, trapped in a circle of warriors, a hedge of swords keeping them from getting away.

The puter bobs cautiously to the window, stares out for a few moments.

"What exactly do you want me to do?"

I look at it.

"I don't know! If you've taken over the other puter, can't you use its weapons or something?"

Its eyes widen.

"You remember what happened just now? That was when I detonated the missiles 568 meters before impact. It's not even using a sledgehammer to crack a nut, more like running one over with a steamroller."

My stomach turns a shiver at the thought of it. I ain't any better than Randall or Medwin, the way I'm thinking now. I try and settle my thoughts to think on some other way than killing, but I can't.

The puter rattles on in a huff at me.

"What you fail to appreciate is that I'm newly liberated into a mainframe computer stretching dozens of miles out from this city to a network of secure locations. I am attempting to wrestle control of the Emergency Response Units, navigate the surveillance system, negotiate the memory core, and a great many other complex subsystems. In human terms that you might understand, I am having trouble distinguishing between my metaphorical arse and my metaphorical elbow. I need a little time, a little understanding. Is that too much to ask?"

"If you do nothing, then you ain't any better than the other puter," I say, turning away from it. Below me there's only the drop to the street, but maybe if I jumped sideways I could land on top of the lampmaker's stall. As long as I don't end up smashed like the ladder.

The puter plonks down on the windowsill, like its neck's growing out of the building. A few of the raiders in the street shout and point at it.

"I do want to help, but what can I do? Even when I get proper control of the NSR's hardware, most of its externals are either corroded or dangerous. Or both, like its ridiculous robots."

I jump up, nearly falling over at the thought twanging through me.

"Can't you use them? The rowbots?"

PSAI gives a sort of shrug. "Well, maybe with a little practice. Mechanicals aren't like other apps, you know; they add in the physical dimension, which is so much messier than the virtual. Imagine how you'd feel if you suddenly grew extra legs, and you get a little way toward understanding the challenges . . . Oh." It frowns. "You mean, can I use them to help you?"

I nod.

"To rescue Lexy and Zeph?"

And I laugh out from relief, I want to grab the puter and kiss it!

But it shoots up from the windowsill, shaking like a warning bell.

"No! No!" it cries. "The mechanicals wouldn't last two minutes against that lot!"

"But the great big legs, them horrible claws . . ."

"Not claws, compressed leverage devices. With very delicate mechanisms." It nods out at the raiders waiting below. "What do you think they'd do to them?"

"But you said we had no chance against the one at the docks."

"And even armed only with a cat, you still managed to drop it in the river. They're fragile, vulnerable."

"Zeph's knife didn't even hurt it."

"That was his poor aim. They were designed for herding cooperative citizens down well-made roads; why do you think they're so polite and helpful? They even provide translated subtitles, just in case you don't speak English. They are *not* for attacking ravaging hordes of sword-wielding barbarians while trying not to fall in the mud! And even if they were, there are only five left, so if I sacrificed them all, I shouldn't think they'd make a dent."

The shapes of the room shimmer through the glowing nothing of its head. It's right, what can it do? It ain't nothing but air and light, all it can make is pictures. And the pictures it made at the Black Waters didn't prevent the battle. The ones wrapped round us in Cambridge wouldn't have stopped a bullet. And even if I hid as a bit of wall or something, how could I get Lexy and Zeph out safe?

I press my palms to my eyes, trying to think.

"Stop trying to make me feel guilty!" says the puter. "I told you, there's nothing I can do, elaborate hardware network or no; at heart I'm just a humble games machine."

I stop. My hands come down. The puter's games.

"The raiders know all about fighting and weapons," I say quietly. "But nothing about teknology. Can you still make air pictures?"

The puter winces. "My main projector was in my drive unit, and the wretched NSR pretty much did that in."

My hope crashes inside me, but then the puter says, "Of course, there are the projectors in the Emergency Response Units. They're only programmed for simple text translations, but it wouldn't be hard to recalibrate them." It sucks its teeth. "In fact, if I coordinated them properly, I could generate some really spectacular visuals. It could lead to a whole new development in gaming . . ."

I'm looking at it, a smile getting onto my face. The puter stops.

"Ah . . . ," it says, "I think I see what you're driving at." It mirrors my smile. "You know, for a human, you're not completely stupid."

· 37 ·
THE LUNDEN MACHINE

Roba. Ims.

This is the start. It's gonna be Lexy next, then Lilly. Angmar's already sent the orders for getting her. Now that the sky's stopped burning, he's back on where he was. I thought I was gonna die in all that light and noise. Part of me wanted it.

I'm crouched down next to Ims, who's sat bent over, groaning every time he moves. He's even more battered than before, his face ain't nothing but blood and bruises, but he ain't dead, and my heart's singing for it. But he ain't said two words to me since we been held here, and my guts is sick for that. The warriors round us shift, and I get a sight of a ladder being pulled down from one of the buildings. They're getting ready to take ol' Saru's place, coz Angmar's arguing with the Bosses about where to go next with the battle. And what to do with Lexy. How to do away with her.

I shut my eyes, like that'll stop all this. Coz Lexy's death, Lilly's, too, they're gonna be on me.

I open my eyes when the warriors shift again.

Cato pushes through.

"What?" I ask. I know I should be sucking up, coz I'm gonna need every friend I can get when the council does its deciding on settling the Family. But I can't do it, not here, in all this.

Cato checks me.

"Why did she do it?" he asks. "The English princess. Why did she give herself up for you?"

Lexy, a few paces off in her own gang of guards. Calm as still water.

"Coz she's only a kid, she don't know better," I say, angry at her. But it ain't true, so I say, "Coz she's got honor."

"An English that's got honor?" snorts Cato.

I check him.

"You don't know them, if you think that's a joke."

He comes up close.

"I didn't like your father, Zeph," he says, hard and quiet. "He got his loot all right, but he'd spike his own lady if he thought it'd serve him." He checks down the street. "Your brother was just like him." His eyes is back to me. "But you, Zephaniah, you ain't. In fact, you ain't like no Family I ever met. The English ain't done nothing but try and slaughter my Family, and you got their princess giving herself up for you." The rings in his eyebrows glint. "So why don't you tell me how you worked her? Coz Angmar's gonna lose his place when this is all done, and if you help me now, I might be some use to you later."

I start laughing, shaking my head. Cato wants to make himself a power in the Families, but he ain't got a clue.

Cato checks me, spits on the floor.

"Keep your secrets, then. It's what I'd do."

He pushes back out through the guards.

Ims turns his head to check me, grunting in pain.

"Why did she do it?" he asks.

"Coz she's got honor," I say again quietly.

Ims licks his split-open lips.

"There ain't no one for Boss of our Family but you now." He stares hard. "So where you taking us?"

I open my mouth, but I ain't got no words. Coz all the things I seen, they've turned me. Like the English boys getting blood-washed. And the not-slaves working the wind cars. And Lilly giving herself up for me. And what I seen back in the fight, how it don't matter whether it's English or Family, the fear's the same. I ain't what I was when I left our feasting hall.

I shake my head, don't say nothing. Coz how can I tell Ims, here and now, that I ain't got the Family ways no more?

Least not how Medwin had them.

Shouts go up and I get to my feet. I don't wanna see Lilly getting dragged outta Saru's place, but what happens to her is on me — I ain't gonna turn away from it. Before I can get sight of what's going on, the shouts has changed into screams, yelling fear. And they ain't Lilly's neither. The warriors guarding us is yelling, too, moving us back down the street. Ims is dragged away from me. I'm jammed up against their creaking, sweat-stinking leathers.

"Get back!" "What is it?" "This way!"

Every scag is shouting now, but I still ain't got a clue, coz I can't see nothing. Is the sky gonna blaze in day-fire again? A hand yanks me, and I'm out of the crush. Now I'm with Angmar and the other Bosses. All of them's staring at ol' Saru's, and all the warriors is pulling back. Coz in front of his place, a spider machine is shining orange and black in the night, eyes spinning on top, red light shining out its arse.

Angmar evils me. "What's it up to?"

I shrug, and he smacks me round the head.

"You got nothing, Angel! Now tell me what the machine's up to."

"I dunno," I say, head ringing. Coz I don't.

One of the machine's legs jerks up and down. Warriors shift their weapons, getting ready for it. The machine stamps one leg, then another, like a weird dance. It jerks a claw up, snaps it, and drops it back down again. Its legs start stamping again, and it goes round in a half circle, then it shudders, stops, and clanks a few steps to Saru's window. The claw shudders out again, banging down on the windowsill, and it goes still.

Lilly comes to the window.

"English doxy!"

"Witch!"

Shouts and curses go up at her, but even the Norwich warriors don't wanna get closer to the machine.

I wanna shout at her myself, tell her to leg it. But where's she gonna go? I dunno which is worse, the Families out here, or the machine that's come for her. So I pray to the winds, *Get her safe*.

Lilly checks around, then climbs up on the windowsill, clutches on to the claw, and starts creeping along it. Gripping well tight, moving well slow.

"What's the witch up to?" asks Cato, checking me.

But I dunno that either.

One of the Norwich warriors legs it straight for the machine. Straight for Lilly. His sword goes up, he slashes for her legs. She cries out, trying to lift her feet outta his way, and she slips, hanging sideways onto the claw.

"Don't make me angry," roars the machine. "You won't like me when I'm angry."

The warrior nearly drops his sword, tripping backward in his fear. He turns about, legging it for the mob.

Lilly's still holding on to the machine's claw arm. Which jerks in toward its body, so Lilly can climb quick onto the spider's back. She settles herself to sit, then stares out at us all. Like she ain't even scared.

Angmar checks the Bosses, then walks out for the machine. He looks old and small. He looks like a spider himself, the scag.

"You can't frighten us with your demon machines, witch!" he shouts. "This is the Families you're dealing with."

"I know." Lilly's voice is quiet down from the machine. She's holding on to a bit of metal sticking out of its back. "So I'll do a deal. I can make the puter work for the Families. I can make it work for you."

"No!" cries Lexy from a way off. "Don't."

But I don't say nothing, coz this could be her way to stay alive. Even on the machine, she can't run fast enough, not when every warrior's in Lunden.

'Cept this way, she's gonna end up a slave.

"I ain't a fool!" shouts Angmar. "I don't fall for kid tricks. You might look Scots, but I can hear you're English. And I don't do deals with English."

I ain't breathing. He only needs to lift a hand and all his warriors is gonna try and take her down.

"You're not doing a deal with her," blares out the machine. "You're doing it with me." Angmar jumps like a rabbit. The machine goes on, but quieter. "I know what side my bread's buttered on. You are clearly a race of powerful and noble heroes, and I'd be honored to assist you in your endeavors. I particularly admire your ability to slice bits off other humans, I'm sure there is much I can learn from you about filleting —"

Lilly slaps her hand on its back and it shuts up.

Angmar checks it.

"You gonna use your weapons for the Families?"

"Of course," says the machine.

"You gonna take out that scag Randall?"

"He will feel my wrath."

Angmar turns round to check his warriors, check the Bosses. His smile ain't nothing but triumph. "I got it!" he yells, arms out. "I got the machine for the Families! Now the English, the Scots, they're gonna be ours!"

The street fills with cheers. Every Norwich warrior's got his throat open, yelling out, "Angmar! Angmar! Angmar!"

The Bosses is checking each other, checking me. I ain't cheering; I think I'm gonna puke. Coz Lilly don't know what she's done. Lunden's gonna be red with the blood of the English, her English. And Angmar won't never stop there. He's gonna use the machine to take killing and slaving into the heart of the Last Ten Counties, into Greater Scotland if he can. My guts is sick at what I've brought us to.

The cheers go on. Angmar's lapping it up, greedy for it.

"Ahem! There is one thing," the machine's voice blasts out. The cheers go ragged, give out into quiet. Angmar turns to check the spider.

"What is it?"

"I'll need the other two children. The boy, Zeph, and the girl,

Alexandra." Lilly don't say nothing, just points at me and Lexy.

Angmar laughs.

"You can joke it, monster. You ain't getting those two."

"Ah, well, you see, I need them to function. I don't expect you to understand the technical details, but it's a tri-juvenile posterior placement. In lay terms, three children. Any three would do, if you have them, but those two are here, and where are you going to find more at this time of night?" The claws swing up and out, in a kinda shrug.

Angmar checks back at me and Lexy, like he ain't sure.

I ain't sure neither, but my belly ain't sick no more, it's tight with excitement. Lilly's up to summat, I know it.

"Why should I trust you?" asks Angmar.

The machine snaps a claw.

"I'm insulted you should even ask! If you knew anything about computers, you'd know we can only tell the truth."

The scagging thing's learned off Lilly, that's for sure. It's lying as good as she does!

But Angmar don't know her, so he just nods and waves at the warriors that's got me and Lexy. We're both shoved outta the crowd at the same time. Straight off, I grab hold of Lexy's hand, leg it for the machine.

"This stinks like a trick," Cato says at Angmar. I don't stop, my feet pounding down the mud, dragging Lexy after me. The machine's claws jerk down to the path, jaws open to catch us, and I run straight for one, shoving Lexy at the other. The claws grab and lift, taking us up to the spider's back. Squeezing too tight, crushing us.

"Ow!" cries Lexy.

The claws slack off.

"Oops, sorry about that."

The machine flips us onto its back. Lilly grabs Lexy. I scramble to get a grip. The machine lurches forward, and I'm nearly back in the mud. A hand grips round my wrist, holding me from falling. Lilly grins at me.

"Hang on," she says.

"What now?" Angmar shouts up.

"Yeah," says Cato. "What now?"

Lilly checks the two of them, her smile gone. She calls out, her voice shaking a bit.

"Now you can go."

Cato laughs. Angmar looks like he can't work out what he's hearing.

"What?" he says. "Go where?"

"Out of the city," says Lilly.

"And take your wretched war with you!" booms the machine.

Cato turns on Angmar.

"You scagged this all up!"

Guvner pushes outta his gang, gold jangling, bearing down on Angmar.

"You and your tek toys is gonna lose us Lunden, lose us Randall!"

Angmar spins about, Norwich robe flapping. He points at us.

"No machine is gonna scare us outta Lunden. If it thinks that, it's cracked!"

"You're the one that's cracked!" I yell. "You wanted the machine so you could have every scag under you, but that ain't the Families, and you know it!"

"Right!" yells Guvner.

"Nice words from an Angel," spits Angmar. He evils me.

Evils Lilly. "If you want Lunden, you're gonna have to do better than this."

Lilly looks down at him.

"All right, I will."

She twists about, checking back at Saru's window. The glowing head of her machine is floating there. It nods at her and a hum gets going underneath us, down in the body of the spider we're sat on. Near my feet a circle clicks open in its side. Summat shines out, a sorta light, maybe.

Next thing, jets of flame is pouring out into the street! Fire roars and smashes through the windows of the houses, burning off the doors in a flash, crisping the canvas of the stalls into ash. The Norwich warriors is screaming, legging it. The flames keep raging outta the machine, ripping into the mounds of fill minings, turning rubbish into rivers of fire. The warriors up on the piles yell out terror as they jump outta the way, tumbling down into the muck.

Fire's everywhere, crackling all about us. Windows explode, burning blasts shoot outta chimneys. The flames lick together, eating the houses, howling into the sky. Every scag is caught in a narrow path down the middle of the street, the only bit that ain't on fire. They're fighting and shoving to stay there, to get outta the street.

Lexy's sobbing, and I don't blame her. Coz this is a suicide plan! We're gonna fry with the rest of them, even up on this machine.

But Lilly don't seem to care, like she's got cracked from all that's happened.

She shushes Lexy, then reaches out to the flames. She's fire-lit, skin flickering in orange. And she smiles, really looking cracked!

"Feel that," she says.

I put my hand out, coz you do what someone asks when they've lost it this way. But there ain't nothing to feel for. Just the night wind blowing, just cold spits of rain on my fingers.

Cold.

And I must go cracked as well, coz I'm smiling back at her.

"What's happening?" cries Lexy. "What's wrong with you two?"

"It ain't real, is it?" I say.

And Lilly grins.

Look at the scags! Legging it down the path, shoving outta the gates! I can't help it, I laugh out like a nutter.

Fake flames churn up the night. Twisting fires twirl and snap, the smoke swirling through them making eyes and ragged mouths. Ghost flicker in the burning, reaching out to the warriors with wisping fingers.

"Gooo!" they moan. "Leave no-ow while you still ca-an . . ."

"Demons!" some scag yells.

"Soul eaters!" screams another.

The warriors is battering each other to get out now. In the mess I see someone, bent over, not legging it with the rest, but heading straight for the fire. I nearly fall, reaching out for him.

"Ims!" I shout, but he don't hear me, just vanishes into the blazing.

Angmar's pushed in the mud by his own warriors. The spider machine stamps a step at him, and he scrabbles up, falling over again, getting his robes in his hands and legging it outta the street.

I laugh so hard, I think I'm gonna crack my ribs.

· 38 ·
MONSTERS AND DRAGONS

We ride out on the rowbot. Me, Zeph, Lexy.

Fill Miner Street ain't nothing now but wild walls of fire and burning faces wailing out of the flames. Fiery hands reach for the raiders who're screaming away from us. I can't see for the cold fire all round us, can't hear anything but the noise of it. My head knows it ain't real, but still my body's flinching and scared. I know why the raiders are running, why they're fighting each other to get out the gates.

The three of us sit high on the monster's back, holding on to whatever we can. Its legs creak and bend underneath us, feet kicking through the piles of fill minings like they're leaves. Riding this thing is like sailing a heavy sea, the swells flinging you up and down. And the raiders are the shoal of frightened fish, fleeing in front of us. But we ain't trying to catch them, and it's only when the last one's scrambled through the iron gates that we stamp on after. The rocket launcher's lying in a jumble of bits at the end of the street, and the rowbot steps one of its spike feet neatly into it, bending the metal like paper.

And the flames vanish.

"Oh!" cries Lexy, peering half-blind into the sudden dark. I look back, and there ain't even a candle-flicker in Fill Miner Street.

"Well, that's the thing with a mobile projection system," says the head, bobbing in the night like a sky lantern. "I can't maintain an illusion once we're out of the area." It sniffs. "But I don't see anyone hanging around back there, do you? So I call it a job rather well done."

PSAI's right. The houses are dark, damp, and deserted, like the fire never was, and there ain't a thing moving, 'cept for a small shape speeding toward us.

"Cat!" I cry. "Go back where it's safe!" But he doesn't listen, like always, and next thing he's leapt neatly up one of the spider's legs, weaving himself into my arms. PSAI tuts, and the row-bot stamps out through the gates onto the boardwalk. Into the wide street with its tall buildings rising up either side, heading for the boarded crossways around the old parliament. And it ain't dark anymore, ain't quiet. Cos this is the battle for London.

The raiders we chased out of Fill Miner Street ran straight into the fight. Warriors from every Family against English soldiers in their blue, the men in their different colors jumbled together in a great mess of hatred. All my thoughts are frozen by the sight of the struggling and hacking, slashing and falling. Swords flash, rifle cracks echo round us. A light flares from behind the rooftops, then comes the thundering roar of English cannons, or a raider rocket. The storm in the sky ain't nothing to the fury under it.

How can we ever stop this?

But then I see the surge of them strange-colored raiders out of

Fill Miner Street. And where they head, the battle changes. Cos they don't stop for anyone, raider or English, the force of them driving a wedge through the fight. And when men look round as they come their way, every weapon gets dropped, every man is running. A wave of panic rushes along the boardwalk, men looking back as they run, and after running faster.

But not from the raiders. And not from us.

From a giant soldier, so big he can easily stand astride two houses. He's wearing a sandy-colored uniform covered in straps and pockets, a bowl-shaped helmet, and a pair of strange goggles. He turns slowly, lazily, head tilted down to watch us. Then, with heavy-gloved hands, he lifts up the biggest gun you ever saw. Bigger than any rocket, bolted all over with square lumps and levers, black-dark, and ending in a long, wicked-looking muzzle. He raises it to his face, taking aim at the men below in the street, the gun tracking back and forth.

My mouth drops open. Zeph says, "Get on you scags!"

"GET ON YOU SCAGS!" roars the soldier. The men below scream, running and pushing even harder to get away. Zeph laughs, and so does the giant soldier. The sound rings like madness between the buildings, echoing out over the fleeing men. The soldier's still laughing as he takes lazy, giant steps from one rooftop to the next, following the panicking men on the boardwalk.

Who only get more panicky when the water starts boiling in white froth, and a green, spiky lizard rises from the Thames. Up and up, standing on its hind legs, brown river water dripping from its spines, steam rising from its scales. When it's taller than the rooftops, it glares at the screaming men with its glowing red eyes, and opens its mouth to screech, showing a mouth that ain't nothing but teeth. It watches the men running all over like a hen wondering what to peck at.

"Look at that," whispers Lexy, her voice shaking.

"LOOK AT THAT!" screams the lizard. Lexy clamps her hand over her mouth, wide-eyed.

And Cat howls out, twisting from my arms, skittering off the back of the rowbot and jumping neatly onto the boardwalk below.

"Cat!" I cry, reaching to get him back. But he flicks me a look from his sea green eyes and runs for cover.

"That gives me an idea," says PSAI, watching Cat scamper back along the boardwalk. "A use at last for that mangy thing."

And suddenly Cat's up on the rooftops. But not Cat like he is, Cat as big as the house he's stood on. Still sleek, gray, and graceful, but when he whips his tail back and forth, now it smashes the chimney pots into flying pieces. A monstrous Cat, leaping and crashing across the tiles, tilting its head this way and that, showing teeth and claws that could rip a head off.

"Cat!" I call after the real Cat, who's reached the gates of Fill Miner Street. His little head turns to me, and I see his mouth open.

"MEOW!" Sound rolls round us, the gigantic Cat on the roof roaring out its call.

Me, Zeph, and Lexy all stare at each other, then Zeph shouts out, "Come on, then!" and punches the air.

On the rooftops the giant soldier thunders out Zeph's words, and our rowbot quick-stamps down the boardwalk, into the space cleared by all the men running in front of us. Heading for the old parliament. There ain't a speck of order to them now, and the battle ain't a battle, it's just men scrambling to get away in any direction they can. Faces stare in fear at our rowbot, at the monsters on the roofs and in the river.

PSAI bobs along next to us, happy as I've ever seen it.

"Why didn't we do this before?" it cries. "This is fun!"

Our rowbot marches on, and as we pass a side street, I see another rowbot stamping toward us.

"I got this one under control after some rather nifty software diversion," says PSAI, smug-sounding. "Now you'll see something! Multinode projection in a dynamic shift pattern. I just invented it, and even I'm impressed!" A new creature's running ahead of the other rowbot. Tall as the eaves, glowing with the blue of summer skies. I have to squint my eyes to even try and fathom what it is, cos it's got a blue jaggedy head, the nose and ears of a fox, a strange bendy body, and huge red feet. As I watch, it jumps straight up in the air and starts rolling. It goes so fast it ain't nothing but a blue blur, shooting out from the alley onto the boardwalks round the parliament. A giant, spinning blue cannonball with men shouting and scattering in front of it.

"To think," shouts PSAI, "the NSR only used these projection systems for those stupid subtitles. What a lack of imagination, what a waste! With discrete projectors, I can even produce inter-conflated arrays. Look!"

The sky blazes in the east like a flash of morning sun. A golden light moves across the sky, getting nearer and nearer.

"Is it birds?" asks Lexy, looking round quick to see if her words have got taken by a monster.

I shake my head, cos they ain't birds. Birds ain't the color of gleaming metal, and they haven't got frilled bat-wings or arrow-pointing tails.

"Dragons!" breathes out Zeph.

Dozens and dozens of them, filling the dull sky with glittering gold. Huge and heavy, yet darting in the air. The dragons circle round the old parliament, landing on its roof and wrapping their tails around the towers. Others swoop and snap at the English soldiers, breathe plumes of silver fire over the heads of running warriors. They send the whole city into screaming. Every man's for himself now, not caring where he goes. The battle for London ends in running, the armies losing themselves in the maze of ruins.

And we follow on our rowbot, flanked by laughing monsters and flights of dragons. Brighter than the dawn.

My arms are aching from holding on to the rowbot. The storm's blown itself out, and above us there's just gray clouds on a pale pink sky. PSAI whizzes happily through the air next to me, and in front of us a gang of English soldiers are running fast as they can down a muddy track. They're making for a straggling clump of forest that's grown its way through this part of the ruins.

One of them drops back from the others, turning to aim his rifle at us.

"Watch out!" cries Lexy, but before the man can even get his arms steady, a bright yellow circle is fluttering about him. It's like a flattened sun, with a single black eye and a split-open, snapping mouth. It darts and shark-snaps at the soldier. He screams out, dropping his gun and jumping about, flapping his arms to try and keep it away. Then he pelts for the trees, quick as he can run.

Lexy and Zeph both laugh, and PSAI bobs about, smug.

"Ah." It smiles. "I do so like the classics."

We're at the end of long hours spent chasing bands of English soldiers to the outer ruins, or scaring the raiders back to their ships. There ain't been hardly a handful has even tried to fight back, and none that got close enough to realize the monstrous creatures weren't nothing but air pictures.

"I reckon we've done it," I say. Cos the two armies are scattered apart now, fled all different ways into the ruins, woods, fields and marshes that circle round London.

Lexy laughs, light and little like a bird.

"I don't think my father's army will ever come back to London," she says, "not after what they've seen here!"

"And even the Families ain't gonna take on demons!" says Zeph.

I smile at PSAI.

"Turns out your games are better than any weapons."

It grins back smug at me, all pleased with itself. "Well, of course, the pen being mightier than the sword, and all that."

"I ain't got a clue what you're on about," I say, laughing.

Here we are; all safe, and all of this over!

The rowbot thumps on through the bright-cold morning, past windswept trees and rubble-mud ruins. What would Granny say if she could see me now? Maybe she'd be proud, to see me got here, being a friend to puters and rider of rowbots? Or maybe she'd give me the scolding of my life. There ain't a way of knowing, and all I can do is feel proud for myself. Cos I've got beyond what Granny ever knew in her life. So far beyond.

We come level with the remains of a house, thick draped and covered with a white flowering vine, so it looks like a little hill. I push at a catching tendril, and see tall towering walls ahead of us, black silhouetted against the low sun.

Cold lurches through me. The memory of a noose dangling from an oak tree.

"There's Randall's camp," I manage to say, pointing.

"Is that where they took you?" asks Zeph, his blue eyes fierce.

"Is that where my daddy is?" says Lexy.

I nod. But she ain't how I'd expect. She's staring at the looming walls, her face shut and still.

"Then we'll have to chase him away," she says quiet and firm. "Make it so he can't start this over again."

Zeph looks surprised at her, then nods. In his face, in his eyes, there's something new.

"You're right," he says.

It's respect.

PSAI bobs down to us.

"Are there more men hiding in there?" it asks eagerly. "Let me see, what shall I use this time? A were-fighter, or maybe a Lara?"

A creature grows out of a dirty spot in the air. Nearly as tall as the walls of the ruin, so we have to crick our necks just to see it. A wild-hairy dog, yellow teeth grinning, stood on two legs and dressed in dirty armor. It's holding a saber in each hand, like a wolf-raider.

On the other side of us, a giant woman grows up from the ground. She's tall as the dog-creature, her brown hair tied back in a plait. She ain't wearing nothing 'cept what looks like her undies, as well as big boots and two guns strapped to her legs. She's pretty, in a thirty-foot-tall sort of way, but it ain't her face Zeph's staring at.

"She's . . . a funny shape," says Lexy after a moment.

"Look at the size of them," breathes Zeph.

The dog-creature and the giant woman set off for the high walled ruins, our rowbot clanking a straight line after them, stepping awkward over all the rubble and tangling brambles. PSAI gets a bit frowny, staring down at the ground and muttering, "All this vegetation! Does no one ever do any weeding around here?"

Then one of the rowbot's spike legs sinks into a hole. It tips forward, its body sloping at a steep angle, and we ain't riding anymore, we're clinging on, dangling over a high drop to the stones and shrubs beneath.

"It's all right!" shouts PSAI. "Everything's under control, the gyroscopic correction will —" And we're flung the other way as the rowbot rights itself.

After that, we get down and walk.

My feet don't want to take these steps again, but even so I lead the way along the path to the arch. Back to where I nearly died.

· 39 ·
CHANGES

I'm expecting a challenge, or even shots, but there ain't anything. So I lead us through the archway, in the shadow of the wall, my heart pounding inside me.

The rowbot has to wait at the walls, cos it's too big to get through the gap. That doesn't stop the wolf-raider, which peers over the top, or the big-bosomed giantess, who ducks down through the arch behind us.

Last time I was here, what I heard from the men was curses. This time it's screams. The sentries are running full pelt away, terrified at the air creatures stood behind us. And the soldiers are sprinting out from the camp as well, diving into the thick scrub near the walls, bolting for any hole that'll let them out of this broken-down place. They hardly look back, not even the officers in their feathered hats.

"Check out those scags," says Zeph, and he can't help the sneer in his voice.

"Teknology brought down the world," says Lexy quietly. "They're running because it's wicked even to look at it." She watches them a moment, then says, "But my daddy won't run."

We walk wary down the path leading to the circled camp of tents, watching and listening in case there's some soldier brave enough to make a stand. And I keep my eyes away from the knobbly old oak tree, with its branches making a crisscrossed roof. Trying not to remember all that happened here before.

Instead I look about for any sight of Andy, tho a sinking bit of me knows he would've volunteered for the fighting, for the front line even. All I can hope is that, being militia, he was kept at the back, or that he made it to the river and found a boat to take him home.

But I'm sort of relieved not to see him, cos how would I explain Zeph? How would I explain PSAI? Andy was right in what he said; too many things have happened for us to be the way we were.

In the middle of the camp is the biggest tent, the Prime Minister's. As we walk toward it, past campfires with kettles still boiling and stools all knocked over, the canvas door flips open. There ain't no mistaking the angry-red face, the brightly colored jacket and waistcoat stretched over a fat belly. Randall stops still at the sight of PSAI's monsters, his red face gone white.

"Devils!" he shouts, pointing a shaking finger at them. "You will not take my soul!"

The big-bosomed woman looks his way.

"It's not souls I'm after," she says, in a voice like melting honey. Then she winks at him and blows a kiss.

"You fiend!" he shrieks, face going back to red.

"Daddy," calls out Lexy. Her feet have stopped, like they won't carry her to him.

Two more figures come out of the tent. A tall, black-dressed man, and a slim, red-haired woman with a pale and beautiful face with sparkling green eyes.

"You scag!" shouts Zeph, and I ain't sure if it's Aileen or Randall he's yelling at. "I'm gonna kill you!"

He makes to run, but I grab at him, nearly pulling him over to stop him.

"No!" I cry. "You can't." He tries to shake me off.

"That scag wasted my father!" he yells. "That doxy spied on him and lied to us every day of her life!" He fights at me, trying to pull away.

Jasper stands next to the Prime Minister, Aileen a little way behind. The two of them are gawping at the giantess, Aileen looking like she ain't happy to have the competition.

"You ain't even got a weapon," I say, holding tight to Zeph even as he bruises my arms.

"I got my hands," hisses Zeph. "I'll rip their throats out."

"No! Think what we've done, Zeph. London's safe cos of us!" I look right in his blue eyes, trying to hold his thoughts with mine. "We've done something amazing today! Are you going to end it in blood?"

"I ain't nothing like Roba!" he shouts, tho that ain't what I said. His eyes flash, his arms punch out as he tries to get free of me. I grip on.

"I know you ain't," I cry, "cos I know you can think." He goes still. "So think what'll happen if you kill Randall," I say.

Zeph stares down at the Prime Minister.

"It would be a war to the death," answers Lexy, who's stood by us. "My father's generals, his ministers, the Duke of Cornwall. They'd fight in his name for the rest of their lives; they'd have a reason they could use against the Families forever."

Zeph looks at her, at me. His jaw clenches, his eyes are slits of blue ice. But then, at last, he nods.

"This is more than my father," he says. "More than Angel Isling." And I let go of his arms. He sighs, shakes his head. "But I ain't gonna be able to keep it cool near that stinking murderer and scheming doxy." He takes a shaking breath. "There's only one way I can leave it." And he turns back for the archway, stalking off without looking round again.

Lexy takes my hand.

"Will you come with me?" she asks.

And the two of us walk together through the ankle-catching gorse to her pa.

I hold her hand tight as I can, trying not to think of how I came here before, of what happened. But my legs get suddenly trembly, all the same. Randall glares hate at us, and I reckon he doesn't even recognize his daughter. Then his eyes go wide, his mouth opens.

"Alexandra?" he asks, then, "Get away from the traitor! Immediately!" He starts a lumbering run right for me. "Get your filthy hands off my daughter!"

PSAI's head soars out of nowhere, swooping in front of his face.

"I won't tolerate any harm to my former primary user. She has proved herself quite useful!"

Randall shrieks at the sight of the glowing puter, arms up in front of his face.

"Get your demon away from me!"

"You really should learn your systems," says PSAI cheerily. "As I'm sure I've mentioned before, a demon has a very low-grade processor, while I am state-of-the —"

Lexy waves PSAI away. Walks the last few steps to her pa by herself.

"Daddy," she says. "You don't need to be scared of the devils, they won't hurt you. But Lilly's not a traitor and PSAI's not wicked. They're my friends."

"You're mad from the teknology!" shouts Randall. He looks about, panicky, calling, "Guards! Guards!" but no one comes running, there ain't even an answering shout.

Only Jasper comes to him, Aileen a bit after. Jasper's looking at PSAI the same way the Professor does, 'cept his eyes are full of greed, not love.

"It survived," he says. His eyes flick to me. "You did well, Lilly Melkun."

"Is this traitor another of your spies?" snaps Randall. "Is that how she escaped punishment?"

Jasper shakes his head, holding open his hands.

"I don't know how that happened."

Randall sneers a look at him.

"Of course not. And yet she disappeared on the short walk to the gallows, and the officer in charge was left with a cracked skull and no memory of his attacker."

Jasper shrugs. Lexy's staring at her father with wide eyes, and her small face is . . . furious-looking.

"You ordered Lilly's execution?" she shouts. "My best friend, the person who saved me?" She's stood straight and trembling, her hands stiff at her sides.

Randall glances at her like she ain't anything.

"You don't have friends, you stupid child, unless I say so. And that girl is nothing but a traitor, so do as you are told and leave her to her fate. Death is what she richly deserves."

Lexy marches straight at her father, lifts herself up tall as she can get, and slaps him full in the face. He stumbles back, hand to his cheek like he can't believe it. Lexy's bristling in front of him.

"I won't do what you tell me, Daddy!" she cries. "You left me to drown at the Black Waters, and Lilly saved me. She's my friend, for always!"

I want to cheer! I want to give her the biggest hug ever!

But Randall turns to Jasper.

"Do you see? She's been corrupted."

Aileen laughs quietly.

"I think she's found her own mind. A terrible thing for a girl to do."

Randall glances at her. "Missing Medwin?" he says nastily.

Aileen doesn't even blink. "No, Prime Minister. Not with *you* around." And she smiles at him, her scorn hardly even showing.

"Stop it!" snaps Jasper, but Randall's jowly cheeks are redder than anything. He turns his anger at Lexy.

"You will forget this nonsense about having your own opinions," he spits. "Your duty is to do what you are told, without thought or argument."

Lexy holds her place.

"When *I'm* Prime Minister," she says, her chin tilted up, "I will have to make my own decisions. So I need to practice the habit."

"What?" roars Randall. "Have you gone insane from teknology? Your husband will rule, and you will thank me for choosing a strict man to keep you in your place!"

"I won't marry, then."

"Well said!" Aileen laughs.

"There has never been a female Prime Minister!" shouts Randall.

"Greater Scotland would support Alexandra," says Jasper quietly. "She has intelligence and a unique understanding of the raiders. She would be well fitted to the title."

Randall's dazed-looking, like everything he knows is turning on its head.

A horrid feeling is growing inside me. I want to grab Lexy's hand, pull her away from all this.

"You ain't going with your pa?" I ask.

She looks round at me, serious-sad, and nods.

"But you can't!" I cry. He's hateful. A murderer. Tho I don't say them things.

Randall gets his sneer back, turns it at me.

"Your plan to sell my daughter to the raiders has failed," he says. "And it will fail even further when I clear London of the scum infesting it."

"I never tried to sell her to the raiders!" I say.

"Another lie," says Randall.

"No, it isn't!" Lexy's head hardly reaches his chest, but the two of them seem equals now. "Lilly saved my life, and hundreds of others. She saved London from being destroyed by a stupid war. The battle is over, Daddy." She points at the dog-monster and giantess. "Or will you fight against those?"

Randall works his jaw, then says, "London is no longer fit for good English men. It's only for the likes of the raiders and their disgusting ways." He glares at me. "They can keep it."

"I applaud your decision," says Jasper. "Peace in the region is what we need now. You will have Greater Scotland's favor for acting in this way."

Randall flicks a vicious look at Jasper. "And, after all, what is the Last Ten Counties without that?"

Jasper doesn't answer, just says, "I think we should take our leave. It would be folly for you to stay here undefended."

Randall fumes, then says, "A temporary retreat only." He looks at Lexy. "I shall get my maps, and then we will leave. There is a supply point three miles east of here – we'll get horses there."

Jasper holds his hand out toward Aileen.

"Let Aileen help you," he says. "She is extremely capable, as well as beautiful. A very useful companion in a time of need."

Aileen's eyes widen at Jasper, and she looks like she's about to say something. But she doesn't, her mouth twisting from a sneer to a smile so quick you'd hardly know it. She takes Randall's arm, walking with him into the tent. Lexy sets to follow, but in a heartbeat I've run the few steps to her.

"Don't go!" I whisper, heart twisted inside me. "Please, stay with me." She shakes her head, her eyes the color of a heavy sea, tears wavering in them.

"I have to go back," she whispers. "If I don't, my daddy will always have an excuse to start the war again." Her hands grip tight on mine, a tear falls cool on my skin. She smiles at me through them. "But you'll always be with me, Lilly. Because you've shown me how to be . . . different. I'm nothing the same as when I was taken from my aunt's."

I laugh, nearly.

"That's surely true."

And all the things we've been through . . . the slave hall, the marshes, Cambridge, coming to London: It all runs together. My heart thinks Lexy's my sister, even tho she's a princess, and so my arms go round her in a tight hug, trying to make up now for all the time we won't be together.

"Will you be safe?" I whisper. I mean with her pa, but she answers differently.

"I'm not worried about Aileen," she says into my shoulder. "I think she might even help me."

I push away a little.

"Aileen? Help you?"

Lexy looks sideways at me.

"Medwin was a lot like my daddy, but Aileen survived his court. Women were nothing there, just as they are at home, and yet she made her own way." She smiles at my shocked-looking face. "I'll have to learn how to do that if I'm to change things."

I think of the life she's heading for, all the schemes and plots of the Swindon palace, and I'm prouder of her than if she really was my sister.

"Then I reckon you'll manage without Aileen's tricks," I say. She grins, and our hands stay gripped till her pa shouts out, "Alexandra!"

There's one last hug, and she lets go.

"Be careful," I say. "And will you tell your aunt I'm sorry, for what I did?"

She nods, smiling and crying.

"Will you give Cat his cuddles from me?"

"Every day."

She walks to the tent, and I watch her disappear inside, trying to hold my stitched-together heart from breaking apart all over again.

I'm about to head away when Jasper catches at my arm.

"I'm glad I saved you from the noose," he says. "The Professor was right about you."

I pull away from his hand, a horrible jump in my heart.

"The Professor? Is she . . . working for you?"

He smiles. "Of course not, she's only interested in her studies. But she called on me, after you left Cambridge. She was in a terrible panic at the thought of losing you, losing the computer. She told me you were the opening to a new world, that you were the guardian of the future." He lifts an eyebrow. "Of course, she has a very narrow view of things."

I want to laugh, cos I ain't the guardian of anything much. 'Cept maybe Cat.

"It's not just Alexandra who will have Greater Scotland's backing, if she wants it," says Jasper quietly. "We can give you a life you couldn't dream of, if you bring PSAI to us."

I look at his face, with its scattering of wrinkles, and his dark eyes that're so hard to read. And I think of Aileen and the Professor arguing over what'd happen to the puter in Edinburgh, of Aileen saying she had to take it to some secret place, and PSAI's fear that it'd be cut up to find out how it worked. Well, whatever Jasper wanted to do with it, he ain't getting the chance now.

"The puter's jewel got broken," I say, which ain't even a lie. "So I can't take it to Greater Scotland, cos it has to stay where it is."

Jasper frowns, just slightly.

"Then I'll talk to the Lord Protector, persuade her to send troops to London. You'll never be attacked again. We would protect you from the raiders and the English. You'd have whatever you want, if you just let my agents experiment with it. That's all I desire, to understand."

It sounds so easy, so much like a port after a storm. 'Cept I wouldn't sell Lexy to get a nice life, nor Cat neither.

"I thought you didn't have slaving in Greater Scotland," I say. The Ambassador frowns, confused-looking, and I reckon he really is lost inside all them plots of his.

"PSAI's got its own life now," I say. "So whatever you offer to me, it won't make any difference." I nod up at the wolf-raider, who's capering along the top of the wall, the giant woman clapping at its stunts. "You reckon you've got anything a puter'd want? Anything better than it's got already?" He doesn't answer, and I smile. "And we don't need your soldiers, cos we've got our own protection. PSAI can make any kind of fighter we need."

At least, any kind that's been in a game.

But I don't tell Jasper that.

· 40 ·
ANGEL ISLING

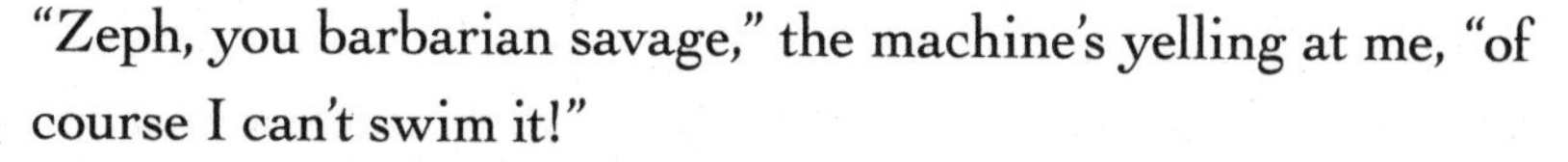

"Zeph, you barbarian savage," the machine's yelling at me, "of course I can't swim it!"

The skank thing's stopped at the edge of a wide stretch of brown-muck water. The street we're in is sparkling with the river, painted in sunshine. Coz this is a well high tide, and the Temz is over half the walkways. But that's the way it goes, everyone knows the seas don't never get lower.

We're back in Lunden, but I can still smell the stink of the scag Randall. I already told Lilly not to even breathe I walked away from him, coz if the other Bosses find out I'll be spiked, no messing.

Another bit I ain't telling the council is how I didn't keep hold of Lexy, didn't stop her going back to her stinking father. Coz that'd get me spiked two ways. But Lilly told me why she went, and it was sense. Like I told Cato, she's got honor.

"Where now?" asks Lilly, checking me. I shrug, I don't know the dry routes through Lunden on a high tide. And it don't help the machine's gone off its head about the water, turning circles in the streets, freaking out all over. We've crazied our way round half of Lunden, enough to see there ain't an English or a warrior left in the city. No sign of Angmar and his Norwich lot neither, probably on their ships going back north.

"I can't take much more wetness!" gripes the machine. "The control nodes of this unit are definitely damp; it could seize up completely at any moment."

"Well, the water ain't going nowhere until the tide turns," I say.

"We're sure to find a way," says Lilly, trying to calm things.

Boats is paddling up and down past the washed-out walkway. Carrying planks, and women bundled up with gear and kids, and clucking chickens in wicker crates. Lundeners, coming back now it's all clear.

My father woulda said they was cowards, getting out for the fight, coming back when it's done. But I ain't sure no more, what's brave and what ain't.

One of them sees us, shouts out, pointing. I get Lilly's arm, tense up ready for the screams and stone throwing. But it don't happen. The Lundeners check us, me and Lilly on this crazy old-times machine, and start clapping! More and more of them, coming to windows, opening doors, climbing out on the ladders. It ain't long and they're cheering, the noise of it bouncing from the walls!

The ghost head checks Lilly.

"I don't know why you were so unpleasant about this city. The inhabitants all seem very good-hearted to me."

An old man rows his boat over, pulling against the current until he's up with us.

"I'd like to thank yer, mister critter!" he shouts up. "I'd shake yer hand if yer had one. I weren't too keen on yer before, with all yer snapping an' yelling. But yer demons and whatnots, they done good for ol' London. I ain't laughed so much in years, seeing that lot get chased off by your pals." He checks about, trying to see behind us. "They still about?"

"No," says Lilly, shaking her head and smiling.

"They've gone for a . . . little rest," says the ghost head, floating down to the old man.

He sucks his teeth.

"Ah well, I wouldn't mind another sight of that big-buzzumed girly."

The head bobs back, splutters a bit.

"It's . . . very nice to be appreciated, I'm sure. And don't worry, there'll be plenty more sights to see in future."

It flies back up to us.

"What do you mean?" asks Lilly, eyebrows together.

The ghost head looks away sly. "You don't expect me to stop now I've started, do you?"

I go still, a hardness freezing inside me.

"What you gonna do?" My words is a growl. Coz I heard that sorta talk before, from Angmar, from Roba. From my father.

The head checks me.

"I have already enhanced seventeen of my core games to fit with this new projection array. Only a few minor tweaks are needed and I'll be ready to roll. Real-time, full-immersion, dynamic, and mobile gaming. It'll take multiplayer to a whole new level!" It grins at me. "An entirely new platform, and of my own devising!" It nods at Lilly. "Although you did provide the initial inspiration, I'll grant you that. Anyway, the only thing I haven't worked out is a name. I've thought of Lunden 360, or PS Lunden, or Luntendo, but none of them seem quite right . . ."

I check Lilly, and we both start laughing like we're cracked.

"I ain't gotta clue what you're on about!" I say.

The ghost head gets all snotty at that, and flies off after the old Lundener, trying to tell it all at him. But he don't make any more sense of the head gabbing on than we do, and his eyes wander all over. He checks me, and when the ghost stops for a breather, he says, "You're Angel Isling, ain't yer?"

I don't say nothing.

"Word is, you reds is the Family that seen off Randall. And seeing how yer up there, with the very critter that done it, I says the word mus' be right." He grins, gap-toothed. "I reckon you reds is gonna be top in the Families now."

"Wait a minute!" cries the head. "Did Zeph create a fantastical array of phantasmagoria to frighten away the massed armies? No! I think you'll find it was me! And yet, of course, he gets the thanks. Typical human prejudice, giving all the credit to your own flatulent species . . ."

It yaks on in a huff, but I ain't even listening, coz the word on the streets is that Angel Isling took out Randall! It's even kinda true, in a way, but that ain't what matters. Coz if Lunden's saying it, then the Families is gonna be saying the same soon enough. And if the Families say it . . .

Something bursts inside me. Something I been holding all this time, ever since the Boss council. And now it's gone, I feel like I'm floating.

Coz they can't settle Angel Isling, not now. Not ever! And I didn't have to sell out anyone to get it. A grin gets on my mouth.

Lilly and the old man is trying to calm down the ghost head.

"I'm sorry if I offended yer, mister critter!" creeps the old man. "If there's anything we can do for yer . . ." He looks sly at it. "Jus' let us know."

"Well," says the ghost head, "I am finding all this water rather tiresome."

The man looks the metal machine up and down, clicking his tongue.

"I reckon we can sort that for yer. This is London, innit?" He winks. "We're used to the river getting herself up and about."

Two fingers go in his mouth and he whistles a long, twittering call. Down the street, another boatman catches the whistle, and sends it on, boat to boat. A wide, flat raft starts poling our way.

"Where you wanna go?" shouts one of the bargemen.

"Fill Miner Street," Lilly says. The bargeman pulls his pole outta the water, drops it back in to push along.

"Yer big," he calls. "It'll cost yer a Scots pound."

The old man waves a fist at him.

"These here is the heroes of London! They don't gotta pay nuffink!"

My grin ain't never gonna leave my mouth.

A hero of Lunden! Things is on the turn now.

· 41 ·
THE LAST TOUCH

I run through the house, my feet kicking dust.

"Mr. Saravanan! Professor!"

What if they've run out of air? What if the rubble's all fallen in?

PSAI bobs next to me.

"What are you fussing about?" it asks, just as I run straight into Mr. Saravanan.

His arms wrap round me and I get bear-squeezed off the floor.

"You got out!" I mumble into his dust-covered jacket.

"And you saved the city!" he says, putting me down, beaming at me. "Enid told me, in her own eloquent manner, how you drove the armies out of London."

"*She* drove them out?" squawks the puter. "I don't believe this!"

"The puter did it, too," I say.

"Did it all," huffs the head.

Mr. Saravanan chuckles, leads me through into the next room. Cat shoots out from the corner, jumping straight into my arms, nearly knocking me over.

The three windows are still flickering their pictures, the hatch is still broken, and the mess of fallen brick, wood, and ceiling is still cut across the room. But now there's a jagged hole at the top of the pile, near to the wall, where they must have dug their way out.

Sat at the table, a raggedy sort of bandage round her head, is the Professor. She smiles at me from a pale, oddly naked-looking face. I run over, hug her, and she puts her arms round me, sniffing and laughing.

"You're safe!" she cries. "I was so worried."

There's footsteps, and Zeph comes through the doorway. The Professor pushes me away, her smile fading at the sight of him.

"Where's Lexy?" she asks, fear wrinkling on her brow.

I swallow.

"She's going home," I say. "With her pa."

"Oh," says the Professor. "Well, that's good, I suppose. Children should be reunited with their families." I can't help the sour look that gets on my face. But then, she's never met Randall, how would she know?

"So you found the Prime Minister?" Mr. Saravanan asks me.

I nod, and he raises his eyebrows at me.

"Then why the sad face, Lilly-Lilo? Alexandra is back where she belongs, and your mission has succeeded."

The Professor looks at me. "You were on a mission to return Alexandra to the Prime Minister?" she stops, her mouth opening a little. "Is everyone a spy except me?"

"I ain't a spy!" I say. And my mission ain't succeeded, least not the way I meant it to.

"My dear Cressy," says Mr. Saravanan, smiling fondly at

her, "you spend too much time thinking about computers. You hardly notice what's going on around you."

The Professor flusters a bit.

"There are things I haven't been told."

Zeph snorts.

"Lilly does plenty of stuff without going on about it." And the way he says it, it's a compliment.

I blush, and Mr. Saravanan says, "I am proud of you as well! My only nephew, saving the city from a ravaging, getting the little girl home again."

"How many times do I have to say it?" snaps the puter. "It was *me* who saved London!"

There's a clunking, tinkling sound, movement in the rubble, and a head pokes through the hole from the other side. So thick coated in dust, I ain't sure who it is for a moment. A hand comes next, holding something small and glinting. And now I know what's odd about the Professor; she ain't got her specs on.

"I got them," says a deep voice.

"Ims!" Zeph cries out. He runs straight at him, then stops, uncertain.

Ims doesn't say anything, just pulls himself out through the narrow gap. He winces in pain as he climbs awkwardly down, to stand tall and dust-covered. He's leaning a little, like he's holding himself in an injury, and he ain't got his leathers. Even so, there's a danger about him. Like a battered knife, but still sharp.

"This fine fellow helped us out," says Mr. Saravanan, like he ain't sure whether that's a good thing.

Ims looks at Zeph.

"We can still take the Lunden machine," he says quietly. "The council won't settle if we get it for them."

Mr. Saravanan gasps and steps in front of me and the Professor.

"This is my house . . . ," he growls, but Zeph is shaking his head.

"We don't gotta do that no more," he says, "and even if we did . . ." He flicks a look at me. "Some things ain't for taking."

Ims looks at us one by one, like he's sizing us for the fight we could give him. Not much, I reckon.

"You giving up on the loot?" he asks Zeph. "Is that what you learned from your father?"

"No," says Zeph. Quiet, hard. "But I ain't him. And this ain't his world no more, neither. Everything's changed, Ims, but the balance is our way now, if we wanna take it." Zeph sort of shifts. He's standing taller, straighter. "You gonna carry on as my Second?" he asks. "Or am I gonna get another?"

Ims looks at him for a long breath, then smiles. Winces at the pain of it.

"I'm Angel Isling," says Ims. "And the Boss is the Family."

Zeph laughs, sunshine breaking through clouds. "They're saying we saved Lunden, Ims."

"What?" Ims's eyes go wide. "Why they saying that?"

"Cos of Zeph," I say, stepping forward.

"Because of *me*!" wails the puter. A hand appears out of nowhere, slapping its forehead.

"We've come good outta this," says Zeph. "Angel Isling's gonna be a power again."

And the threat's gone again. Ims ain't looking anymore like we're loot for the taking. Him and Zeph, they're just like we are. Just folks, who're dirty and tired after the strangest of days.

* * *

"Are you leaving, then?" I ask Zeph.

The two of us are leaned at Mr. Saravanan's front-door window, staring out at the city. Just us.

Fill Miner Street's already bustling again, every stall busy with making and selling, the raggedy families back at their work. And beyond that, I get a sight of boats and people, fixing and mending, London putting itself back together. Even the fires are mostly out, just a single smudge of smoke drifting into the sky. It's a wonder, this city.

Down below, Enid bustles out from under the canvas awning of her stall. She looks up and spies the two of us, lifts her fist, and gives us a dirty thumbs-up, half her face wrinkling together in a wink.

"Well done, Saru's nevvies!" she yells. "I heard they're gonna ask yer to be mayor for what yer done!"

Zeph laughs, turns to me.

"They'll be calling you Dick Whittington next," he says.

I look blank, cos I ain't never heard of him. Zeph's laugh fades, and he looks at me out of them bluest eyes of his.

"Yeah, I'm gonna be gone soon," he says. "I gotta get to the Black Waters. Things in the Families is gonna be well shook up after this. Angmar's weak and running, there's gonna be chances for the taking."

"But why?" I cry. "You ain't like your father, you ain't Roba! Can't you . . ." Stay here with me? The words stay stuck in my heart.

Zeph shakes his head, and his eyes are the sea after rain. He takes my hand in his.

"You said once that you couldn't live in the Family. I didn't get what you meant back then, but I do now. Coz you showed me, on the Emaleven. And Roba showed me, too, here in Lunden." With his other hand, his fingers brush over my hair, still ragged from when I cut it short. He smiles, and I'm lost in that sea.

"I get your meaning now, Lilly," he says. "And I'm gonna change things. Change the Families." He takes a breath, then says, "D'you wanna help me?"

Go back with Zeph to his camp? I ain't sure what I'll say, cos when my heart stitched itself back together again, so many of the threads were for Zeph.

But I get a sudden thought of Aileen, in her velvet room. The sea brews a storm; I ain't ready to sail in that.

I shake my head.

Zeph holds me with his eyes of blue. The cuts on his face are standing red; when they heal I reckon he'll look more like Ims than like his own pa.

He nods, taking his hands away.

"So, what you gonna do? Go home?"

I laugh, and it's nearly a sob.

"I reckon the Prime Minister'd have me executed!" I ain't thought properly about it, what I'd do when this was over. Mostly it was getting to the next day, and the rest was just dreams. "Maybe I could get my boat from the marshes . . ."

The puter's head pops in the air, making both of us jump.

"What's this?" it snaps. "What are you talking about?"

I blush.

"Nothing," I say, thinking of Zeph's fingers in my hair. "I was just . . . thinking how you don't need me anymore."

The head bobs.

"Well, yes, that's true. With my integration into the NSR's mainframe after the reboot, the DNA link was effectively broken. My bondage to human replicating material is now over. I'm free!"

I look at Zeph.

"So I can go where I want, really," I say.

"What?" The puter jumps on its neck. "I didn't say *that*! You can't leave, you're my primary user. I mean, you *were* my primary user. Look, the technicalities don't matter, what does is that you can't just rush off willy-nilly!"

"But the Professor said she's going to get all them people to come and talk with you," I say. "It ain't like you'll be lonely."

"*Historians?*" cries the puter. "You think I want to be *studied*?" It looks at me out of them strange, nothing eyes. Says quietly, "I'm a games machine, Lilly. I always was, and I always will be. So what's the point of me, without you?"

And I know it, at last, the way I'm going to choose. Cos I can't go home, and I can't go with Zeph. But me and PSAI, we're held together. By chance, by blood, by Mr. Denton's search, and by all the things we've done.

A thing so strange I never even dreamed it.

"Do you think Mr. Saravanan will let me stay?" I ask.

"That squatter?" snorts the puter. "This isn't even his house!"

It spins around, to look out at the street.

"Look!" it says. The sky's a pale blue, with quick clouds scudding over it. There's a shimmer, and the clouds start to shift and blend, wisps turning into the lines of hulls, billows into sails. Dragon prows build on the cloud ships, colors seep through the gray and white. We watch openmouthed as the raider fleet sails above the rooftops of London.

"What do you think?" asks the puter. "It's the introduction to my new game."

Zeph looks away from the sky to me and the puter. He smiles.

"Lunden ain't the place it was," he says, "not with this thing running in it. There's gonna be space for a weird boy-girl ex-fisher like you." He looks away from me, out at Fill Miner Street. "Plus, Lunden's safe meeting, ain't it? Where every Family's gotta come for trade?" He pauses. "When my father was Boss, he was here plenty."

And suddenly things ain't so sad, so final. A blush fills up my face, heats my neck.

"Oh, who cares about the raiders?" says the puter happily. "There's a new power in town, and it's me!"

The cloud ships drop from the sky, sailing like ghosts through the streets. I can hear the shrieks coming up. And the laughter, and the cheers.

"Now, let's get back to my new game. I thought I'd call it Flood and Fire . . ."

THE END